SCOT OF RUIN

She was always off-limits but some lines are meant to be crossed.

THE MACKINTOSH CLAN
BOOK 10

LYLA ROSEWOOD

ABOUT THE BOOK

"Ye're nae such a proper lady after all, are ye?"

Agnes MacDonald spent years away trying to forget the man whose love had nearly cost them everything. She thought fleeing him and their mistake was the hardest thing she'd ever done. Until she comes back to Scotland with a secret that still has the power to ruin them both.

And he's right there – more handsome, colder and unforgiving...

Conrad Mackintosh always wondered why Agnes disappeared without a word. When he saves her from a bandit attack, old wounds reopen, and so does his desire for the one woman who was always forbidden to him. Yet, she's hiding something...

And the more she resists him, the more Conrad is determined to uncover what.

But with an old enemy resurfacing and her family against them, Agnes may have to choose between her past, her heart, and a future that may never be hers.

AUTHOR'S NOTE

My lovely Reader,

Welcome to the captivating world of *The Mackintosh Clan series*, where each book unveils the journey of a different person in the Mackintosh family navigating life's challenges, both on the battlefield and in matters of the heart.

What makes this series truly special is that each book is crafted by a different author, bringing a unique perspective and voice to the captivating saga. I am deeply thankful to my esteemed colleagues and dear friends in the Scottish romance genre—*Shona Thompson, Fiona Faris, Juliana Wight, and Kenna Kendrick*—for embarking on this thrilling adventure with me.

This could never happen without them!

Join us as we journey through the enchanting landscapes of Scotland, where passion and danger collide, and love conquers all.

Get ready for an unforgettable adventure!

Warmest regards,

Lyla

FAMILY TREE

My lovely Reader,

Before we delve into the tales of the Mackintosh siblings, take a moment to explore their family tree and to familiarize yourself with the role each character plays in the fictional world we've crafted for them.

Happy reading,

Lyla

FAMILY TREE

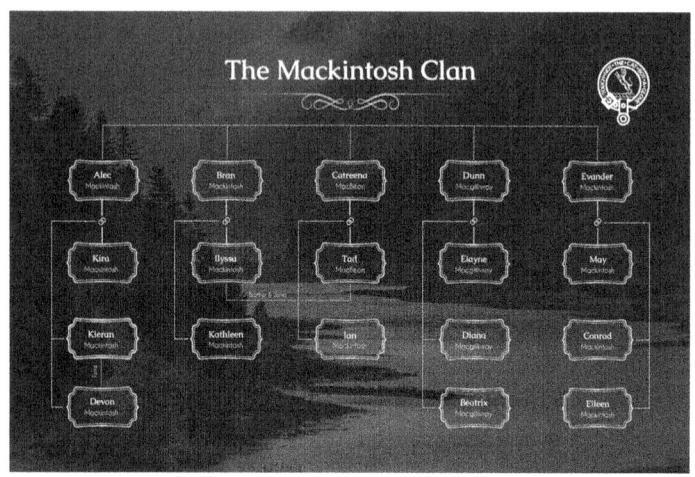

BONUS PROLOGUE

July, Keppoch Castle, Lochaber, fifteen years earlier

"Ach, dinnae be such a baby, Agnes, I'm only gonnae show it tae ye! What are ye runnin' away fer, ye wee goose?" Duncan said, laughing as he chased his little sister along the narrow fringe of gravelly sand at the edge of Loch Machie, with a long silvery eel dangling from his hand.

The four friends were spending the warm July day at the loch, amusing themselves on one of their frequent outings while their parents were otherwise engaged. Eileen and Conrad's father, Evander Mackintosh, war leader of their clan, was talking politics with Agnes and Duncan's father, his old friend, the Laird James MacDonald. Their respective mothers, Lady May and Lady Fiona, also great friends, were spending the day shopping in the nearby Lochaber. Their offspring were at liberty to do as they pleased, and it usually involved a lot of teasing and pranks.

Eileen was sitting on a large rock at the water's edge, fishing for crayfish with a hook tied to a bit of string baited with bread. Furious at seeing her younger friend terrorized, she yelled at Duncan, "Leave her be, ye beast! Duncan, ye ken she hates eels. Ye're scarin' her!"

"I'm nae gonnae dae anythin' with it, just show it tae her, 'tis all," Duncan claimed, laughing uproariously.

"Ye liar, ye said ye were gonnae put it down me neck!" Agnes shouted back at him, running as fast as her legs little ten-year-old legs would carry her, close to tears.

Eileen huffed and jumped from the rock to the sand, to run after Duncan, eager to defend Agnes. "Leave her be, I say!"

Duncan took no notice but continued pursuing his terrified little sister along the narrow fringe of beach, waving the unfortunate eel. "I was jokin'. If ye stop runnin', I promise tae nae put it down yer back. Just have a look at it, will ye," he yelled after her.

"I dinnae believe ye!" Agnes cried. She let out a shrill shriek of panic as he caught up with he and grabbed her arm, dangling the writhing creature over her head.

"Nay, nay! Get it away from me, Duncan! I hate ye, get off of me" Agnes screamed, cringing away from the slimy muscular fish as it brushed against her hair, squirming and gasping for air.

"Get it away from me, ye pig!" She shrank away, desperately batting at the eel with one small hand, repulsed by it, while the other bunched up the neckline of her shift, for she was scared he really would put it down her back.

"Ugh, 'tis all slimy and cold. Think how it'll wriggle when I put it down yer neck," Duncan crowed, holding the eel high and pulling at the neck of her shift.

Agnes exploded with panic, screaming non-stop at the top of her voice, kicking at him to get away. Suddenly, there was a thud, a loud "Oof!", and Duncan and the eel were gone.

With a sideways peep, Agnes saw her brother stumbling backwards into the water, still clutching the eel. He fell backwards and landed with a splash on his backside. The eel flew from his hand and, with a flash of silver, slipped away.

"I hope it bites yer bum!" she shouted at him vengefully through her sniffles.

A tall shadow fell over her, blocking out the sun, and she felt someone crouch down at her side.

"Are ye all right, Agnes," asked the deep voice kindly. Hearing it, the panic and fear began to recede like an outgoing tide. A strong, sun-tanned arm went around her shoulders comfortingly. She looked up into a pair of eyes that were bluer than the sky above and a smile that made her feel warm inside.

"Aye, I'm all right now, Conrad. Thank ye fer savin' me," she murmured, dropping her eyes, suddenly feeling shy. Sniffing, she surreptitiously wiped her nose with the back of her hand, embarrassed at her babyish behavior in front of him. At fourteen, he seemed so grownup. He was her hero.

Eileen skidded to a halt and crashed down onto the sand next to them, panting. "He's a menace, that braither of yers," she puffed.

"Aye, he is," Agnes agreed.

"Grand. Come on, up ye get." Conrad's large hand reached down. She placed hers in it, liking the safe feeling it gave her when it closed around hers. He pulled her easily to her feet, and Eileen got up and helped her brush off her petticoat.

Conrad, arms akimbo, walked down to the water's edge and shouted at her brother, who had by now clambered to his feet and was standing in the loch, squeezing the water from his hair. "Pick on someone eyer own size, Duncan. I told ye before, dinnae scare her like that. She's only wee."

"Aye, she's a wee baby," Duncan said, sloshing out of the water onto the sand. "She's scared of everything," he added, glancing at his sister with boyish disdain.

"Agnes is only ten. 'Tis nae fair tae torment her like that. If ye keep on, she'll be too scared tae come out with us," Conrad pointed out. The imaginary halo Agnes had already placed around his head shone even brighter.

"Ach, it was only a bit of fun, I wasnae really gonnae put it down her back," Duncan protested.

"If 'tis fun ye want, then then why dinnae try puttin' an eel down me back?" Conrad taunted him with a challenging grin.

"Wait 'til I catch another one and I bloody well will," Duncan declared, hurling himself at his friend. Eileen and Agnes stood and watched while the boys fell to the ground and rolled round, wrestling, punching each other, and laughing as they so often did.

"Stupid boys," Eileen pronounced derisively. "Come on, Agnes, let's go and eat some more of that cake." The girls held hands and walked back down the strand, to the blanket spread out there, which contained the remainder of their picnic luncheon.

"Conrad's nae stupid, he's kind," Agnes said, brushing her long dark hair aside as her friend handed her a lump of yellow seedcake. "He rescued me." She bit into the cake with relish.

Eileen chuckled as she set about her cake. "They're both just as bad at times. Ye ken how they love teasin' us. That's the trouble with older braithers. All boys really," she added wisely. "That's why I'm never gonnae get married."

"I think I'd like tae get married one day," Agnes said, secretly eyeing Duncan as he pummeled her brother. No boy was more handsome than him in her eyes, with his strong build and golden hair. She thought of him as a fairy-tale prince, the sort in books that rescued captive princesses and then fell in love with them.

I hate bein' ten, she thought. If I was fourteen, then Conrad might fall in love with me, and we'd get betrothed, and when we're grownup, we'd get married. It was a frequent fantasy of hers, one she would never tell a soul, not even Eileen.

The boys finished their fighting and came to join them, friends again. They plopped down onto the blanket beside their sisters.

"I'm sorry about the eel, Agnes," Duncan apologized. "I was only teasin' ye. I didnae think ye'd be so scared." He ruffled her hair affectionately, and she could not help but smile. She adored her big brother, even if he did tease her. He looked after her as well, and she looked up to him.

"I wasnae scared. I was only pretendin'" Agnes said, not wanting to seem babyish in front of her hero. Embarrassingly, they all laughed at her obvious fib.

"Well, I felt sorry fer the poor eel," Eileen, raising another laugh. Agnes was very grateful to her friend for the distraction.

With harmony restored, they ate some more of their picnic. Then, to make it up to Agnes, Duncan suggested a game of tag, one of her favorites. When at last they packed up their things and began the walk back to the castle, they had not gone very far when an argument broke out between Duncan and Eileen about who was the fastest runner.

"How can ye be faster than me? Ye're too small," Duncan told her. At almost fifteen, he was as tall and strong as their father. He and Conrad had been training with weapons from an early age, and it showed. She and Eileen loved to go and watch them spar together. Eileen, on the other hand, was a mere eleven.

"I may be small, but I'm very fast. Are ye scared too race me in case I beat ye?" Eileen taunted Duncan, never one to back down from a challenge.

Conrad laughed. "Aye, he wouldnae live it down tae be beaten by a lassie," he said.

Naturally, it ended in a race. While Duncan and Eileen sprinted off over the fields, Agnes and Conrad ambled along slowly side by side. Agnes was perfectly content with the situation.

"It's been a grand day out, eh, Agnes? I love spending the day down on the beach when we come and visit ye," he said, looking down at her from a great height.

"Aye, so dae I. 'Tis a shame ye're goin' back tae Moy Hall with yer parents tomorrow. I wish ye and Eileen could live here with me and Duncan. It would be so much fun."

He chuckled, his eyes sparking. "That would be grand. But I think me faither plans tae finish his clan business with yers tonight. Ma says we're all gonnae have a big dinner together after that."

"I ken, and me and Eileen are allowed tae stay up late," Agnes said, feeling tired and wondering if she would be able to stay awake that long. The long day at the beach, all the fun and games, and the hot sun were taking their toll. She did not want to miss a moment of Conrad's company and definitely did not want to fall asleep in front of him like a baby. It would be too embarrassing.

Maybe it was thinking about it that made her want to yawn. Even though she tried to stifle it, Conrad noticed. She was mortified.

"Are ye tired, Agnes?"

"Nay, I'm fine," she insisted.

He gave one of his lazy grins, his eyes crinkling at the corners in a nice, kind way. "Ye wee fibber. Aye, ye are." He stopped suddenly, so she stopped too.

"Come on and hop up on me back, I'll give ye a piggy-back ride the rest of the way home. We dinnae want ye fallin' asleep at dinner tonight, eh, and missin' the fun?" he said, adjusting the cloth bag containing the picnic things so she could climb on his back.

So, Agnes found herself riding on Conrad's broad back the rest of the way back to the castle, her legs wrapped around his waist and her arms curled around his neck, with his blond hair tickling her nose.

She felt like a princess. And in her childish heart Conrad was her prince.

CHAPTER ONE

November 1715,

Keppoch Castle, Lochaber, the Scottish Highlands

"Saoirse, ye're hurtin' me. 'Tis way too tight." Lady Agnes MacDonald exclaimed as she braced herself with her arms against the bedpost while her maid laced her into her corset.

"Yer maither says I must tie it at tight as possible and snatch yer stomach," Saoirse replied, but in her usual kindly fashion, she relented enough to loosen the lacing so her mistress could breathe more easily and stopped feeling pain in her belly. For the moment, at least. "Here, put this on," she added, fetching a voluminous travel cloak from the bed and draping it around Agnes's shoulders. It enveloped her small frame from head to toe. "It'll hide a multitude of sins," Saoirse told her with a wink.

"Thank ye, Saoirse," Agnes told her with gratitude. "Now, have we packed everythin' I'll need?" She glanced around the room to see if they had forgotten anything. The chamber she had occupied for the whole of her twenty years seemed stripped to the bone, all the little personal items she had gathered over the years gone, packed and loaded onto a separate carriage that would follow them the next day. All that was left was the furniture, a few ornaments, some unwanted items of clothing, and a rumpled coverlet on the four-poster bed where she had spent many idle, happy hours daydreaming, reading, and sleeping.

"Nay, I've checked and checked twice already," Saoirse replied, picking up a large tapestry bag that was almost bursting and going to open the chamber door. "We're ready tae go."

Agnes collected her reticule from the vanity and followed the maid out into the hallway with a heavy heart. "I wonder how long it'll be before I come back here again tae me old chambers. Maybe I'll nae come back at all," she said sadly. The thought of leaving the only home she had ever known was both daunting and heartbreaking.

"Now, none of that sort of talk," Saoirse chided gently as they made their way along the hallway in the direction of the staircase. "Of course, ye'll be back. Folks go away from their homes all the time. Look at me, for instance. And they live tae tell the tale, and so will ye, me lady. So stop yer mitherin' and cheer up. 'Tis nae the end of the world. But we'd best keep an eye out when we get downstairs. We dinnae wantae bump intae yer faither on the way, eh?"

That had Agnes quickening her steps as they started down the stairs. She had weathered too many black looks of angry disapproval from her father in the last day or so to last her a lifetime. He must be avoided if at all possible, and she had no expectation he would come and wave her off.

"Besides, 'tis nae as though we're goin' tae the moon. 'Tis only France, and that's just across the water. People go there all the time. I'll be with ye, and ye're goin' tae stay with yer own family as well. Really, me lady, in the circumstances, there's little tae complain of," the ever-practical Saoirse said on the way down.

They reached the bottom of the stairs, their booted footsteps noiseless on the thick rugs as they made their way down the broad, lamplit corridor leading to the castle's main hallway.

"Aye, I ken ye're right, Saoirse, but I cannae help feelin' sad and a bit nervous. I've never been tae France afore, and me Aunt Morag and her family are practically strangers," Agnes confessed to her trusted confidante.

"Aye, and I've never been tae France afore either. At least ye can speak French! I cannae, so I truly will be among strangers. But I've heard the French gentlemen are very handsome and charmin' though, so it cannae be all bad. Maybe I'll come back with a nice French husband, eh? That would be a turn up for the books, would it nae? Think of what me ma would say tae that. She'd have a fit!"

Agnes managed a weak smile at that scenario, being well acquainted with Saoirse's eccentric mother. She was truly grateful for her maid's ceaseless attempts to keep her spirits up, even if they were not entirely successful in easing the general sense of unease that held her in its grasp.

"I must go ahead of ye, me lady, tae make sure the hand luggage has been put in the right carriage," Saoirse muttered, hurrying ahead of Agnes along the corridor, clutching the bulging tapestry bag in her arms as if it were a fat child.

"Aye, all right," Agnes said, pleased to have an excuse to dawdle a little and take a last look at the familiar surroundings, knowing she would not see them again for some time. Years probably. Things had happened so fast since the day before, her head was still spinning, and she had not had time to say goodbye properly to anything or anyone she valued, or so she felt.

She had stopped to take a final look at her favourite painting, when a hand clamped around her arm, and she found herself being pulled backwards.

"What-what—!" she gasped, bewildered when she was dragged bodily into the cupboard on the opposite side of the wall, into stuffy darkness, to be crushed against a large, warm body.

"Haud yer wheesht, sister," came a familiar voice next to her ear, low and conspiratorial.

Relief flooded through her. "Duncan! What d'ye think ye're daein'?" she cried, before he clamped a hand over her mouth. "Wheesht, I told ye. D'ye want Faither tae hear us?" he hissed at her. "Listen, here he comes," he added in a whisper.

Frozen, Agnes listened. Heavy footsteps were coming along the corridor, unmistakably their father's. She and Duncan held their breath, and Agnes wondered why he seemed as concerned as she was that they should not be discovered by him. Duncan was the son and heir, literally the blue-eyed boy in Laird MacDonald's view. The steps passed in front of the cupboard door, and she heard her father's voice.

"Apparently, he's on his way here now," he was saying, sounding none too pleased. "He could arrive at any moment. Dinnae keep him waitin'. As soon as he gets here, show him straight tae me study."

"Aye, me laird." Agnes recognized the voice of Willy Grey, her father's steward, answering him.

Thankfully, the pair continued on past the cupboard and into the depths of the castle. The siblings both breathed out. After a few moments of intense listening to make sure the danger had passed, Duncan opened the door a crack and peeked out. "The coast is clear," he said stepping in to the corridor and giving Agnes his hand to help her out too.

"Duncan, why did ye have tae drag me intae that cupboard?" she quizzed him in irritation as she brushed dust from her cloak.

"Ye must hurry, Agnes," he told her, his voice low but filled with urgency. She grew more irritated when he took hold of her arm again and began pulling her along the corridor, forcing her to trot to keep up with his long strides.

"Whatever fer? There's nay rush," she replied, wondering what the emergency was.

"Aye, there is. I'm nae jokin'. Ye really must hurry. Maither's already in the carriage in the courtyard waitin' fer ye."

"What? Why?" Agnes asked, puzzled as they rushed along.

"Because Faither had a message just half an hour ago tae say that Laird Tavish MacDonnell of Glengarry is on his way here, and he's due tae arrive any minute. He cannae see ye, and ye must be gone before he gets here."

The news was indeed alarming. Realizing that Duncan was right, she had to be away from the castle before Laird MacDonnell arrived—to avoid embarrassing her parents—she stepped up her pace to keep level with Duncan, hurrying alongside him down the corridor, heading for towards the castle's main exit. "What's he comin' here fer anyway?" he asked.

"He wants yer hand in marriage, Agnes."

"He what?!" She suddenly stopped dead, shaking off his grip as shock and disbelief ran through her. She had no idea MacDonnell even knew of her existence. "He wants tae wed me?"

Duncan grabbed her arm again and resumed his rapid pace. "Aye. He wrote tae Faither sayin' he wants tae marry ye, and Faither was keen tae accept the offer."

Agnes bristled with fury. "He was gonnae accept it? Well, what a nerve! He wanted tae wed me tae that man, and he never even consulted me on the matter."

"Dinnae be a child, sister," Duncan said matter-of-factly as they sped along. "Ye're the daughter of a laird. It was tae have been a strategic marriage, a union of alliance between the two clans. Yer opinion would have been neither here nor there. 'Tis nae required that ye should like yer husband in such marriages."

"But he couldnae have seriously expected me tae wed a monster like MacDonnell?" she said, her anger at her father flaring as the full implications of what Duncan was telling her sank in. It occurred to her that, while the situation she found herself was far from ideal, she had in fact had a lucky escape from what would undoubtedly have been a life of misery. MacDonnell was a famously brutal man, warlike and violent.

"Well, 'tis out of the question now. In the circumstances, Faither had nae choice but tae write back tae MacDonnell refusin' his offer fer yer hand," her brother explained, picking up their already rapid pace.

"So, why's he comin' here then?" Agnes asked, puffing along next to him.

"I've nae idea. Maybe because he hasnae seen Faither's letter yet or maybe because he has and he's furious about bein' turned down. It daesnae matter now. Faither has nae choice but meet him face tae face and reject his offer in person."

"Ach, Lord above!" Agnes murmured, furious at her father for arranging such a dreadful match for her. As far as she was concerned, it served him right if he had to suffer the embarrassment of telling MacDonnell to his face that his offer of marriage had been rejected. "I'm glad I'll nae have tae marry him," she added.

"Ach, but it brings us many problems," Duncan said.

"What d'ye mean by that? I suppose ye'd like tae see me wed tae MacDonnell as well, is that it?" she demanded, somewhat hurt as well as offended by her brother's attitude.

"Ach, Jaysus! Of course, I wouldnae, ye wee fool. But d'ye nae ken what sort of man MacDonnell is?"

"Aye, a cruel brute."

"Exactly. He's unlikely tae take the refusal well. He likes tae get what he wants, and if he's thwarted, he'll likely resort tae makin' war against us in revenge."

"Ye mean he could start a feud with Faither?" Agnes asked with a mixture of fear and guilt as the true horror of the situation she had wrought started to dawn on her. Was she going to be indirectly responsible for starting a war where her clansfolk and even her family members could die? It felt overwhelming.

"Aye, 'tis a big risk," Duncan replied as they reached the castle's entrance hall, where Duncan halted them by the main door.

"But what will Faither say tae him?" Agnes asked anxiously.

Duncan let go of her hand. "Wait," he instructed, opening the door slightly and looking outside for signs of the visitor. "He's nae here yet. Come on, hurry." Grabbing Agnes hand again, he pulled her outside and down the steps into the torchlit courtyard.

"He's gonnae tell him that ye're ill and at death's door," he explained as they walked rapidly towards the waiting carriage, which stood a few yards in front of them. The breath of the horses billowed out like clouds of white smoke into the freezing air, and Saoirse stood by the door, hugging herself and stamping her feet against the cold, waiting for Agnes.

"Why is he gonnae tell him that?" a mystified Agnes asked as Duncan hurried her on, scanning the area for hints of the visitor.

"What else can he say? Ye've nae left him a lot of choice. He can hardly tell him the truth." They stopped next to Saoirse. Any misunderstanding between the siblings fell away as Duncan kissed Agnes' cheek, and the pair embraced each other warmly.

"I'll miss ye, Braither," she said truthfully, hating the tremor in her voice. She needed to appear strong.

"Dinnae worry, Sister. France is yer best option now. Ye'll be safe there, and I'll be over tae visit ye as soon as I can."

"Aye, thank ye, Duncan. Take care of yersel' until then," she told him, determinedly holding back her tears.

He opened the carriage door and handed her up the steps, then helped Saoirse in after her. While she and Agnes settled in their seats, he poked his head inside and said quickly, "Goodbye fer now. Have a safe journey, all of ye. I'll see ye soon, Maither, when ye return."

"Aye, Son," Lady MacDonald replied despondently from her seat opposite the two young women. Duncan closed the door and banged on the side of the vehicle to signal to the driver to be off. The carriage moved rapidly out through the castle gates and down the twisting road. They were heading north to the port of Aberdeen where, in three days' time, they would board a ship bound for mainland France.

In the darkness of the carriage, Agnes looked across at her mother. Even at fifty, Lady Fiona MacDonald was still considered to be a beautiful woman. On this cold night, her petite frame was swathed in furs. Her soft, once golden-brown hair, now slightly faded with age, was hidden beneath an elegant fur hat. Her delicate, almost girlish features peeped out from within the nest of fur like the face of a perfect little doll.

But it was her expression of deep sadness and disappointment that struck at Agnes like a knife, because she knew she was the cause of it. She thought it a mercy that the dim light in the carriage prevented her from looking into the blue grey of mother's eyes and feeling even worse about the pain she knew she was inflicting upon her. It was far, far more agonizing to hurt her mother than face the harsh, cold anger of her father.

However, despite all this, Agnes was too proud to abase herself, to cry and beg for forgiveness from either of her parents. No, she was determined to hold her head high, be strong, to show she was not ashamed of what she had done.

So, when she finally spoke to her mother as the carriage bowled swiftly down the well-used and therefore relatively even road, her tone was unwavering and forthright.

"Maither, is it right that ye and Faither are seriously plannin' tae tell Laird MacDonnell that I'm at death's door with some sort of sickness?"

Her mother looked at her sharply. "Well, what else d'ye imagine we could say? The truth? That ye're ruined and can never be a nobleman's wife? Tellin' him yer life is in danger from some sort of illness is the only thing we can say that might, I say might, nae offend him and start a war. The clan is nae strong enough tae fight him. That was why we needed the marriage alliance with him in the first place. Which ye've now wrecked by yer irresponsible actions."

Agnes was once more taken aback by the harshness of her tone, which was so unusual for her. But her mother had not finished it seemed and went on in the same manner. "I mean, with the situation as it is, 'tis nae as though ye can wed another man powerful enough tae take MacDonnell on, is it? If we put it about that ye've died, then we'd risk gossip gettin' out that it isnae true, which if MacDonnell gets wind of, will also likely mean war.

"And it would mean ye couldnae return tae Scotland without putting yersel' and all of us at great risk. Ye've backed us intae a corner, Daughter. This is the only way." She subsided angrily into her furs like a disgruntled chicken with badly ruffled feathers.

Agnes knew it was all true, every word. Yet despite the danger posed by MacDonnell and her feelings of guilt over the situation—or perhaps defensiveness because of it—something in her rebelled against the web of lies her parents were spinning around her, which they expected her to simply accept. Would the truth, though embarrassing to them, have been so bad to admit? Was this farce she was being forced to play out to prevent Laird MacDonnell from making war on their clan? Or was it to save face?

Acting on impulse, she met her mother's angry gaze defiantly. Pulling aside her cloak, she shifted in her seat until her back was turned to Saoirse and said to the maid, "Saoirse, will ye unlace this bloody corset, fer God's sake? I think me maither's tryin' tae kill me. I cannae breathe."

Saoirse looked hesitantly from one to the other of them. But finally, being the faithful friend and helper she was to her young mistress, or perhaps figuring that since she and Agnes would soon be in France, there was little Lady MacDonald could do to punish her, she did as she was asked.

Her mother shook her head. "Ye ken, Agnes, I hardly recognize ye. Where's that calm and dutiful daughter of old, eh? Ye were always sensible, even as a child, stayin' out of trouble, respectful and obedient tae me and yer faither. But now look at ye. A reckless woman with nay regard fer either her own good or that of others, a woman who's made a huge mistake that's gonnae ruin her life and maybe start a war."

Provoked by her mother's accusation, Agnes placed her hand ostentatiously on her belly and said, "Ye can call me what ye like, Maither, but I'll nae allow ye or anyone tae call me bairn a mistake."

Her mother snorted in derision. "Ach, ye're so proud of yersel', are ye nae? But ye're a foolish child if ye believe ye can keep the faither's name a secret forever."

"I'll nae be tellin' ye nor anyone if I dinnae choose tae. I'll keep it a secret if I havetae take it tae me grave!" Agnes snapped back, her nerves at breaking point with the recent news and heartily sick of having been grilled on the subject of the father's identity by both her parents for hours.

And ye can bet that fer as long as I live, I'll nae be tellin' Faither who the faither of me bairn is!

CHAPTER TWO

Five years later,

July 1720, on the road to Keppoch Castle

The carriage wheels kept up a steady rhythm as the vehicle rolled along the road, heading for the home Agnes had not seen for five long years. She was back on Scottish soil once again, unexpectedly.

She had returned because her Aunt Morag, with whom she had been living in France, had succumbed to the feverish sickness which had been sweeping across Europe for several months. The poor woman was gravely ill, and though Agnes hated to leave her, it was decided that she and her four-year old daughter Roisin would be safer if they returned to Scotland until the danger had passed. Naturally, the ever-faithful Saoirse was accompanying them home.

It had been a long and tiring journey and by the time they drew near to Castle Keppoch, it was late. The sun had just sunk below the horizon, staining the sky in startling shades of pink, apricot, and lemon, which were gradually being overtaken by darkness. The July night was warm, and the interior of the carriage felt stuffy to Agnes, although it might have been partly due to her restlessness. She was wide awake, itching to reach the castle and get out of the carriage.

In contrast, Saoirse was dozing, her dark head bobbing against the back of the seat with every turn of the wheels and mercifully, an over-excited Roisin had finally fallen asleep on Agnes' lap. Agnes was absently stroking her daughter's silky hair as she slumbered, her little thumb in her mouth.

In the quietude, Agnes was thinking of Duncan. She was looking forward to seeing him most of all. He and her mother had last visited them in France six months ago, but it seemed like an eternity now. When Roisin had been born, Agnes' mother had been smitten with her granddaughter, and Agnes knew Roisin would never lack for love from that quarter.

Likewise, Duncan had taken to being an uncle like a duck to water. Roisin adored him, and the pair had spent hours playing together. Agnes delighted in witnessing this different side to her otherwise tough brother, a softer, protective side which told her he would make a wonderful father to his own children one day.

And yet, she was filled with trepidation, hence her restlessness. Because there was someone else at the castle awaiting them, someone she could not be sure would welcome Roisin so warmly. Her father. Once she had longed for his approval, but now, she no longer cared very much if he still insisted on treating her coldly. She would happily return the favour. But she would not tolerate any behaviour from anyone that made Roisin feel in the least bit unwanted or unloved. And of all her close family, her father was the one she feared was most likely to do exactly that.

As far as she was concerned, her trepidation was based on sound supposition. He had treated her coldly before she left for France, and he had not once troubled himself to write to her or make the journey to France to see her and his granddaughter in the entire five years she had been away.

He had always been a stern, unemotional father, not given to displays of affection towards his children. He had never been cruel, but he inspired more respect than love.

Agnes had come to realize over her years in France that he had perceived her pregnancy as an attack. It had made him feel he had failed to manage his daughter, and the disgrace she had brought upon him by doing so had been too much to forgive. She suspected that was still very much the case.

Such were the thoughts that were occupying her mind as the carriage rolled ever closer to the castle. She was suddenly shocked out of them by the sound of shouts coming from outside the vehicle, which suddenly drew to a shuddering halt. So abrupt was the stop, that Saoirse instantly awoke. Fortunately, cushioned on Agnes' lap, Roisin slept on.

"Are we there, me lady," Saoirse asked in a voice blurred by sleep, rubbing her eyes and yawning.

"Nay, we've stopped on the road. Listen, there's some sort of ruckus goin' on outside," Agnes told her hurriedly, her anxiety rising. They listened as the shouts of several men grew louder, more insistent, coming from immediately outside the vehicle. Needing to know what was going on and if it posed a threat to Roisin, Agnes sat up carefully to avoid disturbing the child, leaned over to the window, and raised the blind a little.

Peering out, trying to see what the cause of the commotion could be, she heard running feet but glimpsed only fast-moving shadows in the gathering darkness.

"Ach, 'tis too dark tae see anythin' properly," she told Saoirse in frustration, leaning back from the window. Yet still the shouts persisted, hard, sharp, unintelligible bursts of sound that gave Agnes the unsettling feeling of being encircled by a pack of dogs

The two women locked eyes, and Agnes could clearly see her own fear reflected back at her in Saoirse's.

"I dinnae like this one bit, me lady," the maid murmured, glancing worriedly at Roisin.

Agnes called up the driver. "Coachman, what is happening? Why have we stopped? Have we broken down?"

It was slightly reassuring to hear the driver's voice come back strongly, "Nay, me lady, but—" His reply was suddenly cut off by a blood-curdling scream, followed by a loud thud.

Agnes and Saoirse froze, staring at each other in undisguised alarm. "Me lady, I think we're bein' attacked by brigands," her maid hissed.

"Oh, Lord preserve us, Saoirse, I think ye're right," Agnes answered in a panicked whisper, starting to shake. Roisin, startled awake by the scream and confused and frightened by the shouting from outside, started to cry.

She clung to Agnes wide-eyed, her little face white with fear. "Mama, what was the man screamin' fer? Is he hurt?" she stammered, hardly able to speak.

Despite her rising panic, Agnes stroked Roisin's head and tried to reassure her. "Nay, darlin', he's all right. But there's some bad men outside, and ye need tae hide," she said, hearing the tremor in her own voice. She opened her cloak. "Come here, under me cloak. Now, ye must be a brave lass and dinnae make a peep or move until I tell ye 'tis safe, all right?"

Roisin nodded, tears streaming down her face as she scooted beneath the cloak and huddled against her mother, hidden from sight once Agnes folded it over her, thanking the heavens above that Roisin was a smaller child than other's her age.

"What shall we dae? We have naethin' tae defend oursel's with," Agnes whispered to Saoirse. "What are ye daein'?" she asked, seeing Saoirse frantically rummaging in her old tapestry bag, the same one she had brought with them when they had left five years before. It was stuffed with hers and Roisin's things as well as a host of other useful items.

"Aye, we dae, we have these," Saoirse whispered back, handing Agnes a dirk. She had another for herself, it appeared. She unsheathed the blade, while Agnes only stared at hers.

"But I've never used..." She hesitated to say knife in case it frightened Roisin further. So instead, she said, "... one of these before. I dinnae what tae dae with it."

"Well, I'm nay expert either, but there cannae be much tae it," Saoirse said, brandishing the blade in front of her. "I'll take that door, and ye take the other, and if anyone tries tae get in, do this." She demonstrated with a series of quick, darting thrusts at an imaginary enemy before shifting over to station herself at the door where Agnes had tried to look outside. "Ye need tae take it out of its sheath first," she added emphatically, noticing Agnes had not moved and was simply staring at the dirk in her hand.

"Aye, right," Agnes said numbly, pulling the knife out with shaking fingers and gripping the hilt. The blade was about ten inches long and looked frighteningly sharp. But any qualms she might have had about using it on another person or dying in the attempt were overtaken by her motherly instinct to protect Roisin at all costs.

"Aim fer the chest," Saoirse instructed, holding her tall body stiffly between them and the door, the knife in her outstretched hand pointed at it.

Agnes shifted slightly, making sure Roisin was positioned between them beneath her cloak, so she would be protected if they were boarded. The little mite clutched her mother's waist, her small body trembling, but she made not a peep.

"It'll be all right, darlin'," Agnes whispered, her arm around Roisin outside the cloak, trying to reassure the little girl as best she could. Then, the very thing she and Saoirse had been dreading actually occurred, for the carriage door on her side was suddenly wrenched open. Her heart leaped into her throat as she pointed the knife at the man who appeared in the doorway.

He was scruffily dressed, and he was wielding a dirk. When he saw the two women, his dark eyes gleamed, and his unshaven face split into a wolfish grin. "Well, well, well, looks like 'tis our lucky day. Good evenin' tae ye, ladies," he said in a rough voice, leering at them. Agnes felt a wave of fear and revulsion wash over her as his eyes swept over her body. She knew very well what happened to women caught by brigands on the road before they were murdered.

"What a fine lookin' pair ye are. Ye willnae mind if I come and join ye, will ye?" the brigand said, putting his foot on the step and heaving himself up, clearly about to get in. Agnes was shaking so much, she could hardly grip the dirk. She heard Saoirse moving behind her but could not see what she was doing.

"Och, two feisty ones, eh? That's what I like. A bit of spirit," the brigand said, obviously enjoying their terror.

"Dinnae even try tae come in here, ye robbin' bastard," Saoirse swore fiercely at the man, lunging forward protectively in front of Agnes and stabbing at him with the dirk. "Run, me lady, run!" she cried, doing her best to keep the brigand at bay.

"Ach, ye harridan, drop yer blade, or I'll cut yer throat!" the man yelled in pain as Saoirse's knife slashed at his hands and wrists. In a panic, afraid for the maid's life, Agnes dithered for a moment, hesitating to leave her. But when Saoirse shouted again, "Run! Get away!" she realized Roisin's safety had to come first.

Still clutching the dagger and holding tightly to the little body hidden beneath her cloak with one arm, she rushed to the opposite door, unlatched it with shaking fingers, and clambered awkwardly as fast as she could out onto the road. As soon as her feet hit the ground, she took off running into the trees, bent on finding a hiding place in the darkness. A shrill scream of pain from behind halted her, and when she turned to look over her shoulder, she was horrified to see Saoirse grappling with the brigand inside the carriage.

The man had hold of Saoirse's wrist and was twisting it cruelly, making her scream in pain and forcing her to drop the dirk before shoving her violently backwards.

"Saoirse!" Agnes screamed as the maid impacted the side of the door with a thud, fearing she was badly hurt. But Saoirse confounded her and the brigand by recovering almost immediately. Agnes watched as she hurled herself bodily through the door, hitting the ground in a crouch before pinpointing

Agnes in the tree line. "Run, find a place tae hide!" the maid shouted frantically, racing towards her.

But just as Agnes turned to start running again, from the corner of her eye, she saw the brigand leap from the carriage and sprint after them, brandishing his dirk. "Ye may as well give up runnin', ye ken I'll catch up tae ye, and it'll be the worse fer ye when I dae!" he yelled threateningly. Her heart hammering with terror, with Saoirse hot on her heels, Agnes fled. She pushed herself to run faster, clinging to the desperate hope they would be able to outpace him and lose themselves in the forest. Yet she knew her hope of escape was in vain.

Trying to negotiate the uneven forest floor in the dark at speed was proving too hazardous. She sobbed with fear and frustration as she ran, desperately keeping Roisin clasped to her hip with one arm, while tree roots and debris threatened to trip her up with every step. Her skirts snagged on the undergrowth and tore, and she narrowly dodged colliding with tree trunks that loomed out of nowhere. It was as though the forest itself was conspiring to slow her down.

Agnes' terror mounted to hear the brigand crashing after them through the trees, cursing them both roundly as he gained on her and Saoirse. The situation seemed hopeless, but she was determined to keep Roisin safe, no matter if it cost her her life. Even as she ran on blindly, she tried to marshal her thoughts, to come up with some sort of plan to save her daughter.

I still have the dirk, she thought, clutching the handle of the blade tightly in her free hand. *I need tae find somewhere tae hide Roisin, then make a stand. I'm gonnae have tae fight him off somehow and pray that help comes in time!*

She heard Saoirse let out a scream and then the brigand's ragged breathing coming ever closer. "Get away from me, ye bastard!" Agnes shouted at him over her shoulder, her maternal instincts roused to fever pitch. "Or I'll kill ye!"

"Ye can try, ye wee vixen, but ye'll nae succeed!" he shouted, hurling himself after her with renewed energy. Despite Agnes best efforts, it was only a matter of seconds before he came up behind her. She felt a large hand suddenly grip her wrist and, with savage force, twist it. She shrieked in agony, and the dirk fell unseen from her hand.

She could feel Roisin beneath her cloak, hanging on for dear life, her little body trembling violently. All Agnes' instincts told her to disentangle herself from Roisin's grasp and tell the child to run and hide, but there was no time. In a flash, she found herself pinned against a large tree trunk, with the brigand looming over her menacingly, filling her purview. Certain she was about to meet her maker, terrified for her daughter, in a last-ditch appeal for help, Agnes let out a loud, desperate scream.

What happened next was a confusing blur. One moment the brigand was there, snarling in her face with fury. The next, she heard his skull crack as something hit him over the head. He watched uncomprehendingly as his eyes rolled back in his head, and he dropped like a stone to the ground at her feet.

Agnes stared in stupefaction as his place was immediately filled by another man. But this one was far bigger, taller, more powerfully built, his shoulders broad enough to block her view. Unsure if this was a new threat or someone come to save them, she dared not let down her guard. With her heart still pounding in her ears, Agnes tightened her hold on Roisin as the newcomer sheathed his sword then reached down and dragged the clearly deceased brigand up by the scruff of his neck and tossed him aside as if he weighed nothing.

Then, he dusted off his hands and looked down at her, sheathing his sword with practiced ease. "He'll nae be troublin' ye anymore, Miss. Are ye all right?" he asked, his deep, husky voice filled with concern.

The reassuring words should have calmed Agnes, who was shaking from head to foot, having believed only moments before that she was about to die. Instead, the sound of his voice sent a powerful tremor of recognition through her body that set her heart racing afresh. *Nay, it cannae be him. 'Tis the shock. I'm hearin' things,* she told herself, her mind reeling.

"Miss, 'tis all right," the man told her softly, clearly worried by her silence. "I promise, ye're safe now. Did that bastard hurt ye?"

Agnes did not answer but put a hand to her head, still convinced she was experiencing some sort of delusion. *I must have banged it without realizin' it,* she thought, staring up uncomprehendingly at the man's shadowy features. *'Tis the only explanation fer it.*

"Me lady! Are ye all right? Where's the wee yin?" *Saoirse! She's unharmed, thank God!* Agnes thought with relief as the maid hurried towards them. Unable to speak, she could only nod mutely. Pulling aside her cloak, she revealed a shivering, tearful Roisin tightly clasped to her side.

Saoirse clasped her hands to her cheeks and smiled. "Och, thank the Lord above!" Then, as if remembering something, she glanced up at their rescuer and added, "I mean tae say, thank the Lord fer sendin' ye tae save us, Sir."

"Think naethin' of it. I'm only glad I arrived in time," he replied. "Now, let's get out of here and back tae the coach. There may be more of those brigands lurkin' about here. 'Tis nae safe fer ye tae stay."

As they followed him back through the trees to the road, Agnes became aware of the sounds of fighting growing louder as they approached. When she saw the carriage and the coachman slumped insensibly in his seat, both she and Saoirse gasped in shock.

"Is he…?" Saoirse asked, looking up at the man.

"Nay, just unconscious. He's taken a nasty knock tae the head though," their rescuer replied. However, Agnes attention had been snared by the sight of two men engaged in a fierce sword fight a short distance away. Reflexively, she covered Roisin's eyes, not wanting the child to witness any bloodshed.

Suddenly one of the men broke away and ran off down the road, with the other charging after him in hot pursuit. "Braither!" Agnes cried out, instantly recognizing the pursuer as Duncan. And the man he was chasing was clearly another of the brigands. "Be careful!" she called after him fearfully, her heart in her mouth as she watched him slowly gaining on the brigand. Silently, she prayed he would triumph.

Then, as she knew it inevitably would, the familiar deep, husky voice came from her side, breaking into her distraction over her brother and setting her heart throbbing painfully.

"Agnes? Is it ye?"

She made herself turn and look at him, at his expression of utter shock, and her insides turned to water. Five years had scarred and hardened his sculpted features somewhat. His blond hair was longer, curling around his ears. There were a few more lines around his mouth and at the corners of his eyes. But to her dismay, time only seemed to have increased his allure.

He was a fearsome warrior, marked by battle, frightening to look upon. Yet he was without a doubt the most beautiful, desirable man she had ever seen. The sight of him was like a knife twisting in her heart, for she loved him with all her heart but could never let him know it.

His presence threw her into fresh turmoil. *Why is he here? Maither said he'd be away fightin' with Duncan. Ach, this is a disaster! How the hell am I gonnae keep the truth from him now?*

"Aye, Conrad," she eventually replied, trying to keep her voice steady as a storm of emotions coursed through her. "'Tis me."

CHAPTER THREE

"I'm sorry, but as ye can see, the coachman's out of action, and me and Duncan must search the woods tae check if there are any more of those brigands hiding hereabouts. If I unhitch a couple of the horses, will the wee lassie be all right if ye ride tae the castle?" Conrad asked, unable to take his eyes off of Agnes.

"Aye, she loves horses, she'll be fine," Agnes replied, though the little blonde-haired girl she was holding so tightly was still crying, shaking, staring at him mutely, wide-eyed with fear.

"Ye dinnae need tae be afraid, lassie, I'll nae hurt ye," he told her gently, giving the child what he hoped was a reassuring smile. But it failed to have the desired effect, for she looked even more afraid. Agnes spoke to her in low, soothing tones, while the child clung to her neck like a monkey. Who daes the wee lass belong tae? he wondered, confused by how close the pair seemed.

"I need tae fetch the bag from the carriage," the maid said, interrupting his train of thought. She hurried to the open door of the vehicle and reached inside. She came back clutching a bulging tapestry bag in her arms. There was a sudden shout from somewhere out of sight, which Conrad hoped was Duncan finally dispatching the last of the brigands that had attacked the carriage. But he was still worried that more might be lurking nearby, and it made him even more anxious to get the women away to safety. He herded them to the front of the vehicle and hurriedly unhitched a pair of horses from the four standing in the shafts.

He was unprepared for the jolt that ran through him when his hand brushed Agnes' as he passed her the reins. It suddenly hit him that it was the first time they had touched since she had left him five years ago. It shook him up so much, he had to snatch his hand away, and he was certain she felt it too because she did the same. And even in the moonlight, he could see her cheeks redden.

She's more beautiful than ever, he thought, his eyes scanning her pale, tearstained face, a familiar pang of agonizing loss lancing through him. Why did ye leave me like that, Agnes? Why did ye go and never even say goodbye, nae a word from ye in five long years?

Realizing she still had the same effect on him was deeply unsettling, unleashing a whole hornet's nest of deeply buried emotions that threatened to betray his true feelings for her if he did not maintain rigid self-control.

He saw Agnes glance back worriedly in the direction of the cry and knew she was afraid for her brother. "Duncan will be all right, dinnae worry," he told her, but her tense expression told him she was unconvinced.

"Here, take the horses and ride as fast as ye can."

"Aye, thank ye, Conrad," Agnes said, her voice shaking as she grasped the reins tightly, the little girl still hanging onto her for dear life. "Soairse, will ye take her?" she asked the maid, gently disentangling herself from the child's arms and handing her to Saoirse, the tall, capable-looking lass of a similar age to herself that always accompanied her.

Who is this wee lassie? Conrad wondered, confused by the interplay between the trio. Agnes was acting as if he was the mother, but he knew that was impossible. Or was it? She's been away five years. Maybe she met a man in France. Maybe she's even married. Pain twisted in his gut to think of it, the burning pain of jealousy.

"Aye, give her here," Saoirse replied, taking the child onto her hip, kissing and cuddling her while he boosted Agnes up into the saddle. He noticed how the little girl wound her arms around the maid's neck, appearing to take comfort in her caresses.

"Who daes the child belong tae?" Conrad asked Agnes, looking at her searchingly, needing an answer urgently.

"She's-she's—" she muttered.

"She's mine," the maid interjected. "But me lady loves her like her own as ye can see," she added, smiling at him as he bounced the child gently on her hip.

"She can ride with me, Saoirse," Ages said, reaching down for the child. Saoirse handed her up, and Agnes settled her in her lap. She cast Conrad what he thought was an oddly shifty glance as she added, "I'm a better horsewoman. She'll be safer with me than with her maither."

"Aye, she will," Saoirse agreed, putting down the tapestry bag to take the reins of the other horse and allowing Conrad to boost into the saddle. He passed it up to her. "Thank ye. And thanks again fer comin' out tae rescue us," she told him with obvious gratitude before wheeling the horse about.

Well, all right, he thought, his jealousy turning to relief. 'Tis the maid's child. Agnes is soft-hearted and cares fer the wee yin, 'tis all. He looked up at Agnes and said, "Away with ye then, and dinnae stop for anythin'."

"Nay, we'll go straight to the castle," she assured him, glancing worriedly again down the road after Duncan before skilfully wheeling her horse around in the direction of her home. In Conrad's eyes, her anxiety only heightened her pale, delicate beauty. "Thank ye again, Conrad. We're very grateful fer yer help. Bring Duncan home safe."

"Aye, I will," he replied, unable to help gazing up at her, still hardly believing she was back.

"And yersel', of course," she added, looking down at him.

"Ye can be sure of it," he replied, secretly touched by the unexpected show of concern for him but determined not to let her see it.

She's only bein' polite, that's all. Dinnae get tae thinkin' she cares about ye. However much ye wish she did.

"Away ye go now," he repeated.

"All right. Come on, Saoirse, we must hurry and get the little one tae safety," Agnes told the maid, kicking up her horse and setting off at a canter, followed immediately by Soairse.

Filled with a mixture of warring emotions, Conrad stood and watched while the women sped off down the road towards the castle, until they were no more than vague shapes in the darkness.

Agnes rode almost without seeing the road ahead. Her eyes were blurred with tears, her head full of Conrad. Her heart was aching in her chest, not from the ride, but from the shock of seeing him again after such a long time. Unable to cope with the welter of emotions their meeting had stirred up inside her, she tried to push them down as the towers of her old home loomed up before them.

Before they reached the gates, they had already swung open as if to welcome her home. She and Saoirse rode straight into the main courtyard, their horses' hooves clattering noisily on the cobblestones.

Naethin' has changed yet it feels very strange tae be back here again after so long, Agnes thought, glancing around the torchlit enclosure as she and Saoirse reined in near the entrance to the castle keep. She looked around at the familiar scene while she waited for Saoirse to dismount and take Roisin from her.

"She's a wee bit calmer after the ride," she told the maid, who set her bag down on the cobblestones before Agnes carefully handed Roisin down to her waiting arms.

"Aye, she loves the horseys. That's right, eh, little one?" Saoirse murmured affectionately as she let Roisin pet the horses for a moment. Agnes realized that, just like her, Saoirse was hoping Roisin's love of horses would help wipe away the shock of her recent ordeal. Agnes slid from her saddle to the ground and handed the reins over to a waiting groom, who led the horses away.

"Night night, horseys," Roisin called after them winsomely, waving.

"We'll go and visit them tomorrow in the stables, shall we, darlin'?" Agnes asked her. "We'll take them some carrots and apples tae eat. Would ye like that?"

"Aye, Ma, I would!"

"Agnes! Where's the carriage? Why did ye ride in like that? Is everythin' all right?" Her mother came hurrying from the keep towards them.

"Aye, we're all right, Maither," Agnes told her as they went to meet her. "We were attacked by brigands on the road, but Duncan and Conrad and some of their men fought them off. They've gone to check the woods to see if there are any more of them." As they walked towards the open doors of the keep, she explained about the injured coachman being the reason why Conrad had insisted they take the horses.

"Is Duncan all right," her mother asked worriedly as they stepped inside. Duncan was her pride and joy. Deservedly so, Agnes thought.

She silently prayed he was safe, and she did not wish to alarm her mother by telling her that the last she had seen of him, he had been fighting furiously with one of the brigands. So, she just said, "Aye, he's fine. He'll be along shortly, I expect."

"Och, thank the good Lord," her mother exclaimed with obvious relief. Then, she looked at Agnes with a faint air of disappointment and said, "So, ye made it home safely then."

"Aye, we made it home, Maither," Agnes replied, quite used to being the object of her mother's quiet dissatisfaction. It no longer bothered her. All that mattered to her was that her mother loved Roisin.

As soon as Roisin heard her grandmother's voice, she wanted

to go to her. "Grandma!" she cried, reaching out for her. "There were bad men on the road!"

Lady Fiona held out her arms to the child, and Saoirse put Roisin down so she could run to her. The older woman scooped her up in her arms and hugged her tightly, peppering her face with kisses. "Och, me wee angel, I ken. Ye must have been very frightened," she told her little granddaughter soothingly, stroking her hair, clearly hiding her own alarm at what could have befallen her.

"She was very brave," Agnes said, giving Roisin an encouraging smile as they entered the keep. "I was very proud of her." She was rewarded by a bright, gappy smile from her daughter.

"I've had yer old chambers prepared fer ye and a room next door fer Roisin and Saoirse," her mother said as they stood in the vestibule at the bottom of the sweeping mahogany staircase. "We've arranged a special dinner this evenin' in honour of Duncan's safe return from battle. This is the first time he's been home since we came tae visit ye in France."

"He's been away fightin' fer six months?" Agnes asked, surprised. "I'm awful glad he's come home safe. That's cause fer celebration all right." Something else occurred to her then. "Is that why Conrad's here as well? I thought ye said he'd be away when I came."

"Nay, they came back taegether," Lady Fiona replied distractedly. "There was a change of plan, that's all. The dinner will start at seven o'clock, and ye'd best be on time. Ye ken what yer faither's like. He cannae abide tardiness."

Agnes gave a wry chuckle. "Ye dinnae need tae remind me, Maither," she said in answer to her mother's warning look.

"Well, time's getting' on. Ye'd best go upstairs now and get the wee one settled in if ye're tae be ready fer seven," Lady Fiona replied. She put Roisin down, kissed her on the cheek, and said fondly, "Go on now, pet, I'll come and say good night tae ye later, all right?"

"All right, Grandma. Dinnae forget though," Roisin said as Agnes took her hand and they and Saoirse started up the stairs.

"Lord, what a day!" Saoirse sighed as they entered the room next door to Agnes' old chambers. She put down the bulging tapestry bag she had brought from the carriage and rubbed her back.

"Aye, and what a night," Agnes agreed, taking in the small bed that had been set up next to the one Saoirse would occupy during their stay. The family had decided it would save them embarrassment if everyone thought Roisin was the maid's child. Even though Agnes did not like it, she knew she had no choice but to accept it.

"Are ye tired, wee one?" Saoirse asked, looking at Roisin, who was yawning and rubbing her eyes. "I'll put her tae bed. Ye'd best go and get ready tae meet yer faither," she told Agnes.

"Aye, thank ye, Saoirse." While Roisin went over to test out her bed, Agnes leaned closer and whispered to the maid, "And thank ye fer nae givin' me away tae Conrad. I couldnae believe it when I saw him standin' there. Me heart was racin' when he asked ye who Roisin belonged tae."

"Aye, I bet it was," Saoirse whispered back as they stood watching indulgently while Roisin bounced on the bed. "'Tis better that everyone thinks she's mine. It would only be embarrassin' fer ye all if anyone outside the family learned ye're her maither. I dinnae mind goin' along with it fer yer sake, me lady."

"I hate lyin' tae everyone, but ye ken what me family's like. They still look on me as their shameful secret."

"Well, there's bound tae be a few tricky moments, but we'll get through it as best we can," Saoirse told her in her usual practical way. She was the only one Agnes trusted enough to tell the truth about the identity of Roisin's father, and Agnes knew she would keep the secret no matter what. "Now, time's gettin' on, me lady," her friend said, always looking out for her. "Ye'd best go and make yersel' respectable if ye're gonnae meet yer faither at this celebration later."

"Aye, all right." Agnes went over to Roisin, who had collapsed on the bed giggling, and hugged her. "Saoirse will get ye ready fer bed while I go and change, me darlin'. But I'll be back in a little while tae kiss ye goodnight," she promised.

"All right," Rosin said, kissing her cheek and looking at her hopefully. "Can I have some milk and shortbread before bed? I've been very good, and I was very brave when the bad men came."

"Of course, ye can, love. Saoirse will see tae it fer ye. Now, I must go and change."

Agnes left the room and went into her old chambers next door. Lamps had been lit, and a fire burned in the grate, giving the room a warm, inviting glow. Her bed was still there, all made up with fresh linen. It felt strange, but at the same time good to be back.

Despite her trepidation about meeting her father again after so long, she found she was quite looking forward to spending time with her family and celebrating Duncan's safe return. But her anticipation was laced with fear—fear of bumping into Conrad again.

He's bound tae be at the dinner too. Ach, I'll just have tae dae me best tae avoid him and keep him at arm's length. Even if it pains me tae dae it…

CHAPTER FOUR

Filled with resolve, Agnes distracted herself by taking a tour of the room. She noticed a few necessities had been left on the vanity and guessed her mother was responsible. There was a comb and hairbrush, some face powder, a pot of rouge, a small vial of scent, and some other useful things. Unfortunately, apart from the contents of the bag Saoirse had rescued from the carriage, she had nothing else with her. The bulk of her things were coming separately and would arrive in the next day. Or so, she hoped.

In the meantime, she realized she only had what she had left behind five years ago to wear. She opened the wardrobe and leafed through the few gowns still hanging there. They were all out of fashion, but she eventually selected a burgundy-coloured gown she had thought too grand to take with her to France. "It will dae," she murmured, taking it out and hanging it on the door.

"Lace me up, would ye, Saoirse, please," she said half an hour later, entering the room next door, with the back of her dress gaping. "I cannae dae it by mesel'." She hurried over to her maid, starting when the clock on the mantel chimed seven. "Ach, God, I'm gonnae be late fer the dinner. Me faither will be furious. That's all I need," she said, feeling under pressure.

Saoirse had been sitting next to Roisin's bed when she came in, but she got up at once and came over to help.

"Och, she's already asleep, I see," Agnes said, glad to see her daughter was now sleeping peacefully.

"Aye, the poor wee mite was more tired than she wanted tae admit, but as soon as her head hit the pillow, she was out like a light," the maid said with a smile, taking hold of corset strings. "D'ye remember daein' this before ye left fer France?" she asked as Agnes leaned against the bed post, while she pulled the laces of the corset tight and laced her in.

"Aye, I dae, and that's still too tight!" Agnes exclaimed breathlessly before Saoirse chuckled and let it out a little. "Just toyin' with ye," she said.

Once the gown was fastened, Agnes did a twirl and said, "Thank ye. Now, how dae I look?"

"Well, if we were back in France, I'd say that gown is rather old-fashioned," Saoirse replied. "But since we're in Scotland, where 'tis still the height of fashion, I'll say ye look stunnin', me lady."

Agnes could not help laughing at the comment. "Now that's a backhanded compliment if ever I heard one." She glanced at the clock to check the time and let out a little gasp. "Ach, I must hurry. I'll already be in Faither's bad books fer bein' late as it is. Shall I send a servant up fer ye, in case ye want tae get somethin' tae eat or a drink while I'm gone?" she asked Saoirse hurriedly as she rushed to the door.

"Nay, I'll be fine, me lady. I'm tired mesel'. Now Rosin's settled, I'll probably have nap. Wake me when ye get back though if ye would."

"Of course." Agnes paused by the door, looking back at her faithful friend with gratitude. "Thank ye again, Saoirse. I dinnae ken what we'd dae without ye."

"Ach, wheesht, off ye go and enjoy yer supper, me lady," Saoirse told her, waving her away with a modest smile.

She went the back way to the great hall and came out directly behind the laird's table, not wishing to run the gauntlet of walking up the central aisle through the tables, where the majority of the guests were already seated when she arrived ten minutes late. Unfortunately, her lateness made her the centre of attention among the guests at her father's table, a mixture of his advisors and their wives and families, as well as friends and allies. It seemed they all wanted to greet her and were curious to know where she had been and what she had been doing for the previous five years.

Her reply to their enquiries was always the same. "After I recovered from me illness, I stayed in France, lookin' after me Aunt Morag. She's old now, and she needs a bit of help and companionship. She misses Scotland, but she says she's too old tae make the journey home now, so 'twas easier fer me tae go there and stay with her."

It was not entirely a lie, and everyone seemed to accept it. However, she was shocked to hear that some of them believed her to be dead.

"Little Sister, 'tis good tae have ye back!"

Agnes wheeled around at the sound of her brother's voice. "Duncan! Ye're safe! Och, thank goodness." He opened his arms, and she threw herself into them, all her worries fading away in her delight at being reunited with her beloved brother.

"Oof! Hold on there, let me at least breathe before ye break me spine, will ye?" Duncan pretended to complain as she squeezed him with all her might. Laughingly, he lifted her off her feet in a bear hug before finally breaking their embrace. He held her hands in his as he scrutinized her face.

"My, ye look bonny. Are ye well? Is Roisin all right? Nae sign of that sickness poor old Aunt Morag has come down with?" he asked, a flash of worry in his eyes.

"Nay, I'm glad tae say, we're both very well," Agnes replied, unable to stop smiling as she in turn looked him over, relieved to see he had not a scratch upon him. "I think we left France just before it could really take hold ood," she explained. "Ye look well too. I was fearful fer ye when I saw ye fightin' with that brigand on the road."

"Och. He put up a bit of a fight, I admit, but I sent him tae meet his maker soon enough," he told her, pulling her in for another hug.

"Did ye find anymore brigands in the woods?" she asked when they finally broke apart.

"Nay, thankfully. I hate tae think what ye must have gone through. It must have been terrifyin'. I was so worried fer ye and the wee lass. She must have been so scared."

"Aye, she was the poor wee angel." She briefly explained what had happened, and how she had managed to conceal Roisin beneath her cloak while fightin' the attacker off.

"Ye're a brave woman, Sister. I'm proud of ye. Ye fought with more courage than many a man I've kent and kept her safe. Even so, thank God me and Conrad happened on ye, eh?"

"Aye, thank God," she agreed, knowing she owed Conrad her life and Roisin's too but wishing it had been Duncan who had saved them all the same. Not wanting to think about the problem Conrad's presence posed just then, she changed the subject. "What about ye? Maither says ye've been away fightin' since ye came back from visitin' me in France. Is that right?"

"Aye, but we won, and the war's over now fer good, I hope. 'Tis certainly grand tae come home and find ye here with the wee yin. I didnae think I'd be seein' ye fer a while. How's Auntie Morag though? D'ye think she'll pull through?"

"I'm nae sure. Ye ken she's gettin' on in years and isnae as strong as she used tae be. 'Tis a devastatin' sickness, tae be sure, but there are plenty who recover, and she's bein' well cared fer. We must hope and pray she'll be one of them. The plan is fer us tae go back tae France when the sickness is over."

His face fell a little. "Aye, I ken. 'Tis a damned shame. Ye should be here at home. If I had me way, ye would be, and Roisin would be growin' up a Scots lass instead of a French miss."

"Aye, but maybe 'tis better this way. It saves face fer Maither and Faither, and that's important tae them," she said, not mentioning the other more important reason why she preferred to live in France. Saoirse was the only one who knew that, and even though she hated to keep things from Duncan, she knew it was for the best. Again, she steered the subject away from herself.

Duncam glanced over her shoulder and gave a small grimace. "Faither is lookin' this way, and he's nae lookin' very happy," he warned.

Agnes let out a sigh of resignation. "Aye, nae doubt he's annoyed with me fer bein' a wee bit late," she said. "I suppose I'd better go and speak tae him and apologize. I admit, I'm nae lookin' forward tae it. Wish me luck, Braither."

"Aye, of course. I'm gonnae make sure tae enjoy me party, and I want ye tae have a nice time as well."

The siblings hugged once more. Duncan went off to socialize, while Agnes steeled herself and went to greet their father.

James MacDonald was a tall, imposing man. Still strong despite his fifty-five years, his silver-streaked black hair and lined face spoke of years of stern leadership as Laird of Clan MacDonald.

Determined not to be intimidated, Agnes bobbed a respectful curtsey as she faced him. "Good evenin', Faither."

He glowered at her. His hard, steely blue eyes, always sharp and watchful, bored into her. "Ye're late, Daughter," he said accusingly, his voice low and gravelly.

"I'm sorry, Faither. It couldnae be helped." She explained about the brigands and was surprised to see what might have been a flicker of concern in his eyes. But it was so fleeting, she could not be sure. She did not let herself imagine for a moment she was anything but an embarrassing disgrace in his eyes, but she refused to be cowed and insisted on completing her explanation. "Maither told me about the celebration when I got here, but I didnae have much time tae get ready."

He grunted and said grudgingly, "Well, now ye've graced us

with yer presence, ye'd better sit down." He nodded stiffly at the vacant chair next to her mother.

"Aye, Faither," she replied, going to sit down, glad to have gotten the initial meeting out of the way. But her relief was short-lived when she realized who was seated next to her.

Conrad!

CHAPTER FIVE

The moment he saw her, he got up and pulled out the chair for her, like the gentleman he was. Caught in a welter of conflicting emotions, she hardly dared look at him, but a sidelong glance told her his expression was stony. She assumed he would rather not have sat next to her. When their eyes did meet, she feared his piercing, light-blue gaze would see into her very soul and learn the secrets she had been keeping for so long. Feeling her cheeks grow hot, she had to look away, hoping to hide her blushes.

"Thank ye, Conrad," she murmured, summoning a fake smile as she sat down. He pushed the chair in for her, his fingers brushing against her back briefly, sending tingles running up her spine. When he resumed his seat next to her, they were so close, she could feel his heat burning through the fabric of her sleeve to the skin beneath. She perched in her chair, as stiff as a board, digging her nails into her palms beneath the table in an effort to maintain her outward composure.

I cannae bear it, I just cannae bear tae be so close tae him, she thought in despair, desperately trying to think of a way to leave the celebration without seeming rude.

But there was another part of her that yearned to stay at his side, to be as close to him as she could for as long as she could. She had loved Conrad for so long, her heart ached for him. And the fact it was unrequited love made it even more of a painful secret. Her unrequited love was the very reason she was determined to keep an even bigger secret from him, which meant she had to keep him at arm's length... and lie to him over and over again.

Watch what ye say if he asks ye any questions, she told herself. Dinnae slip up, because he must never, ever suspect the truth!

"Wine?" he asked shortly.

"Aye, yes, please." He picked up the jug and filled her glass. As he did so, his hands caught her attention, and her insides melted. Large, strong, square, tan, she could almost feel the hard callouses on his palms from wielding his sword. Her eyes brushed over the many scars she had always fancied to be writing in an unknown language that spoke of hard-won battles, of his strength and capability.

Stop that! Stop it at once! He's nae interested in ye. Stop yer moonin'. Ye' cannae afford tae act like a silly young girl anymore! That's what got ye intae this mess in the first place.

Nevertheless, she found herself transfixed by his hands as he topped up his tankard with ale. He took a long sup, and she took a long drink of her wine. Nervous as she was to converse with him, her gratitude won out.

"I wantae thank ye again fer what ye did fer us earlier, Conrad. If ye hadnae come just at that moment, I fear we'd all be dead by now. Ye saved our lives, and I'll always be grateful tae ye fer that."

Every word was heartfelt. The thought of any harm coming to Roisin was pure torture. But again she wished Duncan had saved them instead, so she never had to face Conrad Mackintosh again, let alone be grateful to him for her life and Roisin's.

He leaned his muscular arm along the back of his chair and skewed his body to face her, his penetrating gaze searching her face. Just looking at his handsome features made her heart race. She lowered her eyes, partly because of the effect he had on her, partly because she was scared of what he would see in them.

"So, ye've come back then," he said gruffly.

"Well, 'tis either that or ye're seein' things."

Why did I say that?

He did not appear to notice her sarcasm. Or he chose to ignore it. "Ye were away an awful long time. How long has it been?"

"Five years." She sipped more wine, trying to hide her face, knowing her cheeks must have been crimson by then.

"I suppose ye're better now, are ye?"

"Better?" Her mind drew a blank. She actually turned to him and met his piercing, blue-eyed stare. His expression was still grim, but she thought he glimpsed a flicker of concern in his eyes. She dismissed the notion as wishful thinking. "What d'ye mean, better?"

"I was told ye were at death's door, and that was why ye had tae go away tae France, tae recover."

Ach, of course. Thank ye Maither, Faither, fer all the lies ye've told about me.

"Oh, aye, I'm all better now, thank ye. Even though I just found out that some folks thought I was dead."

"That daesnae surprise me, the way ye disappeared so quickly."

She scoffed lightly. "I was ill, nae dead. When ye go off tae fight and folks dinnae see ye fer a while, daes everyone assume ye're dead?"

He ignored that too, his eyes still pinning her to her seat. "We're ye poorly the whole time ye were away?"

Keep calm. Just answer his questions, and it'll soon be over. After this, ye can avoid him.

"Nay, once I recovered, I stayed on in France tae look after me Aunt Morag. That's who I lived with while I was there."

"France, eh? I expect 'tis more excitin' than Scotland."

"I'm sure there are a lot more excitin' places than Scotland, nae just France."

"So, did ye go tae lots of fancy parties and the like?"

What? Why is he askin' me that?

"Nay. Aunt Morag lives in the country. 'Tis very quiet."

He nodded, for some inexplicable reason, seeming to approve of her answer. "Grand."

Before he could stop herself, compelled by a pang of ridiculous jealousy, she asked, "What about yersel'? Have ye been tae lots of fancy parties while I've been away?"

The look he gave her then made her feel about two inches tall. "I've been away fightin' most of the time. I havenae had much time fer parties."

"Well, that makes two of us then. In fact, this is the first celebration I've attended in quite a long time."

"Aye, me too. 'Tis good that we can both be here tae honour Duncan then."

"Aye."

An awkward silence fell between them. She hoped he had come to the end of his questions. But he had not.

"Is the wee girl all right after her ordeal?"

Agnes's hackles rose at the mention of Roisin. She looked away, suddenly finding the tablecloth intensely interesting. "Aye, she's fine. She's with her maither, fast asleep now." The lie filled her with guilt, putting her even more on edge.

"Grand."

"Aye."

"Ye left in quite a hurry back then. Without a word. One day ye were there, the next ye were gone. Whatever ye were sick with, it must have come on very quickly."

Damn! I should have thought of that. She scrambled for a believable lie. "Aye. It was a terrible fever that came on all of a sudden, out of nowhere. The healer couldnae dae anythin' fer me."

"But they could in France?"

"They have better physicians there. 'Tis hotter in France too, in the south. They said I needed the sunshine and good weather if I was tae have any chance of recoverin'."

He nodded again and supped some more ale, not taking his eyes off her the whole time. Her nerves were as taut as bow strings.

"Grand. So, ye're well now, are ye?"

"Ye already asked me that."

"Aye, so I did. Anyway, from what I recall, it all happened very fast. It was like ye were spirited away."

"Aye, I suppose it must have seemed like that. I dinnae remember much about it," she lied. She remembered every single moment of heartbreak. "It was all arranged very quickly, by me parents."

At that moment, Duncan, who all this time had been doing the rounds of the guests, appeared behind their chairs.

Thank the Lord, Braither, ye've come just in time tae save me.

Relieved to have some respite from the effects of Conrad's disturbing proximity and awkward questions, Agnes turned and smiled up at her brother.

"Congratulations, Braither. I'm so happy tae be here tae see ye've come back safely from battle. I never kent ye'd been away so long fightin' until Maither told me."

"That's probably for the best, Sister, ye'd only have fretted about me," he replied with a laugh, bending down to plant a kiss on her cheek. However put together he appeared, with his short, neatly combed hair, clean-shaven face, and fine, well-fitting clothes, Agnes could tell he had already had quite a few drinks. His dark-blue eyes, usually so watchful, were dancing with merriment.

"Ye look like ye're enjoyin' yer party," she said teasingly. "What have ye been up tae?"

"Och, this and that, but I'll tell nay tales. Folks seem tae want tae ply me with strong drink and tell me what a good fella I am," he replied good-naturedly.

She laughed. "Well, what's wrong with that? 'Tis what ye deserve," she told him.

"I cannae help thinkin' 'tis a bit unfair that I should have a party thrown in me honour. What about Conrad here? He was with me, fightin' at me side the whole time, and so were plenty of other men. The celebration should be tae honour all of them as well."

Agnes' heart swelled with love and respect for her brother. "Maybe ye're right. Ye could make a toast tae yer comrades, and we'll all raise our glasses tae their health."

"'Tis a grand idea, Sister. I'll be sure tae dae that." He turned his attention to Conrad, giving his friend a mighty slap on the back just as he was supping his beer. The blow made the ale go down the wrong way, leaving Conrad spluttering and coughing violently. Agnes, worried for him, had to resist the urge to pat his back.

Oblivious, Duncan went on tipsily, "This man's saved me life more than once. I want tae show him me gratitude. He's the best friend a feller could ever have. He always has me back, eh, Conrad?"

Conrad finally caught his breath and managed to say, "'Tis lucky fer ye I seem tae recall ye savin' me life a few times as well, man, or ye'd be gettin' a punch in the throat fer half chokin' me like that!"

Agnes could not help smiling when Duncan looked at him, all innocence and said, "Daein' what?"

"Ach, away with ye, ye fool," Conrad told him without heat. "I'll come and find ye later!"

"I'm goin' anyway," Duncan replied, smiling beatifically as his gaze suddenly alighted on a certain point across the hall. "I've just seen an angel, and I havetae go and talk tae her before someone else snaps her up."

Agnes looked in that direction and saw two young women seated among the guests. One of them, a pretty, slender girl in a pink gown with long, light-brown hair, smiled and waved her fingers provocatively at Duncan in response to his admiring scrutiny. His eyes lit up as he waved back in kind. "I'm comin', darlin', just dinnae go anywhere before I get tae ye." He clapped his hands on Conrad's shoulders. "Och, and look, Conrad, she has a wee friend with her as well, a pretty lass she is too. I'll see if I can snag them fer the evenin', shall I?" He leaned down and whispered loudly in Conrad's ear, "Somethin' tae keep us warm later, eh, man?"

Feeling a sudden stab of jealousy, Agnes took in the other girl sitting next to Duncan's "angel," a shapely blonde girl in blue. She had the kind of curvaceous figure Agnes, being very petite herself, had wished for in her youth. The girl had her hand over her mouth, clearly trying stifle her giggles, while her eyes were sparkling with mirth.

Ye have nay right tae be jealous, Agnes silently berated herself as she looked away, 'tis nae yer business who he spends the night with.

But the jealousy burned just the same.

"Wish me luck," Duncan said as he left then and made a beeline for the women, leaving an awkward silence hanging over her and Conrad.

She struggled to tamp down her emotions, casting Conrad a covert glance. She was surprised to see a red flush on his cheekbones and a tic working in his clenched jaw. He seemed embarrassed, but she had no idea why. She thought that perhaps he would have liked to go with Duncan to chat with the girls but felt bound to stay with her out of politeness.

So, she was stunned when he suddenly leaned towards her and looked intently into her eyes before saying in a low voice full of restrained anger, "Ye ken, Agnes, I've never forgiven ye fer runnin' away like that, and nae a word from ye in five years."

"But… but…" she muttered, a wave of guilt and confusion washing over her in the face of his earnestness.

Did he really miss me, did he really care about me?

It hurt her heart to think so, especially knowing how much she had longed for him for five long years. But still, she doubted it.

And even if he did care about me then, 'tis too late now.

"I had nay idea ye were bothered about me leavin'," she forced herself to reply, hating to hurt him but thinking it better that he should withhold his forgiveness for her leaving like that than for giving birth to his daughter and keeping it a secret from him.

"Nae bothered? After what happened?" he exclaimed, sounding both hurt and angry.

As soon as he said it, Agnes was overcome with emotion, and a hot flush spread over her entire body. Instantly, she was transported back in time, to almost six years before, to the cèilidh at Moy Hall, the stronghold of Conrad's family, the Mackintoshes. Their families had always been strong allies, and they often socialized together. She had been an innocent lass of twenty then, and Conrad had been twenty-four, with no idea that she had been secretly infatuated with him for as long as she could remember.

CHAPTER SIX

Five years earlier, Moy Hall, Stronghold of the Mackintosh Clan

"Och, I hope Duncan's gonnae ask me tae dance again," Conrad's sister Eileen said, staring dreamily over at him. "He's such a good dancer." A small frown appeared on her pretty face as she added, "That's the trouble. All the lassies want tae dance with him."

"Hmm, he's very popular," Agnes replied, absently tapping her foot to the music while her own eyes were fixed on Conrad, who was standing next to Duncan. The pair were laughing and joking with each other a few yards away, at the edge of the packed dancefloor. With flushed faces and tankards of ale in their fists, it was clear they were both well into the spirit of the cèilidh.

She loved seeing Conrad looking so carefree, and a thrill of excitement shot through her when he glanced over at her and suddenly gave her a dazzling smile. She returned it, thinking how braw he looked in his smart clothes that showed off his powerful physique, honed by years of training and battle, to great advantage. *He's so tall and strong,* she secretly mooned, *and his hair is so fair and beautiful, I love the way it falls across his brow like that. What would it be like tae touch, I wonder?*

She willed him to ask her to dance, imagining the thrill of having his hand on her waist and his fingers entwined with hers as he twirled her about the floor. *But he sees me the same as he sees Eileen, just another little sister,* she thought sadly, feeling a familiar ache in the region of her heart.

"Agnes. Agnes, what are ye thinkin' about. Why, ye're miles away."

Eileen broke into her thoughts. "Och, sorry, Eileen, I was just wonderin' what the next dance is gonnae be," she fibbed. She did not dare tell her best friend how she felt about her brother, even though Eileen made no secret of her crush on Duncan. Seeking to drown the sorrows her unrequited love for Conrad always brought, she drained her glass of wine and said to Eileen, "Let's get some more wine, shall we, before the next dance starts?"

"Aye, but we'd better hurry if we wantae find partners fer it beforehand," Eileen said, linking her arm with Agnes'. Agnes noticed the longing look her friend cast at Duncan before they went off to refill their glasses, so she allowed herself a quick glance at Conrad as well, inwardly praying he would ask her for the next dance.

However, when she and Eileen were fetching the wine, she saw him and Duncan talking and laughing with two other girls. She was suddenly gripped by jealousy, while at the same time, her hopes sank like a stone. *I might as well face facts and stop puttin' mesel' through all this pain. He's never* gonnae look on me as anythin' but another sister, she told herself again, forcing her eyes away from him and back to Eileen.

"Lady Agnes, would ye dae me the honour of dancin' with me?"

On hearing the voice, Agnes jumped and turned around, to find a thick-set, red-haired young man of about her own age standing behind her. It was Lachlan McClintock, the eldest son of one of her faither's allies. A little vexed at being taken by surprise, she said, "Lachlan, ye nearly made me jump out of me skin, creepin' up on me like that."

He laughed, looking not the least bit apologetic as he held out his hand and said, "The next dance is about tae start. Will ye dance with me or nae?"

A quick look over at Conrad and Duncan told her they were taken up with the other two girls. Spurred by jealousy and disappointment as well as her longing to dance, she was tempted to accept Lachlan's invite. She glanced at Eileen, who gave her an encouraging nod.

"Aye, all right. I'll dance with ye, Lachlan," she said, feeling a little bit guilty for leaving her friend as she took his hand, which she found was rather clammy. The musicians struck up a familiar tune as Lachlan led her to the dancefloor. As they got into position, she was glad to see Eileen joining them on the arm of her cousin Devon and felt immediately better about having deserted her friend.

Lachlan was not exactly a bad dancer, but he was not the best either. There were a few times when he trod on her toes and she had to stifle a cry of surprise out of good manners. However, what he lacked in finesse he made up for in enthusiasm, clearly enjoying himself as he whirled her about, although his hand was a little tighter on her waist than she was comfortable with. But she enjoyed the freedom of the dance as well.

"D'ye ye have a beau yet, Agnes?" he asked her as they linked arms and skipped in semi-circles in time to the music.

"Nay." She twirled beneath his arm.

"I dinnae have a lassie yet either," he informed her for no good reason she could fathom. The tune took off, and he seized her by the waist and held her too tightly while they danced around in a large circle along with the other couples.

"So, there's nay one feller who's caught yer fancy then?"

Agnes hesitated for a second before answering with a lie. "Nay."

"Grand," he murmured, almost to himself, as the dance wound down and finally ended with them exchanging bows and curtseys. "Would ye come out on the terrace with me fer a wee while? I want tae talk tae ye," he said, steering her by the elbow towards the open doors leading to the outside.

"What about?" she asked curiously, intrigued enough not to resist.

He grinned down at her, his dark-brown eyes flashing. *He has a nice smile,* she thought, *and he's nae bad lookin'.* "Say ye'll come with me, and ye'll find out," he replied, his tone cajoling.

What harm could it do to go with him and find out what he has to say? "All right, I'll come, but just fer a few minutes," she told him.

"Grand," he repeated with a smile. He linked arms with her, and they went out onto the large terrace that looked out over the castle gardens. Strategically placed torches mounted on wall sconces provided flickering light in addition to the silvery beams cast by the waning moon overhead, yet it was still surprisingly dark. Several knots of people were already out there, standing in shadow, talking, laughing, drinking, and enjoying the cold air.

Suddenly feeling chilly, Agnes rubbed her bare arms. Clad only in a flimsy ball gown, she was starting to feel the cold and regretting agreeing to go outside. "Why cannae we talk inside?" she asked, noticing Lachlan was manoeuvring her towards a quieter spot away from the other people, near a stone column.

"'Tis so noisy inside, but out here, we can talk more privately," he replied.

"I suppose so. Oh!" Agnes suddenly said, surprised to find herself backed up against the column, with Lachlan unsettlingly close. Alarmed at the position she found herself in, but reluctant to make a scene and let her parents know she had come out onto the terrace alone with him, she said, "I wantae go back inside. I'm cold."

"Dinnae worry, I have a plan tae keep ye warm," he replied with a low chuckle. Before the implications of his words could register, to her absolute shock, he leaned forward and tried to kiss her!

Repulsed and infuriated, she turned her head, making sure he missed her lips. "Ugh! Get away from me!" she hissed, putting her hands against his chest and shoving him away with all her might. As he stumbled backwards, she went on, "Leave off, Lachlan, what d'ye think ye're daein'? Ye said ye wanted tae come out here tae talk, ye liar!"

When he righted himself and looked at her, his smile was gone. "What's wrong with ye?" he snapped, his features dark with anger. A shiver of fear crept over her at the sudden change in him, but she refused to be cowed.

"I didnae come out here so ye could try tae kiss me, that's what, ye cheeky beggar!"

"Aye ye did. Why else would ye come?" he asked scornfully, closing in on her again.

"Ach, how dare ye!" Again, she pushed him away.

"Why, ye're a tease, Agnes MacDonald, with naethin' tae back it up. I'll bet ye've never even been kissed before and ye're scared," he came back nastily.

"So what if I havenae been kissed before?" she retorted, trying hard not to feel she was somehow lacking.

"What, why are ye so afeared of a wee kiss from a real man? How d'ye ken ye'll nae like it if ye dinnae try it?"

"I'll decide who I kiss and when, Lachlan McClintock!"

"Ach, there's somethin' wrong with ye. If ye carry on like that ye'll die an old maid, all dried up and shrivelled. Nay man will want ye then," he sneered.

Temporarily struck dumb by the viciousness of his insults, Agnes stared at him open-mouthed as he went on with his diatribe. "I mean, dinnae try tae pretend anyone's shown any interest in ye. Ye've been of marriageable age fer years now but still nay sign of any man wantin' tae court ye."

"I... I willnae stay here any longer listening tae yer insults!" Deeply offended, Agnes picked up her skirts and was just about to leave, when a huge fist suddenly shot out from over her shoulder and struck Lachlan right in the mouth. One second he was there standing in front of her, the next he was flying backwards, landing with a bump on his backside, blood pouring from a split lip. A large hand laid hold on her arm and whirled her around.

"Conrad!" she cried, realizing who it was, her mind reeling at what had just happened. Conrad did not speak or look at her but simply pulled her along behind him into the shadows at the far end of the terrace. There was a door there leading directly to one the corner towers. From there, one could easily enter the castle's living quarters. Wondering where he was taking her but ready to go to the moon with him, Agnes let him hustle her along until they came to a familiar hallway. In another moment, she found herself inside his chambers, the door firmly shut behind them.

CHAPTER SEVEN

"Are ye all right, Agnes?" Conrad asked, his handsome brow creased with worry as he came towards her.

"Ye saved me," she breathed, looking at him in wonder, only vaguely aware of where he was. Not that she cared. She would have gone anywhere with him, especially now he had rescued her from Lachlan. "Thank ye, Conrad. Ye're me hero." Every word was heartfelt.

"That wee bastard McClintock, why, I should have thrown him off the terrace fer his nerve," he growled, suddenly fierce, his fists flexing at his sides.

"I'm glad ye didnae dae that," she said, smiling up at him adoringly, recalling with satisfaction and amusement the mighty punch that had sent Lachlan flying. "I think a split lip was sufficient. I wouldnae want ye tae get intae trouble because of me."

"Ach, he made me so mad, the things he was sayin' tae ye, the snivellin' dog! I just couldnae go back into the cèilidh right away like naethin' had happened. I needed tae cool down a bit. And I expect ye'd like some time tae gather yersel' after that ordeal back there."

"Aye, of course. That's very thoughtful of ye, Conrad," she said, entranced as always by the startling blueness of his eyes. At the same time, she was glad his gaze could not pierce through her to her heart and see the love she held for him there. If he did, he'd probably run a mile, she told herself, struggling to keep her feet on the ground. *He only saved me because he's kind, nae because he cares fer me.*

"I hope ye dinnae mind me bringin' ye tae me chambers like this, Agnes. I ken we shouldnae be here alone," he told her with an apologetic look. "I dinnae wantae ruin yer reputation."

Thank God he cannae tell how many times I've wished he would! "Well, I dinnae think me Maither would approve, and if me Faither finds out, I'll be dead," she replied, only half joking, fully expecting him to obey the rules of propriety and leave her alone until she felt ready to return to the cèilidh.

But he made no move to go. He simply stood a few feet from her, smiling, looking at her in a way that was making her heart race like her father's favourite hunting dog, Beira, when she was chasing a fox. She looked around the room properly for the first time and realized with delight that she was actually in Conrad's chambers. With Conrad. Alone. It was even better than her regular fantasies about him, waking and sleeping. "I can hardly tell him tae leave his own chambers now, can I?"

"Would ye like some wine, Agnes? Or somethin' else tae drink?" he asked suddenly, a slight edge of tension to his lovely, deep voice. "I have whisky as well. Or ye can have water if ye like." He crossed the room to a console table, where she saw the drink was kept.

Why nae? Why nae make the best of it now I'm here? "Aye, thank ye, I'd love some wine. I think it might settle me nerves."

"Aye, likely so. That was a nasty ordeal ye just went though. I'll join ye as well." He poured them both some wine and handed her a glass. "Slàinte Mhath," he said, his eyes on hers as he raised his glass to hers in the familiar toast of good health.

Agnes held his gaze and smiled as they clinked glasses. "Slàinte Mhath," she echoed, and they both drank deeply of the wine.

"Will ye sit down, Agnes? 'Tis warm by the fire there." He gestured at the hearth where the fire was burning low but still keeping the chamber comfortably warm. "I'll build it up again," he assured her, seeing her solicitously to one of the chairs stationed on the luxuriously thick hearth rug, fussing around her, making sure she was comfortable. Agnes was in a state close to euphoria. Little nervous thrills were chasing around her body from just being near him.

Is this really happenin'? Am I really here with him? Maybe I should pinch mesel' just tae make sure, she thought, looking across at him and marvelling breathlessly at his rugged, manly beauty of his features.

She watched as if under a spell as Conrad knelt by the grate, took up the poker and stirred the embers of the sleeping fire into life before adding some logs from the pile stacked close at hand.

"There, that should keep us nice and warm," he said when it was blazing, replacing the poker and getting up. He then sat down in the chair opposite Agnes, pulling it up closer to where she was sitting.

He leaned forward, his elbows on his thighs, turning his glass round and round in his hands as he looked into her eyes. "I hope ye didnae listen tae any of that nonsense McClintock was spoutin'."

She had almost forgotten all about Lachlan and his insults. Now, they came back to her full force. Old maid. Dried up. Shrivelled. Well past marriageable age. Nae man will want ye. "The things he said were very upsettin', aye."

"He had nae right tae talk tae ye that way."

"He turned nasty when I wouldnae let him kiss me," she explained with a shudder. "Ugh, it was horrible!"

Conrad's gentle expression when he heard that instantly changed to one of fury. "The sleekit wee bastard! I kent I should have killed him when I had the chance, damn him tae hell. Ye wait 'til I see him again. I'll teach him tae show ye some proper respect. I'm sorry I wasnae there tae stop him before he tried anythin', Agnes."

Secretly Agnes found his sudden vehemence exhilarating, and she looked back at him with wonder. It really seemed that he cared about her and wanted to protect her, which was more than she had ever dreamed of. But at the same time, she was a little bit scared of what he might actually do to Lachlan the next time he saw him.

She leaned forward in her seat, until their heads were every close. "Nay, Conrad, ye must promise me nae tae dae anythin' foolish. I dinnae want ye tae get intae trouble fer me sake. He's nae worth it."

"He wants teachin' a lesson," Conrad growled, his eyes flashing like sapphires in the firelight.

"Promise me ye'll nae dae anythin' more tae him, Conrad. If ye hurt him, then me faither might get involved and I'd rather keep him out of it. Ye ken what he's like."

He sipped his wine until, with obvious reluctance, he finally nodded and said, "I dinnae like it, but if that's what ye want, then I'll nae lay a finger on him. But if he meets with a wee accident next time we're out huntin' then I'll nae be held responsible."

Agnes, now feeling more than a little tipsy from the wine, could not help laughing. "'Tis very gallant of ye tae try tae defend me honour," she told him.

"I'm always ready tae defend yer honour." There was no doubting from his serious expression that he meant it.

"Och, thank ye, that's very sweet of ye tae say, Conrad," she said, deeply moved by his obvious sincerity. "I feel a lot safer now ye've told me that," she added jestingly, feeling the wine was making her giddy. Or maybe it was due to Conrad's company.

"I was furious when I heard what he was sayin' tae ye. Besides anythin' else, he must be blind, the bloody fool!"

"Blind? What d'ye mean?" Agnes asked, puzzled.

"Well, 'tis the only explanation fer it. He had nay idea what he was talkin' about, obviously."

Not understanding, she gave him quizzical look.

He gazed at her intently and said softly, "Agnes, ye have nay idea how beautiful ye are, d'ye?"

Agnes felt herself blush all over. "Ach, stop it, ye're teasin' me now."

"I'm nae teasin' ye. Ye're very beautiful, Agnes, the most beautiful woman at the cèilidh tonight."

Shafts of exquisite pleasure pierced Agnes' heart. How she had dreamed of hearing him say such things to her, never for a moment believing it would ever happen. But here he was, telling her she was the most beautiful woman at the cèilidh! Even though it was patently nonsense, it was exactly the sort of nonsense she could take all day from him.

"That's a very extravagant compliment, but 'tis the nicest thing anyone has ever said tae me, and it means a lot comin' from ye. Thank ye fer bein' so nice," she said, hearing the tremor in her voice.

"I'm nae bein' nice, Agnes, I'm tellin' ye the truth," he told her, his beautiful eyes holding her incredulous gaze.

"D'ye really think me beautiful?" she dared to ask him shyly.

"Aye, I think ye're the most beautiful lass I've ever laid eyes on, and I've been a few places."

"Och, Conrad!" Shivers of delight were running up and down her tailbone now. "I never kent ye thought that of me."

"Why would I nae, Agnes? I'm a red-blooded man with eyes in me head. We've kent each other fer years, since we were young. I've watched ye grow up and blossom intae a true beauty, and ye're beautiful inside too." Somehow, he seemed to move closer. Agnes was spellbound. "I've never told ye this before, Agnes, because I wasnae sure what ye felt about me or if Duncan would approve, but I've always cared fer ye."

Agnes' heart soared. "Ye have? Honestly? Ye're nae teasin' me?"

"Dae I look like I'm teasin' ye?"

She looked at his deadly serious expression, the glow of his eyes, and shook her head. "Nay."

"Well, now ye ken me secret."

"I have a secret as well," she said, shifting forward in her chair, certain he was being truthful now. "I've always cared fer ye too, Conrad."

His lips curved upwards, his eyes lit up with warmth, and crinkles appeared at their corners, transforming his expression. Agnes' heart fluttered, quite overcome by how dazzlingly attractive he as.

She watched in fascination as a red tint crept along his cheekbones, a sign of his natural modesty. "But why did ye nae say somethin' before?" he asked.

"I could ask ye the same question. I didnae say anythin' because I always thought ye looked on me as a sister. I was always hangin' around with Eileen, and bein' younger, well, I didnae think ye'd ever take me seriously, I suppose. I never fer a moment thought ye liked me too."

"Jaysus," he said in tones of wonder, "and I thought ye looked on me as another elder braither." He shook his head a little sadly.

"Well, 'tis a shame we're both so good at keepin' secrets from each other, but they're out now," she said without regret.

In the silence that fell between them, she poured them both some more wine, feeling she needed fortification. They clinked glasses again and drank, gazing at each other across the narrow gap between them as though caught in an enchantment. The very air felt charged, heavy with long supressed emotions and things unsaid. Gripped by excitement and a sense of nervous anticipation, Agnes felt goosebumps prickling her skin beath her flimsy gown.

Conrad broke the spell. "Is it true that ye've never been kissed?"

"Ye overheard that did ye?" she asked, her cheeks growing hot with embarrassment and a lingering sense of inadequacy.

"Aye, I couldnae help it. And I must say, I find it hard tae believe."

"Well, 'tis true," she replied a little defensively. "And after what happened with Lachlan, I just wantae get it over with. I never want tae face that sort of mockery again." Before she knew what was happening, Conrad was on his knees in front of her chair, his face inches from hers. He took her glass and placed it alongside his on the hearthstone.

"Is it all right if I kiss ye then?" he asked in a husky whisper.

A thrill shot through Agnes, a mixture of excitement and nerves. *Is it really going to happen at last? Me first kiss is going tae be with Conrad?* It was a dream come true. Trembling, feeling suddenly shy, she murmured, "Aye, if ye like."

She held her breath as, without saying a word, holding her gaze, he angled his head, leaned forward, and pressed his lips to hers.

When she first felt the gentle pressure, Agnes' world exploded into a burst of golden light. She closed her eyes, her lips tingling where Conrad's touched hers, and a wave of heat washed over her. Inexperienced as she was, she revelled in the warm softness of his mouth against hers, so dizzy with excitement, it threatened to consume her. The kiss was everything she had imagined it would be with him, and much, much more. The taste of his lips was so delicious, their touch so tantalizing, a flame of powerful desire for him flared within her, and she wanted the kiss to last forever.

Agnes felt it was all too soon when Conrad broke the kiss, though he only moved back enough to look in her eyes. "How was it, yer first kiss?" he asked, his voice strangely hoarse.

"Och, Conrad, it was... it was..." Agnes murmured, lost for words, trembling before his searching, blue-eyed gaze, already missing the warmth of his kiss. Before she knew what she was doing, she reached out and twined her fingers his hair, pulling him closer. She kissed him eagerly, opening her mouth against his, letting her tongue slide against his, following his lead as he took her deeper into the kiss, his growing passion exciting her further as they explored each other's mouths and lips hungrily. It was like nothing she had ever experienced or could have imagined. It was... wonderful!

When at last their mouths parted, to keep him near, she linked her arms around his neck. Conrad cupped her face in his palms and whispered, "I've waited so long tae kiss ye, Mo Ròisín, and 'tis even better than in me dreams."

"What did ye call me then?" Agnes asked curiously, never having heard the phrase before.

"Aye, it means "Me Little Rose, in Gaelic" he told her, gently stroking her cheeks with his thumbs. "'Tis me private name for ye. Ye've been Mo Ròisín fer many years, in me mind."

"Mo Ròisín," she repeated softly, deeply moved by his confession. "I love it." She pulled him closer, giving in to the urge to kiss him some more. He kissed her back hungrily, his arms slipping around her waist, drawing her forward against his chest.

Their arms tightened around each other as their kisses grew more passionate, and it was not long before they were both on the hearthrug, their bodies melting together, swept away by the overwhelming power of their long-suppressed desires...

CHAPTER EIGHT

"Agnes, where are ye goin'? Nay, dinnae leave like this, come back. Ye at least owe it tae me tae give me some answers and hear me out," Conrad said, his voice low and urgent, wanting to physically stop her from getting up and leaving the table but afraid to grab her in case others noticed something was going on between them.

As it was, he could do nothing but watch helplessly as Agnes walked away from him and went to speak to some other guests. Duncan's celebratory supper was winding down, and folks were standing about in relaxed cliques, chatting amiably, nursing their drinks.

Conrad drank more ale, but his eyes over the rim of his tankard never left her graceful figure as she moved around the room between the various groups, speaking to people as if she had not a care in the world. He watched as Agnes began a conversation with one of her father's council members. Why is she talkin' tae him and nae me? With each passing second, his frustration with the way she was acting increased. I'll nae stand fer it. I'll make her talk tae me whether she likes it or nae, he vowed silently to himself as he sat brooding.

But however much he needed to speak with her and get to the truth of why she had left so suddenly all those years ago, he knew he could not just go over there, interrupt their conversation, and make a scene.

As soon as she leaves, I'll follow her. I'll nae give her the chance tae avoid me much longer.

Suddenly, he saw Duncan coming towards him, with a girl on each arm. His stomach dropped at the sight of them. Duncan had made it obvious earlier on that he had chosen his bedfellow for the night, and Conrad knew the blonde in the blue dress with the generous bosom was meant for him. Good manners forced him to stand up as Duncan arrived with the ladies. However, Conrad covertly continued to watch Agnes.

"What are ye daein' sittin' here on yer own, man? God, ye look fed up. Good thing I found ye. Look, I've brought some pleasant company tae cheer ye up," Duncan said, beaming at him and slurring his words slightly as he presented the women to Conrad.

"This here is Betty." He winked at the dark-haired girl, holding her hand to his lips and kissing it. She giggled delightedly. "Betty this is me friend, Conrad." Conrad smiled politely as he greeted Betty.

"And this here is Shona." Duncan smilingly presented the blonde to him. "Shona, meet Conrad."

"Nice to meet ye, Conrad," Shona said, fluttering her eyelashes at him flirtatiously.

"How d'ye dae, Shona?" Conrad said, careful not to smile or do anything that would encourage her. However, once again, good manners prevailed, and he found himself pulling out a chair for her to sit down. He sat down as well, absently participating in the raucous conversation with the odd word or nod, stoically ignoring Shona's attempts to flirt with him, while continuing to keep watch on Agnes over Shona's shoulder.

At last, he saw her heading for the doors. Seeing his chance, he rose abruptly from the table. "Excuse me, there's somethin' I must attend tae," he told the others, ignoring the surprised look on Duncan's face and not even sparing the women a glance as he strode down to the main floor and followed Agnes.

It did not take him long to spot her walking along the hallway towards the vestibule and the staircase. To his frustration, there were too many people about for him to run after her and grab her by the arm. So, he walked normally and kept his distance, reaching the hallway as her burgundy-coloured skirts disappeared around the corner of the first landing.

There was no one else about, so he took the stairs two at a time, figuring she was on her way to her chambers. He hurried after her, wanting to catch her before she went in and shut the door on him. Not that that would stop him. He had vowed to get her to talk, and propriety be damned. He was up to the landing in a few strides and turned the corner to see Agnes approaching a door at the far end of the hall. She was just entering the room when he came up behind her. She let out a little shriek as he bundled her inside.

"Did ye really think I was just gonnae let ye avoid me all night without speakin' tae me, Agnes?" he demanded loudly, his frustration at fever pitch.

"Shhhhh!" she hissed, "be quiet, will ye?"

"Nay, I'll nae be quiet any lon—"

He was more than surprised when she suddenly reached up and tried to clamp her hand over his mouth. "Ye'll nae shut me up like that!" he exclaimed, grabbing her arm and pushing her hand away. Somehow, she unbalanced and lost her footing, and when she reflexively grabbed at him, she pulled him down as well, and they ended up in a tangle of limbs on the carpet.

There was a sound, a sigh, and a rustling of bedclothes. Feeling Agnes gasp and freeze beneath him, he raised his head and, for the first time, looked at his surroundings. Two beds, one big, one small. In the firelight, he could just make out the shape of a full-sized person sleeping in the full-sized bed. In the smaller one, a slight movement of the occupant showed a little blonde head turning on the pillow. He shot to his feet.

Bloody hell, I'm in a nursery!

By that time, Agnes was on her feet too. She seized him by the arm and bodily dragged him out of the room and into the hallway. Looking about hastily, her eyes settled on a closet door. She threw the door open and shoved him into what proved to be a broom closet, following him inside immediately and shutting the door.

He could hardly stand up straight, and they were crushed against each other in the stuffy, cramped space. Only a sliver of lamplight from the hallway showed around the edges of the door, but it was enough to light up the hazel-eyed glare she fixed on him.

"What d'ye think ye're playin' at? Why are ye actin' like this?" she hissed angrily.

He ignored her question, countering with one of his own. "Why are ye visitin' the maid's child?"

She did not answer at first, seeming to struggle to reply. Finally, she said, "Nae that it has anythin' tae dae with ye, but Saoirse has nae been feelin' well. I just wanted tae call in before bed and make sure Roisin was all right. Now, what d'ye mean by followin' me up here?"

"Ye ken very well why I followed ye. I tied tae talk tae ye at supper, but ye walked off and ignored me fer most of the evenin'. But ye're gonnae speak tae me now whether ye like it or nae."

"Ye keep goin' on about talkin', but what is it ye wantae talk tae me about?" she asked, a line of annoyance appearing between her eyes.

"Agnes, I'm gettin' angry now. Stop playin' this game. I want an explanation from ye fer why ye disappeared overnight without so much as a word five years back, and why I havenae had a single word from ye in all that time."

"I dinnae havetae explain anythin' tae ye," she said in a harsh whisper. "And I already told ye at supper what happened. I was ill. What's so hard tae understand?"

He could have shaken her for her refusal even to acknowledge his hurt. "Aye, ye told me that, but accordin' tae ye, ye recovered from yer illness a long time ago. What stopped ye from writin' tae me then? Ye kent where I was the whole time. Naebody told me anythin'. Did ye nae think for one minute I might have wanted tae ken where ye were and if ye were all right?"

"Ach, dinnae give me that, Conrad," she said scornfully. "Why are ye behavin' like this? 'Tis nae as though ye had any real feelin's fer me back then, was it?"

The way she said it so unfeelingly was like being stabbed in the heart.

Daes she really mean that? Did she nae really care fer me at all? All she said that night, all we did, it was just down tae too much wine and the "moment"?

He was rendered speechless.

"'Tis obvious the only reason ye're actin' like this is because yer male pride was wounded when I left, is that nae the truth?" she went on accusingly.

Feeling as though she had torn his heart from his chest and trampled on it, Conrad mentally retreated and regrouped as the awful truth of the situation sank in. *She never really cared fer me then, and she certainly daesnae now.*

"Aye, ye're right," he lied, covering up his pain. "Me pride was hurt. I didnae have feelin's fer ye or anythin', but it just wasnae right."

"Well, I hope we both ken where we stand now," Agnes said, "and that ye willnae keep followin' me about demandin' I talk tae ye."

"Ye can be sure of that," Conrad replied shortly. "Are ye gonnae let me out of this bloody broom closet now? I feel like I'm gonnae suffocate if I stay in here much longer."

"Aye, I'll be only too happy tae." He heard her grasp the door handle and turn it. But nothing happened. The door did not open. She tried again, rattling the handle, turning it left and right. "'Tis stuck," she said, clearly flustered.

"Let me try." Their movements in the confined space were very limited, and for him to reach the door handle meant sliding his arm between them in the region of her waist. It was unavoidably intimate and embarrassing. But finally, he had his turn on the handle. Even with the extra force he supplied, the door would not budge. "I think it's locked itself somehow, or the lock is broken," he said finally after several unsuccessful attempts to open it.

"Then how are we gonnae get out of here?" she asked, the beginnings of panic in her voice. "Naebody will come this way fer hours, and I dinnae fancy just anyone comin' along and findin' us together like this."

"It'll be hard tae explain, aye," he replied, also eager to get out of the closet and away from her, to seek refuge in his chambers and brood alone. He tried the door again, rattling the handle hard. "Nay, 'tis nae budgin'," he concluded.

"Well, what are we gonnae dae? We cannae stay in here all night until someone finds us. What if me maither comes along? Or Duncan? Or, God forbid, me faither?" Her voice was slowly rising along with her frustration and fear of discovery.

"All right, calm down, there's nae need tae panic," Conrad told her, starting to worry about her. "If there's nae other choice, I'll just havetae bust the door down."

"And how d'ye intend tae dae that?" she asked. "Ye cannae even move in here as it is. Ye can hardly take a run up, can ye? And besides, how would I explain that in the mornin'?"

They continued squabbling for another few minutes before a sound out in the hall caused them to freeze. Agnes' eyes blinked at him, wide with alarm. They held their breath as the key turned in the lock, and finally, the door opened.

"What on earth are ye two daein' in there?" Saoirse asked, standing back and looking at them in surprise. She had a shoe in her hand and saw Conrad glance at it curiously. "There was such a noise comin' from out here, it woke me up. I thought we had rats," she explained, helping Agnes out of the closet. He unfolded his long limbs and stepped out into the hallway, relieved to be able to stretch his legs at last.

"Then I heard ye two arguin'. That lock always was a bit dodgy," Saoirse went on before looking from one to another of them questioningly, a small smirk appearing on her lips. Conrad started to feel uncomfortable. "But why were ye in there in the first place?" she asked.

"Never ye mind," Agnes said tetchily. But Conrad noticed that her demeanour suddenly turned solicitous when she asked the maid, "How are ye feelin', Saoirse? Are ye any better now?"

"Eh?" Saoirse replied, her brows knitting.

"Ye were feelin' poorly earlier on, ye said. Remember?" Agnes asked in a tone which Conrad found strange. But everything about her was strange to him now, or so it seemed, so he dismissed it.

"Och, aye, that's right," Saoirse said as if suddenly recalling something. "I'm fine now, me lady. It was just a wee headache after all. 'Tis quite gone now I've had a nap."

"Och, I'm glad tae hear it. I looked in on Roisin a wee while ago. She was fast asleep. Was everythin' all right while I was at the supper?"

"Aye, I've nae heard a peep out of her. She's been as good as gold."

Once again, Conrad found the interaction between the two women when it came to the child confusing. Why did Agnes fuss so much over her maid's child? It struck him as odd. But again, he was more preoccupied with the rift Agnes had created between them and did not take much notice. In fact, he had no clear idea what he was still doing there.

As if just noticing he was still there, Agnes looked at him, a small frown crinkling her otherwise smooth forehead. "Conrad's goin' now, are ye nae, Conrad?"

"Aye, I'm goin'. Good night, Saoirse. Thanks for the rescue," he said, nodding his thanks to the maid.

"Ye're welcome, me lord. Anytime," she replied, her eyes twinkling with mirth as he turned and strode away down the hallway with as much dignity as he could muster, and a heart trampled upon by Agnes MacDonald for the second time in a row.

Conrad hurried back to his chamber, glad to shut the door behind him when he got inside. The first thing he did after heeling off his boots, stripping off his coat, and laying aside his sword belt was to go to the console table and pour himself a stiff dram of whisky. There was a hollow ache inside him, and he needed something to numb the pain. He drank two drams straight off, one after the other.

The heat of the whisky rushed through his veins, bringing a modicum of comfort but no solace for all he felt he had lost. *Ye cannae loose what ye never had, ye fool,* he told himself bitterly. Unable to find the energy to wash or even undress properly, he threw himself down on the bed just as he was. He lay on his back and stared up at the ceiling for a long time, letting his misery flow through him along with the whisky.

For years, unanswered questions about the past had tormented him. When Agnes had returned, it had been a massive shock, like a scab being ripped from a wound and setting it bleeding again. He had hoped he would at least get some answers to those questions at long last. But all he had was more questions and no answers at all, or none that seemed to ring true at any rate.

He could not help thinking there was something strange about the way Agnes was behaving towards him. She had refused to talk to him at the supper and then tried to avoid him. And later, when he caught up with her, she had seemed antagonistic at times. Buy why? It was she who had left him, not the other way around.

What happened five years ago fer things tae come tae this between me and Agnes? Everythin' should have been perfect. We could have been wed all this time if I hadnae had tae go away tae fight and come back tae find her gone. 'Tis like some cruel practical joke. I just cannae understand what went wrong or why she seems so set against me now.

As he sought for answers, the familiar past came flowing back and engulfed him like a tide, as it had almost nightly since she had left him. It carried him away, to the cèilidh held at his family home, Moy Hall, the stronghold of Mackintosh Clan, five years before, and the night when he had so foolishly let himself believe that true happiness could really be his.

CHAPTER NINE

Conrad woke up smiling. His mind was crystal clear, with no aftereffects from all the wine he had drunk the night before. Rain tapped at the windowpane of his chamber, but in his heart the sun was shining. Finally, what he had dreamed of hopelessly for years had come true. He looked down at his little rose fast asleep in his arms, drinking in the perfection of her sleeping face, her full, rosy lips bruised from his kisses, her wild dark hair spread out over the pillow, and knew he had never felt so happy, so whole in his entire life.

For years he had felt bound to conceal his growing love for Agnes. Partly, because he had had no idea if she would return his feelings. And party because he was not sure Duncan, whom he loved like a brother, would approve of his best friend being in love with is little sister. In the uncertain circumstances, he had put his friendship with Duncan before his own feelings for Agnes.

But in one night, everything had changed. Now that he knew she felt the same as him, he had already decided to ask for

Agnes' hand. He could not envisage ever wanting to be with anyone else but her, so what was the point of delaying when they had already waited for so long?

He looked down at Agnes, at her white shoulder, at her pale, slender arm lying across his chest, feeling the first stirrings of fresh arousal. Besides, he thought, I've allowed mesel' tae indulge in somethin' I should by rights have waited fer. And it was sweeter than I ever could have imagined. It felt so good to know he was her first, that there would never be another. Because now, she's mine forever.

She stirred in his arms, her eyelids fluttering open, her lovely hazel eyes dazed with sleep. "Good mornin', Mo Ròisín," he said, unable to stop smiling as he planted a small kiss on the tip of her nose. She smiled too and stretched her naked limbs against him with a little moan of pleasure before putting her arm back around his chest and cuddling up under his arm again.

"Good mornin'," she replied softly, looking so delicious, he just had to pull her to him and kiss her mouth again.

"How are ye feelin'?" he asked when their lips parted, his heart overflowing with love for her.

"I feel wonderful. How are ye feelin'?" She traced her fingertips along his jaw, sending little tingles racing through him.

"Wonderful." They both laughed and shared more kisses. "I have somethin' important I wantae talk tae ye about," he told her eventually, wishing they could stay like that all day.

"Oh? What's that?"

He had just opened his mouth to tell her he wanted to marry her when the air was suddenly filled by the clamour of bells. "'Tis the alarm, there must be an emergency," he muttered, sitting up in bed, the intrusive metallic clanging shattering the tranquillity of their haven. "I'm sorry tae leave ye, Mo Ròisín, but ye ken I havetae go," he told her regretfully.

"Aye, I understand," she said, sitting up against the pillows and drawing the coverlet up to cover her breasts. With extreme reluctance, he roused himself to leave her in the bed and hurried to dress. He quickly fetched the duffel containing his battle gear and rested his shield against it by the door. Finally, as he buckled his sword belt around his hips, he returned to the bed and leaned down to give Agnes a kiss before leaving.

"We'll talk later, when I get back, all right?" he said, pressing his lips to hers.

"Aye, all right. Be careful, Conrad, dinnae take any risks. I dinnae want anythin' tae happen tae ye," she said, her voice betraying her concern for him. It touched him deep inside.

"I promise, I'll come back tae ye as soon as I can."

"Aye." She reached up and kissed him softly. Then, despite his strong desire to stay, he forced himself to turn away and leave her.

Even though he hated to leave Agnes, his buoyant mood persisted as he strode down the hallway and ran lightly downstairs and out of the keep. In the courtyard, he joined the other men responding to the alarm, making for the stables to saddle his horse. Duncan was already there, mounted on his black stallion, giving out orders when Conrad rode up to his side.

"What's up?" he asked his friend, who looked fresh and wide awake despite the previous night's celebration and the tumultuous night Conrad imagined he had enjoyed with Betty.

"There's been an attack on one of the outlying villages, and we need tae get out there as soon as we can and find out who's responsible," Duncan explained.

"Aye, all right. Any idea who's behind it?"

"Nae yet, but I intend tae find out."

"I hope it aeisnae take too long," Conrad murmured without thinking.

Duncan raised his brows at him and grinned. "That's nae like ye, man. Are ye keepin' somethin' from me? Got somethin' tae hurry home fer this time, have ye?" he asked teasingly.

Conrad felt his face flush. "Nay, I'm just sick of fightin', 'tis all. I'd like tae spend some time at home fer a change," he replied, hating himself for lying to his best friend.

Duncan nodded. "I'm with ye there. I'd like a rest mesel', but duty calls." His chuckle had a hard edge to it as he added, "It'll take as long as it takes, same as always."

Within a half hour they were on the road, traveling to the southern borders of Laird MacDonald's lands. Conrad rode next to Duncan, but he hardly took in anything his friend was telling him about his night with Betty. His mind was almost entirely occupied with Agnes. He could not wait to get back home and go straight away to speak to her father and ask for her hand in marriage…

They were away for weeks and when he had got back, he planned to go visit them at their keep. When he had finally made it over there, he had seen her for a fleeting moment at a council meeting and then Agnes was gone, without a word, without an explanation.

It had changed him irrevocably. There had been no solace to be found anywhere. Survival had only been possible by throwing himself into his duties.

Perhaps the hardest thing about it all was having to conceal his heartbreak from everyone, but most of all from Duncan. In five long years, even though Duncan had expressed worry about the change in him many times, Conrad had not even had the relief of unburdening himself of his sorrow to his best friend and closest confidant. He had kept all the pain and anger and confusion bottled up inside him. It had bubbled away, gradually turning to a dark, corrosive poison that hardened what remained of his broken heart.

Now, the wound had been ripped open again, leaving him with more questions than ever revolving endlessly in his brain. Without answers, the situation was like a puzzle he had no chance of getting to grips with. Fighting, battle, killing, that he understood. But Agnes MacDonald? He despaired of ever being able to understand her.

"Och, she looks so sweet with her wee tartan dress matchin' her dolly's, eh?" Agnes said, smiling indulgently, her heart overflowing with love as she looked over at her Roisin when she entered the nursery the following morning.

The little girl was sitting on the rug by her bed, playing happily with her favourite cloth dolly, Peggy. Both wore identical dresses of MacDonald tartan, both made by Saoirse. "She must be over the moon. Ye've done a wonderful job there, Saoirse, thank ye," Agnes added gratefully.

The maid chuckled. "Aye, she is, but as ye ken, she came up with the idea all by herself. She may be young, but I think she already kens how important it is tae make a good impression on her grandfaither."

"I'm nae sure about that," Agnes replied sceptically. "She just loves her nice dresses, and she wants Peggy tae look pretty too. But who kens? Maybe it'll soften the old man's heart tae see them both wearin' the clan tartan."

"Mayhap it will me lady, which will be a very good thing if ye ask me. 'Tis about time he thawed out a bit with ye. Speakin' of the laird, time's tickin' away. We'd best get ye lookin' presentable if ye're gonnae go and see him this mornin'," the maid remarked in her usual kindly, matter-of-fact way.

Saoirse proceeded to help Agnes dress for the day in a pale-blue cotton gown printed with white leaves, the only gown left in Agnes' wardrobe suited to the summer heat. They were both hoping the carriage containing the bulk of their clothing and Rosin's toys would arrive later that day.

"How daes she seem? Have ye noticed any ill-effects from the hold-up yesterday?" Agnes whispered to Saoirse as the maid tied her petticoat strings and helped her into the gown.

Saoirse shook her head as she adjusted the skirts around Agnes's slender hips so that they flowed elegantly to the floor. "Nay, she slept like a baby, and she's been as right as rain, like she's forgotten all about it."

"Well, thank the Lord fer that!" Agnes exclaimed softly, relief washing through her. "I've been so worried about her, I hardly slept a wink last night. Mind ye, that's nae been the only thing that kept me awake," she confessed, although she chose not to mention the inexplicable attack of jealousy she had suffered after seeing Conrad with the curvy blonde girl at the party. That too had also prevented her from sleeping.

"Och, ye dae look a bit tired, me lady. Have ye been worryin' about the meetin' with yer faither today as well?" Saoirse asked with concern, starting to do up the back fastenings of the bodice.

"Aye, that was playin' on me mind the whole time," Agnes admitted, telling herself to be strong and not let her anxiety and fatigue overwhelm her.

"Aye, I can imagine. I mean, he's a good man and all, but he's nae exactly the welcomin' type, is he?" Saoirse remarked, adjusting the gown's lace collar and standing back to check her efforts. "Ye'll dae nicely, me lady," she added, clearly approving.

"Thank ye, Saoirse. Nay doubt he'll still be annoyed with me because I was a wee bit late fer the feast last night. I expect he'll have somethin' tae say about that," Agnes replied, checking her appearance in the long looking glass and finding it satisfactory, except for the traces of tiredness and strain on her face. "I dinnae care how cold he is towards me as long as he minds his tongue with Roisin. If he says or daes anythin' tae upset her, he'll ken about it from me. I dinnae care how powerful he is, I'll nae allow it."

"That's right, me lady. Dinnae let him get away with anythin'," Saoirse agreed, starting to tidy things away about the room.

"That's why I need ye tae come with me," Agnes told her, slipping her feet into her shoes.

Saoirse stopped what she was doing and turned to her, a mixture of doubt and surprise on her face. "Ye dae?"

"Aye, I need ye tae be on hand just in case he says somethin' and I need ye tae take Roisin out of the room. I think 'tis best if I go in first and speak tae him, while ye and Roisin wait in the hall outside his study. If all seems well, I'll come and fetch ye. But the minute he steps out of line, ye can take her off tae see the horses or find somethin' else tae distract her while I put him straight."

"All right." Saoirse nodded a little warily.

Agnes went on. "I dinnae wantae risk goin' down tae the hall tae eat in case I run intae someone I dinnae wantae speak tae." She flashed Soairse a meaningful look.

"Our erstwhile rescuer, ye mean, I suppose," the maid murmured.

"Exactly. Last night was risky enough, with him askin' about who Roisin belongs tae. I cannae have him gettin' suspicious. I dinnae need tae explain tae ye the importance of tryin' tae avoid him wherever possible while we're here."

"I understand, me lady. I ken how important it is tae ye tae keep things secret. Speakin' of that, d'ye think we should remind the wee lass about the game we're supposed tae be playin' about pretendin' I'm her ma instead of ye?"

"Aye, we'll dae it after we've been tae see me faither," Agnes agreed. "Although the family all kens she's mine, we'll try tae avoid meetin' other people if we can when we go out and about. 'Tis necessary that everyone else around the castle believes she's yer daughter." She added in a whisper, "Especially Conrad."

Saoirse nodded. "All right. We must be on our guard then."

"Aye, we must." Agnes went over to Roisin and sat on the edge of the bed next to her. "My, ye're lookin' very pretty today, Roisin. I see ye're wearin' yer favourite dress."

"Aye, wearin' it fer Grandfaither," Roisin replied, smiling up at her sunnily, the gap between her front teeth adding a hint of mischief to her otherwise angelic appearance. "I'm wantae meet him, and I'm takin' Peggy here tae show him." She held up the cloth doll. "Will he play with me?

Agnes heart welled up with love for her little daughter whilst aching at the same time. She searched her mind for a single memory of her father playing with her and found none. He was simply not that sort of father. But how to explain that to Roisin without hurting her? She smiled down at hr daughter and tucked a lock of long blonde hair behind her ear. "I hope so, me wee darlin', but yer grandfaither's a very busy man, so ye must nae be too disappointed if he cannae play with ye today, eh?"

Roisin's lips made a little moue, and she shrugged in a very French manner that said, "Maybe, but we'll see."

Juts then, there was a knock on the door. As Saoirse went to open it, Agnes said brightly to Roisin. "Are ye hungry?"

"Aye, me tummy's hungry," Roisin admitted, rubbing it before adding with a cheeky grin, "and so is Peggy's."

Agnes had to chuckle. She gently ruffled her daughter's hair and held out her hand to her. "In that case, I think we should all go and have some breakfast," she said brightly, clasping her daughter's tiny hand in hers and leading her over to the table where Saoirse was unloading the breakfast trays. Throughout the meal, Agnes made sure to maintain a cheerful facade, determined that Roisin should not suspect her own underlying anxiety over the upcoming meeting with her father.

Agnes left the nursery first to go and sound him out, with instructions for Soairse to follow with Roisin after a quarter of an hour. They would then await her summons is the hallway outside the laird's study. She was making her way to the landing, about to take the staircase down to the vestibule, when she turned the corner and, to her shock, was almost knocked off her feet by a large person running up the stairs from below.

"Oh!" she gasped, breathless, caught off balance, tottering on her feet. Groping for the banister to save herself from falling, she was surprised when a brawny arm shot out and a large hand gripped her arm firmly, steadying her.

Agnes regained her balance, but when she looked ahead, she found herself facing a wall of naked flesh, firm, ridged with muscle, marked by several old battle scars, with a covering a wiry, dark-golden hair. "Oh!" she repeated, shocked but at the same time entranced by the unexpected sight. How beautiful, came the involuntary thought before she tilted her head back and looked up, into a familiar pair of piercing bright blue eyes.

Her heart jolted, and her pulse began racing.

Nay! Why daes this keep happenin'?!

"Are ye all right, Agnes?" Conrad asked solicitously, his ruggedly handsome face flushed and covered with a pearly sheen of sweat.

Why him? Why now? Why like this?

CHAPTER TEN

"A-aye," Agnes stuttered, putting a hand to her lips in a vain attempt to hide her blushes, unable to tear her eyes away from the superb example of masculine gorgeousness standing inches in front of her. His musky scent flowed up her nostrils and made her insides turn to water.

Omigod! Why must he be so braw?

"Sorry about that," Conrad apologized, releasing her arm. "I was in a hurry and didnae hear ye comin'."

"Oh." Agnes fought to gather the shreds of her shattered composure around her. Directing her gaze to the mail shirt, breastplate, and other items of clothing he was carrying over one arm, she asked, "Why are ye…" She gestured helplessly at his naked chest with her eyes whilst trying not to look at it. "…Runnin' around up here half-dressed like that?"

"I've been sparrin' with Duncan and some of the men at the trainin' ground, and we had a quick break. I just ran up here tae fetch somethin' from me chamber," he explained, his voice husky, his bright blue gaze pinning her. "'Tis very hot work trainin'. I took me things off tae try cool down a bit before I go back out."

"Oh." Is that all I'm capable of sayin'? I sound like a fool. "Well, ye nearly sent me flyin' just then." It was supposed to be accusatory, but it came out without any real heat to it. The heat was all over her body.

"I apologized again. It was an accident."

"Well." Well what?

She could not prevent her gaze from straying over his tousled, damp fair hair and the sculpted contours of his face, the high cheekbones, the hollows beneath, the golden-brown stubble covering his strong, square jaw, the texture of which she could still recall very well from stroking them with her fingertips and kissing them.

Dinnae look at his mouth.

At the same time, she felt him looking at her too, his bright, searching gaze traversing her hair, her features, her neck, all the way down to the neckline of her gown, which suddenly felt far too revealing for comfort. She felt the sudden urge to cover the part of her breasts on show, burningly aware that the air surrounding them was crackling with tension, as though a storm was about to break.

She knew she should leave, but that would mean pushing past him, and she was already struggling with the unsettling effects of his proximity. To actually touch him felt dangerous.

It was something of a relief, initially at any rate, when someone came tripping down the stairs from the floor above, where some of the party guests were still lodging. It broke the spell, and they both turned their heads to look. Agnes was unpleasantly surprised to see it was the curvy little blonde she had seen him with at Duncan's supper party. A familiar spear of jealousy stabbed at her.

A quick glance at Conrad's face told her he was just as surprised as she was to see the girl. But in his case, the surprise was tinged with embarrassment. Seeing it, suspicion fuelled the fire of Agnes' jealousy.

What did he get up tae with her? Did he lay with her like he did me?

The young woman reached the landing and stood next to them. "Good day tae ye, Lady Agnes," she said respectfully, bobbing a small curtsey. Mortified, Agnes could only nod stiffly at her in reply.

The girl's demeanour changed utterly when she turned to greet Conrad. "Hello," she said, beaming at him and fluttering her eyelashes coquettishly. Her big pale-blue eyes suddenly alighted on his bare chest and lingered there for a few moments while her smile widened. "'Tis very nice tae see ye lookin' so… well."

Her lips pursed tightly as she struggled to push her jealousy down, Agnes looked at Conrad. He was now shifting awkwardly from foot to foot and hugging his gear to his chest as if to fend off the girl's lascivious glances. The tips of his ears had turned puce. "Uh, hello there, Shona," he replied haltingly. "Ye, uh, look well too."

She smiled at him expectantly, clearly hoping to continue the conversation. However, he said nothing more, and after a few moments of awkward silence, Shona seemed to realize there was tension in the air. Her smile turning tight, she glanced from Conrad to Agnes. Whatever she saw or sensed, she suddenly said, "Excuse me, may I pass?"

Conrad startled at her words. "Och, aye, of course, sorry." He quickly retreated a few steps and shrank back against the wall, as though trying to get as far away from her as possible. Wordlessly, Agnes also drew back, giving Shona enough room to pass.

"Thank ye," she said, giving Conrad a final, puzzled glance before she hurried past them and down the stairs, not looking back.

Agnes' eyes collided with Conrad's. He smiled awkwardly and shrugged. "An acquaintance," he said. "Duncan introduced us at the party."

Secretly seething, at him, at Shona, but mostly at herself for what she knew was her quite unjustified jealousy, Agnes could not help retorting sharply, "I ken. I saw ye together."

The heat in his eyes was unmistakeable as he lowered his gear, revealing more of his chest in what she suspected was a move calculated to goad her. She could not help her gaze being drawn to the muscular expanse, nor the flash of desire that pierced her like an arrow at the sight.

"D'ye like what ye see?" he asked teasingly.

Seriously flustered by the embarrassing truth, Agnes dragged her eyes away from his chest. "I havenae got time fer this, I have a meeting with me faither" she muttered, desperate to get away.

He bared even more of his naked chest and grinned at her, teasing her. "Ach, come on, ye like it, eh? Why d'ye nae admit it?"

Agnes knew she should have some sarcastic comeback for him, but she was so overcome by her warring emotions, she had none. She knew she had to get away before she cracked.

"Excuse me," she murmured, slipping rapidly past him, taking care not to touch him, and running down the stairs.

"Ach, dinnae be so touchy, I was just jestin'" she heard him call after her as she reached the bottom and scuttled across the vestibule. She did not answer or look back at him, urgently needing to put as much distance between them as she could. She felt his eyes burning into her back the whole way until she turned the corner into the main hallway. There, she slowed her pace, fighting to regain control of her racing heart and her breathing.

By the time she reached the door of her father's study and halted, she had composed herself. Glancing back down the hallway, she saw Saoirse holding Roisin's hand, and the pair were coming in her direction. She waved and smiled at them, and both waved back. She waited for them to reach her.

"Wait f me here while I go and see if me faither's available," she told Saoirse. Roisin was clutching Peggy the doll close to her chest. She beamed up at Agnes, who told her, "Stay here with Saoirse, wee yin, and be a good girl, all right?" Roisin nodded.

"Wish me luck," Agnes murmured to the maid, taking a few deep breaths before she raised her hand and rapped firmly on the door, hoping to project confidence.

"Enter," her father's deep voice rumbled. Agnes went in. As she shut the door behind her she saw her father was seated at his desk and had clearly been working his way through a pile of correspondence and such like. He looked up, and as soon as he laid eyes on her, his already forbidding expression set into a cold mask of disapproval.

Remembering her resolve not to be intimidated, to be strong in front of him, she walked boldly up to the desk and, lifting her chin, stood in front of him, her hands clasped loosely at her waist. "Good mornin', Faither," she greeted him, making sure to keep her voice even and betray no hint of her anxiety.

He put down his quill and leaned back in his chair, regarding her silently for a few moments, his steely blue eyes entirely devoid of warmth.

"What is it, Agnes? I have a rapport I need tae finish, would ye mind coming back a bit later?" he eventually asked, his voice like gravel.

"I apologize fer interruptin' ye, but I trust ye're nae too busy tae spare the time tae meet yer granddaughter," Agnes said clearly. "Ye've never set eyes upon her, and if we're gonnae be stayin' here fer a while, then I think she ought tae ken her grandfaither."

A slight raising of his brows was all that told of his surprise in the brief silence that followed. Though she found it uncomfortable, Agnes did not say another word, having put the ball firmly in his court. "Of course, she should," he finally agreed with a nod. "I wasnae expectin' it, but I suppose now is as good a time as any fer us tae get acquainted. Bring her in."

Agnes stood up, went to the door and waved her maid and daughter in.

Saoirse waited respectfully by the door. Agnes took Roisin by the hand and walked over to the big desk.

"Say hello tae yer gradfaither, me sweet," Agnes said, squeezing her little hand in hers.

"Hello Grandfaither", she whispered shyly, half hidden by her mother's gown.

"Hello, wee yin. I'm very happy tae meet ye. Dinnae be shy, lassie. Come on over here and let me look at ye."

"Go on. 'Twill be all right.

The little girl went over to where he had stood up by the desk.

"My, what a pretty wee thing ye are, tae be sure. Roisin is yer name, is that right?"

Of course, it is, ye've kent her name since she was born!

"Aye, it means little rose."

"Aye, I ken. 'Tis a very lovely name and it suits ye.

He looked shy but pleased. He noticed her dolly and asked, "Now, who have ye got there?"

"'Tis Peggy, she's me best doll and me friend as well."

She passed him the doll and laughed when he took it in his hands to inspect it. "She's wee in yer hands," he said as he inspected it.

Clearly tickled by her observation, he chuckled. "Aye, I suppose she is. She's a bonny lookin' dolly, eh?

"Aye. She's wearin' her best dress today fer ye, Grandfaither. Saoirse made it fer her. 'D'ye ye like it? 'Tis like mine, see?"

My, is that a tear shining in Faither's eye?

"Aye, I certainly dae," he told the child. "Peggy's a proper MacDonald lass, eh? Like yersel'. Ye both look grand in yer matchin' dresses."

"Thank ye. Grandfaither?"

"Aye, wee yin?"

"Dae ye wantae play with us?"

"Well, I'd like tae, but I'm quite busy just now. But I'll maybe see ye later, eh?"

"Aye, all right," Roisin replied with a little nod, her eager smile fading. She flicked a glance at Agnes, who saw her disappointment. Her heart aching for her, she gave her an encouraging smile.

"Roisin, I need tae speak tae yer maither fer a minute," her faither suddenly said. "Would ye like tae sit in me chair and draw fer a wee while?"

Roisin brightened at once. "Aye, please," she answered.

"D'ye? Well, that's grand, lassie. There's some old paper there, ye can use the side that isnae stained, and a quill, and some ink. Will ye be all right with that fer a minute or two?"

"Aye, thank ye, Grandfaither. I'll be careful nae tae get ink on me or Peggy's dress."

"Good lass. Up we go then."

Agnes watched as her father stood up, looking like a giant next to her diminutive daughter, who was small for her age, destined to be petite, like Agnes and her mother. Again, she saw his usually hard glance soften as he picked his little granddaughter up and placed her gently in his chair. It too dwarfed Rosin's tiny frame, but she was all smiles again as he pushed the chair in for her.

It almost reduced Agnes to tears to see how Roisin smiled up at him adoringly, knowing he was unlikely to live up to her childish expectations. "Thank ye, Grandfaither," the child said, drawing up a piece of paper and then dipping the quill pen delicately in the ink pot. "Me and Peggy are gonnae draw a picture of ye."

He said nothing for a moment. Then, he ruffled Roisin's blonde locks gently and said in the softest voice she had ever heard him use, "Is that so, wee yin? I look forward tae seein' what ye make of me then."

He strode over to Agnes. "She daesnae have yer colourin'," he said pointedly. His eyes had hardened again, and she felt them boring into her, as though he would drill down and find the all-important information she had withheld from him all this time—the name of the father.

"Nay. But I think she looks a bit like ye in the face," she lied, wanting to stop him from going down that road in front of the child. "And she takes after me and Maither in her small build."

He huffed at her attempt at deflection. "Aye, she's small fer four, as ye were as a wee bairn." He glanced over at Roisin, who was concentrating hard on her drawing, the tip of her tongue sticking out of her mouth. Turning back to Agnes he said, "I hope ye realize the importance of hidin' the fact she's a bastard while ye're here."

Agnes went cold. Without saying another word to him, she turned to Saoirse. "Soaries, will ye please take Roisin outside fer a moment?"

"But Mama, I havenae finished me drawin' yet," Rosin protested.

"Ye can finish it in a wee while, darlin', and give it tae Grandfaither another time. Go with Saoirse now," Agnes replied, ignoring her father's look of perplexity.

With obvious reluctance, Roisin climbed down from the chair and did as she was told. "Goodbye, Grandfaither. I'll finish yer picture soon, I promise," she said sadly as Saoirse led her from the room.

"Very good, lassie, very good," the laird replied with unexpected gentleness.

Once the door was firmly shut behind them, Agnes looked up at her father, drawing on her fiercely protective love for her daughter to strengthen her resolve.

"What did ye dae that fer?" he asked, his dark brows drawn together. "I didnae ask the child tae leave."

"Because I dinnae want her tae hear what I have tae say tae ye. And ye'd best listen well, Faither, fer I'll nae repeat mesel'."

He looked completely shocked at being spoken to in such a forthright manner.

"Now, ye can speak tae me however ye want, but I'll nae have ye, nor anyone else for that matter, speak of Roisin in any way that might make her feel unwanted. If there's one thing ye can be sure of, that lassie is loved. And ye're never, ever tae speak of her in that way again, d'ye hear?"

He opened his mouth to speak but shut it when she ignored him and continued talking. "Roisin is the biggest gift in me life, and I'll nae have ye makin' her feel bad about hersel', especially since ye've nae even lifted so much as a finger tae try and get to ken her since she was born."

"That's nae fair," he managed to interject. "Have ye forgotten that I'm the laird here? I cannae just up and leave all me responsibilities tae go tae France," he protested.

Agnes scoffed, her hands on her hips. "Are ye honestly gonnae try tae tell me that in almost five years ye've nae had even a few days tae spare tae come and meet yer granddaughter?"

He did not respond to that, but she thought she saw a glimmer of guilt in his eyes before it disappeared and they grew hard again. "I didnae say anythin' unkind tae the lassie tae make her feel bad, and ye cannae run away from the fact that she is a bastard."

Seething at his denial, Agnes' squared up to him, unafraid. "Faither, I had a long time tae think about things while I was away, and I've forgiven ye fer the way ye've treated me."

He gasped in astonishment. "What the devil—"

Her fury was so great, it was like a damn bursting inside her. All the resentment, the hurt, the disappointment came pouring out in a torrent.

"Aye, I've forgiven ye fer bundlin' me off tae France without consultin' me at all, I've forgiven ye fer blamin' me fer the ruined betrothal with McDonnell, which ye arranged behind me back and just expected me tae go along with. I've forgiven ye fer nae botherin' tae come and see me in France, nor writin' me so much as a word in all those years. I've forgiven ye fer spinnin' all those lies about me, tellin' everyone I almost died, fer neglectin' me when I needed ye most, fer puttin' yer reputation above everythin' else. I appreciate ye took care of me but ye could have shown ye care fer me."

She paused for breath, her heart pounding. "What I will never forgive ye is nae tryin' tae be a proper grandparent tae Roisin, fer nae bein' there fer her or protectin' her as she deserves, even though she has only one parent tae look out for her!"

Having said all she needed to say, she picked up her skirts and was about to storm out when she heard him speak behind her.

"Are ye really so surprised at the way I've acted after what ye did back then?" he asked, his voice harsh. Disgusted, without even turning around to look at him, she opened the door and went out, leaving him standing there, not even giving him the satisfaction of slamming the door.

CHAPTER ELEVEN

Five years earlier, the Great Hall, Keppoch Castle

"Maither, where's Duncan, and what's Conrad doin' here?" Agnes whispered in her mother's ear, surprised and secretly thrilled to see Conrad walk into the great hall with her father and occupy the seat where her brother usually sat.

"Duncan's on his way home, but Conrad's faither's needed him tae come home early, tae help him deal with some matters tae dae with the conflict. He came over earlier today and volunteered tae take Duncan's place," her mother whispered back. It was the day when the MacDonald family held their weekly audience, when the clansfolk would come before the laird with their complaints. Her father expected his whole family to be present.

"Oh," Agnes said casually, concealing her nervous anticipation at the prospect of speaking with Conrad. She had not seen him since the night they had spent together more than two months prior, before he had departed. They had not been able to communicate by letter in his absence, due to the undercover nature of his work with Duncan. So, despite her love for him, she was unsure of his feelings for her. And, frustratingly, they had only been able to exchange glances before he sat down at her father's right hand. She only hoped they would be able to speak when the audience was over.

But it dragged on, and Agnes felt increasingly uncomfortable due to the strange queasiness she had been experiencing for the last month.

When they broke for a bite to eat and a drink, she was surprised when her father, usually so unemotional, smiled at her. Disconcerted, she smiled hesitantly back. Then, he leaned across his wife and said with rare good humour, "I have a wee surprise fer ye, lass. Ye've received a marriage proposal. Is that nae excitin'?"

"Who's it from?" Agnes asked without any genuine interest, instantly resolved to refuse the offer. There was only one man she wanted to wed, if he wanted her that was. Conrad.

But she did not hear her father's response, because just then a servant set a crock of stew on the table before her. The smell was so nauseating, Agnes clamped her hand to her mouth and bolted for the nearest door, which led outside. Bursting through it, she ran to some nearby bushes and promptly threw up.

"Agnes, dear, have ye been taken' ill?" Her mother came up beside her, clearly anxious.

As the wave of nausea gradually passed, Agnes leaned weakly against her mother. "Ach, the smell of the food made me feel sick all of a sudden," she explained., dabbing her lips with her hanky. "I've nae been feelin' right fer a while."

After a moment's silence, her mother said, "I think we should get ye tae yer chambers, Agnes. Come along now and tell me all yer symptoms."

Back in her chambers, Agnes felt better and was intent on catching Conrad before he left. She was completely shocked when her mother suddenly asked her outright, "Agnes, have ye been intimate with a man?"

Instinctively, Agnes denied it. "What?! Nay, Maither, of course nae." But even as the lie left her mouth, a truly frightening thought struck her, and she knew she had to tell the truth. She sighed and looked up at her after a moment of silence.

"Maither, I'm sorry, I lied tae ye just then. Aye, I have. But–?"

Her mother's face crumpled. "Ach, omigod, Agnes, what have ye done!" she cried, clearly distraught.

"What is it, Maither? Tell me, please?" Agnes cried, dreading the answer.

"Why, ye foolish lass! Is it nae obvious? Ye're with child!"

It was the last thing Agnes heard before she fainted dead away.

When she awoke, she was lying on her bed, her parents standing a few feet away, whispering. "She's awake," she heard her mother say. They went and stood by the bed. Her father's face was like thunder, her mother's eyes heavy with disappointment.

"What happened?" she asked groggily, before reality slammed into her.

Her father did not mince words. "I never thought a daughter of mine could dae such a thing tae me," he growled. "Ye've shamed me and the whole family. Ye ruined yersel' ferever and ye have ruined the marriage alliance I had planned. Nye nobleman will ever take ye tae wife now ye've gone and done this tae yersel'!"

"Who did this tae ye, Agnes. Who's the faither? He'll havetae marry ye now," her mother demanded.

Agnes was suddenly wide awake. If she told them it was Conrad, they would force him tae marry her. But what if he didn't love her? He was honourable, he would wed her out of duty, but I she could not stand that. It would ruin his life and thus hers.

"I'll nae tell ye his name," she replied, resolved to keep her secret. A bitter argument then erupted, full of threats and pleading from her parents, but Agnes stubbornly refused to reveal the father's identity.

"Ye've brought shame on the family," her father berated her. "If the truth gets out, there'll be a scandal. Me reputation will be ruined. Ye must leave Scotland immediately."

"We're sendin' ye tae stay with me sister Morag, in France," her mother supplied. "I've already written tae her tae tell her what's happened."

"France!" Agnes exclaimed, shaken by how fast they had acted. "But… when?"

"Ye leave tomorrow mornin'," her mother replied, radiating disappointment. Agnes gaped at her, shocked by the lack of maternal warmth coming from her otherwise supportive mother. But then she realized the pain she was causing her, and guilt set in. What else could she expect in the circumstances? What did she think would happen? She didn't want to be sent tae France in disgrace. But she supposed her mother saw it as the best way to protect the family's reputation, and hers as well.

"I've instructed Saoirse tae pack yer things," Lady Fiona continued. "She'll be goin' with ye. I'll travel with ye tae Aunt Morag's and then return home. Ye'd best get yersel' ready. There's nay time tae waste."

With that, they made to leave. Her father paused at the door. Glowering at Agnes, he said, "I kent ye had many bad traits, but I never thought stupidity was one of them. Yer braither will be back here later today. Ye can say yer goodbyes afore ye leave. We'll come up with some lie tae explain why ye're goin' away fer the other people."

He closed the door behind him, leaving a stunned Agnes wondering what they were going to say about her.

That afternoon, with nothing better to do, Conrad spent some time in the training yard, taking out his frustrations one of the practice dummies, punching the suspended straw man it as if it were fighting back, building up his strength and trying not to think about Agnes.

He was so focused, he was startled when he heard a sharp cry behind him. He stopped what he was doing and wheeled around to locate the source of the unfamiliar sound. He was surprised to see the little daughter of Agnes' maid racing towards him across the yard.

As he wiped the sweat from his brow with his kerchief, he could not help smiling to see the way she was speeding along on her little legs. Her sunhat was dangling from it strings, bouncing against her back as he ran, her long blonde hair flying out behind her. She was full of life.

"Hello, wee lassie," he greeted her as she skidded to a halt in front of him. She was so tiny and delicate, with her eager little face shining up at him, she reminded him of a daisy. He automatically hunkered down so he would be at her eyelevel. "My, ye're a fast runner."

"Hello," she replied, puffing as she grinned up at him, showing the gap in her front teeth that somehow tugged at his heartstrings. "Thank ye. I like tae run."

"I can tell. What are ye daein' out here? Have ye come tae learn tae fight?" he asked jokingly.

"Aye. I saw ye hittin' the dolly real hard." She pointed at practice dummy. "Can ye teach me how tae punch like that?" she asked, her bright blue eyes earnest.

"So, ye really do wantae learn tae fight," he said laughing with genuine amusement.

"Aye."

"I can teach ye if ye like. Who are ye plannin' tae punch?"

"Bad men, like the ones who tried tae hurt us."

"Och, that's very brave of ye tae want tae fight them, Little Flower," he told her, deeply touched by her determined attitude. "I hope there'll nae be a next time. All right. I can lift ye up so ye can practice on the dummy?"

"Yes, please!" She said, dead serious, already bunching her little fists in anticipation.

He lifted her up by her waist and held her up in front of the dummy. "Right, now, ye punch with yer right fist and then yer left, one, two, one, two, understand?" She nodded. "When I say one, go. One!"

She began punching ferociously, while he chanted, one, two, one, two. "Aye, ye're a natural," he told her, taken aback at her determination. She joined in the counting as well. He gave her a few tips, which she quickly learned.

"That was very good fer a first go. Ye're stronger than ye look."

"Aye, me maither says that though I'm small fer me age, I'm strong,"

"Is that so?" He reckoned she must be three and a bit, though she was clearly precocious for her young age. "Well, ye have the makin's of a good fighter. Maybe that's what ye'll be when ye grow up, eh? A warrior."

"If I can learn tae fight like ye can, aye." She beamed at him, and he felt an unusual glow inside him.

"Would ye like a drink of water?"

"Aye, please. Fightin' makes ye thirsty."

He laughed and ruffled her hair. "Aye, it daes." He fetched her a ladle of water from the barrel, and while she drank, he studied her. He noticed the precise way she held the ladle, the way she angled her head and smiled, the cadence when she spoke, her intelligence. Something stirred in his mind, and it suddenly struck him how like Agnes she was in her mannerisms. *That's odd, but I suppose 'tis tae be expected when they spend so much time together.*

But as he scrutinized her face, something else even more peculiar occurred to him. Her hair was exactly the same shade and texture as his own, and her eyes were the same bright blue as those he saw in the mirror every morning. 'Tis an extraordinary coincidence. Nevertheless, he felt a connection to her which he could never remember having felt before with any other child he had come across.

She finished drinking and handed him the ladle. "Thank ye. I left some fer ye."

"Och, dae ye remember me name, Little Flower?" he asked.

"Aye, 'tis Conrad," she replied, her bright blue eyes dancing. "I wouldnae forget. Ye saved us." She tilted her head and looked past him. "Och, here comes me maither."

CHAPTER TWELVE

He looked around and saw Agnes and Saoirse walking towards them. As always, his heart thumped when he laid eyes on Agnes. A sudden thrill ran up his spine as he suddenly recalled the tense moment they had shared in the rear pantry before she had run off in a hurry. What sort of mood will she be in this time, he wondered uncertainly, tamping down the storm of conflicting emotions she always stirred up inside him. He put on a neutral expression and braced himself to face her.

The girl skipped over to the approaching women, slotting herself between them and taking both their hands. He watched curiously as Agnes and the girl's mother crouched next to her and the three of them went into a sort of huddle, whispering so he could not hear what they were saying. He felt the several glances that came his way though, saw the smiles of the women as they straightened up, and heard the giggling of the child. What was all that about?

"Good day tae ye, maister. I trust ye're keepin' well," the maid greeted him, her gaze sweeping over him from head to foot before giving him warm smile.

"Aye, very well, thank ye, Saoirse. I hope ye're well too," he replied politely. "Yer we lassie here has been keepin' me company." He grinned at the child, who beamed at him.

"I hope she's been nae trouble," Agnes said, looking slightly worried. He noted she had not even greeted him properly. *Why is she bothered about it? The lassie's nae hers.*

"Nay trouble at all. She's been a pleasure," he replied firmly.

"Conrad's been trainin' me tae fight," the little one said, excitedly swinging from the women's hands like a monkey. Agnes eyes flew wide when she heard that, which confused him.

"Is that so, wee yin?" the maid jumped in before Agnes could say anything.

"Aye, I've been practicin' how tae punch bad people," the girl declared proudly.

Saoirse looked at Conrad with friendly curiosity as she asked her daughter, "Are ye aimin' tae be a great warrior like him when ye grow up then?"

"Aye, I am." She glanced up at her mother and giggled.

"But why d'ye want tae learn that, sweetheart?" Agnes asked, her smile tense.

"So when there's bad men, I can save ye from them."

Saoirse chuckled. "I'm right proud of ye, lass. That's a fine ambition. What ye lack in size ye certainly make up fer in spirit. But we should pray we dinnae meet any more bad men like that, eh?"

"Aye, but I'm still gonnae learn tae fight just in case," the little girl declared staunchly.

"That's very wise of ye, sweetheart," Agnes said with an indulgent smile. But then she cast him a pointed look and added, "But I'm sure Maister Conrad is very busy. He hasnae got time tae teach ye how tae fight, so ye shouldnae bother him."

She daesnae want me tae teach the child, he realized, baffled. "I'm nae so busy I cannae find time tae train a wilin' recruit," he countered, returning her look with a flash of defiance. "I'll make sure she daesnae hurt hersel'.

"See, he has time!" the child said triumphantly. She let go of the women's hands and skipped over to him and took his instead. The feeling that came over him to feel her tiny hand in his was strange. He suddenly knew with certainty that he would protect the mite with his life.

"Can we show them me punchin', Conrad, please?" she asked prettily, gazing up at him.

He looked enquiringly at Saoirse. "Is it all right?"

She nodded enthusiastically. "Aye, go ahead. I'd love tae see it."

"But Saoirse," Agnes chimed in, looking worried. "She might hurt hersel'."

"Nay, I willnae. And Maither says I can," the little girl pointed out, going off into peals of inexplicable laughter at his side. Conrad saw Ages and the maid exchange glances. The maid shrugged, and he assumed the matter was settled, though he was once again puzzled by Agnes' interference.

"Lift me up again, please," the child asked, letting go of his hand.

"All right, Little Flower. Are ye ready? D'ye remember what I told ye?"

She nodded exuberantly. "Aye, one, two, one, two."

"Good lass." And so he lifted her up to the practice dummy once again. "Right, when I say one. One!" Off she went, punch, punch, punching as hard as her little fists would allow, as fierce as anything, chanting the rhythm to herself as she went. It tickled him immensely, and he could not help laughing.

Saoirse started laughing too and then clapping, shouting, "Well done, wee yin! My, ye're strong." Agnes clapped too, but Conrad could not see her face to see her expression.

After a minute or so, he said to his little pupil, "Time fer a rest now. Remember what I told ye before?"

"Aye, I havetae peace mesel'," she replied, puffing as he set her on the floor, her cheeks flushed but wreathed in smiles. They all smiled at her mistake.

"Why, that was amazin'!" Agnes said then in tones of wonder, still clapping. When Conrad turned around, he saw her smile for the child was full of affection and pride. But why pride?

Ach, I suppose she's kent the wee yin since birth and is attached tae her.

However, he still had the feeling of being outside some sort of conspiracy between the trio, though he could not put his finger on exactly why.

It was very hard for him not to keep sneaking glances at Agnes, and he noticed that while she always smiled fondly at the child, she seemed stiff and tense at the same time, as though wary of him. It hurt him, and he could only put it down to her feeling awkward at bumping into him following their encounter in the pantry.

"I think we should leave Maister Conrad tae his trainin' now, wee yin. And ye must nae overdae it on yer first day," Saoirse said, reaching out her hand to the child.

"Dae I havetae?" she wheedled, hanging onto his hand.

"Aye, ye dae," Agnes said insistently. "It'll be teatime soon, and ye said ye want tae see the horses before that."

"Ach, all right," the girl replied with obvious reluctance, letting go Conrad's hand. "Can I come again though, please?" she asked, making his heart clench.

"Aye, Little Flower. If yer maither says it's all right, ye can come when 'tis quiet like this, and I'll teach ye some more, eh?" He ruffled her hair and smiled down at her.

"Thank ye!" She ran off to her mother. "I'll see ye soon, Maister Conrad!"

"Thank ye fer givin' her yer time, maister," Saoirse said, taking the child's hand. "She's clearly enjoyed hersel'."

"I enjoyed havin' her as me student," he told her. "She's a fast learner, and she has a lot of spirit."

He waved at the little one as the trio made to leave. Just before they went, Agnes met his eyes. Something he could not name passed fleetingly across hers as she said, "Thank ye, Conrad. That was very kind of ye."

He nodded, then watched them walk away, holding the child by the hand between them and swinging her along. He missed the child's company already and was sorry to see her go. *I hope her maither lets her come again*, he thought, perplexed by his own feelings. He had always liked children but had little to do with them. However, he knew he had never felt such a bond with a child before. Needing distraction from his thoughts, he turned back to the practice dummy and landed a volley of hard, fast punches.

A short while later, Conrad was in the armory changing out of his gear when he saw Duncan come in. They greeted each other warmly and chatted for a while about the training program they had planned for the men. But since the meeting with Agnes earlier, Conrad's curiosity about her and her relationship to the little girl was plaguing him. Thinking Duncan would be the one to enlighten him, he did not wait long before bringing the subject up. But he took care to phrase his enquiry casually, so as not to alert Duncan to his interest in Agnes.

"Ye sister was out here earlier, with her maid and the wee lassie."

"Was she? She's a livewire, that bairn, eh?" Duncan remarked, his face suddenly brightening with what Conrad thought looked like pride. It stirred his curiosity further.

"Aye, she's a sweet wee thing all right. She daesnae resemble her maither much though," Conrad said, referring to Saoirse, who was dark haired. Duncan seemed taken off guard.

"Her maither?"

"Aye, the maid."

He was perplexed to see something like relief in his friend's eyes. "Aye, Saoirse. Well, bairns dinnae always take on their maither's colourin', dae they? Mayhap she takes after her faither in looks."

"True, true. Well, 'tis nice fer ye tae have yer sister back home after her bein' away in France fer so long, eh?"

Duncan smiled. "Aye, I'm glad tae see her. I've missed her."

"Five years is a long time, and she's still unmarried. But I suppose she's been courted by someone while she's been livin' in France, has she? I mean, it would be strange if Agnes didnae have a beau or two in all that time, d'ye nae agree?"

Duncan gave an awkward chuckle. "I wouldnae ken, me friend. Now, what d'ye think is the best way tae divide up the men up for this trainin'?" Duncan said, abruptly changing the subject, much to Conrad's frustration.

"Twenty or maybe thirty at a time would be manageable, I reckon."

"I have somethin' important I wantae talk tae ye about,"

"What's that then?" he asked, realizing he would get nothing out of his friend just then. But that did not mean he was giving up.

"I've been thinkin' about the attack on me sister's carriage the other night, "Duncan confided. "I was wonderin' if it wasnae just a random attack by those brigands but a planned one instead. What d'ye think?"

Conrad was taken aback and perplexed by the suggestion at the same time. "Why, I havenae even considered such a possibility," he admitted. "I saw nay evidence of it."

"Well, nay other vehicles have been attacked. It got me tae thinkin' that those brigands might nae have been brigands but men in disguise actin' in someone's employ."

"I dinnae understand what ye're drivin' at. Are ye suggestin' the attack was planned tae specifically target yer sister's carriage?"

"Aye, that's exactly what I'm sayin'."

"But that daesnae seem likely. First, who would want tae dae such a thing. And second, what purpose could they have fer daein' it?"

Duncan seemed to consider his next words carefully before speaking and even then, he seemed reluctant. But eventually, he said, "Well, I havenae told ye this before because me faither ordered me tae keep it tae mesel', and if I tell ye, ye must swear nae tae tell anyone else, all right?"

"Aye, of course, I swear. Ye ken ye can trust me tae keep me mouth shut, whatever it is."

"All right." Duncan nodded and lowered his voice. "Fer the past few years, we've been havin' some problems with Clan MacDonnell."

"Clan MacDonnell? Why? What sort of problems?"

Duncan was about to speak when they heard the door opening behind them and looked to see who was coming in. It was Duncan's father, Laird MacDonald.

"Ah, there ye are, son. I need a word with ye. Will ye leave us, Conrad? I need tae speak tae him in private," he said commandingly, holding the door open and gesturing for Conrad to go.

"Aye, me laird, of course'," he said, moving to obey.

"We'll talk more later, eh?" Duncan murmured as he went by.

"Aye, all right," Conrad agreed, stepping outside, watching the door close on him.

He stood for a few moments, deeply curious about what Duncan had been about to tell him.

What the hell has Tavish MacDonnell got against Clan MacDonald, I wonder?

Though his curiosity was roused, he told himself had no choice but to be content with knowing he would find out more about it from Duncan later.

CHAPTER THIRTEEN

It was the lull between luncheon and teatime, and most of the servants were eating in the servants' hall adjoining the kitchens. It was easy for Conrad to steal noiselessly and unnoticed through the back door, down the corridor, to the rear pantry to grab something to eat. The door was ajar, so he pushed it open and was stunned to see Agnes there. He watched unseen while she stood on her tiptoes trying to reach something on the top shelf, but she was so petite, her efforts were in vain.

Feeling mischievous, he crept up behind her silently, reached up over her, and took down what she wanted, a round ceramic crock with a lid, and placed it on the counter in front of her.

She let out a small scream of alarm, her hand flying to her chest as she turned around. When she saw who had her hemmed in, her back to the counter, the look of alarm turned to surprise, then into a small frown. "Conrad! Ye shouldnae creep up on folks like that. I nearly jumped out of me skin!" she berated him.

He took a step back and held up his palms. "Just tryin' tae be of help," he said, feeling the almost palpable awkwardness descending upon them as they stared at each other.

He wanted to tell her how beautiful she was looking, his eyes drinking in the gentle waves of her long dark hair, which provided the perfect frame for her pale, almost elfin face and lovely warm, hazel eyes, her full lips the colour of crushed raspberries. He felt the urge to grab her and kiss her. But he knew he could not do either of those things. So, he just said, "I was feelin' peckish. I came in search of a bite tae eat."

"Aye, me too," she replied, eyeing him and seeming to decide he posed no immediate threat. "Thank ye fer gettin' that down fer me." She gestured with her chin at the crock on the counter before adding a little defiantly, "Although I would have done it by mesel' with the steps over there if ye hadnae come in."

He did not bother to look, finding it hard to take his eyes off her and look at the crock instead. "Well, I saved ye the effort. What's in there?"

"I'm nae sure. I was hopin' somethin's sweet." She turned and lifted the lid. "Och, aye, 'tis half a seed cake." Lifting it out carefully, she set it on the counter. "Hand me a knife, would ye?"

Reaching to his belt, he handed her his Sgian dubh, the small, single, bladed knife generally carried by all for everyday things such as cutting up food and eating. "Ye can cut me a big slice of that, if ye please," he said, secretly admiring her narrow waist and flaring hips as she cut into the cake.

"Will ye pass me some plates?"

"Aye." Wrenching his eyes from her shapely figure, he reached over and took two down small plates, handing them to her. She set the slices on them, a generous one for him and a smaller one for her.

"See if there's some milk in that pitcher, will ye?" she asked, setting both plates down on opposite sides of the scrubbed pine table in the centre of the room. She placed the knife next to his. "I'm thirsty as well as hungry," she added. Snagging two beakers from the dresser, she set them down next to the plates before she sat down at the table.

Conrad did as she asked, bringing the full pitcher of cold milk with him as he took the seat opposite her. He hid the fact he was taken aback to see she had laid the table for two. He bit into the seed cake with relish, looking across at her as she nibbled hers delicately. Considering the tense atmosphere between them and her previous reluctance to answer his questions, he was surprised she was actually remaining in the same room with him. Recalling the incident on the stairs, he wondered how long it would be before she either told him to leave or ran out in high dudgeon herself.

They ate and drank in silence, their elbows on the table, the air in the room becoming more and more fraught with unspoken words.

That was until Agnes swallowed her mouthful of cake, looked at him, and said, "Ach, I cannae bear this tension between us. Are we gonnae be awkward with each other like this forever?"

Taken off guard, he replied a little defensively, "'Tis the last thing I want, Agnes. I dinnae like it any more than ye dae. But after everything ye've done, how d'ye expect me tae act? Ye havenae exactly made me feel welcome in yer presence."

But then, he noticed she was not really listening to him but was instead glancing behind her, a worried expression on her face. Suddenly, she dropped her cake, shot out of her chair, and ran around to his side of the table. "What is it? What's wrong?" he asked, standing up to follow the direction of her eyes. Something moved on the shelves beneath the counter.

"'Tis a rat!" she squeaked, and the next moment, she was in his arms, clinging to his neck, scrabbling desperately to keep her feet off the floor and get onto the table.

"All right all right, there's nay need tae panic," he told her, quite enjoying the unexpected warm soft weight of her against him. 'Tis a wee rat, nae a bloody crocodile. It'll nae eat ye."

"Ugh! I cannae stand the nasty, dirty things. Will ye catch it please, Conrad, and get rid of it?" she begged him.

"I'll try, but they're fast. And I'm nae killin' it." He placed her carefully on the table.

"What d'ye mean ye're nae gonnae kill it? What are ye gonnae dae with it then? Dinnae get it anywhere near me!" Her eyes darted to the bottom shelves, and she let out another little shriek, her hands flying to her cheeks. Then she pointed frantically. "I saw it movin', look, there! There!"

"Wheeshst, woman, keep the noise down will ye? Ye'll have all the servants in here, and it'll nae look good us bein' in here together. Ye must mind yer reputation," Conrad warned, grabbing a burlap sack from a pile in the corner of the room and stooping to investigate the bottom shelves.

"Ye have a cheek tellin' me that," she retorted from the tabletop. "Look, can ye see it movin' behind that pan, the big one."

"Ach, stop makin' such a racket. Ye're scarin' the poor wee thing." He was on his knees now, watching for the slightest movement, the sack poised in front of him. The pan moved, and he pounced, but the sack came up empty. "Damn, missed."

"Ach, hurry up, please, Conrad!" Agnes pleaded.

"Hang on, I just got a glimpse of his tail. 'Tis all fat and pink and scaly," he said teasingly, stifling his laughter when she let out a horrified squeal.

"I have an idea." He picked up a brush that was to hand and poked it around by the pan while positioning the sack at the other end of the shelf. There was a brief commotion as the rat dashed away from the brush, and into the sack. "Got him!" Conrad let go the brush to grasp the sack in both hands. There ensued a struggle with the surprisingly muscular rat, which squeaked shrilly in fear as tried to fight its way out of its prison.

"Have ye got it?" Agnes asked breathlessly, watching his every move.

"Aye, I have it," he replied, wrapping it firmly in the sack, making sure not to hurt it. Once he was sure it could not escape, he held the wriggling bundle at arm's length and let go the laughter that had been bubbling up inside him since the start of the chase.

"Ach, thank God!" Agnes exclaimed with obvious relief before starting to laugh as well. "Dinnae bring it near me!"

"I'm nae goin' tae," he said, standing up and going to the small window at the back of the room, with the rat fighting every inch of the way. He opened the window and threw the whole bundle out into the yard. Then he shut the window firmly. "So it cannae get in again that way," he laughingly explained to Agnes as he brushed his hands off and returned to the table.

"Thank ye so much, Conrad," she said, smiling thankfully at him in a way that made his heart turn over in his chest. "Come on then, ye can get down now." He reached up to lift her down, feeling a tingling in his skin when she put her hands on his shoulders and let him place his hands around her waist. Their gazes suddenly locked, and time seemed to stop.

His heart began beating loudly in his ears as they remained poised like dancers in some graceful ballet, unmoving, their faces so close, he could feel her warm breath tickling his cheek. His eyes moved to her mouth, her lips were slightly open. He looked into her eyes, and the heat he saw there sent a tremor racing through him like a lightning bolt. She trembled beneath his hands. Something hit him with certainty then, something that wiped out the past.

I'm gonnae kiss her, she wants me tae kiss her.

A sudden crash followed by an annoyed shout coming from the depth of the kitchens broke the spell. The moment was gone, like a burst bubble. Agnes stiffened and pulled back from him. "Ye can lift me down now, thank ye," she said, her tone formal.

"Aye." He placed her gently on her feet and steadied her. She practically snatched her hands from his shoulders. "All right now?" he asked, withdrawing his hands, feeling strangely bereft.

"Aye, thank ye again fer gettin' rid of the rat. I must go now."

"But ye havenae finished yer ca—" Before he finished his sentence, she was gone in a flurry of skirts, leaving him staring after her open-mouthed. Confused, his heart aching, not knowing what else to do, he sat down at the table and finished off both plates of cake.

Later on, as promised, Agnes went with Saoirse and Roisin to the stables, to visit with the "horseys."

"Och, 'tis a joy tae see her so happy'," she said, smiling indulgently at her daughter, who had found a friend in young Will, one of the grooms. He was introducing her to all the horses one by one, telling her stories about them, showing her how to feed them bits of apple and carrot on the flat of her little hand as they went. She was in seventh heaven.

"Aye, I think she's gonnae be horse mad when she gets a bit older. She'll likely wantae start learnin' tae ride before long," Saoirse said.

"Nay, she's far too small. It would be dangerous!" Agnes exclaimed, quite shocked.

"She'll be five soon. I was already ridin' a horse by that age. Had tae, growin' up on a farm," the maid pointed out.

"I suppose I had me first pony at that age as well," Agnes mused, looking at her slip of a daughter. She seemed so fragile, it was impossible to imagine her controlling a large animal, yet she knew Roisin was stronger than she looked. And she was resilient. Her quick recovery after the run-in with the brigands had proved that. Moreover, she was quick minded too. So she made a decision. "Well, dinnae put any thoughts in her head just yet," she told Saoirse, "but if she decides fer herself she wants tae learn, then I'll arrange it fer her."

After an hour or so at the stables, they returned to the nursery. They all had tea together, munching on sandwiches, honey cake, and bannocks, which reminded Agnes that she had run out on Conrad without finishing her seed cake. While Roisin had a nap, she related the whole incident to Saoirse, leaving out the moment when time had stopped, and it had been just her and Conrad on the verge of… something so she would not allow herself to dwell on. She was mortified by her own behaviour, and the sheer force of her desire for him.

At any rate, by the time she had finished telling the story of Conrad catching the rat, Saoirse was wiping tears of mirth from her eyes with the hem of her apron. Even Agnes could not help laughing. Nor could she help remembering the molten feeling in her belly when she had looked into Conrad's eyes.

But she did her best to put it out of her mind when Roisin awoke from her nap. She scooped her up and wrapped her in her arms, gently brushing her damp blonde curls from smooth little brow.

"Och, ye smell lovely," she told her as she dried her off. "In fact, ye smell good enough tae eat. Yum, yum, yum!"

Swapping kisses for bites, she playfully pretended to eat Roisin, eliciting gales of laughter from the child, along with cries of, "Nay, Mama, stop, it tickles!"

They spent some more of the afternoon together playing with her dolls and taking a walk in the garden. She then sat with the girl as she had her dinner and when it was time for Roisin to get into bed, Agnes sat with her and told her a story, and old Scottish tale of maidens and monsters and heroes, the sort Roisin loved. The little girl was asleep before the story was finished.

"She was more tired than she wanted to let on," Saoirse said, coming over to the bed and smiling fondly down at the sleeping child.

"Aye, bless her," Agnes said, struck as always by her daughter's perfection. She bent and pressed a small kiss to her forehead. "Sleep well, me wee angel."

They moved into the adjoining room so as not to disturb Roisin.

"Ye ken, me lady, she looks an awful lot like Conrad," Saoirse murmured.

Agnes did not reply, for her heart suddenly felt very full.

"Ye've nae idea how difficult this is fer me, Saoirse. 'Tis so hard fer me tae look him in the eyes and nae tell him he's her faither. But I ken 'tis for the best," she confessed, sadness mingling with guilt inside her.

"Conrad's a man of honor, me lady. I'm certain that if ye told him the truth, he'd marry ye like a shot. He'd wantae dae the right thing fer Roisin."

"Aye, of course, he would. D'ye think I dinnae ken that?"

"Then why nae tell him?" the maid asked.

"Because that's exactly what I wantae avoid."

"What? Ye wantae avoid him marryin' ye?" Saoirse asked, her brow furrowing with puzzlement.

"Aye. The whole reason I've kept the truth from him is because I never wanted him tae feel he hastae wed me just tae "dae the right thing" by Roisin. That would make it an obligation, nae a choice. I never wanted tae tie him down with a child. I wanted tae be chosen by him."

"Ah, I understand now," the maid said, her dark eyes full of sympathy. "That's a nasty bind ye've put yersel' in there, me lady. I mean, keepin' it from him means he'll nae be able tae choose one way or the other, will he?"

"There's more tae it than that, Saoirse," Agnes argued softly but with force. "I'm afeared fer Conrad. Can ye imagine how furious me family would be if they found out he's the faither after all this time?"

"Lord, yer faither would go off his head," Saoirse replied, lines of concern appearing around her eyes.

"That's right. And what about Duncan? He'd feel betrayed by his best friend. I'm afraid that if they found out the truth, they might dae something stupid. That's why they must never find out. Neither them nor Conrad. 'Tis safer fer everyone that way."

I already feel bad fer lyin' tae him about Roisin, but I love him too much tae tell the truth and put him at risk.

CHAPTER FOURTEEN

That evening, Conrad met Duncan in the great hall and had a couple of drams and a few pints of ale with him along with some supper. They did a lot of talking, but Conrad wasted little time in bringing up the topic that he had been wondering about ever since Duncan had first mention it to him in the armoury.

"Hey, ye were tellin' me about yer idea that the attack on Agnes' carriage was planned, but ye didnae finish," he said. "Ye mentioned havin' some issues with Clan MacDonnell. Are ye gonnae fill me in?" He took a big bite of his bread and ham.

"Ach, put that thought on the back burner fer now, lad. It was just an idea knockin' about in me head, but I've nae proof," Duncan replied dismissively.

"Ach, all right," Conrad agreed, feeling somewhat disappointed. "But ye still thingkthis business with the MacDonnells has somethin' tae dae with it?"

Duncan took a long drink of his ale then said, "I'm nae sure yet. But the scouts are due back any time, so we'll see what they have tae say first before jumpin' tae conclusions."

Knowing his friend well enough to realize he did not want to talk about it further, he changed the subject and applied himself to his ale. But his curiosity lingered. It seemed to him that lately, when it came to the MacDonalds, there were secrets in the air that he was not privy to. It was not a pleasant feeling, but being the stoical, loyal type and very patient when he wanted to be, he supposed he would find out what they were sooner or later.

It was already quite late when he wended his way back from the great hall. He was far from drunk but feeling pleasantly tipsy, having had just enough whisky to push his problems to the back of his mind.

He was passing along one of the hallways, heading for the stairs, when the sound of music unexpectedly wafted to his ears. He paused, listening intently. Recognizing the tune, he hummed the refrain. He went a little further along the hall, following the sound, and was finally able to recognize the instrument being played. It was the harpsichord. The distinctive sound instantly transported him back to past. And Agnes.

She had learned to play as a child and was a very skilled player, spending hours practicing and entertaining him and his sister Eileen with her virtuoso renditions of their favourite tunes. He recalled with a faint smile how she had tried to teach them both to play. Eileen had done quite well for a time, but she had soon given up, and even though he liked music and loved Agnes, he had proven to have no talent for it at all.

He stood for a moment, simply enjoying the music, then became curious about who was playing. He continued down the hallway, the music becoming louder and clearer as he progressed, and soon came to the door of the music room. It was ajar, so he peeked through the crack, not wishing to disturb the player by his presence.

To his astonishment, he saw Agnes sitting at the stool in front of the instrument, her fingers flying over the keys. Her eyes were closed and she appeared to be completely lost in the music. She looked so ethereally beautiful, he felt his longing like a physical pain in his belly. He remained there as she played on, transfixed by her. But after a few minutes, he began to feel bad for spying on her and wondered if he should leave.

"Ye dinnae havetae sneak around out there, tryin' tae hide. Ye can come in if ye like."

He almost jumped out of his skin at the sound of her voice. She continued playing, while he stood there, frozen, feeling rather foolish.

How the hell did she ken I was here? Can she see through bloody doors now?

He wanted more than anything to go in.

Affecting casualness, he sauntered in. Agnes looked over at him but continued playing faultlessly. He went to her and leaned on the edge of the instrument, feeling the notes vibrating though his body. It was almost as if she were touching him. He tried to focus on the music that flowed from her fingertips as if by magic. But it was impossible.

She ended the tune with an impressive flourish and sat back on the stool, regarding him coolly. Almost instantly, Conrad felt the tension in the atmosphere. Their gazes locked, the air fairly crackling between them.

He cleared his throat. "That was lovely. Ye still play as well as I remember."

She smiled doubtfully. "I'm a bit rusty. I havenae played fer years. Nae since I went tae France. Aunt Morag daesnae have a harpsichord. I hadnae realized how much I missed playin'."

He nodded, struggling to know what to say next in the heavy silence that fell.

Maybe she felt awkward too because she broke it. "I think I remember this bein' one of yer favorites." She began playing again, a version of an old traditional reel he knew at once. It was a lively tune, and the memories it brought back made him smile and tap his foot. But beneath the surface, he felt a little pang of hope "I'm surprised ye recall me likin' this one," he told her truthfully.

Daes she remember because she cares fer me?

"I remember those days quite vividly," she replied, her hands moving skilfully across the keyboard as she flicked him a glance. He watched her carefully, but her face gave nothing away.

"Aye, we used tae dance tae this, d'ye remember, when me and Duncan and ye and Eileen used tae practice our dancin'?"

"I wouldnae be playin' it if I didnae remember now, would I?" she replied a little tartly.

"Aye, I suppose nae." There was enough of an edge to her voice to provoke the return of other, less pleasant, memories to his mind. Like her leaving him so suddenly and maintaining a wall of silence, putting him through hell for five long years. The need for answers to the thousand questions he had rose up inside him like a loch-bound monster poking its head above the surface of the water, hunting for prey.

His enjoyment in the music gone now, he waited for her to finish. When she did, he clapped his hands in appreciation. "Very nice." She gave him a nod and a small smile, then closed the lid of the instrument. "I think that's enough fer now," she said, flexing her hands. "I'm so out of practice, me fingers are startin' tae ache."

But she did not get up, though she avoided meeting his eyes. Conrad leaned his elbows on the harpsichord. "Agnes, ye still havenae properly answered me questions about ye leavin' like that and nae writin' tae me."

"I disagree."

"Agnes, why did ye nae write tae me?" He heard the plaintive note in his voice and hated it.

With an impatient huff, she abruptly rose and made to move past him. He blocked her way. She frowned up at him. "Will ye let me pass?"

"Nay, I willnae. I deserve an explanation," he insisted.

"But we've already been through this, Conrad. I ken I hurt yer pride, and I'm sorry fer it. But I cannae change the past now, can I?"

"What was this mystery illness ye suddenly came down with overnight?"

"I told ye," she replied her eyes flashing with defiance. "It was a fever. The doctors in France said so. Ye think ye're all right, but then the symptoms come on very suddenly. It can kill ye within hours."

"Why dae I nae believe ye?"

"I've nae idea. 'Tis the truth."

He shook his head. "Nae, I can see ye're lyin'."

"Ye can see naethin' of the sort. Believe what ye like. It daesnae matter now."

In desperation, he found himself grabbing her upper arm and pulling her closer. She gasped as he bent and put his face directly in front of hers, so she could not avoid his gaze. "Agnes, we spent the night taegether, and I ken I was gone fightin' much longer than I thought I would be when I was called away. I'm sorry fer it, but I couldnae help it. But all the time I was away, I never forgot me promise tae return tae ye, and as soon as I could, I did!"

"Aye, two months later," she hissed, trying to free her arm. He tightened his grip.

"D'ye remember that day when I came here and sat in fer Duncan on yer faither's audience?"

She nodded, looking utterly miserable. "Aye, of course, I dae. Me maither said ye'd come back early because yer faither needed ye at home."

"That was a lie I told yer faither, an excuse. I came back fer ye. But before I could even get a chance tae speak tae ye, I was told ye were at death's door, and ye'd gone tae France. Can ye imagine how confusing that was? How devastated I was?"

Tears welled up in her eyes, and he hated himself.

"Conrad, I'm sorry, but I cannae change things now. Too much time has passed. Things have changed. 'Tis too late," she said her voice breaking. "Please, let me go."

"Ah, things have changed, have they? Daes that mean ye have a beau in France, is that it?" He had to know, even though he knew he was making her unhappy. She looked at him, eyes wide, clearly startled by the question.

She shook her head vehemently. "Nay! There's been nay one, there's nay beau!"

Her denial rang true, and he felt a sort of relief wash over him. He let her go, and she ran out of the room. He leaned on the harpsichord, his breath coming raggedly as he listened to her feet running down the hallway until the sound dissipated. He felt like a brute, but another part of him believed what she had told him, and in that moment, it was enough.

There's nay beau in France.

Conrad did not see Agnes at all for the next two days. He was too busy with his duties, which suited him perfectly, or so he told himself. The emotional strain of being near her was hardly bearable. When he was, he either wanted to shake out whatever it was she was hiding from him or kiss her and take her to bed.

On the morning of the third day, he went down early to the great hall for breakfast and was glad to find Duncan seated at the laird's table alone, eating.

"Mornin'," he said as he strode up to him. "Mind if I join ye fer a bite tae eat?"

Duncan's mouth was full of toasted bannock, but he nodded and gestured at the seat next to him. Conrad sat down and started piling a plate with food from the platters laid out on the table. "I was thinkin' of going fer a ride before trainin'.

Wantae come?" he asked, getting out his knife and buttering a hunk of bread.

Duncan shook his head and visibly swallowed his mouthful of food. "Ye're nae goin' anywhere, me friend. Ye're needed at this mornin's council meetin', by order of me faither," Duncan told him, spearing a bit of ham with his knife.

Conrad paused with the bread halfway to his mouth. "I am? Fer what reason? I'm nae usually invited," Conrad replied, surprised.

"'Tis about that business I mentioned tae ye the other day in the armoury."

"About the attack on Agnes' carriage and MacDonnell, ye mean?"

Duncan nodded. "Aye. The scouts came in late last night. They'll be reportin' at the meetin'. We need ye there because ye were with me durin' the attack and may have some useful insights tae offer. It should be an interestin' gatherin'."

"All right, I'll be glad tae be there and hear what the scouts have tae say," Conrad replied. "D'ye suspect MacDonnell may have somethin' tae dae with the attack then?" He wondered again what beef Tavish MacDonnell could have with Laird MacDonald. Although to be fair, the man was a born troublemaker and fond of starting a fight over very little.

"I'm keepin' an open mind at the moment. Until I hear different, I'll draw nay conclusions," Duncan told him before heartily eating a bannock stuffed with bacon.

Following suit, Conrad applied himself to his breakfast, keen to get to the meeting and find out what news the scouts had brought back. The idea that the attack had been planned was quite chilling, and the possible involvement of Tavish

MacDonnell even more so. He silently thanked God that he and Duncan had arrived in time to save the women and the little girl that night. But he still could not imagine what reason MacDonnell could have for attacking Clan MacDonald.

CHAPTER FIFTEEN

"I'm sure we're all eager tae hear what Dan and Colin have got tae report tae us now they're back from the field. Go ahead, lads," Laird MacDonald directed, gesturing at the two scouts seated to his right to take the floor. Dan and Colin Black were brothers and expert scouts. Conrad knew them both well and was unsurprised when Dan stood up to relay their report, Colin being renowned as man of few words. The room went quiet as Dan began speaking.

"So, tae sum it up," Dan said a few minutes later, "we have many witness accounts tae support our original suspicions, that there's been a lot of movement in recent weeks of what appear tae be parties of MacDonnell's men on our western borders as well as smaller numbers closer tae home. MacDonnell's up tae somethin', Me laird, nay doubt about it." Dan sat down while his alarming news sank in.

"Hmm, this just increases me suspicion that MacDonnell was behind the attack on me daughter's carriage the other night. It seems tae me that he's been keepin' a watch on us and that his spies found out about her return from France. It seems more and more as if he was targetin' her specifically, which is very worryin'."

Conrad was very puzzled. "Me laird, I'm sorry tae interrupt, but I'm nae clear on why ye think MacDonnell would have an interest in targetin' Agnes in particular. Is there somethin' I'm missin'?"

It was Duncan who answered, and what he said shook Conrad to the core. "Because he made an offer fer her hand that was refused."

Dumbstruck by this information, Conrad heard little of the rest of the meeting. The news itself was shocking enough, but he also suspected that this was one of the secrets the MacDonalds had been keeping. Even Duncan had never mentioned it to him, which hurt because it felt like his best friend did not trust him enough.

But why would they dae that?

He remained quiet for the rest of the meeting, but as soon as they were out in the hallway, he asked Duncan about it. "When exactly was this marriage proposal from MacDonnell? Was Agnes actually promised tae Tavish? I've never heard anythin' about an engagement between them."

"It was right before Agnes got sick," Duncan replied, tight-lipped, clearly worried. "Faither had it planned tae go ahead because he wanted an alliance with MacDonnell. He figured that bein' an ally of the man would protect the clan. But the whole thing was all called off when Agnes became ill and had tae be sent abroad for medical treatment."

Conrad's blood turned cold. "Christ, Duncan. Are ye sayin' that MacDonnell's found out she's back and he still wants tae wed her?"

"Looks like that's a strong possibility," his friend answered, his face grim.

Light dawned in Conrad's brain. "So, ye were right all along. It was nae a random attack. MacDonnell was waitin' fer her tae come home, and he staged the attack on her carriage. It wasnae a robbery. He wanted tae abduct her and force her intae marryin' him!"

Duncan halted by the door to his father's study. "Keep this tae yersel', man. And for God's sake, dinnae mention a word of it tae Agnes, whatever ye dae."

Conrad was stung by that. "What d'ye think I am?"

"Sorry, I'm just worried about her," Duncan apologized, running a distracted hand through his neatly shorn hair. "Now it looks like we have tae deal with MacDonnell, and he's a bloody madman, with a much bigger army than ours. Look, Conrad, I havetae talk tae me faither now. We'll catch up later and talk about it some more."

"Aye, all right," Conrad agreed, leaving him to it and walking off down the hallway, with no idea of where he was going.

Back in his chamber, feeling the urgent need to blow off some steam and get his thoughts straight, he grabbed his gear and headed out to the training field. On his way past an enclosed part of the castle gardens, he caught the sound of childish laughter and women's voices. He looked over a hedge and saw Agnes, Saoirse, and her daughter sitting on the lawn.

He stopped to watch them for a moment, struck by what a pretty picture they made in their bright summer dresses. Agnes was looking particularly fine, he thought, in a pale pink dress embroidered with flowers, her long dark hair flowing down her back like a river of silk.

"Let me put it on fer ye," the little one was saying, standing before Agnes and carefully arranging her hair before placing a crown of daisies upon it. When she had done so to her satisfaction, she threw her arms around Agnes' neck and kissed her on both cheeks. In return, Agnes peppered her face with tiny kisses and tickled her. The little girl shrieked with laughter and leapt away. Once again, it struck him how close they were.

He made no sound or movement he was aware of to alert her to his presence. Yet, as though sensing his gaze upon her, she suddenly looked up and met his eyes. To his surprise, considering their last acrimonious meeting, she immediately leaned over to Saoirse and whispered something in the maid's ear. Saoirse glanced at him nodded.

Agnes slipped around the bushes while the child was not looking and came over to him. Without saying anything, he followed her over to the other side of the path, where she stopped next to a large myrtle bush aflame with red blossoms.

"Ye and the lassie have a close bond," he said.

"I've kent her since she was a baby. She's a very affectionate child."

"Aye, she's a sweet little thing." he had to agree, recalling the fragile little body he had held up during her fighting lesson.

"How long have ye been watchin' us?" she asked, her lovely hazel eyes glittering in the sun.

"Nae long. I happened tae be passing and heard ye laughin'."

"Oh, ye happened tae be passin', did ye?" she asked sceptically. "Ye seem tea have a habit of turnin' up. Are ye spyin' on me and followin' me about?"

"I am nae!" Conrad shot back defensively. "I dinnae ken what ye mean!"

"Well, this is the second time I've caught ye spyin' on me. Like when ye were lurkin' outside the music room the other night." She idly picked a myrtle blossom and began methodically shredding it.

"I wasnae lurkin'!"

"Ah, ye just happened tae be passin', I suppose?"

"Aye, I was. And anyway, I could say the same of ye. Ye always seem tae appear, whatever I'm doin'," he countered, rattled by her accusation.

"Well, ye neednae worry about that fer much longer since I'll be returnin' tae France very soon." He threw away the last of the myrtle flower. Ye ken I only came back tae avoid the sickness that's been spreadin' through France. It was always intended that I'd return once it passes and me auntie is better," she explained, her eyes on his.

Pain lanced through him because she seemed so happy to be leaving him again, choosing her French relatives over him. Fighting to maintain his composure, he said, "Right. Well, in that case, if ye're so set on leavin' because ye miss all the people ye have in France then perhaps 'tis best if we keep our distance from each other while ye're still here. I mean, since ye'll be gone soon anyway."

"Aye, I agree," she said blithely, tossing her head as she walked away. He caught himself staring after her and gave himself a mental shake.

I'll nae bloody watch her walk away from me again. I'm off tae let off some steam.

He stalked off apace to the training ground, where he enlisted one of the men to spar with him and gave the unfortunate fellow a thrashing.

For two days since their meeting in the garden, Agnes had been trying her hardest to avoid bumping int Conrad. She had even dined alone in her chamber or with Saoirse in the nursery, refusing to go down the hall, but on the third morning, both she and Roisin fancied porridge for breakfast, so she decided to risk going down to the kitchen to fetch it herself.

"Would ye mind putting a big blob of jam in the middle please?" she asked the kitchen maid who served her.

"Jam, me lady?" the girl asked, goggle eyed, spoon poised in mid-air.

"Aye, jam. Ye should try it. 'Tis very tasty," Agnes informed her.

The door opened, and a large shadow fell across the stone flagged floor. The girl smiled at whoever had just come in. "Good day tae ye, maister," she simpered, her face going bright red.

Agnes cringed inwardly.

Why is this always happenin'? What are the odds of him comin' in here right at this very moment?

"Mornin', Mary. I've just come tae pick up me lunch."

That voice! It always sent shivers down her spine.

"'Tis all ready fer ye. I'll just serve me lady here, and then I'll fetch it fer ye," Mary replied, clearly thrilled to oblige him. Agnes felt a twinge of jealousy.

"In both bowls, me lady?" Mary asked, turning her attention back to Agnes.

"Aye, please."

"Any flavour jam in particular, me lady. We have plum and blackberry, I think."

"Blackberry," Conrad said from behind Agnes. "That's what she likes best in her porridge," he added.

"Blackberry it is," Mary said, going off to fetch it.

Agnes turned her head and looked at him, pursing her lips, yet her heart fluttered at the sight of him. He looked absolutely gorgeous, his blonde hair curling about his ears, his handsome face tanned by the sun, his eyes as bright as sapphires as they held hers. "I see ye still eat yer porridge the same way as ye used tae," he observed with a small smile.

Agnes could have cursed the heat that flooded her cheeks at that moment, knowing they must be turning bright pink. "Aye."

"Why two bowls though? Is one nae enough fer ye?"

Reluctant to strike up conversation with him again, unable to trust her own response to his proximity, she could see no choice but to answer him. "One is fer Saoirse's little girl."

"Is that so. What a coincidence that ye both like tae eat yer porridge the same way."

She detected an odd tone to his voice that put her on edge. She looked at him sharply, searching his face for signs he had guessed the truth. But she saw none. "Nae really. She just likes it as well, 'tis all."

"I must say again, ye and the wee yin are very close, eh?"

Rattled, Agnes was glad when Mary came back with the pot of jam at that moment and plopped a big dollop into the centre of each bowl of oatmeal. "Thank ye," Agnes told her as she picked up the tray with the bowls on it and turned to leave. But she was riled and could not resist answering him. "Ye keep sayin' that, but I dinnae ken what ye're drivin' at. I told ye, I've kent her since she was born. Why would I nae be close tae her? She's a sweet bairn. Excuse me, please," she said irritably, desperate to get away.

He opened the door but partially blocked the entrance with his body so that she would have to squeeze past him if she tried to leave. She gripped the tray tightly, the only thing separating them, her heart fluttering madly in her breast. Summoning a little defiance for strength against the effect he was having on her, she looked up and met his eyes. That proved to be a big mistake. They pierced her, pinned her to the spot, setting her pulse racing madly. Something passed between them, some crackling undercurrent that heated her blood.

"Christ, man, get out of the way, will ye? What are ye daein' blockin' the doorway. Can a man nae even get intae his own bloody kitchen when he's hungry?"

It was Duncan, standing in the doorway, hands on hips, his eyes flicking between them. "Are ye all right there, Agnes?" he asked, clearly wondering what he had interrupted.

"Aye, Braither," she replied hastily, summoning a smile for him. "I was just leavin'. Me porridge is gettin' cold." She swept past the both of them and hurried down the hallway, praying Conrad would not follow her. Thankfully, he did not, and she breathed a sigh of relief as she went as fast as she could up the stairs.

CHAPTER SIXTEEN

*D*uncan was attending a clan meeting for some urgent matter and had told Conrad to take a few hours off for himself that afternoon. He welcomed the thought of few hours alone to think. He had decided to take a leisurely ride down to the nearby Loch Machie, where he had spent a lot of time with Agnes, Duncan, and Eileen in their youth.

He had arranged for a packed lunch to be made up for him to take along, which was how he had happened to bump into Agnes in the kitchen that morning. It had been a chance meeting he had not been prepared for at all and, as always, the encounter had stirred up a storm of emotions inside him.

One of them was suspicion. The more he witnessed the interactions between Agnes and Saoirse's little girl, the more his suspicion had grown. But it was as yet a nameless thing, without form, which nagged at him but refused to be pinned down.

With such thoughts occupying his mind, it seemed to him that fate was playing a cruel game with him when he crested the grassy hillock that would take him down to the sandy strand at the edge of the loch… and saw Agnes and the little girl already there.

Agnes was walking slowly along the edge of the loch, watching and laughing while the little one was paddling and splashing in the water, dressed only in her shift. It was a lovely picture that both warmed and pierced his heart, while simultaneously sending his suspicions soaring.

He watched them for a while, sitting astride his horse, wondering if he should go before they saw him, when the child spotted him. "Maister Conrad! Come and play with us!" she shouted, leaving the water and racing towards him across the sand.

Why daes this keep happenin'. 'Tis like fate is throwing me and Agnes together and havin' a damn good laugh.

He smiled despite himself as the little girl ran up the hill to meet him.

"Come and have a paddle," she invited him, blue eyes flashing in the sunlight, her smile irresistible. It tugged at his heart strings. He could not refuse her anything. Before he knew what he was doing, he reached down to her. "Come on up, Little Flower," he said. "Ye like horses, eh?"

With a little laugh of delight, she caught his hand. He lifted her easily up into the saddle in front of him. She settled her warm little body against his chest, her face wreathed in smiles. "Click yer tongue, like this." He demonstrated. "And he'll go forward."

She followed his instruction, clicking her tongue. At the same time, he heeled the horse's flanks, urging it forward down the shallow bank towards Agnes. She was standing, a slender sprite framed against the majestic background of water and sky, shading her eyes with one hand, watching them approach.

Nay doubt she'll be annoyed tae see me here.

"What about Agnes?" he murmured to the child. "Will she nae mind me interruptin' yer time together?"

"Nay, she'll be happy. She likes ye," she replied simply.

He laughed, taken aback, knowing it could not be true. "I dinnae think so, lassie."

"Aye, she daes. I can tell." The bald statement, uttered with a childish lack of artifice, stunned him. The girl carried on stroking the horse's mane, clearly fascinated. "What's his name?"

"Davey."

"Hello, Davey. I have an apple fer ye tae eat." She looked up at Conrad, giving him a jolt when he looked into her eyes. They were so like his own. "We brought our luncheon tae eat by the loch. Davey can have me apple," she explained.

"He'll like that. He loves apples."

"Ach, then I'll get some more fer him next time."

Next time? If Agnes has her way, there'll nae be a next time.

The thought made him sad.

They drew level with Agnes, and he slid from the saddle. "Down ye come, Little Flower," he said, carefully lifting the child down on to the sand. "I'll fetch me apple," she said and ran off to the small pile of things they had brought with them.

"What are ye daein' here, Conrad? Ye are followin' me," Agnes said, her cheeks turning unaccountably crimson as her sunlit eyes bore into his.

"Ach, dinnae be daft, Agnes. I am nae. I had some time off, and I thought I'd come here and have some peace. I had nae idea ye'd be here. I was gonnae leave, but the wee yin saw me. I couldnae say nay tae her. I've nay wish tae be where I'm nae wanted. I'll just stay a short while, and then I'll find an excuse tae go," he said, seeing no point in not being truthful.

"All right. I suppose I can hardly throw ye off the beach," she said grudgingly, turning away from him. The girl ran back, clutching the apple. "Can I give it tae Davey now, please, Maister Conrad?"

"Ach, just call me Conrad, Little One," he told her, and was rewarded with another gappy grin. "But he needs a drink first. Then, we'll take him up tae the trees over there." He nodded at the tree line a few yards away. "There's grass there fer him tae eat and a bit of shade. He daesnae like tae get too hot, ye see. Then once he's settled, ye can give him the apple, all right?"

"Aye, all right. I'll come with ye," she replied, taking his hand. It surprised him how good it felt to hold her little paw as they walked Davey to the edge of the water and let him drink. He could not help but be touched by the way the little girl stroked the enormous horse's neck and prattled to him the whole time, as though he were a person.

Once Davey had drunk his fill, she was thrilled when Conrad let her take the reins and lead him up to the shade of the trees. Conrad showed her how to hitch the reins to a tree, impressed once more by how quick she was to learn new things. Though he knew she was Saoirse's child, it reminded him of Agnes.

"Och, ye're as bright as button, Little Flower," he told her. "Go on then and give him his apple. He'll love ye forever then." Davey whickered and chomped the apple happily, while the little girl giggled. When the horse repaid her generosity with an affectionate nuzzle, she lit up with pleasure, rubbing his velvety nose and planting small kisses on it. Conrad's heart clenched at her sweet innocence.

They returned to Agnes, who was sitting on the sand facing the water, her arms wrapped around her knees. "All right, me darlin'?" she asked, raising a smile for the child.

"Aye, I gave Davey the horse me apple fer his lunch," the little one explained with childish earnestness.

"I'm sure he enjoyed it," Agnes told her.

"Aye, he's me friend now. I'm goin' tae play in the water." Off she scampered, to clamber over the big rocks at the edge of the water, completely oblivious to the tense atmosphere between the two grownups. Conrad could not resist glancing over at Agnes covertly, noticing how tense she appeared.

"She's as sharp as a tack, that one," he said eventually, to break the silence.

"Aye, too sharp fer her own good sometimes."

What did she mean by that?

"How come ye're here with the lassie on yer own. Where's her maither today?"

"She's busy. 'Tis a nice day, so I said I'd take the lass out fer a walk by the loch tae keep her occupied."

"Ye mean ye walked all the way here?" he asked, amazed.

"Aye, 'tis nae far. We walk a lot further than this at home in France."

"Is that so? What's the wee yin's name by the way?" he asked, realizing he had never felt the need to know before. Little Flower seemed to suit her fine.

As she seemed to do with unusual frequency, Agnes hesitated before giving him an answer. "Her name's Roisin." Her cheeks went bright pink.

"Roisin?" Conrad echoed, staring at her in surprise. "That's quite a coincidence," he added, a memory of Agnes naked in his bed, of him whispering his secret name into her ear. Mo Ròisín. Agnes looked away, as though to hide her blushes, and he suddenly knew she remembered as well.

"Nae really. Saoirse liked the name," she replied, her voice laced with irritation. Unexpectedly, she rounded on him, her face still flushed. "Look, since the day I've come, ye are asking me questions constantly and I really dinnae ken what ye expect me tae answer. I'd prefer it if this constant interrogation ended, because it makes me feel uncomfortable." She flicked her eyes at Roisin before turning her flashing gaze back to him. It struck him that she seemed scared. But what was she scared of, he wondered, his suspicion flaring once more.

Suddenly, the silence was shattered by a shrill scream and a splash. "Omigod!" Agnes was on her feet and racing down to the water before Conrad. "I'm comin' darlin', I'm comin'" she shouted, picking up her skirts and plunging into the loch without hesitation.

CHAPTER SEVENTEEN

Conrad was just behind her and saw how she threw herself towards the little girl, who had obviously slipped from the rocks and fallen into a deep part of the water where her feet could not reach the floor. She was panicking, thrashing hysterically, but then Agnes was there beside her, struggling to calm her and lift her from the water. Conrad swam to her side in a few strokes and helped her, his heart in his throat to see how the child coughed and spluttered, clearly having swallowed a lot of water.

"'Tis all right, I've got ye, ye're safe now, 'tis all right, me angel," Agnes crooned as they waded back to the strand, holding her between them as the paroxysms of coughing shook the fragile body. As soon as they got to dry land, Agnes sank down onto the sand, her hair plastered to her face as water ran off her. She put the coughing little girl over her shoulder and patted her back vigorously. Roisin sobbed in distress as she coughed up water convulsively, gasping and struggling to catch her breath all the while.

"That's it, darlin', cough it all, up and spit it out, there's a brave lass," Agnes urged her frantically over and over, tears of barely restrained panic rolling down her cheeks as she encouraged her to expel the water from her lungs. It took a few minutes before she had coughed it all up, but sobs still shook her small body.

Now all the water had come up, Agnes cradled the little girl to her chest and rocked her like a baby. "There, there, me wee angel, that's better, eh? That's all the nasty water gone now. Ye had a wee accident, but 'tis all right now. Och, what a fright ye gave me." She stroked the child's wet hair from her face and kissed her repeatedly.

Conrad watched in awe Agnes calmed the child, marvelling at the way she had thrown herself unhesitatingly into the water to save Roisin, as determined and protective as a mother would be.

"She needs tae be kept warm," Conrad said, dashing back to the horse to fetch a blanket. He wrapped it around them both, tucking the ends in carefully so they would not get a chill. The water was very cold, and though it was a warm day, there was a fresh breeze blowing in across the water.

They sat there for a while, drying off in the sunshine. Agnes rocked the little girl against her breast until he slowly settled, her eyelids fluttered closed. "She's sleepin' now," Agnes said quietly at last. "I need tae get her back tae the castle as soon as possible. I want the healer tae check on her and make sure she's all right."

"Aye, we'll take me horse. It'll be quicker," Conrad replied, getting to his feet at once. Agnes looked up at him, doubt fleetingly crossing her face. It stung him, but he swallowed the hurt. "Come on, Agnes, ye ken it makes sense. We'll get there in a quarter of the time it'll take ye tae walk." He reached out a hand to help her up.

"Aye, all right," he said with obvious reluctance but seeing it was for the best. She held Roisin with one arm while taking his hand with the other and letting him pull her to her feet.

"Ye'd better ride in front with her," Conrad said as they approached the horse.

"Aye, all right," she replied, sounding hesitant. But she allowed him to put his hands around her waist and lift them both up into the saddle without protest, clearly prepared to put their differences aside for the sake of the child. He swung himself up behind them, arranging the blanket around them again and waiting while Agnes settled herself as comfortably as she could with the child cradled on her lap.

It felt terribly intimate when he put his arms either side of her to take the reins, and she had no choice but to lean against his chest. He hoped she could not feel how fast his heart was beating at the close contact.

Though the situation called for speed, he dared not go too fast in case the child awoke and got upset. So, he went at a fast walk, burningly conscious of Agnes' seated between this thighs, her soft, warm body gently bumping against him with every one of Davey's powerful strides. Thankfully, the little one was so worn out by her ordeal she slept soundly the whole way.

Back at the castle, it did not occur to him to leave Agnes by herself. She did not send him away either, so he escorted her to the infirmary, striding along the hallway ahead of her to knock at the door and gain immediate admittance by the castle healer. He held the door open for Agnes, who rushed past him into the room. Then he followed her in and closed it behind him.

The healer was a thin woman called Una, who could have been aged anywhere from thirty to fifty, with strawberry blonde hair, freckles, and intelligent pale-blue eyes. As soon as she saw the child, she beckoned Agnes to carry her over to the bed on one side of the room, listening intently as Agnes explained what had happened.

"The poor little thing, that was a nasty thing tae happen," Una murmured sympathetically, frowning as he made some preliminary checks on the sleeping child, gently lifting her eyelids, laying a hand on her forehead, then checking her pulse.

"Will she be all right?" Agnes asked frettingly, holding Roisin's hand.

"Wheesht a moment," Una said, taking a tube made of horn from her apron pocket and placing one end to the little girl's chest, then putting her ear to the other. She listened intently, while Agnes and Conrad waited on tenterhooks in silence.

Conrad let go the breath he had been holding when, after what felt like an eternity, Una straightened up and said, "I cannae hear any water in her lungs, which is a very good sign that she's nae come tae any serious harm. She's very healthy, and at her age, she'll likely bounce back in nye time." She smiled kindly at Agnes then at him. Suddenly, Una's brows rose. "Och, God, ye're Lady Agnes," the healer quickly bowed. "I apologize fer nae realizin' it earlier."

Conrad watched as Agnes's cheeks turned pink. "'Tis all right, I havenae been home fer a long time. D'ye think she'll be all right?" she asked Una again.

"Aye, she'll be fine. She might have a bit of a sore throat for a while though, from coughing up all that water. Honey and hyssop will soothe it. I'll give ye a mixture before ye go," the healer told her kindly.

"Shall I keep her in bed?"

"I should put her tae bed right away and let her sleep it off. Hopefully, she'll wake up none the worse fer her ordeal. But if there's any sign of fever or sickness, call me right away."

Conrad watched the tension visibly drain from Agnes. His heart went out to her as he sighed with relief. "Och, thank ye, Una, I'm very grateful tae ye," she said, smiling for the first time since the mishap.

"I'm glad 'tis good news, me lady," Una replied. "Now, I'll make ye up a flask of the mixture tae soothe the wee yin's throat." He went to her work counter and began preparing the medicine.

"That's grand news, eh, Agnes?" Conrad asked, surprising himself with how relieved he felt at the positive outcome. She nodded at him distractedly as she sat on the edge of the bed, still holding the child's hand and gazing anxiously at her.

"Aye, it is. Thank ye fer bringin' us back, Conrad, but there's nae need fer ye tae stay now," he said without looking at him.

Trying his best not to feel slighted by her dismissal, he said, "I'm glad she's all right."

But Agnes did not have time to reply because at that moment, Roisin stirred and opened her eyes. As soon as they alighted on Agnes, she reached out her little arms to her and cried out, "Mama!"

Conrad's heart thudded in his chest. He stood in stunned silence, staring at the pair as they embraced tenderly. All his suspicions came home to roost, and he mentally kicked himself for not realizing the truth sooner. He felt a fool. Though it was a shock to find out this way, it seemed so obvious now. Agnes' shiftiness, the odd dynamic between her and Roisin and Saoirse… it suddenly all fell into place.

The question he had been trying, and failing, to get a response to out of Duncan for days was now answered loud and clear. Not only had Agnes been courting another man in France, but whoever he was, she had also given birth to his daughter.

He could not prevent the painful stab of jealousy that went through him, nor the hollow feeling of loss that squeezed his heart. Loss was a familiar companion, after all. Neither could he stop himself from asking the question that was now burning at the forefront of his mind. "She's yet daughter, is she nae?"

This time, Agnes decided not to lie and he saw her expression shift as she almost whispered the word "yes."

I shouldnae ask who the faither is, should I?

"Who's the faither?"

Damn it!

"'Tis nae important, Conrad," Agnes replied, cradling Roisin and rocking her as a mother does her beloved child, whilst simultaneously warning him with her eyes not to ask questions in front of Una and the child. The little one rested her head against her mother's breast. At any other time, it would have been an affectionate scene. But that was far from Conrad's thoughts.

The child is how old? She's small, so she's nae much more than three or four, for sure. That means Agnes must have met another man just a year or two after moving to France. He felt crushed to think how little he must have meant to her.

"I'm only askin'. Is it a secret then?" he asked, struggling to keep his voice even.

"There ye go with yer questions again."

"I understand now why ye're so eager tae return tae France."

"Aye, that's right. There's really nae need fer ye tae be here, Conrad. Roisin's all right now, so ye can go."

"Aye, I suppose nae. Now I ken she's all right, I'll leave ye alone then."

He let himself out into the hall and stood there, his mind reeling.

Questions, questions, and more bloody questions, that's all she's given me in the last five years. And now she's back, 'tis even worse. She's never really cared fer me at all. The sooner she goes back tae France the better. I wish she'd never come home. But what I cannae make out is why she would lie tae me like that, tryin' tae pass Roisin off as Saoirse's daughter. I mean, why go through all that charade tae keep it from me? It daesnae make sense at all. And what's all the secrecy about who the faither is?

He recalled the shock of learning about Tavish MacDonnell's marriage proposal to Agnes, which had been deliberately kept from him.

And now this. But that's the MacDonald's fer ye. Secrets all over the place, and I'm nae tae be let in on any of them!

Relieved that Conrad had gone, now equipped with the flask of soothing medicine Una had made for Roisin, Agnes took her back to the nursery. There, she promptly put the little girl to bed and dosed her with the mixture. The child soon dozed off again and she and Saoirse sat on either side of the bed whispering to each other so as not to wake her. Agnes explained to Saoirse what had occurred.

"What are ye gonnae dae now Conrad kens ye're Roisin's maither?" the maid asked, her kindly face creased with concern.

Agnes shrugged. "I'll nae dae anythin'. 'Tis obvious he's assumed the faither is some man I met in France, and that's the way I intend tae keep it."

"But, me lady, how can ye be so sure he'll keep yer secret and nae tell anyone else Roisin's yer daughter?"

It suddenly hit Agnes that she had failed to do so. "Ach, I was so distracted, I forgot tae ask him that!" He sprang to her feet, feeling the urgency of the situation. "Saoirse, hold the fort while I go and talk tae him straight away."

Saoirse nodded, while Agnes hurried from the room to seek out Conrad and ask him to keep her secret.

But why would he dae that?

CHAPTER EIGHTEEN

"What d'ye want, Agnes? Why are ye here?" Conrad asked bluntly, not sounding at all pleased to see her when he opened the door.

Omigod!

For several long moments, Agnes could only stare open-mouthed at his shocking state of undress. All he had on was a towel wrapped around his waist, his hair was wet, and his face and body shone with droplets of water.

Her cheeks burning, she hastily dropped her gaze to the flagstones. "Can I come in?"

"What fer?"

To her further discomfiture, he seemed determined to keep her out in the hallway where anyone could come by at any time and see her outside his door.

What will they think?!

Not knowing which was worse, someone seeing her there or being alone with a half-naked Conrad in his chamber, out of urgent necessity, she chose the latter. "I need tae talk tae ye, in private. 'Tis important, about Roisin," she said hurriedly.

After a moment's hesitation, he stepped back and held the door open wider for her to enter the room. She went inside and wheeled around to face him as he shut it behind her. The sight of his muscular body shining with drops of water sent a pang of desire shooting through her. Instantly hot and flustered, she quickly averted her eyes and knotted her fingers nervously at her waist, as though unable to trust them not to reach out and try to touch him.

"I'm busy, so say what ye need tae say," he said, standing a few feet away from her, not bothering to cover himself.

Agnes said awkwardly, "Conrad, could ye nae… could ye put some clothes on, please?"

"Ye interrupted me while I was changin'. Ye must take me as I am. 'Tis nae the first time ye see me like this, so I dinnae see why ye should be turnin' red."

Determined not to be drawn into an argument, for she needed his cooperation, she managed to meet his eyes. "I need ye tae promise me nae tae tell anyone else the truth about Roisin bein' me daughter and nae Saoirse's," she said. "Me and me family's reputation will be ruined if it gets out."

His handsome features creased into a frown. "Is that all ye came fer? D'ye think I didnae realize that? I'd never dae anythin' tae hurt ye or yer family, Agnes, and ye should ken that."

Relief washed over her. "Thank ye. I'm grateful tae ye."

"Aye, well, there's nay need tae be. And ye dinnae need tae worry about me asking ye awkward questions anymore either. I'm leavin'."

"Leavin'?" Agnes was shocked. For the first time since entering, she looked around the chamber and saw he was in the throes of packing up his things. There were bags piled up and clothes on the bed. It was for the best, she thought, but even so, she could not stop the dismay that suddenly filled her. "Why so soon?"

"I goin' home tae Moy Hall. I reckon the time's past due fer me tae take up me position as me clan's war leader as me faither wishes. I've been away from home fer too long, what with all the recent fightin'. I'm gonnae spend some time with me family."

"Oh, I see." Agnes replied, a pain suddenly flaring in her chest. She knew she was being contrary, having already told him she was returning to France shortly. But deep down she did not want him to go and could hardly bear the thought of not seeing him again.

Stop bein' so foolish, 'tis better that he should go.

She told herself that harshly, digging her fingernails into her palms to stop herself from doing anything stupid.

"Well, goodbye then," she forced herself to say. Unable to stand the tension between them any longer, she headed past him for the door. She did not expect it when, at the last moment, Conrad stepped in her way.

Surprised, she looked up at him questioningly, her skin prickling with heat to realize how close they were.

"Before ye go, Agnes, just tell me one thing. Why did ye call yer daughter Roisin?" His voice was soft, probing.

Filled with unease, Agnes scrambled for a reply. "'Tis just a name."

Conrad stepped right up to her, so close, she could feel the heat of his body on her bare skin, his breath on her hair. "I dinnae believe that fer a moment," he said, taking hold of her chin gently and tilting her face up to look deeply into her eyes. "Tell me the truth. Did ye dae it because ye remember the night we spent together?"

Shaken by his perceptiveness and caught in the piercing gaze of his bright-blue eyes, Agnes found she could not move. Her heart began racing, her chest fluttering as her breath caught in her throat. Before she knew what was happening, Conrad seized her by the shoulders and pulled her to him. When his lips went down on hers so forcefully, so demanding, the years flew away.

A fire ignited in her belly, and her blood turned hot as it coursed through her body, her very flesh and bones reliving the passion they had shared all those years before. Unable to resist the desire which overtook her, she surrendered herself totally to the kiss, reaching up and twining her fingers in his hair, drawing him closer, opening her mouth to meet his with a fierce fervour she had not felt since their fateful, forbidden night together. Except in her fantasies.

'Tis just as wonderful as it was before!

Filled with pent-up longing, the kiss intensified, and she would have been happy for it never to end. But then, a sudden noise from the hallway outside dragged her back to the present.

Nay! This shouldnae be happenin'!

Panicked, she abruptly released Conrad and sprang away from him, thankful that he did nothing to stop her as she wrenched the door open and ran out.

She was out of breath when she slammed her chamber door behind her and stood with her back to it for a few minutes, her mind reeling, wondering if what had just happened was real or a dream. But the tingling of her lips and the glow of warmth in her belly told her the kiss had been all too real. "Ye fool," she muttered to herself angrily. "How could ye have let that happen?!"

Leaving the door, she began pacing the floor, thinking of the enormous risk she had taken just by being alone with him in his chamber like that, with him almost naked. But that only got her hot and bothered thinking about his body.

His gorgeous, beautiful body.

In five years it seemed to her that he had only gotten more desirable, his body harder, stronger, more powerful than before.

"Ach, stop thinkin' about him like that! I should have pushed him away when he kissed me, nae kissed him back like a wanton hussy," she chided herself aloud, clenching her fists as she paced, furious with herself for the way she had responded. But the touch of his lips, his tongue entwined with hers, had peeled back the years, and the pent-up wanting had been unstoppable.

I dread tae think what might have happened if I hadnae heard someone in the hallway and come tae me senses. 'Tis good that he's leavin', the sooner the better. 'Tis what's best fer all of us. I'll waste nay more time worryin' about him.

The following day, Agnes was relieved to find that after a good night's sleep, Roisin seemed to have already bounced back from half drowning in the loch. It was another warm, sunny July day, and the little girl begged her mother to go out and play. Wanting to make up for the disappointment of the previous day, Agnes had an idea for something they could do together which she knew Roisin would enjoy.

Roisin happily spent the morning with her grandmother. Then, at around noon, the two of them set off hand in hand for a walk to the nearby castle woods. Over her arm, Agnes carried a wicker basket full of sandwiches, cakes, apples, and freshly made lemonade, a picnic courtesy of the cooks.

She had chosen the castle woods as being far enough from the castle for them not to encounter anyone, and there were no guards to bother them.

"This looks like a nice place fer a picnic, Ma," Roisin declared, skipping ahead as they came through the fringe of trees and emerged into a grassy clearing. It was an idyllic spot that soothed Agnes' troubled soul. Birdsong serenaded them, and sunlight danced across the grass like fairy lights as it filtered down through the leaves, which shifted gently in the light breeze.

"Aye, this is perfect, me darlin'. This is where me and Duncan and Conrad and his sister Eileen used tae play often when I was a wee lassie like ye," Agnes told her daughter, shaking out a blanket and spreading it over the grass. "We made a camp in that tree there." She gestured at a large, ancient elm with branches low enough to safely sit on. "It was our special tree. We had lots of fun and games together in this spot," she added, smiling a little sadly at the fond memories.

"I'm gonnae make a camp too," Roisin said, running over to sit astride one of the branches as if it were a horse, bouncing up and down happily.

"That's a very good idea. Ye make the camp while I get out our tea. Are ye hungry?"

"Aye, I am, but first I'm gonnae collect some leaves and make a nice comfy place for us tae sit in me camp. It'll be our secret place, Ma. But I'll show it tae uncle Duncan. He can come here if he likes, after we go back tae Auntie Morag's."

"Och, I'm sure he'll come here a lot and think of ye. Maybe we'll leave a wee present for him tae find, eh?"

"Aye, that would be grand! We could leave him a cake, but if it rains, it might go all soggy. I'll find somethin' better fer uncle, as a surprise."

Agnes laughed as the little girl jumped off the branch and began running around the clearing, full of enthusiasm. She busied herself foraging for fallen leaves and various bits and pieces that she found interesting, gathering them all up in her pinafore.

"I think I'll tell Conrad about the secret camp as well, and I'll find a surprise tae leave fer him too," Roisin suddenly said, taking Agnes completely by surprise. She had been trying very hard to put all thoughts of the kiss out of her mind. But there was no denying Roisin had taken a shine to him.

"Well, Conrad's goin' home tae see his family soon," she told the child gently. "He willnae be comin' back here fer a while. Maybe ye could leave his present with Grandma or Duncan, eh? They'll give it to him when he comes back, but we'll likely be in France by then."

Roisin stopped what she was doing and looked at her mother. "But he cannae go without me sayin' goodbye," she said, her bottom lip starting to quiver.

Agnes sighed inwardly. "All right, we'll go and find him when we go back ate the castle later. Ye can say goodbye then."

With luck, he'll already be gone. I'll find some way tae distract her then.

Roisin's smile immediately reappeared. "Good. Conrad's me friend, and friends dinnae leave without sayin' goodbye," she said in her precocious way.

From the mouths of children and infants, Agnes thought, remembering the words of the old psalm.

They spent a delightful couple of hours together, making the camp, picnicking, playing ball, then Agnes showed Roisin how to make little dolls out of sticks and grass.

"One fer Duncan and one fer Conrad," the child pronounced as her little fingers nimbly tucked in the last grass stalk and he stood the small figure against a stone, admiring it.

"Ye've made a good job there, wee yin," Agnes told her proudly, putting the already-finished doll next to Roisin's. "I'm sure they'll both be delighted with their presents."

"I'll take Duncan's and hide it in the camp for him tae come and find when we've gone back tae France," the child announced, taking one of the stick men and running over to the elm. While her daughter engrossed herself in her small world of make-believe, humming merrily to herself, Agnes remained sitting on the blanket. Suddenly, she noticed the birds had fallen silent. A shiver of unease ran up her spine as she cast around the clearing, seeing nothing untoward but having the unnerving feeling of being watched.

Over the next few minutes, the sense of unease became so strong, the hairs on the back of her neck stood up. Starting to feel scared, she stood up. "Roisin, I think we should pack up our things and go back now," he called to the child. "'Tis getting late."

"Ach, Ma, can we nae stay just a wee bit longer, please?" the child wheedled.

Agnes was already throwing the remains of the picnic into the basket. "Nay, lass, we must go now. I promised Saoirse we wouldnae be back too late," she said firmly, her anxiety levels soaring by the second. She hurriedly latched the basket, folded up the blanket, then looked around for Roisin's ball. It was nowhere to be seen.

"Is this what ye're lookin' fer?"

The man's voice coming from her right was so unexpected, Agnes heart almost burst out of her chest with shock. Her head snapped around, and he gasped to see an armed man standing at the edge of the clearing. He was grinning at her, and he was holding out Roisin's ball.

Out of the corner of her eyes, Agnes caught movement, and when she looked away from the man and around the clearing, her blood turned icy cold. They were surrounded by armed men, who seemed to have materialized out of the shadows between the trees. She looked over at Roisin. She had her head down among the gnarly roots of the elm and clearly had not noticed the men. Frightened for her daughter but not wanting to scare her, Agnes moved swiftly in her direction, calling out, "Roisin, come here at once, darlin'." She was mentally preparing to grab her daughter and run.

But the man with the ball had other ideas. "Stay where ye are, lady," he told her in a calm, commanding voice. He walked towards her, a thickset man with a black beard and a long scar across the bridge of his nose that underscored his cold black eyes. She ignored his order and began running towards Roisin, but he caught up to her easily and took hold of her upper arm in an iron grip, halting her in her tracks. The other men began to close in.

"Let go of me this instant. Who are ye? What d'ye want?" she demanded of her captor, determined not to show weakness.

"Ma, who are those men?" Roisin asked, looking alarmed as she popped up from her nest between the tree roots.

"Naebody, sweetheart. Come over here, love, right now." Agnes said as calmly as he could. "Let me go now or me faither will hear of it," she hissed at the bearded man, trying to shake off his grip. But he merely tightened it, his fingers biting into her.

"We've been watchin' ye fer days, and it's taken us a long time tae get ye alone like this. I'm nae lettin' ye go after all the trouble we've been tae. Ye're comin' with me. Laird MacDonnell really wants tae see ye, and I cannae wait tae finally deliver ye tae him personally."

Agnes' heart stopped. "MacDonnell! I'm nae goin' anywhere near that monster!" she screamed at him, punching him in the face as hard as she could, feeling her fist connect with his mouth. While he reeled back and in pain and shock, she tore herself away from him and raced towards Roisin. "Roisin, run, run back tae the castle! NOW!" She shouted to the bewildered child.

The words had hardly left her mouth before she was violently tackled from behind and thrown face first to the ground. As she went down, she saw one of the men grab Roisin. "Leave her! Dinnae dare touch her, ye bastard" she screamed, kicking at the man whose body was now pinning hers to the ground. "If ye hurt a hair on her head I'll kill ye!"

"If we dinnae kill her first."

CHAPTER NINETEEN

"When d'ye think I'll see ye again?" Duncan asked Conrad. It was late afternoon and they were in the stables. Duncan was lounging against a post, arms crossed, watching while Conrad saddled up Davey in preparation for leaving Keppoch Castle and returning to his home to his father's lands.

"At yer weddin' tae the buxom Betty maybe?" Conrad replied jokingly, hiding his true preoccupation—Agnes. Ever since their kiss, his emotions had been in turmoil. Even now he was having to force himself to leave.

Duncan burst out laughing and slapped him on the back. "Ach, we'll both be dead if ye wait that long, man. It'll never happen! Well, maybe I'll ride over tae see ye before too long. I'll miss yer company."

"Ach, dinnae be so soft, me friend. Ye'll have me cryin' if ye keep on like that," Conrad told him with a grin. Then, pretending a casualness he did not feel, he asked what he really wanted to know. "D'ye ken when Agnes and the bairn are goin' back tae France?"

Duncan shrugged. "Nay idea. She's said naethin' tae me about it. Why?"

"I just wondered is all. She mentioned tae me in passin' that she'll be goin' back soon. 'Tis a shame she's nae here because I havenae had a chance tae say goodbye tae the wee lassie. I've taken quite a shine tae her."

"Aye, she's a bright spark, that one," Duncan replied with a fond smile. "I'll tell her ye said goodbye if ye like," he offered.

"Thanks," Conrad replied with a nod of gratitude. Now, he understood the odd flashes of pride for Roisin that Duncan had displayed on several occasions—he was her uncle. But it hurt to know his best friend had not trusted him enough to confide that fact in him, though he knew it was to protect Agnes' reputation as well as the family's.

He tightened the girth strap and stepped back to make sure the saddle was secure, and that was when he heard the scream. It was faint, but there was no doubt it was a scream. He tensed immediately and looked at Duncan. "Did ye hear that? Someone screamed."

Duncan shook his head. "Nay, I heard naethin'."

Conrad held up a palm. "Wheesht! Listen." He strained his ears to hear. After a few moments, it came again, a shrill scream of terror. The sound sliced through him like a rapier, putting all his nerve endings on high alert. "There it is again," he told Duncan, swinging himself into the saddle. "Someone's in trouble. I'm goin' tae find out what's goin' on." Without wating for Duncan, he manoeuvred Davey out of the stables and set off apace through the castle gates.

Once outside, he kicked Davey into a fast gallop and raced towards the source of the screams, the castle woods. A few minutes later, he heard Duncan coming up behind him and was glad of it. However, he thought it best not to tell his friend what he suspected—that the screams had come from Agnes.

A minute or two later, they reached the treeline and plunged down the main trail leading to the clearing where they had played as children. They thundered into and came upon a group of men, five he counted, and they had Agnes surrounded! She was fighting as hard as she could to get free, but as he drew closer, Conrad could see her hands were tied behind her back.

"Agnes! I'm comin'!" he shouted, his blade singing as he tore it from its scabbard, fear and fury rushing through him in equal measure as he headed straight for the men holding her. He would save her if it was the last thing he did!

As soon as she saw them both, Agnes screamed and began struggling harder to get free of her captors, but in vain. "Conrad! Duncan! They have Roisin!" she shouted frantically. Conrad glanced across the clearing and was horrified to see Roisin in the grip of one of the men. He had his hand clamped over the child's mouth to stifle her screams, but she was wriggling furiously in an attempt to make him let her go. Another man stood close by, his sword already drawn.

"Dinnae worry, Sister, I'll get her back," Duncan yelled, pulling out his sword and brandishing it aloft as he made a sharp turn towards the man who had hold of Roisin and his comrade. "Get yer filthy hands off her, ye bastard!" Duncan snarled as he bore down on them. The man reached for his sword but could not keep hold of the little girl as well, and she dropped to the ground.

"Hide, Roisin, hide in yer camp!" Agnes screamed at her daughter. Roisin, though clearly terrified, immediately dived in between the tree roots and vanished from sight. Meanwhile, Duncan launched a vicious assault on the two men.

Knowing the pair were as good as dead, Conrad directed all his efforts to saving Agnes.

"Get the woman out of here!" yelled the bearded man who was apparently in charge. He drew his weapon and blocked Conrad's path to the two others behind him, who were now dragging Agnes towards some waiting horses. Conrad slashed with his sword at the man in his way, but the fellow ducked skilfully and dodged out of reach. He snatched a dirk from his belt and chased after Conrad, grabbing at the reins while stabbing at Conrad's arm and shoulder, clearly aiming to unseat him.

Conrad was so pumped up, he hardly felt any pain as the blade entered his flesh, but the attack on Agnes and Rosin had infuriated him. "Ye cowardly cur, I'll teach ye nae tae hurt women and bairns!" he snarled at his assailant. With a powerful downward stabbing motion, he pierced the man's neck just by his shoulder, then immediately retracted his blade. The man fell away, obviously mortally wounded.

Without pausing to inspect the damage, Conrad urged Davey forward with his heels, racing after the two riders who had taken Agnes.

"Conrad! Help me!" Her terrified screams echoed through the woods, each word lancing through him like a knife blade in his guts.

I havetae get tae her, I'll nae let anythin' bad happen tae her!

"I'm comin' Agnes, I'm comin'!" he called to her. Fast thought her abductors were, he had the advantage of knowing the trail well and soon caught up to them. The one in front with Agnes thrown over his saddle raced ahead, while the other lagged slightly behind.

Fuelled by his determination to save the only woman he had ever loved, Conrad accelerated and drew level with the rider. Leaning across, he delivered a mighty downward blow with his sword that sliced straight into the man's shoulder. He shrieked in agony and toppled sideways from his horse. Panicked, neighing wildly, it ran on, dragging its injured rider by his foot, which had caught in the stirrup.

Conrad saw the other rider ahead, frantically kicking at his horse's flanks in an effort to make it go faster, while Agnes bounced violently in the saddle behind him. With no time to waste, Conrad drew his dirk with his free hand, aimed it, and threw. The foot-long blade thudded with deadly accuracy into the kidnapper's back, leaving the handle protruding from it.

To his disappointment, the rider jerked and cried out but still kept going. "Damn ye," Conrad cursed. He urged Davey to go faster, desperate to finish the fellow off and save Agnes.

The riderless horse, now minus its injured rider, raced past him, veering dangerously close. "Conrad, fer God's sake be careful!" Agnes screamed at him as he swerved out of the way to let it pass safely.

He was coming up beside them now, wielding his sword as he prepared to take down Agnes's abductor. But to his surprise, the man suddenly crumpled and fell sideways from the saddle to the ground. Conrad sheathed his sword, realizing the dirk had taken a little time to do its work.

But the danger was far from over. The terrified horse, now also riderless, plunged after its companion, with Agnes bouncing violently on its back. Aware she could be thrown off and severely injured or even killed at any moment, Conrad powered ahead in its wake. It took several heart stopping minutes before he managed to get close enough to lean over, grab the reins, and eventually bring the beast to a halt.

Conrad leapt from his horse and lifted Agnes down from the saddle. She collapsed against him as he hurried to free her hands. "Ye're all right now, Agnes, ye're safe, they're all dead, dinnae worry any more. I've got ye now."

He threw the ropes aside, and they embraced. His heart went out to her, for her whole body was trembling uncontrollably. She clung to him, sobbing against his chest. "Roisin, where's Roisin? Is she all right?" she gasped, looking up at him with tear-filled eyes.

Just then, Conrad heard a shout, and when they looked over, they saw Duncan running from the trees towards them, with Roisin in his arms. "She's safe," Conrad told her, holding her close, sending up a silent prayer of thanks that the child was unharmed.

"Och, thank God, thank God," Agnes murmured, tears of relief streaming down her face.

"She's safe, ye're both safe now," Conrad murmured, wanting desperately to comfort her. "Are ye hurt?" he asked anxiously.

He shook her head. "Nay, just bruises and rope burns on me wrists," she told him, her sobbing starting to subside. "As long as Roisin's all right, I dinnae care about anythin' else."

"Aye, of course," he murmured, reflexively stroking her hair, admiring her fierce maternal instinct for her daughter's safety.

Duncan reached them and placed Roisin straight into her outstretched arms. His comfort no longer needed, Conrad stood up.

Agnes looked up at her brother as she cradled the crying child in her arms, doing her best to comfort her. "Duncan, are ye hurt?"

"Nay, dinnae worry about me, I'm fine," her brother told her, shaking his head dismissively as he went closer and kissed his sister's head.

"Who were they? Is it who we think?" Conrad asked, now starting to feel the painful throb of the wounds to his arm and shoulder. He had sustained far worse before in battle and so had brushed it aside. However, he noticed his blood had stained Agnes' dress.

"I'm nae sure, but I'd take an educated guess that they're MacDonnell's men," Duncan replied, frowning heavily as he pulled the blade from the dead kidnapper's back and wiped the blood on the man's coat before handing it to Conrad.

"Aye, so they said," Agnes replied. She quickly filled them in on what the bearded man had told her about taking her to MacDonnell.

"Jaysus!" Duncan exclaimed, pacing about, running his fingers distractedly through his short hair. "I cannae believe this. The man's mad. He still wants tae marry ye after all this time, Agnes. Even though he must ken ye have a child." Conrad noticed the slip up but said nothing.

He was more concerned to learn who was behind the attempted kidnap. "This was MacDonnell? Ye're sure of it?" he burst out, replacing the dirk in his belt.

"Aye, I told ye what the man said," Agnes replied, still rocking Roisin like a baby.

"I havenae told ye this before, Sister, but I figure it was MacDonnell who was behind the attack on yer carriage," Duncan told her, sounding reluctant.

"Ye mean it wasnae brigands?" she exclaimed, staring up at him, her eyes wide with shock.

"I've nay proof, but I reckon so," her brother explained, telling her his theory. "But this is a new low even for him. Tae come onto our lands and try tae snatch ye like this, 'tis brazen."

"Aye, and there could be more of them nearby. I think we'd best get Agnes and Roisin back tae the castle and report tae yer faither at once," Conrad suggested. "I'll postpone me departure until he decides what action he wants tae take against MacDonnell. He needs tae put an end tae this business."

"Aye, I agree," Duncan replied with a nod. He looked down at Agnes. "Sister, can ye ride?"

"Aye, of course. Help me up, will ye?" She reached up to Conrad, who took her hand and helped her to her feet. She stood with Roisin balanced on her hip, with the little girl clinging to her neck, still crying softly. Agnes thanked him, then added, "Roisin will ride with me."

"Aye, ye can take me horse. Conrad and I will bring these two," Duncan said, gesturing at the horses the MacDonnells had left behind. "There were five of those men, so there's likely three more horses tethered in the woods somewhere as well. I'll send some of our men back tae find them." He shot a glowering glance at the slumped body of the slain MacDonnell soldier who had taken Agnes before adding, "And clear up the mess."

Within the hour, a worried Laird MacDonald had called an emergency council meeting, with both Duncan and Conrad present to explain what had happened and how close Agnes had come to being abducted.

"I'd already told ye that I reckon MacDonnell was behind the attack on Agnes's carriage. In me opinion, that was his first attempt tae abduct her disguised as a robbery by brigands. But there can be nae mistakin' what happened this afternoon fer anythin' but a blatant attempt at kidnappin'."

"Aye, they had her on a horse and were already makin' off with her by the time we got there tae stop them. Plus, they scared the little one half tae death. If we'd been five minutes later, they would have taken Agnes and been gone," Conrad put in, his fists flexing as he tried to control the rage he felt for MacDonnell. He was secretly praying that Duncan's father would give the order to attack MacDonnell immediately.

"Aye, it was that close," Duncan agreed angrily. "We cannae let this outrage go unpunished, Faither. We must take measures against MacDonnell at once and put a stop tae this."

"Hold yer horses there, lad. First, I wantae thank Conrad fer savin' me daughter and the little one, once again. Me heartfelt thanks tae ye, Conrad. I'll nae forget what ye did."

Conrad nodded in acknowledgement of the laird's thanks, but he wanted far more than that. He wanted revenge on

MacDonnell, just as he knew Duncan did, and he was itching for the laird to say the word.

"I wantae tae put a stop tae this as well, we all dae. But ye must see that we cannae just march intae MacDonnell's lands and attack him without so much as shred of proof."

"But Agnes has already said that one of the men told her outright that MacDonnell wanted tae see her and that he was gonnae deliver her tae him personally," Duncan argued.

"That's nae proof. This man she spoke of could have been workin' for himself, a bounty hunter. I need proper proof before I can sanction retaliation against MacDonnell," his father insisted, much to Conrad's frustration.

"So, what d'ye think we should dae, me laird?" he asked. "Because it seems tae me that MacDonnell's nae gonnae give up until he gets what he wants. He thinks he's been cheated out of a bride. Tae dae naethin' will likely result in another attempt tae kidnap Agnes. She's nae safe at all."

"Aye, I realize that, Conrad. Even so, I'm nae prepared tae accuse MacDonnell without proof unless I give him the chance tae defend himself. If the council agrees, I suggest I write tae MacDonnell askin' him tae justify his actions," the laird said with an air of finality. There was a brief discussion among the council members. Ultimately, they all backed the laird's suggestion.

Conrad exchanged frustrated glances with Duncan, but he knew the laird had the final say, so that was that.

When the meeting broke up, he and Duncan strode down the hallway side by side. "I'm very disappointed tae say the least," Duncan admitted, clearly annoyed with his father and as worried for Agnes as Conrad was.

"Aye, the thing is, until MacDonnell is stopped, Agnes will be in constant danger of being abducted. Ye should maybe consider puttin' a guard on her and the lassie," Conrad suggested.

"I'll talk tae Faither about it directly," Duncan replied. "As it is, she'll nae be able tae leave the castle at all until we ken what MacDonnell intends. He's as sly as he is rotten. Most likely, he'll deny havin' anythin' tae dae with what's happened."

"And we'll be right back tae square one," Conrad agreed, thinking he would postpone his departure indefinitely so he could keep an eye on Agnes and Roisin and protect them if needed.

The pair went their separate ways, Duncan to see his father in his study, Conrad heading for the kitchens to order bathwater to be sent up to his chamber. Next, he called in at the infirmary, where he asked Una for some supplies to see to his own wounds. After that, he went to his chambers and had a couple of strong drams as he waited for the water to arrive, longing for a good, hot soak to wash of the attackers' blood as well as his own. But all his thoughts were with Agnes.

A while later, just before bathing and seeing to his wounds, he was surprised by a knock at the door. Thinking it was the maids come back to empty the tub, he called out, "I'm nae done yet. Can ye come back a wee bit later?" Instead of the reply he was expecting, the door opened a crack, and a familiar face appeared around the edge.

Startled, he burst out, "Agnes? What are ye daein' here?"

CHAPTER TWENTY

"Can I speak tae ye for a minute? 'Tis important," Agnes asked, a hot flush racing over her skin when her eyes alighted on Conrad's exposed torso.

Ach, he's bloody half-naked again!

She averted her eyes from the compelling sight and tried to ignore the fluttering of excitement in her belly. She tarried by the door instead.

Conrad waved her in, clearly surprised to see her there. "Aye, if ye must, but come in before someone sees ye. Ye shouldnae be in here at all. Besides, as ye can see, I'm about tae take a bath'," he replied.

Ignoring the voice in her head that was yelling at her to leave, she slipped inside his chamber and shut the door behind her. "Aye, sorry. 'Tis just that I wanted tae thank ye properly fer savin' me this afternoon," she said, trying and failing to stop herself from peeking at the enticing view. "That's twice now that ye've saved me and thrice Roisin. We owe ye our lives, and I'm very grateful tae ye."

"I dinnae need yer gratitude. Ye ken I'd never allow anythin' bad tae happen tae ye. Nor the wee lass, obviously."

Agnes nodded, secretly admiring his muscular arms and only then noticing with a jolt the bloody cuts on his upper arm. "Conrad, ye've been hurt!" she cried, concern for him eclipsing all else as she rushed over to him to take a closer look.

"Ach, 'tis naethin'. Just a couple of scratches," he said dismissively, about to move away.

"Stay still and let me see," she told him, laying her hands on his arm to keep him still while she inspected the wounds, angry with herself for not realizing before that he was injured. "They are nae just scratches. They're very deep cuts, and there's a lot of blood. They need tae be cleaned up right away before they get infected," she declared.

"Aye, I ken that. That's why I have all the stuff Una gave me over there on the table," he told her, jerking his chin in that direction.

Agnes went over to the table, seeing cloths, a pot of salve, and clean dressings already set out there. She made up her mind in an instant and began rolling back her sleeves as she looked back at him. "It'll be better if ye let me dae it for ye. After all, 'tis the least I can dae, considerin' what ye've done fer us."

There was a moment of silence as they held each other's gazes, during which Agnes became very aware of the tension in the room ramping up, along with her temperature. Conrad shrugged in a non-committal way and said, "All right. If ye like."

"Come and sit here," she instructed, patting one of the straight-backed chairs by the table. Conrad obeyed, while Agnes went and wetted a clean cloth in the steaming bathwater. She returned to him and began carefully cleaning the blood away from the many wounds with it, doing her best not to actually touch his skin with her hands. She feared what might happen if she did.

However, though she tried hard to keep her focus on the task in hand, having his semi-naked body only inches away was deeply distracting. Her eyes kept wandering from his chest to the fine line of dark golden hair that led from his navel, down his flat, muscle-ridged belly, to disappear enticingly beneath the waistband of his trews.

To her embarrassment, she felt her nipples hardening against the fabric of her gown.

Stop this! Ye have a job tae dae, so get on and dae it, and then leave!

She prayed Conrad would not notice how he was affecting her. That illusion was dispelled when he suddenly smirked at her and said teasingly, "Go on, ye can look as much as ye want. Or ye can even touch if ye dare."

Agnes melted into him as he seized her waist, pulled her onto his lap, tangled his hands in her hair, his kiss filling with the hungry intensity of a pent-up desire that matched her own.

She met his ardour with heat, tangling her tongue with his in a frantic dance of exploration, her body alight with desire. As if making up for lost time, their hands roved over each other's bodies. Craving the feel of his skin, Agnes ran her palms all over every bit of his flesh she could touch, excited beyond reason by the feel of his muscles flexing beneath her hands. The chair creaked complainingly as she moved to straddle his lap, entwining her arms around his neck, pulling him closer still as their kisses grew fiercer and more demanding.

Conrad eased down the neckline of her dress, groaning appreciatively deep in his throat as her breasts tumbled out. Agnes gasped, spears of pleasure lancing through her as he filled his hands with them, squeezing and hefting their soft weight in his palms. His lips broke from hers, to trail small, hot kisses down her throat and neck until he took her already hardened nipples into his mouth and sucked and nuzzled at them. Agnes threw back her head and moaned, trembling with anticipation for what was to come.

Conrad's lips and mouth continued to tantalize her breasts while he slid his hands beneath her skirts and all the way up her legs, cupping her behind in both hands, his fingers provocatively skimming her sex.

Carried on a wave of sheer wantonness, she opened her thighs, inviting him in, moaning when she felt his fingers parting the soft, curling nest between her thighs that was already wet and burning with wanting. A small moan left her lips as two of his fingers slid inside her, thrusting deep, while another found her rosebud and teased it until the only way she could stifle her moans was to kiss him with all the passion he was stoking inside her.

Before long, she knew she was close to the edge, so it was a surprise when Conrad suddenly stood up, holding her in place with one hand under her behind while he swept everything off the table and laid her down there on her back. He pushed up her skirts, baring her completely, and then his hot, questing mouth descended between her legs, greedily plundering her sex, his fingers holding her open while his tongue flickered like lightening over the hot flesh and in and out of her.

Now hot enough to melt, Agnes opened herself farther, her calves resting on his shoulders, her hands reflexively clutching his hair, her hips bucking beneath the onslaught of pleasure he was giving her with his mouth and tongue and hands. Powerful waves of ecstasy began rising from her core and sweeping up over her body.

"Och, Conard, it's so good, dinnae stop, please, dinnae stop," she murmured, writhing in ecstasy as he took her by slow, deliberate degrees to the ultimate peak. She finally came in sudden, blissful rush that shook her entire being.

"Omigod," she whispered breathlessly, unwinding her fingers from Conrad's hair as he rose up from between her legs and their eyes met. Still caught up in the moment, she smiled at him and murmured, "Bein' with ye is just as sweet as I remember."

"Aye, ye still taste as sweet," he mumbled, busy kissing and nibbling at the insides of her thighs.

She chuckled, finding her appetite for him only whetted. "I'm glad if ye find me so, but I think 'tis yer turn now," she said, determined to give him the same pleasure as she had given her. She sat up on the edge of the table and wrapped her legs around his waist, then boldly put her hand on the erection she knew she would find bulging at the front of his trews.

"Och, Agnes, what are ye up tae?" he murmured almost nervously, trying to pull back. But her desire had been unleashed now, and she tightened her legs around him, refusing to let him go. Their mouths clashed fiercely as she undid his trews and snaked her hand inside, taking his length in her fist. The low groan he gave out as she stroked him only fanned the flames still burning hot inside her.

Sliding to the floor, she knelt before him and peeled his trews down over his hips, daringly kissing the tip of his erection as it was revealed to her, dazzled by its size and the level of excitement she could bring him to.

'Tis just as it was before… incredible.

She caressed him once more as she had dreamed of doing for five long years.

"Jaysus, Agnes, och, Christ Almighty," he mumbled, burying his hands in her hair as she sowed tiny kisses up and down his length. She slipped the head of his erection into her mouth, caressing it with her lips and tongue, revelling in the groans falling from Conrad's lips and the dazed look in his darkened eyes as he gazed down at her teasing him. Sensing his approaching climax, she increased the speed of her mouth and hands, as he had shown her the first time they had lain together.

She sensed his climax was near when his body stiffened and he clutched at her hair more tightly. "Ach, Agnes," he groaned at last, and a few moments later, he came across her naked chest, then pulled her up, holding her against him as he panted to catch his breath.

Then, he picked her up and carried her over to the bed. There, he laid her down and then lay next to her, drawing her to his side and tucking her under his arm. She snuggled against him, one leg thrown over his, her fingers stroking his chest, trying to preserve the moment and not think about what would come next.

Even as Conrad held Agnes and looked on her beautiful, flushed face as she laid her head against his chest, the words she had uttered in the throes of passion were going around and around in his head.

Bein' with ye is just as sweet as I remember, she said. But there was somethin' about the way she said it that made it sound like she'd never been with anyone else. But if that were so, then how would that explain Roisin?

It was at that moment that he had an epiphany of sorts, and all the moments of formless suspicion that had gone before suddenly coalesced into an astounding possibility.

"Agnes?"

"Mmm?" She looked up at him, smiling, her fingers wandering idly through his chest hairs.

"What ye said, about how bein' with me is just as sweet as ye remember. Did ye mean tae say that ye've nae been with anyone else since ye went away?" He felt her body stiffen, and she looked away, as though to hide her face. But she was not quite fast enough for him to miss the flash of guilt in her eyes. He held his breath as he waited for her to answer, knowing that, despite what had just happened between them, she was about to lie to him.

"Nay. How can ye even ask me that?" she said.

Conrad took hold of her chin and tilted her head up, forcing her to look him in the eyes. In hers, yes, there was guilt. But there was fear too.

Fear?

"I dinnae believe ye, Agnes. I ken ye're lyin' tae me now, and I think ye've been lyin' tae me all along," he told her.

"I dinnae ken what ye mean. Lyin' tae ye about what?" she protested, squirming to get away from him. But he clamped her to his side and held her chin firmly in place.

"Tell me the truth now, Agnes." He finally asked the question that was burning inside him, which he had to have the answer to at once. "Is Roisin me daughter?"

CHAPTER TWENTY-ONE

Agnes' eyes filled with tears. They fell in fat drops and rolled down her cheeks. Moved by an irresistible force that suddenly gripped him, Conrad let her go and got off the bed. He grabbed his trews from the floor and pulled them on. Then, he turned to face her. She was looking up at him, her face wet with tears.

He braced his arms on the bed and leaned closer to her. "Is she? Say it!" he demanded, needing her to voice the words even though he knew it must be true.

She nodded. "Aye. Roisin is yers." It came out in a sob, followed by more tears.

His mind reeling from shock, Conrad began pacing the floor, running his hands over his face and through his hair. Beset by an anguish he had never felt since she had left him, he wheeled around and confronted her again. "Why did ye lie tae me? Why did ye nae just tell me the truth in the first place?" he asked, his anger rising.

"I was-I was scared, Conrad. Scared of what would happen if everyone found out ye were the faither," she admitted, her face a picture of guilt.

"Ye were scared, so ye decided all by yersel' nae tae tell me I have a daughter! In five years!" He advanced on her again, pinning her gaze with his. "When were ye gonnae tell me, Agnes?" he shouted, barely keeping his temper as he read the truth in her eyes. "Ach, dinnae bother answerin'. I can see it written all over yer face. In fact, it explains the way ye've tried tae keep me at arm's length the whole time ye've been here. Never! Ye were never gonnae tell me I have a daughter, were ye? Ye'd rather let the lass go about a bastard than tell me she's mine." He started pacing again distractedly. "Jaysus! This is unbelievable. Five years, and all that time, ye've kept her from me."

"I'm sorry, Conrad, I didnae want things tae be like this. I was only tryin' tae dae what I thought was best," Agnes replied through her sobs, but he felt no sympathy for her at all, only anger.

"Best? Best fer who? Because 'tis certainly nae best fer the child nae tae even ken she has a faither and grow up a bastard!"

"Dinnae keep usin' that word!" she exclaimed with a flash of defiance.

He rounded on her again. "Why should I nae use it? 'Tis what she is. 'Tis what everyone else will call her. God Almighty, Agnes. What did ye think ye were daein'? I never though ye could be so selfish as tae dae somethin' like this."

"I didnae dae it fer selfish reasons. If ye'll just calm down a bit and let me explain," she cried beseechingly.

"Calm down? Ye're jokin', eh?" he shot back furiously.

"Please, Conrad, I ken I deserve yer hatred, but ye dinnae ken what happened. Please, just hear me out," she begged.

Breathing heavily as fury coursed through his veins, he continued pacing, clenching and unclenching his fists, trying to reason with himself and keep a hold on his temper.

I shouldnae have lain with her before we were wed. 'Tis me fault as well as hers. But this, nay, I can never forgive her fer this.

When he had outwardly composed himself enough, he went over and stood by the bed. "Go ahead then, explain it tae me. Ye can start with what happened after we spent the night together, when I was called away," he told her, folding his arms.

Agnes nodded, making a visible effort to rein in her emotions as well and stop crying. She dashed the tears from her face with the back of her hand and hugged her knees. "All right. I'll tell ye everythin'."

During the next few minutes, Conrad listened with a growing sense of incredulity and anger. But he had calmed down enough to move from standing over the bed to sitting on the edge, his head in his hands.

"So, ye see, Conrad, the same night I found out I was with child, I was banished tae France. I left that next morning."

"So, wait, when did ye find out about the marriage alliance with Laird MacDonnell?" he asked, taking his head from his hands to look at her.

"I kent naethin' about it until Duncan told me just as I was leavin'. Faither had arranged it all behind me back, probably because he kent I'd refuse tae go through with the marriage."

"Duncan said yer faither had tae tell MacDonnell ye were at death's door tae avoid him takin' offence and startin' a war yer clan had nay chance of winnin'."

"Aye. Faither still blames me fer ruinin' his plans and puttin' the clan in danger, as well as the disgrace I've brought on the family by havin' a child out of wedlock."

"But that still daesnae explain why ye simply didnae tell them I was the faither. We could have got married right away!"

"Nay! Ye make it sound simple but think about it. Ye would have been forced tae marry me then, and I didnae wantae ruin yer life."

"But—" Conrad began, about to say he had already intended to ask for her hand back then anyway. But he stopped himself, pausing to consider her words. "Aye, I suppose Duncan would have seen his best friend gettin' his sister with child out of wedlock as the worst sort of betrayal," he admitted. "It would have destroyed our friendship."

"Aye, nae tae mention how angry and disappointed our parents would have been as well," Agnes replied. "And that's why I'm beggin' ye tae keep me secret, Conrad. Please, dinnae tell me family ye're Roisin's faither. It'd cause ructions," she added more urgently.

Conrad, furious and sick at heart, knew she was right. But in the end, it made no difference to him. "I dinnae care about all that. I refuse tae let me daughter grow up a bastard when I'm right here, ready and willin' tae be a faither tae her," he said. "There's only one way tae resolve the situation. We need tae get married as soon as possible."

Agnes' eyes flew wide with fear. "But-but if we marry now, everyone will suspect the truth. What will Duncan say? And our families too? The scandal would kill them!"

"There must be a way of gettin' around it," Conrad replied, thinking fast. Then, the answer came to him. "We can tell them ye're afraid of MacDonnell and that ye believe the only way tae stop him is fer ye tae marry someone else. And as we've always liked each other, it makes sense fer it tae be me."

She looked dubious. "D'ye think that would work?"

"Why would it nae? MacDonnell is such a threat tae ye and the whole clan, yer family will likely be relieved tae see ye safely wed tae me, someone they trust tae protect ye. It'll work all right."

She opened her mouth to speak, but he held up a hand to stop her. "Nay, dinnae bother arguin' with me. That's what's gonnae happen, so ye'd best get used tae it." He turned a dark look on her as he added, "But ye'd best be aware, Agnes, that even though we're gettin' married, I'll never forgive ye fer keepin' me from me daughter fer five years and lettin' the world think her a bastard. Never."

The look of sorrow that appeared on her face then almost made him regret his words. But he meant every one of them, and whatever happened between them after they were wed, he decided he would not take them back.

So, me worst fear is comin' true after all, Agnes was thinking, her heart weighed down with sorrow after hearing Conrad's angry declaration.

We're gonnae be married, but nae fer love. He's made it very clear he's only daein' it because he feels obligated fer Roisin's sake. He daesnae even like me, let alone love me. Look at his face! 'Tis obvious he nay longer wants anythin' tae dae with me, and he's never gonnae forgive me fer what I've done. Even though we'll be wed in the eyes of the world, and I love him still, we'll both be livin' a miserable sham fer the rest of our lives.

With the passionate intimacy shattered, the air now full of acrimony, and her heart aching with sadness, Agnes watched Conrad moving around the room, his manner business-like as he got dressed and outlined his plans for their marriage.

"If we keep it small, it'll be easy tae organize quickly. This will also keep ye both safe from MacDonnell. Once yer faither agrees, we should be able tae have the ceremony in the next few days. Nay point delayin' it, is there?" he said as he pulled his padded leather vest over his shirt and fastened it.

"Nay, nay point at all," Ages replied dully, getting off the bed and attempting to repair the ravages their earlier passionate encounter had wrought on her appearance. She wanted to leave as soon as possible.

"We only need a couple of witnesses tae make it legal. There's nay need tae bother much with guests apart from family."

"All right." Though she felt she had no choice but to go along with it, to Agnes, the ceremony he was planning sounded like a rushed, hole-in-the-wall kind of affair, almost as if she were with child and had to get married fast to cover her shame. What he was planning was a soulless business transaction, devoid of love, affection, or romance.

But dae I deserve any of those things after what I've done?

"It'll be in the chapel here at the castle," Conrad was saying as he put on his coat. "Once the date's been set, I'll go and see the minister and arrange fer him tae conduct the ceremony."

"Aye, grand." Agnes went to the washstand and splashed cold water from the jug on her face in a vain attempt to wash the redness of crying from her face.

"Of course, I'll havetae speak tae Duncan about it first. Even though I'll be lyin' tae him, I'd like tae get his blessin'."

"Of course," Ages responded, putting down the comb and turning to watch him as he pulled on his boots—her gorgeous husband-to-be who despised her. "And I'll speak tae Roisin," she managed to get out, fighting down the urge to weep again.

How will she take it? Will she be happy or sad?

"Grand. How d'ye think she'll take the news she's gonnae have a faither?" he asked, his face unreadable.

"Well, she's nae used tae havin' a faither in her life, but she already likes ye. Mayhap she'll be happy about it," Agnes told him, searching for the silver lining in the cloud of misery hanging over her. "And she'll enjoy wearin' one of her pretty dresses fer the ceremony. But Conrad, ye must promise me one thing."

"Oh?"

"Aye, ye must promise me that even if ye're daein' this out of obligation, Roisin will never ken a moment's unhappiness because of it."

"What d'ye take me fer, Agnes?" he asked, frowning at her. "I'll be a good faither tae her, dinnae ever worry about that. I'll never give her cause tae be unhappy about anythin' if I can help it, and ye should ken that without even askin' me tae promise."

"I'm sorry if I upset ye, but I havetae be sure," Agnes told him, not apologetic at all. "She's me world. Her happiness matters more than anythin' else tae me. But I believe ye."

"And so ye should," he replied brusquely. "Now, I have things tae arrange fer the weddin'. Ye'd best leave first in case anyone sees ye. I'll wait a few minutes and then go. I'll let ye ken when I've spoken tae yer faither and Duncan, all right?" He opened the door a crack and checked the hallway. "Go on then, 'tis safe." He waved her out and immediately shut the door.

Relieved to be alone with the maelstrom of emotions she was barely managing to control, Agnes picked up her skirts and hurried back to the nursery, wondering what Saoirse would make of this momentous development.

CHAPTER TWENTY-TWO

The next morning, Agnes was rudely awoken from sleep by Conrad barging into her room. It took her a few moments to realize what had startled her awake, and when she saw Conrad approaching the bed, she gave a little squeal of alarm at her state of undress.

"What are ye daein', bargin' in on me like that without so much as a knock?" she protested, sitting up and clutching the covers to her chest indignantly. "Where are yer manners? What if I'd been in the middle of gettin' dressed?"

"Haud yer wheesht, woman," he said, coming to lean against the bedpost, his eyes raking over her. "What's with the false modesty? 'Tis naethin' I've nae seen before."

"That's nae the point," she protested, blushing furiously because she knew he was right. There was not an inch of her he had not seen—or had his hands all over—before.

So, why am I so embarrassed? Because he despises me, that's why!

"The point is, we'll be man and wife soon. Ye must get used tae sleepin' in the same room as me," he went on. "By the way, I had a drink with Duncan last night. I told him about the weddin', and he's given us his blessin'."

"Oh?" She was glad to have Duncan's approval but felt bad for keeping the real reason from him. She hated that her marriage to Conrad, the only man she had ever loved, was based on his feelings of obligation as well as more secrets and lies. "So, he believed what ye told him then, that we're doin' it tae stop MacDonnell?" she asked.

"Of course. He thinks 'tis a good idea."

"I hope Faither sees it that way too. Is that what ye woke me up tae tell me?" She wished he would go away so she could have some time to order her confused emotions.

"Nay. I said I'd come and let ye ken when I'd arranged fer us tae speak tae yer family, so I can officially ask yer faither fer yer hand."

"Offer tae wed me, ye mean," Agnes murmured cynically.

"If ye want tae put it that way, aye. At any rate, ye must get up and get dressed, because that's exactly where were goin' now."

"What? Right now?" she asked, taken aback, once again feeling swept along by events she had no control over.

"Aye, right now," he told her. "We've already waited five years. There's nae time tae waste."

"Well, I wasnae expectin' anything like this," James MacDonald said from his seat behind his desk. "So, let me get this straight, Conrad, ye're prepared tae wed our Agnes because ye think that once MacDonnell learns she has a husband he'll stop all his shenanigans against us?"

"That's exactly right, me laird," Conrad confirmed with a nod.

"But we still dinnae have any definite proof pointing tae MacDonnell's guilt," the laird replied doubtfully. "What if it turns out he's innocent of any involvement in the attack on Agnes' carriage and the abduction attempt? Ye'll have married her fer nay reason, lad."

"I'm sorry tae doubt ye, me laird, but I cannae believe he's innocent," Conrad replied. "I believe that as long as Agnes remains unwed, he poses a great threat tae her safety, and 'tis only a matter of time before he tries something even bolder tae get his hands on her. I care about her and I couldnae live with mesel' if that happened. The only way I can be sure of her safety is as her husband."

"Well, all right, but what does Agnes think about it?" The laird fixed his steely eyes on Agnes.

"I agree with Conrad, Faither. The leader of the men who tried tae abduct me told me he was gonnae deliver me tae MacDonnell. I dinnae think he's gonnae give up unless he finds out I'm already married. It'll be safer for all of us once Conrad and I are wed. And as me husband, I ken I can trust Conrad tae protect me whatever happens. We've been fond of each other fer years, I am sure he will take good care of me."

"I think 'tis a good idea, as long as the both of ye are willin' tae go along with it," Duncan interjected.

"Aye, we are," Conrad replied firmly. Agnes nodded obediently in confirmation.

"What's yer opinion, Fiona?" the laird asked his wife.

"Well, even if MacDonnell wasnae in the picture, I'd be glad tae see Agnes respectably settled. And, of course, I'd be proud tae have Conrad as part of our family officially." She paused to beam at Conrad, who acknowledged the compliment with a nod and a smile. "And besides that," she went on, "the union would cement the long-standin' ties of amity between the Mackintoshes and the MacDonalds, which would be a very good thing if MacDonnell daes decide tae cause trouble. Conrad's parents will likely be pleased by the news as well. So, if Conrad and Agnes are prepared tae go through with it and think they can be happy together, then I think they deserve our blessin'," Lady Fiona replied.

"Very well put, Wife, thank ye. All right, Conrad, Agnes, ye have our blessin'," the laird declared.

"Thank ye, me laird. I'll dae me very best tae make her happy and protect her," Conrad promised.

"Aye, thank ye, Faither, I'm very grateful," Agnes said, inwardly sagging with relief at having gotten thought the worst part of the lying ordeal successfully.

"But all that aside, Conrad, there's somethin' we havetae tell ye that might affect yer decision tae wed our Agnes," her father said with some reluctance, casting Agnes a sidelong glance. "As ye ken, ye're very dear tae our family, and we wouldnae want ye tae feel like we've hidden somethin' important from ye."

"Aye, that's right, Husband, Conrad must ken the truth before he decides," Lady Fiona agreed, her smile marred by the small, worried frown between her brows.

"Oh? I appreciate yer concern, but what is it ye think I should ken?" Conrad inquired, playing his part perfectly.

"That Agnes has a child," her father said baldly, with the air of a man who had just lit a fuse and now nervously awaited the forthcoming explosion.

"Oh! Aye, I ken all about Roisin," Conrad replied blithely. "It makes nae difference tae me at all. Agnes loves the wee lass, and that's good enough fer me."

His words warmed Agnes heart.

I wish he did love me. But a least I ken he means what he says, and he'll always be a good faither tae Roisin. That's all that really matters.

The next moment, she had to fight down the urge to laugh hysterically at the amazement and relief that appeared on her father's face, and on her mother's too.

Aye, they cannae believe their luck. The family disgrace is gonnae be a respectable married lady at last, and yer grand-daughter willnae be a bastard any longer.

Her father was staring at Conrad wonderingly. "Ye mean ye dinnae mind that the lassie's another man's child, born out of wedlock?" he asked.

Conrad shook his head. "Nay," he said reassuringly, casting Agnes an affectionate smile that she wished with all her heart was genuine.

"But, Conrad, I havetae tell ye, we have nae idea who the lassie's faither is." Her father's annoyed glance flicked over Agnes before returning to Conrad. "Agnes has always refused tae tell us his name. Has she told ye who it is?"

Agnes held her breath, fearing Conrad was about to tell them the truth. She only breathed out when he shook his head and replied, "Nay, but I respect her decision tae keep it a secret.

'Tis all in the past now anyway." Agnes was so grateful for the lie, she almost kissed him again.

"Ye're a good man, Conrad, a very good man," her father said, finally cracking a smile.

"In the circumstances, Agnes and I think it would be best tae have the weddin' as soon as possible," Conrad informed them. "Tomorrow if ye have nae objection. I've already spoken tae the minister, and he's agreed tae officiate at the ceremony. Obviously, it'll just be a small affair. Then, after a week or so, me and Agnes and Roisin will leave fer Moy Hall fer good. Hopefully, MacDonnell will cease troublin' any of us after that."

"Tomorrow? That's a bit sudden. But all right, I agree. I suppose the quicker ye're man and wife the better," her father said. He looked at his wife inquiringly. "Is tomorrow enough time fer ye tae make ready, Fiona?"

"Well, 'tis a bit short notice, but with a bit of help, I think we can dae it, aye," Lady Fiona replied, smiling at Agnes, her former disappointment replaced by the kind of pure, maternal affection Agnes had so sorely missed. "We must find ye somethin' nice tae wear, Daughter, so ye look yer best goin' up the aisle. And Roisin as well. And I'll arrange fer us all tae have a wee feast after the ceremony tae celebrate."

"Thank ye, Maither, I'm sure that will be lovely. Naturally, I'd appreciate yer help," Agnes told her, rather touched by her mother's words.

"Tomorrow it is then. Well, if 'tis all settled, I'll write tae Conrad's family right away tae inform them," her father said with an air of finality.

"Aye, thank ye, me laird," Conrad replied. "I'll write tae them as well, tae tell them when me and me new family will be arrivin'."

Her father insisted on them all toasting to the happy couple's happiness with a dram each, and then there was a brief flurry of congratulations before Agnes and Conrad finally managed to leave the study.

Once out in the hall, arm in arm, like the happiest of betrothed couples, they made their way upstairs to their respective chambers.

"I'll go and tell Roisin what's happenin' now. And Saoirse too. Can she come with us tae Moy Hall?" Agnes asked anxiously, worried for her loyal friend's future.

"If ye wish it and she's willin', of course," Conrad replied.

"Thank ye," she replied, relieved. "Me and Roisin would miss her too much tae leave her behind."

"Aye, after all, she's like a second maither tae the lass, eh?" Conrad shot back as they paused outside his door.

"Very amusin', I'm sure," Agnes replied, feeling sure she could look forward to a lifetime of such jibes. "I'll tell Saoirse first, and then I'll take Roisin out to the gardens and explain tae her about us gettin' married. If ye wantae spend some time with her, ye could meet us where ye saw us before, by the myrtle bushes, in about an hour's time," she suggested.

"Aye, all right. I'll be there," he agreed with a nod, going into his chamber. "After I've written tae me family about the news."

Agnes hurried to the nursery, rehearsing in her head the best way to explain to her little daughter that her mother was going to be married the following day... and that she was about to gain a father.

"Conrad! Mama says ye're marryin' and that ye're gonnae be me faither. Is it really true?" Roisin ran to him across the lawn, her doll dangling from her hand, stretching up her arms to be picked up.

Unable to help smiling, he swept her up easily and lifted her up, holding her in the crook of his arm where they could see eye to eye. "Aye, Little Flower. Is that all right with ye?" he asked, no longer wondering why her hair and eyes were exactly the same colour as his. *She's me daughter. Of course, she looks like me,* he thought with a flash of what he supposed must be fatherly pride.

"Och, I'm very happy. And so is, Peggy," she assured him, giving one of her captivating, gap-toothed grins as she brandished her dolly at him.

"Well, that's grand news," he told her, glancing at Agnes, who was smiling at them both. Conrad fancied she seemed a little misty eyed but quickly dismissed the idea, thinking it more likely that she had something in her eye than being moved to see him with his daughter. "I'm very glad ye and Peggy are happy," he told Roisin, basking in her smile.

"Aye, and Mama says me and Peggy can both wear our prettiest dresses at the weddin', and Saoirse is gonnae dae our hair in ringlets 'specially," she informed him, adding, "and if I'm good, I'm allowed tae stay up late fer the party as well." She finished by hugging his neck and rubbing her soft cheek against his stubbly one.

A huge lump rose in his throat, and for a few moments, he was overwhelmed and could not speak. All he could do was cuddle her fragile form against him, his heart aching to think he could not yet tell her he really was her father. *But the day will come when ye'll ken it,* he silently vowed as he cuddled her closely.

"We brought some games tae play," Agnes put in, gesturing to the small pile of playthings lying on the grass.

"Aye, let's play battledore and shuttle cock!" Roisin declared, wriggling to get down from Conrad's arms. He placed her on the floor, and she immediately abandoned poor Peggy, grabbed a ball and three wooden bats from the pile. She handed one each to him and Agnes and kept one for herself. "I'll start," she cried excitedly, snatching up the shuttlecock. "One, two, three!" she cried, tossing it into the air.

And so, the game of pretending to be a happy family began.

CHAPTER TWENTY-THREE

"Have ye finished crushing those almonds, Agnes?" Lady Fiona asked, peering across the table from her mixing bowl to look into the large mortar where Agnes was patiently crushing the peeled white nuts to a powdery consistency. It was now early evening, and she and her mother were closeted in the still room, where the air was deliciously scented with the precious sugar and spices stored there for making exotic desserts.

"They need just a wee bit longer, Maither," Agnes replied, brushing the slight sheen of perspiration from her forehead with her sleeve, continuing to laboriously grind the almonds. "'Tis surprisingly hard work."

"I'll fetch the raspberry jam," Fiona said, wiping her hands on her apron as she went to the dresser and lifted down the jar of rich, red preserve. Returning to the table, she began spooning a thick layer of it on the bottom of the pastry case they had already prepared. Agnes looked over at her mother, pleased to see her smiling as she worked.

"'Tis nice tae see ye so happy, Maither," Agnes remarked.

"Aye, well, I am happy. Ye're tae be wed on the morrow tae one of the best men I ken. Ye and Roisin will be settled at last, and the past will be the past. Why should I nae be happy?" her mother asked.

"I'm glad. 'Tis such a long time since I've done somethin' tae make ye smile," Agnes could not resist saying, grabbing the spoon from her mother and childishly licking the jam off it before laying it aside.

Lady Fiona sighed. "It may seem that way tae ye, Daughter, but it broke me heart when we had tae send ye away like that. It was hard fer all of us. Honestly, I never thought ye'd find a husband at all. That ye're marryin' an honourable man like Conrad is everythin' I could have hoped fer. Besides," she added, flashing Agnes a smile, "I'll be able tae visit ye and Roisin whenever I please now instead of havin' tae go all the way tae France. Aye, I'm content fer the first time in years." She finished her mixing and began piling the filling on top of the jam in the pastry case, spreading it out evenly.

Agnes understood perfectly why her mother was pleased with the way things had turned out. Conrad was a catch by anyone's standards, a son-in-law to be proud of.

I suppose that even though he despises me, I'm lucky he's prepared tae marry me, even if 'tis only out of obligation fer Roisin's sake. I shouldnae feel sorry fer mesel' but try tae make the best of things.

"At any rate, Agnes, this weddin' couldnae have come at a better time," her mother went on, artfully arranging almonds in a pattern atop the tart.

"Oh? D'ye mean because of MacDonnell?" Agnes asked, starting to tidy up.

"Aye. Yer faither didnae wantae say anythin' fer fear of scarin' ye, but the scouts have reported seein' more soldiers on our southern borders, in numbers too. Tavish MacDonnell's soldiers."

Agnes heart filled with cold dread. "Now, I'm scared," she admitted, suddenly wishing she could marry Conrad right then.

"Aye, we're all scared, lass. We must pray that, once the weddin's made public, MacDonnell will have nay use fer ye and give up. Yer faither and Duncan think it unlikely he'll try anythin' once ye and Conrad are wed. He'd havetae take on the MacDonalds and the Mackintoshes combined, and he hasnae got the strength tae win, they say."

"I hope tae high heaven they're right about that," Agnes said, suddenly struck by shocking thought. MacDonnell was more than capable of making her a widow by killing Conrad, then forcing her to marry him instead. But she said nothing of her fear to her mother as they took the tart to the kitchen for baking. And as they went upstairs to her chambers to choose what she would wear for the wedding, she made a silent resolution.

If the worst happens, then I'll give mesel' up tae MacDonnell in exchange fer sparin' Roisin and Conrad's lives.

"Och, yer maither makes a bonny bride, eh, wee yin?" Lady Fiona asked her granddaughter as she entered Agnes' chambers the following morning and saw her daughter standing before the long looking glass in her wedding dress.

"Aye, she's très belle, the bonniest mama ever," Roisin agreed heartily, blowing a kiss at her mother's reflection in the long looking glass before spinning around to face her grandmother. "And what about me and Peggy, Grandma? D'ye think we look belles as well? Look, Saoirse did our hair all in ringlets, like we're sisters." She pranced about like a miniature pony, tossing her mane of fair ringlets, clutching Peggy in her hand.

"Ye make a very pretty picture, me darlin'," Lady Fiona assured her, gliding further into the room in her spectacular yellow silk gown. She stood and watched approvingly while Saoirse skilfully put the finishing touches to the bride's toilette.

"Thank ye, Grandma, and ye look very nice too. I like the flowers on yer dress," Roisin said, coming up to hold her hand and gaze at Agnes admiringly. Agnes blew her a kiss and smiled at her.

"Thank ye, sweetheart," Lady Fiona replied, her voice trembling slightly. She got out a small square of lace and dabbed at her eyes.

"Maither, are ye cryin'?" Agnes asked, moved by her mother's emotional state. She was a bundle of confused emotions herself, the main one being an eagerness to hear the minister pronounce her and Conrad man and wife and so reduce the chances of MacDonnell making trouble.

"'Tis the weddin' of me only daughter. I've waited a long time fer this. I'm entitled tae shed a few tears," her mother said with a sniff.

Agnes put her arms around her and patted her back gently. "'Tis sweet of ye, Maither. Of course, ye snivel all ye like, but nae durin' the ceremony or the minister will throw ye out," she said teasingly, making them all laugh, even Lady Fiona herself.

"Now, me lady, ye must be careful nae tae crush yer dress," Saoirse warned, smoothing the swags of Calais lace adorning the bell-shaped, richly embroidered overskirt of the fabulous gown. Agnes had worn it but once before, to a Christmastide ball in Granville, a big town in Normandy a few miles from her aunt Morag's house. It had languished in her wardrobe ever since.

Of French design, it was of sea-green silk, with a lace-edged low-cut neckline and off-the-shoulder, tight-fitting three-quarter length sleeves, also sprouting lace, that made for a spectacular decolletage.

"I can hardly believe 'tis me," Agnes breathed in wonder, staring at her image. "Thank ye so much fer all ye've done, Saoirse. I really appreciate all yer efforts at such short notice."

"Ach, 'tis me pleasure, me lady," Saoirse replied, beaming, making minute adjustments to Agnes's hair. She herself was looking her best, her dark auburn hair caught up in a sparking net, her willowy figure shown off to advantage in a beautiful pink gown. She stood back to admire the results of her hard work. "'Tis nice tae be able tae put some of the skills I learned in France tae good use. Ye look absolutely beautiful, even if I dae say so mesel'. Ye could grace the French court, so ye could."

"Aye, I'm sure Conrad will appreciate it as well," Lady Fiona said with a girlish giggle that made Agnes chuckle.

"I think it must be time to go soon," Agnes said, glancing at the mantel clock, driven by a sense of urgency. "We have a quarter of an hour before the ceremony. We should hurry. Ach, I need me ribbon fer the handfastin'," she added, casting about for it.

"I have it, Mama, let me tie it on fer ye," Roisin said, coming up to her and tying the ribbon painstakingly around her mother's wrist.

"Thank ye, darlin', that's a grand job," Agnes told her, kissing the top of her daughter's head while surreptitiously tying the ribbon a little tighter. "Come then, we must go if I'm tae make it tae me own weddin' on time. Roisin, ye almost forgot Peggy."

With the doll retrieved, mother and daughter held hands, and the bride's party set off, heading downstairs and out of the castle, to make the short journey across the grounds to the little family chapel where generations of former MacDonalds had said their vows. Agnes was moved by the number of servants and workers who stopped to wish her good fortune and, as tradition dictated, many strong bairns as she passed by.

The question of future children had not really occurred to her before. *How will we have bairns if Conrad willnae forgive me and wants naethin' tae dae with me?* she wondered. She was not nervous about the wedding itself, but the talk of bairns started to make her feel very nervous about the wedding night. And that was on top of her fear of MacDonnell. It was not exactly the happy wedding day she had envisioned as a girl for her and Conrad.

Her father and Duncan were at the chapel door to greet them. Duncan looked her up and down in wonder. "Why, can this sophisticated lady really be me little sister?" he asked teasingly, giving her a peck on the cheek. "Ye look gorgeous. Good luck, Sister."

"Thank ye, Duncan," Agnes replied.

"And look at this fine wee lassie in her pretty dress," he addressed Roisin, who rushed to give him a hug.

"Daughter. Ye look lovely." Her father had come up next to her and threaded her arm through his, ready to walk her up the aisle. She was surprised by his compliment and the look of pride he gave her as they approached the chapel door. Everybody was happy she was marrying Conrad, it seemed.

As Duncan opened the doors, Agnes stooped down and said to Roisin, "Ye must go with Grandma and Saoirse now, sweetheart. Be a good girl, like I told ye."

"Aye, Mama," the little girl assured her pertly. They exchanged kisses before Lady Fiona and Saoirse spirited her away inside the chapel.

"We'll give them a few minutes and then we'll go in," her father told her, patting her hand with uncharacteristic warmth. "I'll admit, lass, I never thought I'd see this day."

"Aye, I'm sure ye didnae, Faither."

"It's all worked out in the end, eh?"

"That is if MacDonnell daesnae take it intae his head tae attack us or murder me husband," she blurted out, finally voicing her worries.

Initially, he looked shocked, but then he nodded. "MacDonnell is a dangerous man, there's nay denyin' it. But dinnae fret. He's nae as powerful or clever as he thinks, lass. Ye have all of us here tae protect ye and the lassie. And soon ye'll have a fine husband tae look out fer ye. There's nae need tae fear. We'll keep ye safe. Now, let's get ye wed, eh?"

Feeling slightly better for her father's rare reassurance, Agnes nodded and squeezed his arm. "Thank ye, Faither. Aye, let's go in."

The chapel was tiny, and it was only a few yards from the doors to the altar. With only her family, Saoirse, her father's advisors and their wives present, the tall, broad-shouldered figure waiting at the altar stood out. When she set eyes on Conrad, looking so devastatingly handsome in his full kilt in Mackintosh colours, his curling blonde hair neatly combed, Agnes went weak at the knees.

Ach, God, why daes he havetae look so braw?

Her heart started to pound as she drew nearer.

'Tis too cruel, havin' such a beautiful husband who willnae wantae touch me because he hates me.

CHAPTER TWENTY-FOUR

As if hearing her thoughts, Conrad turned slightly, and their eyes locked. The sunlight streaming through the high windows ignited the bright blue of his eyes, and he smiled at her. A brief moment of hope flared in her chest. But it died when she reached him, and her father handed her over to his care. She she could see Conrad's eyes were cold. For the benefit of her family, she raised a smile as he took her hand in his, but sorrow settled inside her as the minister began the service.

It seemed to go by in a blur, though she managed to recite her vows without stumbling. The hardest part was the handfasting, when Conrad made the cuts in both their palms and pressed them together, mingling their blood and Duncan tied the ribbons around their wrists into a symbolic knot. The solemnity of the ancient ritual set against the falsity of their union did not sit right with Agnes, not when she knew what Conrad really thought of her. Not when she loved him with all her heart.

Just when she thought it was all over, the minister intoned, "I now pronounce ye man and wife," and her heart sank. Her eyes locked with Conrad's, and he bent his head and pressed his lips against hers. She expected no more than a dry peck, but the kiss was surprisingly sweet and took her aback, hope flickering in her breast.

But when she looked at him, trying to gauge his thoughts, he avoided her gaze. Hope died as he tucked her arm in his and led her down into the aisle, where they were greeted by her family. Agnes could not help noticing the sense of collective relief that underpinned the otherwise hearty congratulations of her father, mother, and brother.

"It'll turn out all right, me lady, dinnae fash yersel'," Saoirse whispered as she hugged Agnes warmly. "Sir Conrad is a good man. He'll come around, ye'll see."

"I wish I could share yer optimism, Saoirse, but I thank ye," Agnes whispered back, hugging her old friend back, with both gratitude and sadness in her heart. Soairse was the only one who understood how conflicted she was over Conrad, and she had tried her best to offer comfort when Agnes had revealed how tormented she was by his vow never to forgive her for what she had kept from him.

"Ach, take nay notice. He was angry when he said it. Once yer married and livin' together, he'll soon forgive ye, ye'll see I'm right," Saoirse had confidently assured her the previous day, when Agnes had told her about the wedding. "It might take a little time, but I'm sure ye can find happiness taegether in the end."

"Thank the Lord ye're comin' with me tae Moy Hall, Saoirse, I cannae dae without ye, and nor can Roisin," Agnes had replied. "I'm very lucky tae have ye as me friend."

They stepped outside the little chapel, and as soon as Lady Fiona let go of Roisin's hand, the child skipped happily up to Agnes and Conrad.

"Congratulations, Mama, ye're married now!" she cried, hurling herself at Agnes' and hugging her waist tightly, burying her nose in the expensive silk gown.

"Aye, darlin', we're married. Ye were very good in the chapel. Did ye like the ceremony?" Agnes asked, forgetting cold reality for a moment in the rush of maternal affection that washed over her. She stroked Roisin's hair and smiled down into the small pair of blue eyes that peeped up at her, almost perfect replicas of Conrad's.

"Ummm, aye, I liked the bit when Uncle Duncan did the knot, and when ye and Conrad kissed at the end!" She giggled, clearly finding the kiss hilarious, which set Agnes laughing as well. To her surprise, Conrad joined in. Grinning mischievously up at him, Roisin abandoned her mother's skirts and instead held her arms up to him.

"Come on up then, wee yin," he told her, sweeping her up and putting her on his shoulder as though it were the most natural thing in the world. Despite her underlying worries about her future as Conrad's wife, it warmed Agnes' heart to see how happy Roisin was with him.

I can trust him tae always protect her, whatever happens.

She was comforted enough by the thought to manage a genuine smile.

They eventually arrived in the great hall, where the small family wedding breakfast had been laid out. "Aye, here we are, Little Flower," Conrad assured her, seeming to enjoy being her beast of burden. "And there's gonnae be all sorts of nice things tae eat and drink."

"And Mama says there's gonnae be music and dancin' as well."

"Well, it wouldnae be much of a party without the music and dancin', would it? But there's a few wee things yer ma and I havetae dae first before the party can really get started. So, I'll havetae put ye down fer a wee while."

"Aye, all right. But will ye dance with me later on, Conrad?" she begged once her feet were on the floor.

"Of course, I will. Wild horses wouldnae stop me," he told her, ruffling hair with a tenderness that made Agnes' almost want to cry. "Now, go and bother yer Uncle Duncan fer a wee while." He chuckled as she shot off towards Duncan.

"We'd best dae our duty as bride and groom," Conrad told Agnes, escorting her over to a table, where a small barrel of whisky and the ancestral quaich had been set out. The MacDonald quaich, the traditional two-handled lover's cup, was made of finely chased Irish silver and had been in the family for many generations. Duncan, now with Roisin riding on his hip, went over and ceremoniously filled the cup with whisky.

Her family gathered around whilst Agnes and Conrad each took one of the handles and lifted the cup to their lips. She could not help smiling as they drank together of the strong liquor. It warmed her insides, but not as much as when Conrad unexpectedly returned her smile, sending a little shiver of anticipation through her.

Maybe he's forgotten he said he'd never forgive me. Maybe Soairse's right, he only spoke in anger and didnae mean it at all.

But she knew Conrad too well to really believe it was possible, and her nervousness about the wedding night only grew.

Fresh congratulations and good luck wishes accompanied their sharing of the loving cup, which Duncan immediately topped up and passed around, according to the ancient tradition. It put the seal on their union as well as the joining of their two clans.

Next, following yet more Highland tradition, Conrad had to pay the waiting piper his traditional dram before the fellow would pipe him and Agnes, with their party following behind, to the laird's table. When they were all seated, the wedding breakfast began in earnest. Beautiful harp music played in the background as the feast was served, servants rushed to fill everyone's glasses and tankards with ale and wine, and the atmosphere quickly became convivial.

I just wish I felt more like celebratin', Agnes thought, keeping her smile pasted in place.

She and Conrad sat on decorated chairs next to each other at the laird's table. There was nowhere for Agnes to hide at all. Naturally, as newly-weds, they were expected to hold hands and regularly exchange languishing looks and even kisses and endearments, if they so wished, which proved to be quite a strain.

Roisin had her own chair in-between her grandmother and Saoirse. "We'll keep her occupied so ye and Conrad can enjoy yer celebration in peace," her mother had told Agnes kindly when they all sat down to dine.

"Thank ye, Maither, that's thoughtful of ye," Agnes had replied. Though, frankly, she could have used the distraction her daughter would have provided just then. But Roisin seemed so happy where she was, being spoiled by her grandmother and picking out all her favourite foods to eat, Agnes let her be.

She picked at her food, and when she finished off her second glass of wine, Conrad refilled her glass immediately. Before long, the wine began to go to her head. Or more to the point, other parts of her, for it began to stir her desire for her new husband.

It wouldnae be so bad if he didnae look so braw in his fine clothes, she thought to herself as he leaned across her to pour the wine, his delicious, musky scent filling her nose, almost making her swoon. Her eyes were drawn to his hands, his muscular arms, the glint of his fair hair in the sunlight spilling through the windows. Knowing what was hidden beneath his fine clothes made her rue the past and sigh inwardly with longing.

But what good is it tae feel this way about him when he despises me? I cannae even touch him, let alone kiss him. Ach, what I wouldnae give fer him tae want me again, like I want him.

Her pride made her lift her chin and smile despite her sadness, though her nerves stretched tauter as the evening wore on. The feast was consumed, and the harpist was eventually replaced by a trio of musicians skilled on fiddle, pipes, and drums. The dancing was about to start, and Agnes wished she could share in the rising anticipation among the others.

The band struck up the opening strains of a familiar reel. "I think the bride and groom are expected tae open the dancefloor," Conrad murmured to her. Agnes glanced around and saw her family looking at them expectantly, including a beaming Roisin.

"Well, we'd best nae keep them waiting then," she said. He stood up and offered her his hand. Though she kept her smiling façade firmly in place, determined to conceal her state of confusion, she was inwardly shaken by the tingles of excitement that raced up her arm as she placed her hand in his and he led her to the dancefloor.

They took their positions in the middle of the floor. As was the custom, Conrad bowed to her, and she responded with a curtsey. For all her outward poise, when the music started up and Conrad seized her by the waist and took off, whirling her exuberantly around the floor, an involuntary burst of joyous laughter left her lips.

"Ye still like tae dance, eh, Agnes?" he murmured, smiling down at her, his eyes sparkling as though he were having the time of his life, dancing with his new wife.

"Aye, when I get the chance," she replied, trying to sound non-committal. However, her excitement was so great that for a few precious minutes, she allowed herself to forget it was all a pretence and simply enjoy having his strong arm clamped around her waist, her body melded to his, their fingers entwined as he skilfully spun her about the floor in perfect time to the beat of the drum.

"Ye look very pretty in yer dress," Conrad said unexpectedly as they flew onwards, noticing her parents coming to join them on the floor. "'Tis very grand. Just right fer a weddin'. It suits ye."

Agnes was taken aback by the compliment. "I'm glad ye think so," she replied, concealing how happy it made her feel. Maybe it was the wine she had drunk as well as the dancing, but her head was spinning. Before she could stop herself, she smiled up at him and said, "Ye're lookin' braw yersel'."

He continued to smile, but his eyes suddenly blazed with cold fire, striking a chill into her heart. "I hope yer nae tryin' tae get around me with yer flattery, Agnes, because it'll nae work."

Stung by his words, Agnes replied indignantly, "That's nae very fair, seein' as how ye just told me ye like me dress. Am I nae allowed tae pay ye the same compliment?"

"I'm just lettin' ye ken that flattery willnae work with me. I'll nae forgive ye fer what ye've done," he stated, twirling her beneath his arm.

"I can live without yer forgiveness," she lied, her fixed smile hiding her wounded pride and aching heart. "Ye're daein' a very good job of playin' the happy bridegroom, I must say."

"Oh, ye think so? Ye're nae daein' such a bad job yersel'. Look at ye. Quite the radiant bride, are ye nae?"

Agnes gave up. "If ye say so," she replied dully, her former exuberance crushed by his harsh attitude. Her enjoyment gone, she remained silent and struggled to keep her smile in place until the dance ended.

However, the sight of Roisin running towards them boosted her flagging spirits.

"I wantae dance as well. Ye promised tae dance with me, Conrad," the little girl cried over the loud music, gazing up at them excitedly. Agnes looked questioningly at Conrad, but he was already laughing and scooping up Roisin in his arms.

"Why, of course, ye must dance, Little Flower," he told her, sitting her on his hip. To Agnes he said, "Looks like we're dancin' again, Wife."

"It would seem so," Agnes agreed, smiling at Roisin, who was glowing with happiness. She was clearly as taken with her new father as he seemed to be with her. For all their earlier disagreement, Agnes was deeply moved by Conrad's gentleness and patience with their daughter. Of course, they looked so alike, and she marvelled at how close the pair already were and how well and quickly Conrad seemed to have adjusted to being a father. Despite her misgivings about their own relationship, his goodness only added fuel to the love that secretly burned in her heart for him.

The love I must hide from him every single day of me life from now on.

CHAPTER TWENTY-FIVE

The music started up again, and the three of them danced together, with Roisin's childish laughter infecting both her mother and Conrad as they spun around the floor. When that dance came to a close and Agnes wanted to rest to catch her breath, Roisin protested.

"I'm nae tired, Mama, I wantae dae some more dancin'!" she declared, hanging onto Conrad's neck.

Agnes spotted Duncan approaching. "Well, I think there's a prince comin' tae ask ye tae dance, m'darlin'," she told the excited child.

"Ye've come just at the right moment, friend," Conrad said, setting Roisin on her feet. "This young lady is in need of a partner."

"I'd be honoured if she'd dance with me," Duncan said, grinning playfully at Roisin, who clapped her hands with glee when her uncle bowed grandly to her. "Will ye dae me the honor, Lady Roisin?"

"Aye, Sir Duncan, I'd love tae," Rosin replied as decorously as any noble court lady, taking her uncle's hand and dropping into a perfect little curtsey. Before moving away to take up their positions for the upcoming dance, Duncan cast a curious glance at Conrad. "The way ye treat the wee yin, man, anyone would think she was yer own," he remarked.

Conrad laughed, as if to brush off Duncan's words, but Agnes detected the trace of unease in it. "And why nae?" he responded a little too jovially. "She's a grand wee lass. 'Tis fun havin' a bairn in yer life."

"She's taken a shine tae her new daddy all right," Duncan replied, a seemingly harmless remark. But there was something knowing in her brother's smile that alerted Agnes to danger. "Come, Conrad, let's go and get a drink. I'm thirsty," she said, pulling on her husband's arm.

"Aye, I'm comin'," Conrad replied. "Enjoy yer dancin', wee yin," he told Roisin, exchanging smiles and waves with her whilst allowing Agnes to lead him off the floor.

"That was a bit close," he murmured when they were standing to one side with drinks in their hands. "I really thought he was about to guess the truth then."

"That's why I pulled ye away. I dinnae want a nasty scene at our weddin'," Agnes said, feeling rather shaken by the incident.

"Me neither. But Duncan's nae stupid. I reckon there's a good chance he'll guess before too long."

"Well, he will if ye keep makin' such a fuss of Roisin," Agnes pointed out, knowing she was being unfair.

"And I intend tae keep makin' a fuss of her. I'm her faither. 'Tis me right," he shot back, sounding irked despite his smile.

"Well, why d'ye nae get up on the table there and announce it tae everyone then?" she said under her breath, feeling under pressure.

"Maybe I will."

The look of hurt that flashed across his handsome features made her instantly contrite. "Ach, I didnae mean that, Conrad. I'm sorry. I'm worried about how it'll affect yer friendship with Duncan once he finds out ye really are her faither. He'll nae forgive ye, and I ken how unhappy that would make ye both."

"And ye dinnae wantae feel responsible fer that as well as keepin' me daughter a secret from me, is that it?"

Aye, somethin' like that. How much guilt and misery can a person bear before it kills them?

Her pride would not let her answer him, instead she hid her heartache in a sip of wine.

Eventually, worn out by all the excitement, Roisin fell sleep on Agnes' lap. "I'd better put her tae bed," Agnes told Conrad, eager for an excuse to escape the celebration, even if only for a short while.

"I'll come with ye," he said to her surprise. Before she could argue, he rose to his feet and gently took Roisin from her lap, cradling her in his arms. They briefly explained to her parents where they were going and left the hall, the sounds of merriment echoing behind them as they walked down the hallway.

Once they had put the sleeping child to bed, they left her in the maid's care and left the room. Agnes thought they would be returning to the wedding feast and started off down the hall. She was startled when Conrad put a hand on her arm and stopped her outside her chambers.

"They'll nae miss us if we dinnae go back. Let's stay up here now. We can sleep in yer room," he said, opening the door and pulling her gently in behind him. Her heart started to pound as he closed the door behind them, wondering what was going to happen now.

Taking the tinder box from the mantel, he lit the candles in the candelabra scattered about the room. Warm, yellow light flickered off the walls, giving an illusion of warmth. "I'll move me things in here tomorrow. We'll be sharin' these chambers and sleepin' in the same room from now on," he told Agnes, flicking the burning spill into the grate.

Her anxiety levels rising, Agnes stood looking at him nervously as he sat on a chair and began taking off his boots. "In the same bed?" she asked.

"Unless ye have a spare bed hidden away somewhere, aye," he replied sarcastically. "But dinnae worry. I'll nae touch ye, of course."

"Ye're right about that," Agnes burst out, flustered at the thought of sharing a bed with him, but for a different reason than she figured he supposed.

Look at him! He looks like a Greek god out of some painting! 'Tis nae fair. How hard is it gonnae be lyin' next tae him, the only man I've ever loved and lain with, when I cannae even touch him because he hates me?

She could have wept with frustration. And even though she had expected rejection, his words still hurt. "And ye dinnae havetae worry either fer I'll certainly nae be touchin' ye," she shot back defensively.

"Grand."

"Aye, grand."

Indignant, fueled somewhat by the wine, Agnes marched over to the bed and gathered up the coverlet and several pillows. She rolled the coverlet into a long sausage, then she lifted her voluminous skirts and got up on the bed, arranging the sausage lengthwise down the middle of the mattress.

Conrad put his hands on his hips and asked, "What the hell are ye daein'?"

"What daees it look like? I'm dividin' the bed in two," Agnes huffed. "That way, we can both be sure we'll nae touch each other by accident durin' the night." She finished with the coverlet and built the barrier up higher with some spare pillows, until there was a little wall between the halves.

"Why, that's plain ridiculous," Conrad scoffed, discarding his sword belt and starting to take off his lovely wedding clothes, throwing them carelessly over the back of a chair. Agnes refused to look at him. She drew the curtain on her side of the bed and hid behind it. Too embarrassed to change into the lace nightdress her mother had gifted her for her wedding night in case Conrad thought she was trying to tempt him, she decided to sleep in her shift.

Mercifully, the bodice of her gown had front fastenings and she was able to get herself out of it and then step out of the voluminous skirts and petticoats. However, escaping her tightly laced stays was not so easy. It took a lot of effort and cursing under her breath to finally undo the laces and push the stays down over her hips. By the time she finally managed it, she was out of breath. Not wishing to take the risk of crossing the floor to the wardrobe in her state of undress, she draped everything carefully over the back of the chair by the side of the bed which she deemed her own.

She heard Conrad moving about the room, and as the light began to dim, guessed he was snuffing out the candles. Until only the light from the candles on her nightstand was left. Then, she heard the bed creak beneath his weight and knew he had gotten into bed. On his side of the barrier, she hoped. Slowly, she pulled back the curtain and saw him.

He was laying with his back to her, on the other side of the divider, one husky arm out of the covers, which were bunched in his fist. For a few moments, she let her gaze linger on him, on the way his unruly golden curls spread across the pillow, glinting as the last of the candlelight danced over them. He was so beautiful, her dutiful husband, that it broke her heart all over again to know he despised her.

The only sound now in the oppressive silence of the bedroom was his soft, regular breathing.

Is he still awake?

She listened carefully. The breathing seemed a little too regular.

Of course, he's awake. What is he thinking?

With no clue as to what occupied his mind and too proud to ask, she blew out the candles and slid warily under the covers, onto the furthest edge of the mattress.

"Good night, Conrad," she whispered hesitantly into the silence, as aware of him as she would be of a bonfire burning in the bed next to her.

"Good night, Agnes."

His response and the sound of his deep, husky voice provided her a small crumb of comfort as she turned on her side, away from him.

'Tis nae much of a weddin' night, she thought miserably, swallowing back a few tears of self-pity and silently chiding herself for them. But 'tis best this way fer Roisin. I must put a brave face on things fer her sake, whatever happens.

Conrad lay in tense silence, his eyes wide open, staring into the darkness. His heart was aching in his chest, while his body burned with frustration, knowing Agnes was lying next to him, just across the nonsensical barrier she had built between them.

Daes she really think that would stop me if I wanted tae claim her as me wife?

It was so hard not to give in to his urge to possess her it bordered on torture.

He could not stop seeing her in his mind's eye, looking so beautiful in her wedding gown, her face alight with joy as they danced. It had felt so good to have her in his arms again, as her husband this time, wishing with all his heart that the celebration of their union was as joyous as they both pretended it was.

But that was a torment too.

Because she daesnae want me, she daesnae love me as I love her, and she never will. She hid me daughter from me fer years and let her live as a bastard. I cannae allow mesel' tae forgive her fer all that. However much I love her.

He closed his eyes and tried to let the wine and whisky he had drunk consume him, so he could forget about Agnes lying so close. But it was impossible. She had not moved an inch since getting into the bed, and he could not hear her breathing either.

Is she awake or has she fallen asleep?

Too proud to ask her, lest he betray his love, he eventually willed himself to sleep.

Conrad smiled contentedly as he surfaced from a dreamless slumber, just far enough to register how supremely comfortable he was, how his arms were wrapped around something pillowy, and how his regular morning erection was pressed up against something soft and smooth and warm… and wonderfully inviting.

Wondering if he could be dreaming, careful not to move, he slowly cracked his eyelids open. To find his nose buried in a mass of silky, dark hair, breathing in the scent of roses. His eyes opened wider as he realized the entire length of his body was spooning with Agnes', his arms encircling her slender, sleeping form.

Their limbs were entwined, and his right hand was enclosing her left breast, which rose and fell gently as she breathed. His chest was pressed against her back, and his throbbing manhood was resting in the crevice of her behind as it nestled in his groin.

He lay motionless, revelling in the feeling, afraid to move and break the spell, wanting to stretch out the moment for as long as he could. All would have been well if not for the urges sweeping through him as the temptation to slip his erection between her legs and inside her grew ever more powerful.

The two warring voices in his head started up.

Nay, ye dinnae have the right. She'll only hate ye fer takin' advantage of her while she's sleepin'.

She's yer lawful wife, man, 'tis yer right tae claim her as such!

As it turned out, he did not have to choose between the two, because Agnes woke up. And as soon as she realized what was happening, she gave a little scream and startled away from him. She turned on him like a wildcat, her eyes wide with shock.

"Ye-ye barbarian!" she exclaimed, giving him an almighty shove. And the next thing he knew, he landed with an almighty bump on the floor, jolting his hardness painfully.

"Ow, what did ye havetae go and dae that fer? I wasnae daein' anythin'," he protested, getting to his feet, cupping his aching manhood.

"So what was that stickin' in me back?" she demanded angrily, pulling the covers up to her chin.

"I'm a man. What d'ye expect?" His ardour firmly dented, he yawned, sat on the edge of the bed, and rubbed his face and hair briskly with his hands. They smelled of rose perfume.

"Ye said ye wouldnae touch me, but I see ye broke yer word," she said accusingly, waving at the dislodged coverlet and the scattered pillows. "Ye clearly sneaked over tae me side of the bed in the night."

He turned to face her, irritated. "Or was it ye who sneaked over tae me? There's nae way of tellin', is there?"

"I think I'd remember."

"Nae if ye were asleep."

She scoffed. "Ye're tryin' tae say ye did it while ye were asleep? Ye ken naethin' about it, I suppose?"

"Who says it was me? And aye, that's right, I dinnae ken either way. And neither d'ye. So quit yer mitherin' and leave me alone."

She huffed loudly, while he stood up and stretched until his bones cracked. Then he sauntered over to the washstand and, just to annoy her, pulled his shirt off over his head and slid his trousers down and stood stark naked, his back to her. Her gasp told him she was watching.

"Ye can always look away if ye dinnae like what ye see," he told her brusquely, starting to wash in cold water. "We're man and wife now, so ye'll havetae get used tae seein' me this way," he added, finding the whole experience strangely enjoyable.

When he looked in the mirror to see if he needed to shave, he saw her reflection staring at him. Her mouth was slightly open, and she was clearly unaware he could see her looking at his nakedness. But it was the heated look in her eyes that really surprised him. If he did not know any better, he would have thought that she liked what she was seeing very much indeed.

CHAPTER TWENTY-SIX

"Ah! Look, Faither, 'tis the newlyweds. Good day tae ye, Maister and Lady Mackintosh. I trust ye slept badly, eh?" Duncan bowed theatrically in greeting before winking at Agnes, who blushed crimson. Duncan proceeded to elbow Conrad playfully in the ribs. "How's married life so far, man?" he asked.

"What's it like bein' so bloody nosy?" Conrad replied, grinning as he punched his friend's arm. They laughed and rubbed their sore spots in brotherly camaraderie.

Later, with Roisin occupied with her grandmother, Conrad had suggested that he and Agnes should take a walk, to promote the illusion of being happy newlyweds. They eventually came to a wide lawn between two hedges and saw Duncan and her father already there. They were practicing shooting their bows, and several targets had been set up a few hundred yards away for the purpose.

They waited respectfully with Duncan until the laird had taken his shot before greeting him. "A very good shot, me laird," Conrad congratulated the old warrior, who had hit the bullseye dead on.

"I still have an eye fer it," the laird said with a satisfied nod, cracking a rare smile and clapping Conrad on the back. But Conrad could see lines of strain on his face and guessed he was worried about MacDonnell's reaction to the marriage as well. But he only said, "Welcome tae the family, lad. I'm glad tae have ye as a son-in-law."

"Thank ye, me laird. I'm honored tae be part of the family," Conrad replied sincerely.

Her father nodded approvingly before turning to look at Agnes. "Good day tae ye, lass. Are ye well? How d'ye like wedded life so far?" he asked, his steely grey glance flicking over her face searchingly.

"I like it fine, Faither, thank ye," she answered with a demure smile. Conrad thought the ethereal pallor of her face effortlessly added credence to the expectation they had been enthusiastically engaged between the sheets all night. But naethin' could be farther from the truth, he thought sadly.

"Where's the wee yin? She's nae with ye?" the laird asked, glancing around for Roisin.

"Nay, she's with Maither and the other ladies up in the solar," Agnes explained. "I think they're teachin' her tae play cards and gamble."

That drew a laugh from her father and Duncan, who knew of Lady Fiona's love of cards. The two men took a break from their practice, and the four of them spent a few minutes talking about how well the wedding feast had gone and what a good job Lady Fiona had done to organize such a grand event at such short notice. Conrad made sure to mention the frangipane tart appreciatively twice.

As Conrad had thought it would, the conversation soon turned more serious, focusing on the announcement of the marriage and how long it would take for MacDonnell to find out about it.

"I've made sure the news has been spread far and wide," Duncan told them, leaning on his bow.

"Then we should be on our guard," Conrad put in, worried for Agnes' safety. "There's nay tellin' what MacDonnell might dae once he finds out."

"Surely, he'll go elsewhere once he finds out I'm wed," Agnes said, clearly doing her best to sound confident. But he could tell from the small line between her brows that she was nervous about it. He had an idea that he thought might help to make her feel more confident about the situation.

"Maybe I should teach ye how tae use a bow," he suggested to her. "Ye'd be able tae defend yersel' then."

Duncan nodded in approval. "Aye, teach her tae shoot. I'd have taught her mesel' years ago if I'd kent MacDonnell was gonnae prove such a problem."

"None of us could have foreseen we'd have tae deal with such a madman," the laird remarked with obvious regret. "But can a wee lass like Agnes ever hope tae be able tae be useful with a bow? She's nae strong enough."

Conrad noticed the familiar flash of defiance in Agnes' eyes at her father's words. Of course, she saw it as a challenge coming from him. "I may be small, Faither, but I'm strong too." She looked up at Conrad so appealingly, his heart thumped in his chest. "I'm sure Conrad is skilled enough tae teach me," she said, as if hinting that her father was not.

"Well, there's nae harm in tryin', I suppose," the laird conceded. "But take care she daesnae get hurt, Conrad."

"I will, me laird," Conrad replied. "Agnes has always been a fast learner," he said, earning himself a look of gratitude from her. A small nugget of excitement lodged in his gut.

"Show her how it's done, lad," Duncan encouraged him.

"Aye, show me how ye shoot, Conrad," Agnes said.

"All right, watch carefully how I stand," he instructed her. She stood nearby watching, and he felt her eyes on him as he took up a bow from the rack, nocked an arrow, and fired off a shot. The arrow flew straight, hitting the bullseye and splitting the laird's arrow in two.

"Och, well done!" Agnes cried clapping her hands. However, Conrad suspected her appreciation was more because he had destroyed her father's arrow rather than his own skill.

If she expected his display of prowess to rile her father, she was disappointed because the old man only laughed. "Fancy shootin', lad," he said.

"Ach, he's just showin' off tae impress his new wifey, is that nae right, Conrad?" Duncan put in teasingly.

"Ye think so?" he asked, nocking a fresh arrow and aiming at an unused target. But at the last moment, he pivoted and let it fly. It landed with a thwack into the ground and stuck quivering between Duncan's feet.

Duncan yelped in surprise and leapt backwards, laughing. The laird laughed as well.

"Conrad! What are ye daein'? That's dangerous!" Agnes cried, clearly shocked.

"'Tis all right, Sister. He kens what he's daein'," her brother assured her. "I was in nae danger."

Even so, the fear on Agnes' face made Conrad regret his action. She had no idea of the daring, dangerous games he and Duncan had played with their weapons since they were boys, hardening their courage for battle. He sought to distract her. "Come over here and pick a bow, Agnes," he invited her, gesturing to the rack.

He was relieved when she did as he suggested, though her lips remained pursed with disapproval. "Bein' quite slight, ye need a bow that's both light but strong." He took one from the rack and handed it to her. "Try this one. How does it feel? Is it too heavy?"

He was relieved when her look of disapproval was overtaken by curiosity as she took the bow and tried it out. "Nay, 'tis nae heavy at all," she said.

"We'll start with that one then and see how it handles," he told her, grateful when Duncan and the laird diplomatically moved over to use the other targets and began shooting again, giving him and Agnes a modicum of privacy. "Now, take yer arrow and come and stand here by me."

Conrad stood close behind her, his knees bent, and put his arms around her, guiding her hands with his, showing her how to hold the bow and aim with the greatest accuracy and precision.

Agnes did her best to pay attention to his instructions, but having his strong, warm body pressed to her back and his muscular arms around her made her as tense as the drawn bowstring. Her heart was racing and, worse, heat was pooling between her thighs.

Daes he ken what he's daein' tae me?

Her cheeks flared with heat.

Is he daein' it on purpose, tae get back at me fer pushin' him out of bed this mornin'?

Determined not to let him suspect how he was affecting her, she fought to keep her composure as she took a few practice shots. It took a few attempts, but with Conrad adjusting her stance and hold each time, she finally managed to hit the target. But nowhere near the bullseye.

"I'm disappointed with mesel'," she admitted, downcast by her poor performance. "Maybe Faither's right. I'm nae strong enough tae be a good archer."

"Dinnae be so hard on yersel', Agnes," Conrad said. "'Tis yer first time. I've been shootin' a bow since I was five years old. Of course, I'm good at it. Ye just need tae practice. Anyway, ye dinnae have tae shoot like me tae defend yersel'. Just hittin' yer enemy could be enough tae buy ye a few vital moments."

"I appreciate yer encouragement," she replied, a small smile curving her full lips.

"Besides, I ken ye'd hate tae prove yer Faither right," he murmured conspiratorially, wringing a chuckle from her. "Ye ken me too well. I never said I was givin' up," she said with fresh determination, taking another arrow and nocking it.

With Conard's unsettlingly close guidance, the next arrow she shot landed much nearer the centre of the target. "Well, that was a big improvement," she exclaimed, pleased with herself. Elated, she unthinkingly leaned her head back to smile at him... and immediately froze, struck by the intense expression on his face.

He was bending low, his arms encircling her, his eyes level with hers. Their gazes locked, their lips inches apart. In that moment, the world around them seemed to disappear. There was only her and Conrad, their bodies melded together as one, their heads slowly moving closer.

Omigod, is he really gonnae kiss me?!

Her whole body tingled.

But at the last second, Conrad pulled back, as though realizing what he was doing. He moved away from her slightly and cleared his throat. Agnes was mortified with herself, feeling his rejection all the sharper because she knew how much she had wanted that lost kiss. To hide her blushes, she turned her head back to the targets and fiddled with her bow, struggling to bring her racing pulse under control.

"Shall we continue?" she finally managed to ask, desperate for a distraction from the unsettling tension between them.

"Aye, take another shot," he replied, snatching up another arrow and giving it to her, clearly also eager to put the embarrassing moment behind them.

They resumed the practice, and though Conrad kept a little distance between them this time, the air between continued to sizzle with a heat the hot summer day could not wholly account for. They remained stiff with each other for some time. However, as her training progressed and she started to show improvement, her father and brother began to notice how well she was doing and called over encouragement. That broke the tension somewhat. Agnes became engrossed in the challenge, and the awkwardness between her and Conrad was forgotten.

"Well, I must say, I enjoyed that very much, Conrad. Thank ye fer initiatin' me intae the delights of archery," she told him when they finished and made their way back to the castle. While the memory of the almost kiss still burned in her mind, she tried to focus instead on her genuine pleasure at how well she had done in a short time. "I'm lucky tae have such a good teacher," she told Conrad as they walked across the gardens, for she was keen to maintain the more light-hearted mood she felt had established itself between them.

He gave a gorgeous, lopsided smile that made her heart flip. "Maybe so, but ye did well fer a novice. It seems ye have a good eye fer a target. Even what ye've learned today could save yer life one day if ye havetae defend yersel'," he told her with a knowing glance, which she understood referred to MacDonnell.

"Aye, I remember tryin' tae fight off that brigand with the dirk Saoirse gave me. I had nay idea what tae dae with it," she admitted with a shudder.

"I seem tae remember ye were daein' yer best tae fight him off when I got there. Nae many lassies would be so brave," he said, pleasantly surprising her by threading her arm through his.

Secretly thrilled by the gesture and his praise, she replied honestly, "But me best wasnae good enough. Ye'll never ken how grateful I was when ye saved us."

Even if seein' ye again was one of the biggest shocks of me life!

He shrugged off her words in his usual modest way. "Well, I'll always protect ye, ye ken that. But I worry about ye if I'm nae there," he confessed as they came to the main courtyard and approached the doors of the keep.

Even if she knew he would protect her out of duty and not love, Agnes appreciated his assurance. "Thank ye, Conrad. That's very comfortin', though I'm still very grateful fer ye takin' the time tae teach me tae shoot. Bein' able tae fight fer mesel' and protect Roisin if I havetae makes me feel safer. I'll keep practicing. Maybe I'll surprise ye."

"Och, I've nae doubt ye will," he replied enigmatically as they entered the vestibule, leaving her wondering exactly what he meant by it.

After supper that evening, the family gathered in the private drawing room, along with Saoirse, to keep an eye on Roisin. They drank wine and whisky, chatted about inconsequential things, exchanged gossip, and played cards and various games to entertain Roisin. The uncertainty over MacDonnell receded for a few pleasant hours as the family scene played out.

Watching Conrad and Roisin playing together warmed Agnes heart. It seemed to her the perfect example of the sort of happy, stable family life Agnes wanted for Roisin.

As she watched him smile and laugh with their daughter, she could not help thinking how incredibly handsome and charismatic her husband was. The memory of the almost kiss returned forcefully when Saoirse took Roisin up to bed and Conrad went to sit next to her on the settee. Her heart began racing as, she supposed for the benefit of the others, he reached over and clasped her hand in his large, warm paw, resting it on his thigh. The thigh that was now pressed intimately against hers.

Now and then, he would rub his thumb over her palm or squeeze her fingers lightly, in what she assumed must be a show of marital affection for the others' benefit. The caress sent tingles careening up her arm and around her body. The heat coming off him and burning through her clothing was intense, while his musky scent was so enticing, she had a hard job just concentrating on the conversation. All she could think of was how much she wanted him.

"Well, 'tis gettin' late," he said finally, looking at her with an inquiring smile. "Are ye ready tae retire, Agnes?"

She blinked at him, hesitating to answer for a moment. She hated the thought of going up to their chambers, of casting aside the illusion of happiness to sleep together but separately in the same bed. But what choice was there but to agree?

"Aye, of course."

So, they said their goodnights and made their way upstairs. They stopped by the nursery to say a few words to Saoirse and look in on Roisin, who was already asleep. Agnes' heart squeezed to see Conrad bend over their tiny daughter and plant a small kiss on her delicate brow.

Even if he daesnae care fer me, he's startin' tae love Roisin. That's the most important thing.

When they were alone in their bed chamber and began preparing for bed, her anxiety levels began rising once more.

"So, are ye gonnae build yer wee wall between us again tonight?" he asked, starting to undress.

I willnae if ye ask me nae tae.

She sat at the vanity brushing out her hair before the mirror, covertly watching him divest himself of his clothes. "Why should I nae? Naethin's changed between us, has it?" she asked, a glimmer of hope flickering in her breast that he would answer her question with a passionate kiss.

"Nay, naethin' has changed," he replied, going to clean his teeth at the washstand in just his trews.

Her hope died. "Will ye help me with me dress?" she asked with a small sigh of resignation.

"Aye, when I've done this."

She took off her shoes and stockings, her jewels, and waited patiently for him to finish, fiddling purposelessly with the items on the vanity as she continued to watch him in the mirror, fascinated by the interplay of muscles rippling across his broad back and shoulders as he cleaned his teeth and washed his face. When her eyes suddenly clashed with his, she realized he was watching her from the mirror above the washstand, his eyes flashing bright blue in the candlelight. She looked away fast, cheeks blazing.

"I saw ye lookin'," he said, turning around to her, rubbing his face and hair with a towel.

"Lookin' at what?" she asked, pretending innocence but furious with herself for being caught out. She quickly got up and went to the bed. Once again, she rolled up the coverlet and built the flimsy barrier supposed to keep them apart, feeling foolish for even bothering with it.

I mean, it didnae exactly work last night, did it?

But she had to do something to distract herself from the crushing tension in the room.

"Ye were peepin' at me in the mirror," he said, a smirk playing about his lips as he came over to her.

"How d'ye ken that?" she asked, climbing off the bed to face him, annoyed by the smirk. "Were ye spyin' on me in the mirror?"

The smirk vanished, and the tips of his ears turned pink. "I wasnae!"

She scoffed and turned her back, gratified to have turned the tables on him. "Undae me dress, please."

He stood very close to her, as close as when he had been teaching her to shoot, so close, his warm breath tickled her neck and made her knees turn to jelly. Even if she had wanted to, which she did not, she could not have moved an inch. The subtle brushing of his fingers upon her skin as he worked on the fastenings set little fires racing up and down her spine.

And embarrassingly, when he lifted the bodice away and his hands brushed her shoulders, her nipples stood out like chapel coat pegs. Thank God he cannae see, she thought in mortification, folding her arms across her breasts in an effort to hide the evidence of her desire.

To her amazement, he actually started humming a tune while he untied her stays and loosened them for her. The sensitive flesh between her thighs grew hotter with each fleeting touch of his hand on her waist.

The tension crackling between them was suddenly too much, and her frustration burst out. As soon as he had finished undoing her stays, she rounded on him. "Are ye daein' it on purpose?" she demanded.

He lifted his palms and backed off a little, a picture of innocence. "Eh? Daein' what?"

She narrowed her eyes at him suspiciously. "Ye ken what I mean. Touchin' me like that."

"What? I dunno how ye expect me tae undae yer dress if I cannae touch ye."

"Ye seem tae be makin' a meal of it."

"Those fastenin's are fiddly things, especially with hands like mine." He held up the hands in front of her. The big, scarred, capable hands that had roamed over every inch of her body. She stared at them for a moment, then at his naked chest, fighting the urge to hurl herself at him and devour him.

"Well," she said, dragging her eyes off of him, clinging to her composure. She silently resolved never to ask for his help in undressing in future.

I'll sleep in me dress if I havetae.

It was just too infuriating. Too thrilling. Too frustrating.

"Thank ye."

"Ye're welcome."

She went behind her curtain and changed into a high-necked nightgown before sliding into bed. She sat up against the pillows, the covers drawn up to her chin. Her eyes simply refused to keep off of him, and she watched him through half-closed lid as he started going around the chamber, putting out the candles. Then, he took a clean shirt from the wardrobe, slung it over his shoulder and sauntered over to the sideboard.

"Fancy a dram?"

"Why nae?"

I could use one. Or three.

Watching him pour, the last of the flickering candlelight playing over his skin, Agnes could not help remembering the thrill of waking up in his arms that morning, with his hand cupping her breast and his arousal pressing against her behind. For a few blissful, sleep-blurred moments, she had simply lain there, luxuriating in his warmth, his strength, his obvious desire.

Wanting him too, she had been on the verge of parting her legs and maneuvering herself so he would slip inside her when reality had hit like a shower of cold rain. Suddenly terrified lest he should think she had deliberately engineered the situation during the night to lure him in some way, she had panicked and ended up by shoving him to the floor, blaming him to cover her own guilty feelings.

He handed her the dram and put his own on the nightstand. She tried not to look as he pulled on the clean shirt and shed his trews. He sighed as he got into bed next to her and lay against his pillows, on the other side of the flimsy divider. "Well, it's been quite a pleasant day, all things considered," he said, reaching for his whisky and sipping it.

Agnes took a deep swallow from her glass and tried to pull herself together. "Aye, it has. It was nice seein' ye and Roisin playin' together this evenin'."

"I love playin' with her. I've never felt such joy as when I'm with her. Or fear. The world is a dangerous place, and she's so wee. All I want tae dae is protect her. God only kens what I'll be like when she's old enough tae wed. I can already see mesel' interrogatin' any lad that dares tae look at her. I think I'm startin' tae understand why ye guard her so fiercely."

Agnes smiled. "Aye. I think ye're findin' out what it is tae be a parent."

To her surprise, Conrad chuckled and leaned across to clink his glass against hers. "Tae parenthood, eh?" he said with a smile.

"Tae parenthood," Agnes replied, returning it with one of her own.

They finished their drinks and wriggled down beneath the covers. Agnes lay on her back in tense, hopeful longing, not daring look at him. The air around them thickened with a thousand things unspoken.

Everything in her wanted to go to him. If he made one move to show he wanted her, she would be there in a second. But none came. Not knowing what else to do, she leaned over and snuffed out the candles on her nightstand.

Darkness engulfed them, almost suffocating in its palpable intensity.

A husky "Good night, Agnes" came out of the dark.

"Good night, Conrad."

Miserably, she turned on her side, away from him. She heard and felt him shifting too, on the other side of the bed.

So tantalizingly near. Yet so very far away.

CHAPTER TWENTY-SEVEN

The sound of fast hoofbeats made Laird Tavish MacDonnell remove the spy glass from his eye. He and his man-at-arms, Captain Donnel Corcoran, turned in unison from the rocky promontory where they were standing and looked down into the camp below.

A scout was riding in, his eyes scanning the mass of men for his commander. The captain gave a piercing whistle, attracting the scout's attention and waving the man up the hill towards them. The scout slipped from his saddle and ran the rest of the way up to join them on their vantage point. He took off his cap and stood before MacDonnell.

"Well?" his commander barked.

"They say she wed, me laird, just a few hours ago, in the castle chapel," the scout relayed.

"What?! Who?" MacDonnell hissed, his lips twisting in anger.

"The son of Evander Mackintosh, they say, me laird. The nephew of the great Laird Alec Mackintosh," the scout informed him, hesitantly speaking the name of his commander's bitterest enemy.

"Mackintosh." MacDonnell hissed the name as if it were a curse as he turned back to the panoramic view laid out before him and put the spyglass to his eye once more. In the distance, three miles away as the crow flew, he could see the towers and roofs of Castle Keppoch in surprising detail. His MacDonald bride was in there somewhere. "A pack of cheatin', snivellin' curs, the whole lot of them," he growled and spat on the ground.

Everyone knew how he had feuded for years with Alec Mackintosh over possession of valuable lands out at Glen Roy. Ever since losing the lands to Alec, he had hated the man and all his clan.

And now I hate this nephew of his, this Conrad. He has just tried to steal me rightful bride in some sham marriage ceremony, nae doubt intended tae make me give up me claim tae her hand. But Tavish MacDonnell daesnae give up so easily when his honor's been besmirched.

"'Tis Conrad she's gone and married then," Corcoran put in, confirming his own thoughts. "He has a reputation as a fearsome fighter, me laird. He'll nae be so easy tae kill if he thinks he's protectin' his wife's honour."

"He thinks himself a fearsome warrior, nae doubt. He's a dead man, that's what he is. This marriage ye speak of 'tis nae lawful. Agnes MacDonald was promised tae me. She belongs tae me. By marryin' her, Conrad Mackintosh has just signed his own death warrant. But it makes nay difference tae me. He'll be dead by sundown, and I'll be marryin' a pretty, young widow."

"But ye'll call off the attack now, eh, me laird? I mean, we havenae enough strength tae take on the MacDonalds and the Mackintoshes together," Corcoran pointed out.

MacDonnell lowered the spyglass and rounded on his captain, pinning him with hard grey eyes. "What's the matter, Corcoran, lost yer balls, have ye? Would ye like it better if we all gave up and went scurryin' home like cowardly dogs with our tails between our legs?"

"Nay, me laird, of course, I wouldn—"

"Then shut yer infernal hole. If I want yer opinion, I'll ask ye. Look around. D'ye see any Mackintosh troops hereabouts?"

"Nay, me laird."

"Nay, me laird. That's because they're all miles away. There's only MacDonald men defendin' the castle. Now is the perfect time tae strike."

"Aye, me laird," Corcoran acceded, sounding like he was going to the gallows.

"This is a momentous day, Corcoran. I've waited too long fer me rightful bride, but today she'll be mine at last. And when she's mine, the fun will begin. Once I wed his daughter, I'll have me revenge on old James MacDonald, on his worthless family, on his entire clan. Mayhap he thinks I've forgotten how he cheated me five years back, when I offered him an alliance on good terms in exchange fer the hand of his daughter. He leapt at the chance and he promised her tae me. And then," he clicked his fingers, "she was gone. And that mealy mouthed old swine had the gall tae tell me tae me face the agreement was off. All those lies about the lass bein' at death's door of some sudden mysterious illness and havin' tae go away tae France? I didnae believe a word. Well, Tavish MacDonnell is nae a man tae be trifled with. I never forget an insult. And I always pay them back. Aye, when Lady Agnes is Lady MacDonnell, the fun will really start. The old bastard will be clay in me hands then. He willnae want tae see his wee, delicate daughter hurt, will he?"

"Nae, me laird," Corcoran replied, his voice edged with doubt.

"Aye, so he'll dae exactly as I say, like a wee puppet."

"If ye can keep her, me laird. There's nay way both clans willnae come against us, whether she's dead or alive. And if ye kill their sons… We could be wiped out," Corcoran warned.

MacDonnell shook his head and gave a twisted, confident smile. "I dinnae think so, Corcoran. Her faither willnae risk it. He'll behave. Now listen, here are yer orders. Kill Duncan MacDonald and that Conrad Mackintosh. Kill him as well. As fer the lassie, find her and bring her tae me. And the bairn too. If I have the bairn, the lassie will dae anythin' I say."

He gave a little laugh before adding with relish, "So will they all, MacDonalds and Mackintoshes together, in the palm of me hand. Not that there'll be many of them left, eh?"

Without answering, Corcoran turned to the waiting scout and asked, "D'ye see any signs they're prepared fer an attack? Dae they ken we're here?"

The man shook his head. "'Tis hard tae say, Sir. There's nay obvious signs of steppin' up security, but 'tis always possible they've heard of our presence and are daein' it on the sly."

"Aye," Corcoran conformed with a nod.

"I can see well enough with this," MacDonnell said, brandishing the spyglass. "They have nae idea we're here."

"But we cannae be certain of that, me laird. Which means, the advantage of surprise may be gone. They could have a force approachin' our camp right now fer all we ken. An attack is ill-advised, me laird. We could very well lose," Corcoran said bluntly.

MacDonnell laughed and clapped his second on the shoulder. "Wheesht, man! None of yer defeatist talk now. If we lose, we die. 'Tis up tae ye tae make sure we win. Ye have yer orders. Now away and prepare the men. I want them ready the moment I give the order tae march."

When Agnes awoke, Conrad was gone. In a way, it was a relief. She got out of bed, put on her robe, and went straight next door to see Roisin. To her surprise, the room was empty, Roisin's bed rumpled.

"Roisin? Saoirse?" she called, checking the anteroom to see if they were there. But it was empty too. "She must be with Saoirse," she told herself, feeling the first flutterings of anxiety. She paced while she waited for them to return. A few minutes later, the door opened, and Saoirse came in, holding a breakfast tray in her arms.

She smiled as soon as she saw Agnes. "Good mornin', me lady. Have ye come fer breakfast?"

Agnes peered around her, expecting Roisin to skip across the threshold. But she did not. She saw Saoirse's smile change to puzzlement as she looked around the room.

"Where's Roisin?" they both said at exactly the same moment.

"I thought she was with ye," Agnes said, the flutterings of fear in Agnes' chest becoming the urgent flapping of wings.

"I sent her tae yer chambers, me lady, while I went tae fetch breakfast," Saoirse said, hurriedly putting down the tray on the console table, the color draining from her face.

"I've nae seen her. I just woke up," Agnes told her.

"Ach, maybe she didnae wantae wake ye. I expect she's gone tae play or she's hidin' somewhere. Ye ken how she likes tae dae that. She cannae be far away, it was only a few moments ago," the maid replied, her confident tone edged with doubt.

They spent the next quarter of an hour turning the nursery upside down, to no avail. They moved into the hallway, scouring every closet, every cupboard and alcove, behind every tapestry. Nothing. Agnes was growing increasingly agitated as they thoroughly searched Agnes and Conrad's chambers, under the bed, inside the wardrobe and the blanket box, until there was no place left to look.

"Saoirse, we need help. I'll get dressed and go and fetch Conrad. Ye keep lookin' up here. Get the servants to search as well. She must be around here somewhere," Agnes told the maid before rushing to dress. Not bothering with stockings, not even stopping to comb her hair, she pulled on a simple gown and ran barefoot downstairs, telling each servant she met to go and help Saoirse look for Roisin and asking them if they had seen Conrad. None had. Thinking he might be having breakfast in the great hall, she picked up her skirts and raced down the main hallway. She burst through the doors, and straight into her husband's arms.

"Conrad, 'tis Roisin, she's disappeared, we cannae find her anywhere," she panted, collapsing against him. Duncan came up behind him.

Conrad did not ask questions. "All right, simmer down now. She'll nae have gone far. We'll find her, dinnae fret," he assured her calmly, taking charge of the situation.

"What's happenin'?" Duncan asked, clearly disturbed to see his sister so frantic.

"The wee yin, she's wandered off somewhere, and they cannae find her," Conrad told him. Then he asked Agnes where she and Saoirse had already searched. While she explained, Duncan ran to tell their parents. Within minutes, Conrad had organized the servants into pairs and sent them off to search the various sections of the castle. Within a few more, the whole family and all their retainers were hunting for the child.

"Go and help yer maither look fer her. I'll go and see if she's in the garden," he told her.

Conrad ran into the main courtyard and stopped, looking around for this daughter, but there was no sign of her. He questioned the guards. None had seen her either, but they quickly joined the search. With his heart threatening to burst out of his chest with fear, Conrad wracked his brains to think where Rosin could have gone. When it suddenly came to him, he kicked himself for not thinking of it sooner.

When he entered the stables and heard her little voice, he almost sank to his knees to offer up a prayer of thanks there and then. There she was in front of Davey's stall, the tiny blonde sprite he would die for, in her dressing gown and slippers, chattering away to the horse as she fed him apple pieces off the flat of her hand, just as he had taught her. He could have cried with relief.

He pulled himself together and gave a little cough, so as not to startle her. "There ye are, Little Flower," he said, going up to her with a big smile. "Ye ken yer Ma's been lookin' fer ye. Ye've given her a bit of scare."

"Hello, Conrad." She beamed at him, then frowned. "Och, Mama was asleep, so I came tae see Davey and give him some apple," she explained with heart-breaking earnestness.

"I think he's had enough fer the time bein'," he told her, holding out his arms to her. "If he eats too much, he'll get too fat fer me tae ride, eh?"

Giggling, she reached up to him to be picked up, nestling into his arms happily. He let her say goodbye to Davey before carrying her swiftly indoors.

"Roisin!" Agnes cried when she saw them, running to them and taking Roisin from him to hug and kiss her frantically, as if to reassure herself she was real. The family gathered around, all thankful to see Roisin safe.

"Och, thank ye fer findin' her and bringin' her back safe, Conrad," Agnes said to him above the hubbub, over Roisin's shining blonde head. Her lovely hazel eyes were shining with heartfelt gratitude and relief, and her smile was so dazzling, Conrad's heart jumped in his chest.

Later that evening, after putting Roisin safely to be, they went to their chambers. He was surprised when Agnes collapsed into a chair and rubbed her temples. A small sob escaped her lips. "I'm so glad we were together when she was missin'," she said in a strained voice. "I dinnae think I could have borne it without ye at me side."

"Hey, now, have a wee cry, go on, it'll dae ye good," he told her gently, going over and squatting by her chair, putting an arm about her shoulders for comfort. He was deeply moved by her admission that she needed him. It felt good. "She's safe and sound now, dinnae fret."

It was then that he began to question how much longer he could continue being angry with the woman he had loved for as long as he could remember.

CHAPTER TWENTY-EIGHT

*A*gnes' clothes were dripping.

What was supposed to be a normal bath turned into pure chaos, because Roisin was in a mood and had decided she didn't want to get in the tub. Yet, Agnes couldn't get angry with her. It was the best thing to see her daughter so joyous while they were "wrestling" to get her inside even if it ended with Agnes inside the tub too with her gown on.

She walked into her bedroom where Conrad sat perched near the fireplace, yet she could still fill the chill in the air.

"A fire in August. That's the Highlands fer ye right there," Agnes said as she kicked off her shoes and fumbled clumsily behind herself with fingers, trying to undo the fastenings of her wet gown.

"What happened? Is it pouring outside?" Conrad asked as he took her in slowly, causing a crimson blush on Agnes' cheeks.

"Roisin happened. She's a little devil, is what she is," she answered still battling the fastenings but to no avail. "Ach, I'm sorry, Conrad, I cannae undae me dress and I am getting very cold. Will ye help me, please?"

"Aye, all right, hang on," he replied, putting a few more logs on the fair so that the flames blazed up. Satisfied, he stood up and pulled off his leather vest, heated from the blazes. "I shall order a bath fer ye tae warm up after I've helped ye."

He went out into the corridor, stopped a maid and asked her to bring a tub and hot water fer his wife. Then, he returned and with his trews clinging to his powerful legs, he went over to her. Agnes tried not to stare as he approached. She turned her back, as much to hide the warmth in her cheeks as to give him access to the fastenings.

When he began working on the fiddly fastenings, the chill on her skin soon began to dissipate under his touch, and she found herself holding her breath.

"Nay wonder ye couldnae dae this by yersel', these buttons are tiny, and there are so many of them!" he exclaimed softly, making Agnes' skin tingle as his fingers accidentally brushed her neck. She shifted uncomfortably, for the heat coming off his body seemed to burn through her wet clothing.

For the Lord's sake, hurry up! I'm nae sure how much more of this I can stand!

Gradually, the back of her dress loosened. She let out a silent exhale of relief, imagining the torment was almost over. She was wrong.

"So, Roisin didnae want tae take a bath?" he asked, but the change of subject didn't dissipate the tension in the air.

"Aye. Sometimes she daes that and I always end up in the water with her. Next time I'll send ye tae help Saoirse."

"I wouldnae mind that at all," Conrad said and brushed her skin again. "Nearly done," he murmured, his warm breath tickling her skin and playing havoc with her senses. "That's all the buttons. Let me help ye," he added, offering her his arm to lean on as she stepped out of her dress and damp petticoats.

"Thank ye, I can manage from here," she murmured, now clad only in her shift. It was damp, too, so it clung to her shape. She blushed furiously, feeling she might as well be naked as his gaze moved slowly over her form. When his eyes finally met hers, the heat she saw in them turned her insides to water.

"I dinnae think so," he replied, his voice low and husky. "What about yer stays? I'd best undae them fer ye as well whilst I'm here, eh?"

Her heart pounding in her ears, Agnes looked away.

If I refuse, he'll maybe guess how he's affectin' me.

"Er, aye, all right, thank ye," she managed to say, holding her breath again. With every touch of his hands at the back of her waist, she trembled.

"I enjoyed our time together," he said as he worked on the laces. "It is good… bein' like a family."

"I'm glad. Roisin is certainly enjoying it too," Agnes replied, feeling the usual tension rising between them again.

Or is it just me? Ach, hurry up, please!

"Roisin's a lot of fun tae be with," he went on, showing no signs of hurrying to complete his task.

"Aye, she is. It is more fun fer her with ye there," she admitted. "I'm sure she gets a wee bit bored just bein' with me."

She turned her head around slightly to glance at him, and froze again to see the intense expression on his face.

A spear of desire stabbed at her. "Aye ye done yet?" she asked, desperate to move away from him, even more fearful of making a fool of herself now that they seemed to be on friendlier terms.

"Nay, there's a knot, and the rain has gotten intae the strings and made it fiddly tae undae. Be patient a while longer," he replied.

Agnes frowned.

"I'm certain she daesnae get bored with ye at all. I'm a novelty at the moment, 'tis all," he went on, seemingly no nearer to undoing her laces.

Despite the tense atmosphere, his humility made Agnes chuckle. "I think ye're much more than that. Ye underestimate how good ye are with her, Conrad. She thinks the world of ye, and it fair warms me heart tae see ye playin' together," she told him in a burst of honesty.

"Aye, 'tis strange, but I felt a special bond with her from the first time I saw her. Like somethin' inside me knew she was mine."

"Oh?"

"I had nae thought of bein' a faither. But now I am, I like it. A lot. There ye are, ye're free at last."

Agnes breathed out, relieved. "Thank ye again," she replied, shimmying out of her stays on her way to the wardrobe, where she grabbed a robe and slipped it on, belting it tightly around her waist. Feeling less vulnerable now, she turned to smile at Conrad, to find him watching her with the same disturbing intensity as before.

"Well, I dinnae have much experience of what a good faither is like, but ye make Roisin happy, and that's what counts with me. I think ye're a natural," she said, confused by his behaviour. Being nice when Roisin was a round was one thing. This was quite another. She sought distraction by fetching a clean towel from the washstand before taking refuge in an armchair and starting to dry her dripping hair.

"D'ye really think so?" he asked, standing before her, running wet fingers through his hair. It stuck up in adorable golden spikes.

"I'm nae blind. She smiled and laughed all day long with ye fer the past days," Agnes said, her fingers itching to stroke his unruly hair.

"I seem tae recall ye laughin' and smilin' a lot as well," he said, coming to sit in the chair opposite her.

"Aye, I did."

What's he getting' at?

His bright blue eyes fixed on her unnervingly. "So did I."

She nodded a little hesitantly. "Aye, I believe ye did."

"So, it seems like we all had a nice time. Our wee family."

It was the second time he had described them as a family, she noticed, on guard for one of his barbed remarks. "Aye, we are a family now, in the eyes of the world," she ventured a little nervously.

"It isnae just Roisin I enjoyed bein' with. It is ye as well, Agnes."

Agnes felt as though a hand had reached into her chest and was squeezing her heart. Afraid to speak, she could only look at Conrad mutely.

"I ken what I said before, that I'd never forgive ye fer keepin' Roisin from me and lettin' everyone think her a bastard," he went on, his gaze holding hers. "But this time with ye both has shown me that I cannae just keep on livin' this way and denyin' that... that I care about ye."

Agnes had no idea where the tears that sprang into her eyes came from. She struggled to hold them back, so overwhelmed with emotion, it hurt to breathe.

"D-d'ye mean it, Conrad?" she whispered, searching his eyes with her own for any signs he was toying with her. She saw only sincerity.

"I wouldnae say it if I didnae mean it, now, would I?" he replied. "Nae after what we've been through."

What we've been through? We? Nae what I've put him through?

It took her a few moments to be able to speak without bawling her eyes out. "I didnae expect ye tae say anythin' like that, Conrad," she admitted.

"Aye, I surprised mesel'. But that's how it is with me, like it or nae," he replied with a shrug of finality, as if he expected her to argue with him.

Scared he might change his mind, Agnes moved forward in her seat. "I dae like it. I like it very much, Conrad."

A tentative smiled curved his lips. "Ye dae?"

Agnes looked at him almost with disbelief, amazed that he could not see her love for him shining from every pore of her.

Me heart burns fer ye day and night, and ye ask me if I care for ye?

She hoped he was trying to tell her he had forgiven her. Yet she was still cautious.

"Aye. Ye're Roisin's faither. Of course, I care about ye."

"I wasnae takin' about that, Agnes. I was talkin' about me and ye. I care about ye... still."

She saw in his eyes that he was referring to the feelings they had shared on that fateful night they had spent together, a night full of confessions.

"I've never told ye this before, Agnes, because I wasnae sure what ye felt about me... but I've always cared fer ye."

"I have a secret as well... I've always cared fer ye too, Conrad."

Following her heart, she threw caution to the winds. "I care about ye too, Conrad... still."

CHAPTER TWENTY-NINE

*J*ust then, there was a knock on the door, and several girls proceeded to carry in a tub and fill it with buckets of steaming water. As soon as they were done, they curtsied and left, closing the door behind them.

"Get in and warm up," Conrad said, his eyes ablaze, watching her every move.

She approached the bath, sliding out of her robe. "'Tis very thoughtful of ye tae let me go first, Conrad."

He swallowed hard as she lifted the hem of her shift, flashing a lot of smooth white flesh as she stepped into the water. Not that the flimsy garment hid much. If anything, the way it clung to her curves only added to the mysteries of what he knew lay beneath.

Och, and there goes the shift... on the floor... she's kens what she's daein' tae me, he thought, watching enthralled as the curvaceous mermaid that was his wife slid naked beneath the waters with a sigh of contentment, her breasts bobbing all pink and white like dumplings in a stewpot.

"Och, 'tis bliss," she murmured, catching his eye and smiling at him enticingly through the wisps of steam. His manhood stirred in its nest as his excitement ratcheted up in line with the tension in the air, certain now that she wanted him too.

I'll nae leave her wantin', he vowed silently, smiling back at her and asking, "Would ye like some wine while ye're in the tub, Agnes?" he asked, sauntering over to the sideboard to fetch it.

"That would be heavenly," she replied, stretching her legs out and resting them, ankles crossed, on the end of the tub. Steam rose off her long, shapely legs, distracting Conrad so much, he almost spilled the wine as he poured it into goblets for them.

"There ye are." He handed one to her, drinking in her naked form along with the wine as she reclined lazily, the water lapping at her body as he would very much have liked to do himself. Long twisting snakes of dark hair floated tantalizingly around her, teasing, tempting him as they shifted, offering glimpses of her soft curves.

He moved closer, until he was standing right over her. She eyed the noticeable bulge in his trews, which magically grew bigger.

"Could ye help me wash me hair? But before ye dae, I think ye should take that off." She gestured with her eyes at his shirt. "It might get wet."

"That old thing," he said, ripping it off and tossing it aside carelessly.

"And yer trews. Here, I'll help ye." She sat up, water sloshing, breasts bobbing, and leaned over to undo the fastenings at his hips. The hungry fascination in her eyes as she slid them down his muscular thighs and his almighty erection, solid as a club, leapt free in front of her eyes sent his libido soaring.

"I want ye so badly," he whispered, and suddenly she reached up and pulled him into tub with her, with an enormous splash that sent water flying everywhere. They thrashed around for a few moments like a deranged four-legged animal, giggling as they righted themselves.

Finally, they sat facing each other, legs entwined, lip to lip, their kisses soft and teasing, hands everywhere.

"Now, stay still, lass, fer I have a mind tae help ye bathe," Conrad murmured happily, selecting a washcloth and a small pot of soft soap from the nearby washstand. "'Tis a husband's duty tae tend tae his wife's needs after all. And I wouldnae want tae fall short."

"Honestly, I dinnae see any danger of that happenin'," Agnes said, her fingers teasing his bobbing erection, eliciting a low chuckle.

"Now, lean back," he instructed, his eyes hungry as they raked over her. She obeyed, shivering with anticipation as he deliberately soaked the cloth and lathered it before gently starting to wash her neck and shoulders, grazing the tips of her breasts from time to time. She hissed with pleasure as they hardened, thrusting them at him. But he would not be tempted, it seemed.

Instead, he continued to lather the cloth, next carefully lifting her arms and washing them, then her armpits and her hands.

"Stand up," he told her, and she thought she would melt into the water, she was so aroused. With wobbly legs, she obeyed, the water sliding from her skin. "Turn around." Her heart in her throat, she did as she was told. She felt him stand up behind her, humming a little tune, lathering the cloth once more. With minute attention, he washed her back, then the cloth crept down to her waist, Conrad reaching around her to slowly wash her belly, then her hips, turning her into a quivering, panting jelly.

"Conrad," she moaned, "are ye trying tae drive me mad?"

He chuckled. "Maybe just a little," he confessed, lathering the cloth once more and washing her behind, then her thighs and legs. "Just the way ye have been driving me mad fer days." When she felt his fingers on her inner thighs, prising them gently apart, she eagerly succumbed, feeling she would swoon any moment. He lifted one of her thighs and placed her foot on the edge of the tub, and when the cloth found the now molten flesh between her legs, parting the folds, rubbing across her rosebud, she almost overbalanced, but he held her there with one strong hand on her waist.

She heard the cloth fall into the water, and moments later it was replaced by his fingers. Slippery with soap, they methodically explored every tiny part of her secret places, stroking, teasing her rosebud until she could think of nothing else but her burning need to have him fill her. His soapy fingers slipped inside her, and she gasped aloud, desperate to have him, pushing herself wantonly against his hand. As if sensing her need, he added another finger, thrusting them in and out of her in a gentle rhythm that was intoxicating.

She was dripping wet now, urgently pushing against his thrusts. The same rising wave of intense pleasure was building at her core, and she leaned back against him, giving his one hand free reign to tease and caress her breasts, while the other strummed her rosebud and dove into her.

Driven to distraction by his touch, Agnes moaned and reached behind her, grasping his manhood firmly, her hunger further stoked by his groans of pleasure. Slowly, with Conrad lifting her easily, she guided him to her soap-slick, soaking entrance, then pushed backwards, hearing his gasps of pleasure through her own moans as his entire length pierced her to the hilt.

Locked together, Conrad's mighty arms wrapped tightly around her as if he would never let her go, thrilling her with his strength and power. His hands took possession of her, squeezing and fondling her breasts, toying with her rosebud, fingers sinking into the soft flesh of her behind as they began to move against each other in a slow, sensual rhythm. To feel him filling her again and again gave her a deep sense of satisfaction.

When he grunted low in his throat, and his thrusts grew harder and faster, she felt herself going over the edge, with him soon to follow.

"Ah, Conrad! What ye dae tae me! I love ye, I've always loved ye," she moaned, shuddering against him as her took her to the heights, and kept her teetering there for a few blissful moments, his grip on her tightening.

"I love ye too, Agnes, always have. Ye broke me heart when ye left, I felt like I couldnae go on livin' without ye. Ye're mine, ye belong tae me alone, and naebody else can ever have ye," he ground out in a husky groan against her neck, his hand strumming her frantically, so that she came again just as he climaxed inside her with an almighty final thrust of his hips, his hot juices filling her, then mingling with her own.

After a while, they slowly recovered their breath and turned to embrace each other, breast to breast, covered in soap still as their kisses lingered.

"This water's getting a wee bit chilly," Conrad said at last, scooping her up in his arms and stepping out of the tub. They dried each other, then he carried her to the bed, where they got under the covers and snuggled together, laughing like children as they kissed each other and held each other as close as they possibly could.

Agnes had never felt such a deep sense of peaceful contentment as she did then, lying in his arms. Gradually, they fell asleep holding each other tight.

CHAPTER THIRTY

The following afternoon was fine and sunny.

"'Tis a good chance tae continue yer archery practice," Conrad said over an early luncheon.

"Aye, all right, that'll be fun," Agnes agreed with enthusiasm, excited by the idea of getting close to him again under any pretext. "But what about Roisin?"

"She can come too. It'll dae her good tae get out in the sun and fresh air."

And so it was that a short time later, the little family made their way out into the gardens and wandered by a circuitous route in the direction of the archery butts. Roisin preferred riding on Conrad's shoulders to walking, and it once again moved Agnes deeply to see the child so radiant with happiness with him and know he would always keep her safe. His carefree laughter as he amused their daughter also delighted her.

They soon came across Lady Fiona and her faithful lady's maid Jane sitting on a blanket on the lawn. The pair were well supplied with tea and a plate piled high with raisin cakes. They appeared to be thoroughly enjoying the balmy weather as they gossiped and worked on their embroidery. Duncan was reclining on the grass next to them, looking sweaty and ruffled, obviously fresh from training.

The two parties greeted each other warmly.

"Where are ye off tae?" Lady Fiona asked, smiling at the trio warmly.

"Conrad's gonnae give me a shootin' lesson," Agnes explained, and they chatted for a few minutes until Roisin's excited shouts drew their attention.

The little girl was excitedly urging her "horsey" to gallop around the lawn, and Conrad was laughing as he enthusiastically obliged. Their laughter was infectious, with Agnes, Lady Fiona and Jane joining in. Duncan laughed too, but when Agnes happened to glance at her brother, she felt a small fission of fear. His laughter did not seem to reach his eyes, which were firmly fixed on his friend and niece as they played. Agnes was sure she saw a flash of suspicion in them, which gave her a very bad feeling.

There had been several occasions recently when she and Conrad had been worried that Duncan was on the verge of realizing Conrad was Roisin's father. This was yet another of them.

"We should go if I'm tae get some practice in, Conrad," Agnes called to him, feeling deeply uneasy and thinking it would be best to leave as quickly as possible.

"Aye, all right," he agreed, slowing down his galloping, much to Roisin's dismay, so that they came to rest next to Agnes.

"Can I stay here?" Roisin asked, to Agnes's surprise.

"D'ye nae wantae come and see me shoot some arrows then?" she asked the child, conscious of her brother's intense gaze upon Conrad as he stood with Roisin on his shoulders. Conrad showed no sign of noticing Duncan's piercing looks, but Agnes knew that did not mean he had not.

"Um, I'd rather stay here and have cake," Roisin admitted, pointing at the raisin cakes.

The women tittered. "Of course ye can stay, sweetheart, and ye can have as many cakes as ye like," Lady Fiona promised indulgently.

"All right, ye can stay, but nae too many cakes or ye'll be sick," Agnes warned, taking Conrad's arm and flashing him a warning glance. He clearly understood something was amiss and joined her in making quick farewells before leaving for the archery butts.

"What is it?" he asked as soon as they were out of earshot.

"Duncan. Did ye nae see his face? He was watching ye and Roisin like a hawk the whole time. Och, Lord, I'm scared, Conrad. I'm sure he's close tae working out the truth."

"Ye should have let me tell him, Agnes. He's gonnae be furious that we've kept it from him. Trouble's brewin', I can feel it."

Agnes silently agreed. But despite their fears, neither of them was prepared for what was about to happen.

They had just reached the archery butts when they heard a

shout behind them. They turned in unison, to see Duncan striding towards them across the grass.

"Are ye followin' us, man'?" Conrad asked light-heartedly as Duncan came to halt in front of them. The dark look on her brother's face told Agnes the humour was misjudged. She began to tremble.

"I have a question fer ye two," Duncan said brusquely, looking between them, hands on hip.

Conrad shrugged. "All right, go ahead."

"And I want the truth," Duncan said warningly. "I want tae ken if ye were taegether years ago. Five years ago tae be exact."

Agnes blood ran cold. "Now, Braither, what d'ye—" she began, intending to deny it and pretend indignation. But he cut her off abruptly.

"There's somethin' off about all of this. The timeline daesnae make sense," he said, his tone hard. "I've been watchin' ye with the wee yin, Conrad, and I reckon ye and Agnes are hidin' somethin'. Now, are ye gonnae come clean? Or am I gonnae havetae force it out of ye?"

"What are ye talkin' about, man?" Conrad asked affecting puzzlement.

"The way ye've both been actin' is strange. Conrad, anyone lookin' at ye would think Roisin's yer own bairn. And she looks just like ye as well. 'Tis too much of a coincidence."

A tense silence fell between them, punctuated only by Duncan's harsh breathing as he stared at them piercingly in turn. Agnes stood rooted to the spot, hardly able to breathe, so afraid she could not even speak to deny it. And it appeared that Conrad was equally dumbstruck.

"Ach, ye dinnae havetae say a word. I can see from yer faces that I've hit on the truth," Duncan spat in disgust, his face contorting with fury.

"Duncan, ye dinnae understand—" Conrad began.

Duncan's rounded on him with terrifying speed, his voice like gravel as he said accusingly, "Ye bastard, Mackintosh! Tae think I trusted ye all these years, never dreamin' ye could dae somethin' so cold as tae go behind me back like that and ruin me sister. I counted ye as me braither!"

Agnes had never seen him so angry and feared he would have some sort of attack. "It wasnae like that, Duncan, if ye'll let us—" she tried to interject.

But Duncan ignored her and continued railing at Conrad, his eyes wild. "Yer friendship's worth naethin', Mackintosh. Ye ruined me sister! She's been living away, hidden in a secret fer years and fer what? Because ye couldnae hold it in yer pants?! Duncan screamed and pushed Conrad in the chest. "Ye've lost a friend and gained an enemy fer life, ye lyin' dog. And I promise ye, ye'll nae live long after this!" His weapon sang as he unsheathed it.

Agnes' terror for both of them soared to fever pitch. "Nay, Duncan, nay! Put yer sword away, fer God's sake, dinnae dae anythin' rash, I beg ye," she cried frantically.

Duncan acted as if she were not there, focusing his fury solely on Conrad. "Now, ye're gonnae answer fer yer lies. If ye have any honor left in ye, then draw yer blade and fight me like a man!" he taunted his former friend, brandishing his sword in both fists menacingly at Conrad.

"Stop it, Duncan!" Agnes cried in distress, trying to get between them to shield Conrad. "Ye cannae just blame Conrad. The fault was mine as well."

"Leave, Sister. This is between him and me," Duncan snarled.

"Come out of the way, Agnes, let me deal with this," Conrad commanded, taking her by the upper arms and moving her like a gaming piece behind him, out of harm's way. Her struggles and protests fell on deaf ears as he thwarted her attempts to reach Duncan by standing in front of her.

"I'll nae fight ye, Duncan," he said, holding his palms out placatingly. "I ken I deserve yer anger. I'm sorry fer keepin' the truth from ye all this time. I hated mesel' fer it, but I didnae wantae harm Agnes' reputation or loose yer friendship. Me and Agnes, it was a mistake. It shouldnae have happened."

Despite her distraught state, his words twisted like a knife in Agnes' gut.

"Ye're dead right, it shouldnae. And dinnae try tae tell me ye care about me sister's reputation when ye were the one that ruined it, ye treacherous bastard. What ye did is unforgiveable. Ye're dead tae me, Mackintosh. I'm gonnae kill ye fer this!"

That was too much for Agnes. Using all her might, she pushed past Conrad and confronted Duncan. "He's me husband, Duncan, and he's Roisin's faither. I'll nae let ye hurt him!" she cried fiercely, disregarding the lethal point of his sword swinging inches away from her chest and the hands on her shoulders pulling her backwards.

Then she felt strong hands on her again.

"Agnes, fer God's sake, get behind me!" she heard Conrad roaring at her, attempting to get in front of her again. She struggled to shake him off, but his grip was too strong. Tears of fear and frustration streamed down her face as he forcibly dragged her back and pushed her behind him again before turning back to Duncan.

"Dinnae try tae defend him, Agnes. He's the one that ruined ye, and he's been lyin' tae me all these years. If I'd kent the truth, I'd never have let him near ye, let alone wed ye. He's a bloody disgrace, and he deserves tae die. Now, either leave or stay back out of the way. This is between me and him, and I've nay wish tae hurt ye," Duncan growled, his blazing eyes never leaving Conrad.

"He's right. I'm responsible, Duncan, and I'm sorry fer lyin' tae ye but I had feelings fer her fer so long," Conrad argued, his brow furrowed with anguish but clearly trying to remain as calm as he could. "Ye have every right tae be angry. But even so, whatever ye might think of me, I love ye like me braither, and I'll nae fight ye."

"All right ye coward, if ye willnae draw yer blade then I'll kill ye with me bare hands," Duncan spat, hurling his sword to the ground and rolling up his sleeves.

"I told ye, I'll nae fight ye," Conrad repeated, folding his arms.

"Then I'll kill ye anyway, and ye'll die like the coward ye are!"

Agnes screamed as Duncan swung at Conrad, landing a cracking blow to his chin that sent him stumbling back a few paces. He righted himself but did nothing to fend off the repeated vicious blows Duncan rained on him, dodging them where he could and making not a sound when they connected.

Horrified to see Conrad's face being battered and blood flying from his lips as his head snapped to and from beneath the blows, Agnes sobbed uncontrollably and screamed out, "Stop, Duncan, stop!" But her pleas went unheard and the one-sided fight continued.

"Stay out of this, Agnes," Conrad said between her brother's blows.

Conrad continued trying to evade as much of Duncan's onslaught as he could, but Duncan was just as much of a hardened fighter as he was, and his fury made him relentless. Seeing Conrad dazed, swaying on his feet, his face swollen and bloodied from the repeated blows was too much for Agnes. "Fer God's sake, defend yersel', Conrad, before he kills ye!" she urged him.

"Aye, come on, ye gutless bastard, defend yersel'. It was because of ye she got sent away. Fight back before I finish ye off!" Duncan roared, his face red and sweating, the veins in his neck writhing like ropes. His next blow connected with Conrad's cheek and almost toppled him, wringing another scream of anguish from Agnes.

But then, Duncan's swinging fist landed on Conrad's temple. Conrad's eyes rolled back in his head, and he fell unconscious to the ground. Agnes rushed to him, while Duncan stood over him, panting raggedly.

"Look what ye've done!" Agnes shouted up at him from the ground, where she was cradling Conrad's battered head in her lap, tears pouring from her eyes. Panicking that Conrad might die in her arms, she struggled to lift the dead weight of her husband. "I need tae get him tae the healer now. Help me, fer God's sake, Duncan. Dinnae let him die!" she begged.

Breathing harshly, Duncan wiped the sweat from his eyes with his sleeve and stared coldly down at his former friend, making no move to help her.

"If he dies, I'll never forgive ye. Ye'll never see me nor Roisin again, I swear it!" she screamed at him in desperation, struggling in vain to lift Conrad alone.

Perhaps it was the naked panic her brother saw in her or shock at what he had done to his friend that made him relent. "All right. Get out of the way. I'll carry him tae the infirmary," he growled. He shoved her aside and stooped down to pick Conrad up, slinging his insensible form roughly over his shoulder. He stalked off back to the castle, leaving Agnes to run behind him, barely able to control the terror gripping her heart in its icy fingers.

A short while later, a devastated Agnes sniffed back tears as she perched tensely on the edge of a chair in the infirmary. Silently, she urged Una the healer, to hurry and finish examining Conrad, needing to know if she was to be a widow and if Roisin was to lose the father she had so recently gained.

In another chair a few feet away sat Duncan. Agnes glanced at him occasionally to see him leaning forward, head down, his hands clasped between his knees. She realized that despite his anger over their "betrayal," he was worried for him.

Conrad was lying prostrate on the bed, and when Una straightened up from examining him, Agnes noticed Duncan's head snapped up to look at her as well. "That's quite some fight he was in," she remarked.

"Is he gonnae be all right?" Agnes blurted out in a sob. She sprang up and approached the bed, looking down on Conrad's swollen face. She could hardly recognize him.

"I wish I could tell ye either way," Una replied, her pale blue eyes meeting Agnes' across Conrad's motionless body. "At this stage, it all depends on whether he wakes up or nae. He's taken quite a beatin' in the head. I'll be able tae see more when I've cleaned him up a bit. But I think 'tis likely he has a concussion, which can be very dangerous."

Agnes let out an agonized sob. Taking hold of Conrad's hand, she raised it to her lips and kissed it tenderly, holding it to her cheek. "Please wake up, Conrad, please!" she begged under her breath "I love ye so much, I cannae be without ye. Come back tae me, please."

I've ruined everything. Me family, Conrad's friendship with Duncan, Roisin's future, and any chance I might have had fer happiness.

Agnes sobbed, pressing Conrad's hand to her cheek once more and sending up a silent prayer for him to open his eyes.

Una went to prepare what she needed, while Agnes remained with Conrad. Duncan appeared at her side. His face was grave, his eyes fixed on his former friend.

"Why did ye nae tell me he was Roisin's faither, Agnes? Why did ye lie tae me, the both of ye?" he asked in a low voice, clearly conscious of Una within earshot.

Agnes let out a small, bitter sob. "Because I kent this was exactly how ye'd act, and I had tae protect him. I'm beggin' ye, Duncan, please dinnae tell Faither and Maither he's Roisin's faither. Ye ken what'll happen if ye dae."

He remained silent for a while, leaving her tenterhooks. Eventually, however, he murmured, "I'll nae tell a soul."

Relief flooded through her. "Thank ye. I ken they'll havetae learn the truth sometime, but Conrad and I will work that out together. If he wakes up that is," she added, biting her lip to keep the tears at bay as she looked down at her love lying helpless on the bed.

Duncan looked on with anger but also guilt shadowing his face.

Finally, after a long silence he turned to Agnes and, squeezing her shoulder before crossing to the door and letting himself out, he said "I'll leave ye now, but tell me as soon as he wakes up."

When he had gone, Agnes welcomed the distraction of assisting Una as best she could while the healer gently cleaned away the gore from Conrad's face."

When it was done, she asked, "Can I stay with him?"

"Of course," Una said with a nod. "Stay as long as ye like."

CHAPTER THIRTY-ONE

While Una quietly went about her business, Agnes pulled a chair up to the bed and sat with Conrad, holding his hand and whispering endearments to him. There she remained as the evening came, night fell, and the hours passed like an eternity, with no sign of Conrad waking up.

Eventually, Una went into the adjoining room to rest. "But call me if he wakes," she told Agnes before shutting the door behind her.

Agnes leaned across Conrad, clutching his hand tightly in hers, never taking her eyes from his face. In the darkest hours just before dawn, unable to keep her eyes open any longer, she fell into a doze, her face pressed to the coverlet.

A small sound jerked her awake, and she started up, to see Conrad looking at her out of his two swollen eyelids.

Her heart leapt in her breast. "Och, ye're awake at last, thank God!" she cried, jumping up, wringing his hand, almost hysterical with joy and relief.

"Where am I?" he mumbled through cut, swollen lips, stiffly turning his neck to look at his surroundings. "What happened?"

"In the infirmary," she told him. "Duncan knocked ye out, but then he helped me bring ye here."

"He helped ye?" he croaked, grimacing as his brows shot up in surprise.

"Aye. He's worried about ye as well."

"What? Even after tryin' tae beat me tae death?"

"Aye, I ken, 'tis hard tae believe, but 'tis the truth. Och, Conrad, ye dinnae how happy I am ye've woken up. I was so worried fer ye," she gushed, curbing the urge to hug and kiss him with all her might, lest she hurt him.

He complained his throat was dry, so she helped him to drink some water, much of which spilled down his front because of his swollen lips and sore mouth. Once he had drunk his fill, he looked at her soulfully through slitted eyelids and squeezed her hand. "I'm sorry fer all the trouble I've caused ye, Agnes, truly, I am. Everythin' that's happened, 'tis all me fault."

"Nay, nay, dinnae say that. 'Tis nae true," she chided gently, knowing she was to blame.

"I should have had the sense tae confide in Duncan as soon as I found out I was Roisin's faither and taken the consequences. He was right. I was cowardly."

"Haud yer wheesht now," she said, pressing his hand to her cheek once more, wanting to soothe him. "Nay more of that nonsense. Ye're nae a coward, Conrad. Left tae yer own devices, ye would have told him. Ye only kept it from him because I begged ye tae, and ye respected me wishes."

"Agnes?"

"Aye?"

"I want tae kiss ye."

A wave of intense love for him crashed over her, and a smile came unbidden to her lips. "I wantae kiss ye too, but yer lips are all cut and swollen. It'll hurt ye."

But his hand came up and cupped the back of her head, pulling her inexorably towards him. "I dinnae care about that. I'm gonnae kiss ye anyway," he murmured thickly.

Her heart fluttered like a mad thing as, very gingerly, their lips met in a sweet kiss before Una interrupted them just a few second later.

Agnes was so mesmerized by the tingling sensation on her lips, that she didn't even hear the conversation between the healer and Conrad, who was now swallowing a painkilling concoction Una had prepared for him before discharging himself from her care. "'Tis a beatin', nae a mortal wound, fer God's sake," he insisted, striding about the infirmary, boots on, strapping on his sword belt.

"Very well, but remember, ye could have a concussion," Una warned gently, echoing Agnes' own concerns. "Any dizziness or nausea?"

"Nay. Just a bit of a headache," Conrad replied with classic understatement. Agnes suspected he was playing down his symptoms in his desire to get out of there. Una proceeded to ask a series of simple questions designed to test Conrad's mental powers. He answered them all clearly and concisely.

Una nodded. "Ye're nae showin' any signs of confusion or memory loss," she said. "Mayhap ye have a thick skull and ye've been lucky tae get away with naethin' more serious," she added with a smile.

Agnes breathed a sigh of relief at the news. Considering the battering he had taken, she was amazed at Conrad's powers of recovery, although his beautiful face was a mess.

"But it would be unwise tae go tae sleep fer several hours. Stay up as long as ye can, and ye shouldnae be alone either," Una added.

"I'll be with him," Agnes said before listening carefully to Una's advice for observing Conrad.

"Ye'll be out of danger in a couple of days. I'll give ye some more salve fer yer face and something more fer the pain that willnae make ye too sleepy. After tomorrow night, willow bark tea will be fine tae dull the pain while ye heal. It'll help ye sleep too," the healer told him in conclusion.

She gave Agnes the medicines, and after she and Conrad had heartily thanked Una for her help, she took Conrad's arm, and they left for their chambers.

They ordered strong tea and made themselves comfortable on the bed, staying up talking and playing cards for hours. Later that evening, having seen no sign of concussion, Agnes finally allowed Conrad to go to sleep. Resolving to wake him again in an hour or so just to be sure, she remained awake as long as she could, watching over him and replaying their kiss from earlier again and again.

The next morning, Conrad was sitting with Roisin, Agnes, Saoirse and her grandparents in the parlor. He and Agnes had fabricated a story of how he had encountered a couple of brigands attacking some travelers on the road near the castle and had intervened tae help. Agnes had informed Duncan of their story, so that they would not raise suspicions.

When Duncan joined them after his training, he caught Conrad's eye and gestured to a quiet corner of the chamber. Conrad followed him over there warily, while the others remained focused on Roisin.

The entire conversation took place in harsh whispers.

"Dinnae fash yersel', I'm nae gonnae hit ye again," Duncan told him. "By the way, ye look like shite."

"Thanks, but at least I have a good reason for it. What's yer excuse?" Conrad countered, fairly confident Duncan was not going to start any trouble inside the chamber. Outside was another matter though.

"Ye're feckin' lucky ye have me sister tae thank fer bein' alive. All that weepin' and wailin', I could nae take it. I had tae carry ye tae the healer mesel' just tae shut her up."

Conrad nodded, secretly gratified to hear about Agnes' weeping and wailing. "Aye, so I heard. I'm grateful tae ye fer that much at least."

"I still think ye're treacherous bastard."

"I've nae doubt ye dae. I dinnae expect that tae change any time soon, so ye'll be pleased tae learn that me and Agnes and the wee yin will be leavin' soon fer Moy Hall. Ye'll only havetae put up with seein' me on high days and holidays."

"Ach, shut up, man. Ye ken why I'm angry with ye, and I have every right tae be."

"I told ye that before ye mashed me face," Conrad replied. "Ye should have listened first and then battered me."

Duncan stepped closer and lowered his voice even further. "Damn right. I still feel like punchin' ye now. The only reason I'm holdin' back is fer the bairn. D'ye ken what really gets me about all this? Ye were me best friend, me braither, and yet ye betrayed me by lyin' tae me about bein' the bairn's faither."

"Oh, ye mean like when ye were me best friend and ye lied tae me about the real reason Agnes was sent away tae France? Fer five feckin' years, I never had a bloody clue where she was or what had happened tae her," Conrad replied cooly, mindful of his sore face.

Duncan's brows flew upwards. "But why would I tell ye? I had nae idea there was anythin' between ye. Besides, me faither swore us all tae secrecy because of the disgrace. But ye and Agnes, behind me back, Christ!"

"It was one single night, I swear, Duncan. The next mornin', I was goin' tae go and see yer faither and ask fer her hand. But if ye recall, ye and me were called away tae fight. Ye were summoned back earlier, but I stayed and couldnae even write tae her. By the time I got back, she'd vanished. It broke me heart. None of this would have happened if we hadnae been away undercover."

"Ach, me God, what a bloody mess!" Duncan raked a hand across his short hair frustratedly.

"Well, ye may as well ken it now. I love Agnes, I've loved her since I was a lad. I've always wanted tae wed her."

"What?! And ye kept that from me too? But why, man, why?" He seemed truly pained, which surprised Conrad but moved him also. Perhaps Duncan did not hate him quite as much as he said he did.

"I wasnae sure ye'd approve. I was scared of loosin' yer friendship. And Agnes was scared of breakin' us up. We didnae even tell each other how we felt because of it."

"Oh, making me feel like the monster, eh?" Duncan scowled. "So, ye decided between ye that I wouldnae approve of me best friend, practically me braither, and me sister bein' in love and gettin' wed? Ye deserve a beatin' fer that alone, ye bloody fool. And it still daesnae excuse ye fer nae tellin' me ye're Roisin's faither."

"I only found out mesel' two days before the weddin'. I had tae work it out fer mesel', just like ye did. And then I had tae force the truth out of Agnes. She was never gonnae tell me. She was gonnae let the wee yin stay a bastard her whole life. I couldnae allow that."

"I ken I'm gonnae regret askin' this, but why would she dae that?"

"Like I said, 'tis complicated. Ye'd best ask her. The thing is, of course, we want everyone tae ken I'm Roisin's faither. We're sick of all the secrets and lies as well. But ye got in before we could work out the best way of daein' it. And this is the result." He pointed to his face. "Look, I understand if ye cannae forgive me. I'm sorrier than ye'll ever ken fer nae trustin' ye. But I did want tae tell ye once I found out. Agnes begged me nae tae. She was too scared of how the family would react."

There was a pause while the air rippled with powerful, unexpressed masculine emotions.

Duncan sniffed. "So, how are ye and Agnes gonnae break it tae the families? Faither's nae gonnae like it when he finds out, but Maither'll come round. She's always liked ye, and she'd dae anythin' fer Roisin. But then there's yer parents tae consider as well."

"I'm nae sure yet. What with everythin' that's happened these last few days, me and Agnes havenae had the chance tae talk about it. But we will taenight. I'll let ye ken."

Duncan looked and Conrad and then said in a voice so low, Conrad could barely hear him.

"I didnae want tae beat ye so much… I apologize fer it, and I take me words back. Ye are me friend and ye always will be." With that, he walked off and joined the others. Conrad waited a moment, stunned by what had just happened, before following him.

CHAPTER THIRTY-TWO

After putting Roisin to bed that evening, Agnes and Conrad retired to their chamber. Conrad surprised her by handing her a letter.

"'Tis from me parents," he told her. "Read it."

She scanned it quickly before looking up at him, her anxiety levels rising. "'Tis nice yer family's comin', Conrad, ye ken I like them very much, and it'll be wonderful tae see Eileen. It's been so long. But I havetae tell ye, I'm nervous as well. They'll be askin' all sorts of questions."

"That's why we need tae use this opportunity of having both our families together tae tell them I'm the Roisin's faither," he told her as she handed the letter back to him.

A shock of fear went through Agnes. "I ken ye're right, they havetae ken the truth. But I'm so scared of how they're goin' tae react, Conrad," she replied, her fingers twisting in agitation. "They're all goin' tae be angry, but 'tis Faither I'm really worried about. He's goin' tae like we've betrayed him, just like

Duncan, only much worse. I'm afraid of what he might dae tae ye."

Conrad came and put his arms around her and stroked her hair. She clung to him for comfort and strength.

"'Tis sweet that ye're scared fer me, Mo Ròisín, but yer faither, though he'll doubtless be fumin', will dae naethin' tae hurt his granddaughter. I'm already Roisin's stepfather fer him. They've all seen how happy she is tae have a daddy. They'll nae wantae upset her. I promise ye, it'll nae be as bad as ye think when we tell them the truth and explain how it all came about. There's bound tae be some fireworks, but at the end of the day, they'll havetae accept it, even yer faither, trust me," he persuaded gently.

Agnes looked up into his eyes and found truth and earnestness in them as well as love. It gave her strength and resolve. She nodded. "Aye, all right. I must put me fears aside, fer Roisin's sake and ours. I'm sick of the lies. As long as ye're at me side, I can dae anythin'. I agree, when yer family get here, we'll tell them together."

"That's me brave lass," he murmured, smiling, catching her up and lifting her up to plant a tender kiss on her lips. She put her arms around his neck, returning his kiss with warmth.

When their lips parted, Conrad looked into her eyes and said, "Agnes, I want ye tae ken that even when I was angry with ye fer leavin' me and keepin' Roisin from me, the love in me heart fer ye was true. It always has been, and that'll never change as long as I live. I've always loved ye, and I always will."

"Och, Conrad, it does me heart good tae hear ye say so. I never stopped lovin' ye since I had tae leave ye. I'm hopin' that once the truth is out, we'll have a chance tae put the past behind us and be truly happy together."

"Ye can be sure of it, Mo Ròisón," he murmured, lifting her until their faces were so close, their breaths mingled into one. A hungry passion overwhelmed Agnes, who closed her eyes as their lips collided, savouring the feel and taste of him as they explored each other's mouths, their tongues entwining in a frantic, erotic dance.

Conrad's arm slipped around her waist, holding her close against him, and she felt his erect manhood pressing against her. To feel his building excitement spurred her own desire, and she cleaved to him, pressing her hips and breasts against him, reveling in his strength and power as their kisses grew in intensity, their movements more frantic.

"I need tae touch ye, Conrad, tae feel ye," she murmured, squirming against him, eliciting a chuckle from Conrad.

"Likewise, Mo Ròisón milis," he replied in his low, husky voice, his fingers flying to undo the front of her bodice. "Agnes, me sweet little rose."

Agnes felt it like a caress. "Och, I love it when ye call me that… mo chuisle, me heartbeat," she sighed, working intently on freeing his shirttails from his trews. Conrad paused to raise his arms so she could pull it off before finally losing the top of her gown and the shift beneath, so that her breasts came tumbling free.

She helped him to scramble out of his trews, and they fell on each other like wolves, completely caught up in their unquenchable desire for each other. Feeling herself growing wetter and hotter between her legs, gripped by a bold, needful impulse, Agnes lifted her skirts and straddled him.

"Och, Mo Róisín, aye, come tae me, ye wee witch," Conrad groaned in his excitement and pulled her firmly onto his lap, ravishing her naked skin and breast with kisses and soft, sucking bites. Agnes panted with wanting, feeling the head of his now rock-hard erection nosing at the entrance to her already slick sex.

Reaching down, she took hold of his length and guided it inside her, then slowly sank down upon it by slow degrees, looking into Conrad's eyes, moaning with the exquisite pleasure of him filling her to the hilt and the blissful expression on his face.

Slowly, she began to ride him, her fingers entwined in his hair, arching her back to give him all the access he wanted to her breasts. Conrad smiled at her wickedly, moving his hips in time with hers, burying himself deeper and deeper inside her, clearly enjoying her moans of helpless pleasure. At the same time, he feasted on her breasts, driving her to the edge of delirium with his mouth, nipping and nuzzling her nipples until they grew hard as diamonds.

"Och, I want ye so much, mo chuisle," Agnes sighed, her breasts bouncing wildly, riding him faster as her need for him escalated into burning want that only he could satisfy.

"As long as I live, I'll never have enough of ye, Mo Róisín," Conrad panted, stepping up the speed and depth of his thrusts, gripping her hips tightly, pinning her in place with a mastery that fanned the flames of her desire even higher.

"Faster," she urged raggedly as their movements quickened, sensing their mutual climax fast approaching. With a deep growl, Conrad obliged, increasing his speed until she was bouncing upon his rigid shaft, her walls clenching him tightly as he drove his length into her again and again.

Clutching at each other, urging each other on, they peaked at exactly the same moment, their lips clashing in the throes of ultimate bliss.

In the afterglow, they lay tangled together on sheets dampened by their passion, content to lay in each other's arms, sharing kisses and gentle laughter.

"Ye give me such pleasure, Conrad, the way ye love me. And ye make me feel so safe," Agnes murmured against his chest as she snuggled up to him.

"'Tis the same fer me, Mo Róisín. And now, we're free of the past, we have a whole lifetime of such pleasures tae look forward tae," Conrad whispered huskily. "Ye're mine, and ye can be certain that I'll always love ye and protect ye, fer as long as I live."

Agnes sighed happily, feeling as though she had come home at last, now that she and Conrad were one body, one spirit, one soul.

When the Mackintoshes' entourage rolled up to Keppoch Castle in the late summer afternoon two days later, Eileen was the first through the carriage door. The minute she spotted Agnes, the pair flew into each other's embrace, laughing and smiling.

"Och, Eileen, I'm just thrilled tae see ye, I've missed ye so much," Agnes said, sniffing back tears of joy at being reunited with her old friend.

"Me too, lass, and I cannae believe ye've gone and married me braither! Ye must be daft as a brush. But my, ye look bonny. Ye have nae aged a minute. What's yer secret?"

"Bein' wed tae yer braither of course," Agnes said playfully, but she meant every word.

Eileen screamed with laughter. "We always wanted tae be sisters, and now we are! 'Tis priceless. We're all over the moon about it. Congratulations."

"Thank ye, Eileen. We can have a good catch up later on, eh?"

"Ye can be sure of it, lass."

She turned her bright blue eyes on Conrad. They flew wide. "What the hell happened tae yer face? Did ye have a fight with a barn door or did Agnes dae that tae ye?" she asked.

"I certainly didnae!" Agnes burst out.

Conrad cracked a grin, which was still quite painful for him. "Och, how I've missed yer razor-sharp wit, Sister."

"Did ye get in fight or what?" Eileen persisted, scrutinizing him closely. "If ye did, then I hope the other feller looks worse than ye do. "

"I had an encounter with some brigands'," Conrad lied.

"Some encounter," his sister replied. "I hope it daesnae spoil yer pretty looks, eh, Agnes?"

Agnes just smiled, exchanging a worried glance with Conrad as he and his sister hugged. They both knew they were going to have to tell the same lie to his parents, and neither of them were relishing it. They had already run the gauntlet of lying to Agnes' parents, which had been particularly hard with Duncan standing right next to them. But he had at least kept his promise to Agnes not to say anything to them.

"Agnes, lass, how are ye?" Lord Evander Mackintosh asked, striding forward to greet them jovially.

"I'm very well, thank ye." Agnes dropped Conrad's father a neat curtsey and immediately found herself smothered in a vast bear hug.

"Ah, me bonny new daughter-in-law. I couldnae have picked a better one mesel'," he rumbled in his deep bass voice as he finally released her.

"'Tis lovely tae see ye, Laird Evander," she told him a little breathlessly. Evander was a fearsome figure, tall and broad, his powerful warrior's body impressive and sporting a tattoo for every man he had killed.

Conrad had inherited his build but not his long blond hair, which he always wore tied up on his head. He was handsome in an austere sort of way. His green eyes missed nothing. In character he was similar to her father, which was probably why they got along so well.

But Agnes knew that when it came to his family and friends, Evander was not as frightening as he looked. He liked children and could be affectionate and a lot of fun in a way her own father never had been. Nevertheless, he was canny and watchful. And terribly dangerous to his enemies.

"Bloody hell! What have ye done tae yersel', Son?" he asked when he turned to Conrad, clearly taken aback at the state of his face. Conrad threw Agnes a sidelong glance that said, "Here we go again."

"Just a run in with some brigands, Faither. It looks worse than it is. 'Tis just bruises, that's all."

"Why, lad, ye're back and blue. I advise aye tae be more careful next time, eh?"

"Aye, I will Faither. 'Tis good tae see ye. I'm glad ye decided tae come and visit us."

"Yer maither insisted on it, lad, since we missed yer weddin'. But I suppose ye couldnae wait, eh?" he asked and grinned at them both. Agnes' cheeks grew warm with embarrassment, which she hid with a small cough.

"Aye, that's right," Conrad replied.

"Ye look a right mess, but I'm very happy with ye," Evander went on. "By marryin' Agnes here ye've brought our two clans even closer. Nae one will dare threaten the Mackintoshes and MacDonalds now we're allies by marriage."

Father and son embraced and clapped each other's backs with true affection before breaking apart.

"Och, the dear Lord, Son, what have ye sone tae yersel'?" cried Conrad's mother Lady May, rushing up to them alongside Lady Fiona, examining Conrad's face worriedly.

"Hello, Maither, 'tis grand tae see ye." Conrad smiled as much as he could and went through the same lying rigmarole as before.

"Well, ye must take more care, Son. Look at yer lovely face, all bruised and swollen," May crooned, always a doting mother to her only son. At forty-seven, she was a decade younger than Lady Fiona, with long, silky blonde hair that made her look youthful. Both women were beautiful and petite, always impeccably turned out. They loved it when Conrad and Duncan would tease them, calling them the two dollies, for that was what they resembled, perfect little dolls.

But as well as being beautiful and elegant, they were both warm-hearted, intelligent, kind, and passionate card players. They got on like a house on fire.

"Quit fussin', Maither," her pride and joy told her affectionately, opening his arms and giving her a huge hug.

"Dinnae tell me nae tae worry about ye, Conrad," she scolded him when he let her go. "Ye're still me wee bairn." She turned to Agnes next, with a fond smile. "Agnes, m'darlin'. Why, ye look bonnier than ever. I'm so thrilled ye two decided tae get married. Ye make a lovely pair. I'm so proud. I'm only sorry we couldnae get here in time tae be at the weddin'."

"We were as well, Maither," Conrad said, "but once we'd decided on it, we couldnae see the point of waitin', eh, Agnes?"

"Aye, that's right," Agnes agreed with a nod and a smile, feeling as though she and Conrad were getting more and more enmeshed in a web of lies. On one hand, she was dreading telling everyone the truth, fearing the repercussions that might follow. On the other, she was sick of living a lie and wanted to get it over with come what may.

May smiled understandingly, though Agnes thought she detected a glimmer of disappointment in her mother-in-law's eyes and felt even worse. "Well, it was a shame, tae be sure. But tae make up fer it, we plan on throwin' a big party fer ye when ye come and take up residence at Moy Hall, tae celebrate ye bein' man and wife," she told them.

"Thank ye, Maither, Agnes and I would love that, eh, Agnes?" Conrad said, enfolding his beaming mother in a vast hug and kissing her cheeks.

"Aye, we will, thank ye very much, Lady May," Agnes agreed, embracing and kissing the older lady in turn.

With the reunion and all the greetings out of the way, they went into the castle and Conrad and Agnes showed his parents up the set of chambers they'd been allotted so they could rest after the long journey. They were due to all meet up again at seven thirty in the private dining room for intimate family dinners, where she and Conrad planned to drop their truth bomb.

CHAPTER THIRTY-THREE

*I*f all went well, they would have Saoirse bring Roisin in to meet her new grandparents.

They were both very nervous when they escorted Evander and May down at the appointed time, and the two families sat down to a lavish meal. The atmosphere amongst the old friends was relaxed and convivial, with the help of some excellent wine and food.

Amid the gaiety, Conrad and Agnes held hands under the table to give each other courage. They had agreed that Conrad would make the announcement no later than eight o'clock. That left enough time for the dust to settle if and when they introduced Roisin to her father's family, so she would not end up going to bed very late. Thus, they were both watching the clock in nervous anticipation.

It turned out to be Evander who gave Conrad the opening just before the mantel clock struck eight when he wielded his goblet of wine and embarked on a sort of speech in the middle of the conversation.

"I can see why our Conrad's been absent from home for so long. Agnes is enough fer any young man tae want enter intae the holy state of matrimony and settle down. Ye've done us proud lad with yer choice. And I'm delighted that the Mackintoshes and MacDonalds are now officially one big happy family. I'm sure I'm nae the only one at this table who's lookin' forward tae bouncin' some braw wee grandbairns on me knee. Eileen's a dead loss in that respect, so Conrad and Agnes here are gonnae have their work cut out makin' up fer it!"

Conrad abruptly stood up. All eyes swung to him expectantly, while Agnes trembled in her seat. "Thank ye, Faither. That was a very nice wee speech, but ye're makin' me wife blush." That elicited some laughter, for which Conrad paused, and then went on. "So, I hope ye willnae mind if I interrupt ye. Agnes and I have somethin' very important we want tae tell ye."

Agnes caught Duncan's eye, and he raised his eyebrows at her, as if in warning of the coming eruption. Already sick with nerves, as Conrad reached the critical part of the announcement, she dug her nails into her palms to stop herself from running from the room.

"Tis somethin' we've waited tae have ye all together tae say because, well, 'tis a wee bit delicate," he said. Agnes' eyes were on her father as Conrad concluded, "The fact of the matter is, Agnes and I have a daughter."

There was a stunned silence. Then uproar.

Her father stood up, glaring at Conrad and then Agnes furiously. "Ye mean tae say he's the faither? He's the bastard who ruined ye, and ye've kept it from us all this time?" he demanded furiously of Agnes.

"Aye, Faither. But he's nae a bastard. He's me husband and, aye, he's Roisin's faither. But he did nae even ken it himsel' 'til just before the weddin'," she answered as calmly as she could. "And when he found out, I made him swear nae tae tell a soul."

"This explains why they were in such a hurry tae get wed," Evander chimed in.

"Aye, we thought it strange at the time," May said. "We were disappointed nae tae be at our only lad's weddin', but we put it down tae them bein' keen. We never would have dreamed anythin' like this."

For a few moments, it was utter confusion, with the shocking discovery bringing on a barrage of questions. In answering them, Conrad and Agnes outlined the circumstances surrounding her banishment to France and Roisin's birth.

"I cannae believe the deceit," her father said, aghast. "Did ye ken about this, Fiona?" he asked his wife.

Lady Fiona shook her head "I'm as shocked as ye are. But thinkin' on it now, lookin' at the wee yin, she looks just like Conrad," she replied.

"That's nae the bloody point, woman!" he exclaimed angrily.

"So, what is yer point, James?" Evander broke in. "What daes it matter now they're man and wife? They've gone about things a bit backwards, aye, but that was because of circumstances. They're a respectable family now in the eyes of the law and the Lord. The child's nae a bastard anymore, so there's nay problem as far as I can see," Evander pronounced. Agnes felt a huge warmth towards her father-in-law.

"I couldnae agree more, Faither," Eileen chimed in. "They're nae the first couple in love tae slip up. Least said soonest mended I say. I'm thrilled tae learn I'm an auntie."

"I dae love me wee granddaughter," her mother said, glancing at her glowering husband but continuing fearlessly. "And ye will too when ye meet her, May and Evander. She's as bright as a button. I wouldnae part with her fer the world. I think 'tis very brave of Conrad and Agnes tae come out and tell us all this. 'Tis a shame it happened this way, fer all of us, but especially them and the wee yin. All of this could have been avoided had it nae been fer the bad timing and Conrad having tae leave fer battle. But 'tis all in the past now. We should be glad Roisin's legitimate now. Things have turned out for the best as I see it."

"Och, Roisin, what a lovely name," May volunteered, her face animated. "And she looks just like our Conrad, does she, Fiona?"

The three women started up a separate conversation, expressing their excitement at having Roisin in the family. "Och, get her in here, I wantae meet her," May begged Agnes and Conrad.

Evander stared to laugh at her father's obvious discomfiture, and Agnes saw him wink at Conrad. "I reckon ye're fightin' a loosin' battle on this, James."

Her father turned to Duncan. "Am I the only one who cares that me daughter was ruined by this man here," he stabbed a finger at Conrad, "who had me trust and the trust of all me family? Son, ye must agree with me surely? She's yer sister. What about her honor? What about her disgrace?"

Agnes could feel Conrad's fingers tightening around hers. They were both on tenterhooks, waiting to hear what Duncan would say.

Duncan shrugged. "I understand yer feelin' of betrayal, Faither, really, I dae. 'Tis never nice tae be lied tae, especially on important matters such as this. But things are what they are. Maither's right. There's nay point in draggin' up past insults and outrages, holdin' grudges. That'll only hurt the wee yin, and I'll dae naethin' tae harm the lass. We all love Roisin. We've all seen her with… her faither. I say we accept it, make the best of it, and get on with our lives."

Her father sat down, his angry expression wavering as his eyes fixed on Conrad. Agnes and Conrad looked at each other with a mixture of amazement and hope.

"That went better than I expected," Conrad whispered to her. "Shall we fetch Roisin in? Me family are dyin' tae meet meet her."

"Aye, Faither seems tae have subsided, and even Duncan's accepted it. In public at least," she whispered back. So, with the ladies' collusion, Saoirse was summoned to bring Roisin. But she was still nervous when the door opened and Roisin came in. She was holding Saoirse's hand and carrying her doll Peggy clutched to her chest.

Agnes and Conrad spent the next hour with their hearts swelling, proud parents together as their little daughter effortlessly won hearts and minds with her smiles and sweet ways. Even Grandpa MacDonald ended up lifting her onto his lap and letting her eat from his plate.

When it was time to take Roisin up to bed and the others were fussing over her, Agnes' faither intercepted her. "I'd like tae have a word with ye, Agnes."

"All right," she agreed, leaving Conrad for a moment and going to join her father and mother, with a heavy heart.

"Agnes, we wantae ken why ye didnae tell us at the beginnin' that Conrad was the faither," he said, not unkindly, she thought, taken aback.

"I was afraid of how ye'd react, of what ye'd dae tae Conrad," she admitted.

She was very surprised when he said, "Agnes, I ken I have a hard time showin' it sometimes, but I've always wanted, and I still want, what's best fer ye. I appreciate ye as me daughter, and wee Roisin as well, as me granddaughter."

A big lump rose in Agnes' throat. Tears pressed at the back of her eyes. This was what she had been craving her entire life, her father's approval. Her mother was smiling and nodding at her.

Finally, she managed to say, "Thank ye, Faither. That means a lot tae me. I was so afeared that ye and Duncan would hurt Conrad if ye found out. And when I discovered I was with child, he was away in battle and we didnae have a chance tae talk… it was all so complicated. I never wanted tae lie tae ye, believe me."

He embraced her, his eyes soft for a change. Then Agnes walked away, back to Conrad and Roisin, with a profound sense of peace settling in her heart.

The next morning, Agnes and Conrad woke up feeling happy and light of heart.

"The truth's out now, and we dinnae havetae hide from anyone any longer," he said as they snuggled up together in bed before breakfast, their limbs entwined.

"'Tis such a relief, Conrad, a weight off me shoulders that I've been carryin' around fer years," Agnes said. "And it wasnae half as bad as I feared it would be. Even Faither has accepted it." She had immediately relayed to Conrad what her father had said to her and how it had made her feel as soon as they left the room the previous evening.

"Aye, now we can really be happy at last." He sighed contentedly and pulled Agnes close to his chest. "'Tis what I always dreamed of, Mo Ròisín, bein' wed tae ye and havin' a family together. But when ye left like that, well, it broke me heart. I've loved ye so long, I couldnae never love anyone else. So I pushed all me dreams away and dedicated mesel' tae bein' a good warrior in defense of me clan. If I'm honest, it was quite a cold existence."

She stroked his cheek tenderly, deeply moved by his confession. "I understand all too well," she told him, looking into his eyes. "I thought of ye every day and every night when I was in France. I could never love anyone but ye, Conrad, never. I didnae think I would ever be truly happy again. So, 'tis like a dream come true now. I'm lookin' forward tae spendin' the rest of our lives together."

They kissed, and the kiss soon became passionate, their bodies cleaving together in love and desire. But their loving was suddenly interrupted by a sharp rap on the chamber door.

"Who the bloody hell is that at this hour, Conrad grumbled, detaching himself reluctantly from Agne's embrace. She hid under the covers while he pulled on his trews and opened the door.

"I'm sorry tae disturb ye, Sir, but ye're needed urgently. Lord Duncan is askin' fer ye tae report tae the courtyard and join him at once. There's been some sort of disturbance," said the guard standing in the hallway apologetically.

"Christ almighty," Conrad complained, cursing under his breath as he shut the door and went to explain to Agnes that Duncan needed him urgently.

"Fer God's sake, be careful," Agnes begged him as he hurriedly dressed, her heart filled with misgivings. It reminded her painfully of that morning years before, after their night of lovemaking, when he had been torn from her by circumstance, and years of heartache had ensued. "Come home safely tae me."

"I promise I will this time, Mo Ròisín," he told her, pressing a goodbye kiss to her lips before departing. He remembers it too, she thought, her heart contracting with fear as he left her once again.

Why dae I feel like I've been through this before? Conrad wondered, with a sense of foreboding as he hurried to obey the summons, hating to leave Agnes and Roisin behind.

"What's goin' on?" he asked, joining Duncan and a party of the clan's best fighters, who were gathered in the stable yard.

"Fires have been sighted over tae the southwest," Duncan explained, loading his gear onto his horse.

"Fires?" Conrad said curiously. "Like forest fires, ye mean?"

"The reports dinnae give many details, but there are several of them, they say. Most likely forest fires from the hot weather, I reckon. But we need tae ride out there and find out."

"D'ye think it could be somethin' tae dae with MacDonnell?" He had bad feeling about it and was unhappy about leaving Agnes and Roisin back at the castle without him to protect them if anything happened.

Duncan shrugged, his expression grim. "I guess we'll find out."

They rode for about ten minutes before spotting the first plumes of smoke rising above the tree covered hills a half a mile or so away. Unable to see the cause, Duncan and Conrad decided to ride up onto a promontory to get a better view. Once they reached the top, the reason for the fires became obvious.

Small groups of men could be clearly seen starting fires and then riding away. Their uniform colors were easily recognizable even from a distance.

"Those are MacDonnell's men!" Conrad exclaimed, his mind instantly going to Agnes and Roisin back at the castle. "We need tae get back fast."

"Aye, but what's the purpose of it?" Duncan wondered aloud as they turned their horses back down the track to rejoin their waiting men. But they had not gone very far when there came a shout from below, and one of their men appeared gesticulating wildly.

"Gentlemen! Gentlemen! It's decoys, gentlemen. The castle's afire, and we can hear the alarm bells. We think there's an attack goin' on!"

"Jesus!" Conrad exclaimed, panicking inside as they cantered down to the bottom of the promontory.

"Ride!" Duncan shouted, and they all rode with fury back the way they had come. Conrad stood up in his stirrups, urging

Davey forward across the uneven ground, and to his horror was soon able to see that pasts of the castle were ablaze, smoke billowed from the towers, and MacDonnell's men were like a sea lapping higher and higher up the walls, with some spilling over the top.

He rode faster than he had ever ridden before, his heart threatening to pound its way out of his chest.

I havetae get tae them before MacDonnell daes!

Because he knew that was why MacDonnell was attacking the castle—he wanted Agnes for himself!

CHAPTER THIRTY-FOUR

Agnes was in the nursery with Roisin, reading her a story book Eileen had gifted her. Roisin had woken up and asked for her mother. She was enjoying the story, but she was unaware that Agnes' main purpose in reading to her was to distract herself from her worry over the safety of Conrad and Duncan.

They had gone to investigate some fires outside the castle, and she felt very uneasy about it. Besides she did not feel safe without Conrad with her.

She and Roisin jumped out of their skins when the alarm bells began clanging frantically all around the castle. Already agitated by the alarm, Agnes' heart started pounding as one name dropped into her mind: Laird Tavish MacDonnell.

Has he finally come tae claim me? Conrad's nae here tae protect me… Please Lord, let it nae be him!

It was a terrifying thought, but she pushed her fear aside, knowing she had to protect Roisin above all else.

The alarm bells continued their loud clamoring, making it hard to think.

"What is it, Mama? I dinnae like it! I want Conrad, where's Conrad?!" the frightened child exclaimed, putting her hands over her ears to shut out the din.

Ach, Conrad, where are ye? Please be safe and hurry back. We need ye!

"'Tis the alarm, darlin', it means there's an emergency. It's probably naethin' serious. I'm sure Conrad's on his way, dinnae fret. I've got ye. But we must go and find out what's goin' on."

She grabbed a cloak just in case there was danger and she had to hide Roisin, then hurried outside to the main courtyard. She was shocked at the chaotic scene, soldiers and scared-looking people were running everywhere. Smoke was billowing from above, adding to the chaos. Looking up, she realized fires had broken out all over the castle.

More frighteningly, soldiers were amassing at the gates, and there was a loud roaring and pounding coming from the other side, as though some gigantic beast was trying to get inside.

"Mama, I'm scared," Roisin shouted above the alarm bells, clinging to Agnes tightly. "I want Conrad."

So dae I!

"I ken, darlin', I'm sure he'll be here soon, dinnae fret," Agnes tried to soothe her. "I am here, I will never let anythin' bad happen tae ye."

"Me lady! Are ye and the wee yin all right?" Saoirse ran up to them, her face white with fear.

"What's happenin'?" Agnes shouted to her.

Thankfully, at that moment, the alarm stopped, but the pandemonium around them continued.

"'Tis the McDonnells, they've attacked us, with Laird Tavish MacDonnell at their head!" Saoirse gabbled frantically. "Those fires Sir Conrad and Sir Duncan went to deal with were merely distractions, tae lure our best men away before the attack. We've been caught by surprise, me lady! Quickly, intae the keep!"

They pushed their way through the panicked throng towards the keep and ran straight into her parents.

"Thank the Wee Man ye're safe," her father said, looking fearsome in full battle gear yet clearly relieved. "Fiona, ye go with them and stay in the keep until I say so," he commanded her mother.

Roisin wanted to get down and hold her grandmother's hand, but moments after Agnes put her down, the little mite was torn away from her in the crush. Agnes screamed and dived after her, but Roisin disappeared into the forest of hurrying legs! The three women rushed to search for her. Terrified the child would wander into the fires, Agnes fought through the people, shouting Roisin's name, panic threatening to overwhelm her.

The smoke from the fires that were now rapidly being extinguished made it hard to see. For several agonizing minutes, she desperately searched, her fear rising, until she caught a flash of bright pink, the colour of Roisin's dress. Hope flaring inside her, she ran towards it, pushing folks aside in a bid to see if it was her daughter. Relief washed over her like a wave when she saw Roisin hiding under a stone bench, frightened but safe.

"Come on, darlin', we must get inside quickly," she said, pulling Roisin into her arms. They were both coughing from the smoke, so she tucked her under her cloak to protect her from the worst of the fumes and turned back towards the keep. As she did so, a heavy hand seized her by the arm. Hoping it was Conrad, she spun around, and was horrified to see it was an enemy soldier, with a group of others milling around him.

"She's a noble, all right, lads, and she fits the description!" the man shouted to his companions, who rushed to his aid.

"Let me go!" Agnes screamed at them, struggling as best she could to get free, but they only gripped her tighter and dragged her off across the courtyard towards the gates.

"Where are ye takin' me?!" she shouted, terrified for Roisin, who was still clinging to her beneath her cloak, hampering her efforts to shake the men off. She did not know what to do, whether to let Roisin go and tell her to run or keep hold of her. She decided the former was too dangerous, with the battle raging all around them.

"Ye're comin' with us, me lady, tae see the laird," one of her captors snarled at her as they pulled her through the gates, and into the hellish scene of battle going on outside.

Agnes' blood turned cold with fear for Roisin. She clutched They're takin' me tae MacDonnell!

As MacDonnell's men yanked her along roughly, in the heat of the moment she had no choice but to hold fast to her daughter for dear life, desperately trying to keep her out of sight.

"Dinnae make a sound, m'darlin'," she whispered to Roisin. "Mama's gonnae keep ye safe, I promise." She felt Roisin's little body shaking and her arms tighten about her neck under the cloak.

"Me laird, is this her?" her original captor asked the broad-shouldered, imposing figure clad in black and shining half-armor, who was standing with his back to her amid a group of enemy soldiers, barking orders, some meters away from the castle.

He turned around, and Agnes found herself looking into a pair of cold, deep-set, hard grey eyes set below thick black brows. Beneath a gleaming helmet, dark auburn hair framed a terrifying visage.

His complexion was weathered and ruddy, his thin lips etched into a sneer that made him appear perpetually displeased. An ugly jagged scar puckered his left cheek, pointing to a violent past.

'Tis MacDonnell himself!

Frozen with fear, Agnes stared back as he stepped towards her, his cold glance sweeping over face like fingers of ice.

"Aye, 'tis her all right. I've seen her portrait," he said in a deep, growling voice. "Ye're lady Agnes MacDonald, right?" he demanded of her tersely.

Agnes thought about lying, but she was too afraid for Roisin to take any chances. This was the moment she had been dreading. But she had already decided long ago that she would do anything necessary to save the ones she loved the most. Even if it cost her her life.

Determined not to show fear, she pulled herself up to her full height and lifted her chin proudly. "I used tae be Agnes MacDonald. But now I'm wed, I'm a Mackintosh."

MacDonnell let out an unpleasant, grating laugh. "Ye may be now, lass, but as soon as I find yer husband, ye'll be a widow. And tomorrow, ye'll be Lady MacDonnell."

"All right, if ye're happy tae take the risk of havin' a wife who'll kill ye the minute yer back's turned, go ahead and take me by force," she said boldly, quaking inside, praying he would buy her threat.

She saw lust in his eyes as he came close to her and looked at her curiously, circling her like a beast with prey, making her every nerve ending stand on end. But she stood her ground. The stakes were too high for her to fail.

Without warning, he snatched her cloak aside. Agnes' heart tore in two as Roisin let out a small scream of terror and clung to her more tightly.

A hideous smile formed on his misshapen lips. "Well, well, what have we here? So, this is yer bairn, eh? Ye thought ye could hide her from me."

"Dinnae touch her," Agnes snarled, her protective instincts rising to the fore.

MacDonnell went to grab Roisin's arm, and Agnes leaped backwards. "I said, dinnae touch her," she hissed, eyeing the dirk in MacDonnell's belt.

If I could get it, I could kill him.

But she knew the retribution that would earn was too great a price to pay, so she clutched her daughter to her breast, determined to protect her with her life.

"Ye were promised tae me as me wife by yer faither. He said naethin' about another man's bairn," MacDonnell replied. "But she'll be useful tae me, so I'll take her as well." He signalled to two of his men. "Take the bairn and keep her safe," he commanded them. They rushed at Agnes.

"Nay!" she cried, moving backwards, "keep yer hands off of her!" She looked at MacDonnell and in desperation said, "I'll make a deal with ye... if ye swear tae leave her here with her faither and let them both live."

MacDonnell waved his men back. "Oh? And what deal is that?"

Steeling herself, Agnes looked into his eyes. "If ye swear tae let me husband and daughter go unharmed, then I'll come with ye willingly right now. I'll walk up the aisle with ye, I'll be a good wife tae ye and faither ye bairns. 'Til death dae us part."

CHAPTER THIRTY-FIVE

Standing up in the stirrups and urging their horses to go faster, Conran, Duncan, and the other fighters accompanying them streaked across the pastures towards the castle. Conrad was terrified. All he could think of was Agnes and Roisin being inside the besieged castle, at MacDonnell's mercy.

And I'm nae there tae protect them!

He cursed himself silently for his failure.

He was desperate to get through the gates and search for them immediately, but inevitably, they were soon caught up in the fierce battle that was raging all around the castle between the defenders and MacDonnell's troops. Conrad was shocked to see the number of enemy soldiers present.

MacDonnell must be determined tae get Agnes this time, fer he's brought his whole bloody army with him!

On the other hand, it looked like most of the fires inside had been extinguished, and the MacDonald fighters, though taken unawares, were putting up determined defense. Through the gates, he spied more furious fighting in the courtyard and realized with dismay that enemy had penetrated the castle itself.

But he's nae won yet.

Conrad crashed into the fray on Davey, wielding his sword left and right to carve a path through the enemy towards the open gates. His blood was boiling with the need to cut MacDonnell to pieces, to put an end to his evil pursuit of Agnes forever.

He had almost reached the gates, determined to get inside and find Agnes and Roisin, when he happened to glance to his right at the battle that had speared across the pastures, and thought he saw a woman.

Women did not belong on a battlefield, so he did a doubt take. And was stunned to realize it was Agnes.

What the hell is she doin' out here?!

But as he drew nearer, he noticed something else his that made him sick with fear.

Roisin!

Terrified, determined to get his wife and daughter to safety, he immediately wheeled Davy around and started to make for them. As he smashed his way through the fray towards her, he saw Agnes was clutching their daughter and talking to a tall man in black whose armor flashed in the sun. Conrad went cold all over, for he knew exactly who it was. His worst nightmare, Tavish MacDonnell.

"That's me wife and bairn ye have there, ye bastard. Get away from them before I kill ye!" Conrad roared, standing up in the saddle, swinging his sword, riding straight for MacDonnell.

MacDonnell swung around in obvious surprise. When he saw Conrad coming towards them, his face broke into a leering grin. He grabbed Agnes by the arm, and Roisin's screams of panic sliced through Conrad like knives as MacDonnell shoved them violently towards his men, who seized them both and held them fast.

"So, this is the husband, eh? The famous warrior, Conrad Mackintosh," MacDonnell jeered, unsheathing his sword with a flourish. "Say goodbye tae them, man," he shouted at Conrad, "because this is the last time ye'll ever see them. Consider this an annulment." He laughed evilly at his own wit, clearly looking forward to the fight, convinced he would win.

Fueled by fury, Conrad thundered towards him, and within a few feet of MacDonnell, he slipped from Davey's back and hit the ground running.

"Conrad, leave me, just save Roisin!" Agnes screamed at him, her face chalk white with fear. It made Conrad's blood boil to see how scared she was.

I'll kill him, and I'll get them back safe!

"I'll kill ye before I let ye take what's mine, ye bastard, MacDonnell!" Conrad raged, closing on the rogue laird, set on killing him.

Agnes screamed at him, sobbing, "Conrad, please! Ye dinnae understand! Take Roisin and go. It diaenae matter about me, as long as ye're both safe. I couldnae live if anythin' bad happened tae ye."

"He's nae takin' ye!" Conrad insisted furiously.

"I'm nae takin' her. She's comin' with me of her own accord. She kens a better man when she sees one. I'll keep her satisfied once I've sent ye tae hell," MacDonnell mocked, his eyes locked on Conrad as they squared up to each other, blades swinging.

That gave Conrad pause. "She's me wife, and she'd never go with ye by her own will."

"Oh, but she will. We've made a deal, yer wife and me. I've sworn tae let ye and the bairn live, and in return, Agnes has sworn tae be a good wife tae me. I cannae wait fer the wedding night tae claim me husbandly rights."

Fuelled by rage, Conrad rushed at him, smashed into him like a battering ram with his shoulder. MacDonnell was taken off guard and was knocked to the floor. He rolled and sprang up, sword at the ready. He grinned at Conrad. "Try again, man, it'll take more than that tae best me."

Conrad lunged forward, his weapon arcing down toward MacDonnell's head. But MacDonnell parried the blow, forcing Conrad's blade aside. Quick as lightning, Conrad swung it upward, and before MacDonnell could block it, the tip sliced thinly across his exposed neck.

Snarling with rage, he leapt backwards, then thrust at Conrad's midriff, only for his strike to be blocked by Conrad's blade, leaving his own body unprotected long enough for Conrad to take advantage. He kicked MacDonnell hard in the gut, sending him flying backwards. He staggered but somehow remained on his feet.

Out of the corner of his eye, Conrad became aware that Duncan and some of the other fighters were engaging with the men holding Agnes in an attempt to free her. He wanted to kill MacDonnell quickly so he could go and help. In the meantime, he trusted Duncan like no other to free her and keep her safe.

In that momentary slip of focus, MacDonnell mounted a ferocious attack on him. The first blow caught Conrad's ribs, slicing through his leather vest. He felt nothing and moved back smoothly, expertly blocking MacDonnell's blows, sustaining cuts and nicks to his arms and wrists. He parried defensively for a while, intent on letting MacDonnell exhaust himself.

When he saw the man was tiring a little, he began to push back, advancing foot by foot, his sword singing through the air in silvery arcs. Finally, MacDonnell's sword arm buckled, and his blade flew from his hand. As he lunged to retrieve it, Conrad did not hesitate. In one fluid stoke, he bounded forward and thrust his blade into his MacDonnell's throat. It went right through. Conrad relished the look of shock frozen on the man's face before pulling it back with force.

MacDonnell dropped his weapon, swaying on his feet. Blood fountained from the arteries and veins Conrad had severed, pulsing with each beat of his dying heart. Conrad watched with satisfaction as MacDonnell's eyes glazed over and he fell forward, his face impacting the ground with a jarring thud. He lay motionless, like toppled pine. Conrad stood over him and turned him over with the tip of his boot.

"Now ye can go and find a wife of yer own… in hell," he muttered with an air of finality.

"Och, Conrad, thank God ye're nae hurt!" Agnes was running towards him, her face alight with joy and relief. Her cloak flew open as she ran, revealing Roisin clinging to her mother beneath. His heart squeezed with love and pride.

"And thank God ye're both safe," he told her, relief pouring through him. He put his arms around them both, while Agnes pressed her face to his chest and squeezed him tightly around the waist, heedless of MacDonnell's blood staining his front.

Duncan appeared behind her, panting, dripping with enemy gore. His teeth flashed white in his red-stained face as he grinned at Conrad.

He looked down at MacDonnell's body and said, "Good riddance," and spat on the corpse with derision. "That was the best day's work ye've ever done, lad," he added, slapping Conrad's back.

Agnes looked up at Conrad with shining eyes. "Thank ye fer riddin the world of that menace, Husband. It feels like a much safer place already." Then, to his delight, she stood on her tiptoes and kissed him.

"The tide's turnin' now," Duncan put in, surveying the battlefield. Conrad looked around and saw that with MacDonnell's death, his men were in retreat, many being hunted down by Agnes' father's army and slaughtered. The attack was over.

Agnes kept Roisin beneath her cloak, to shield her eyes from the carnage as they walked back into the castle courtyard. The cobblestones were slick with blood, but a clean-up was already in progress, the bodies of the slain enemies being stacked for removal. "Takin' out the rubbish," as Duncan put it.

In the courtyard they met up with the battle-stained laird, Lady Fiona, and Saoirse. There was much hugging and quiet jubilation for the victory they had won. And a moment of respect for those who had perished. When Roisin emerged from her hiding place, shaken but unhurt, she wanted to go to

Conrad. When he reached out to take her, he felt a sharp pain in his ribs and winced.

"What is it? Let me see," Agnes demanded at once. He tutted as she handed Roisin to Saoirse and inspected him.

"Omigod! Ye must see the healer at once," she declared.

"Tis naethin' but a scratch. Stop fussin'," Conrad protested.

"Ye're comin' with me now tae see Una, now," Agnes insisted. "I dinnae care what ye say. If that cut gets infected, ye'll be in trouble. Come on and stop arguin'."

"Will ye stop mitherin' if I go with ye?"

"Aye, that's the whole point."

So, he let her drag him to the infirmary, with the entirety of the two families following as well, anxious to make sure the hero of the hour was well taken care of. Una inspected his wounds and pronounced them minor except for the long, deep cut to Conrad's ribs that was worrying Agnes and Lady May the most.

Conrad, half naked, complained while the healer cleaned and dressed it carefully in front of everyone. Una instructed him not to do anything too strenuous until it healed.

"Aye ye satisfied now?" he asked Agnes when it was all over as she helped him back into his clothes.

He was easing into his coat when Duncan went up to them and without a question, hugged Conrad.

Agnes watched in delight as Conrad's blood spattered, bruised face split into a huge grin. He embraced him even tighter and patted his back in a touching show of masculine affection, even though she knew it must be paining him because of the wound. She supposed he was so happy to have his friend back, he did not feel the pain.

When Roisin went up to them both and wrapped her little arms affectionately around the mighty legs of her papa and uncle, a collective "awww" went around the room, and hardly an eye was without a tear.

In that atmosphere of love and family unity, came yet another surprise. She was completely stunned with what Conrad did next. It was not something she was expecting in the slightest.

In front of everyone, he suddenly took her hand and declared to everyone present, "I never want Agnes tae be in the position where she's mistaken fer nae bein' me wife again."

He turned to her, and with pure love shining in his bright blue eyes as he looked into hers, said, "Agnes, the first time we got wed, it was in a hurry. I want tae give ye the weddin' ye deserve and dae it properly this time. I want us tae renew our weddin' vows in front of all our guests. Agnes, will ye marry me again?"

The room seemed to hold its breath...

But Agnes did not hesitate. "Aye, I will!" she declared. She threw herself into Conrad's arms, and they shared a sweet, loving kiss. Their families clapped and cheered and wished them all the luck and happiness the world. And many strong bairns, of course.

EPILOGUE

September, Moy Hall, one month later…

"Ye may now kiss the bride," the minister intoned and slammed his bible shut.

Agnes gazed up into Conrad's beautiful bright blue eyes. They sparkled as he smiled at her, pulling her to him by the waist and lifting her clean off the floor, to fold her in his arms, kissing her tenderly, searchingly, warmly, so that she felt all the love in his heart flow into hers. She clung to his neck, kissing him back with equal fervor, buoyant with the knowledge that by renewing their vows, they were truly setting the seal on their love.

They were locked in a bubble of bliss and only emerged, breathless and dizzy, when the walls of the great hall at Moy Hall reverberated with the applause, cheers, hooting, and stamping of many feet that expressed the congregation's joyous approval of the proceedings.

She floated on a cloud of happiness on Conrad's arm as they stepped away from the makeshift altar and were immediately crowded by their family and the many guests who had been invited from far and wide, to help celebrate what they referred to as their "proper" wedding.

"I never thought it was possible tae be this happy, Conrad. I feel fit tae burst," she told him as they walked towards the end of the hall, regaled by smiles, kisses, well wishes, and congratulations.

"Me neither. This is the best day of me life," he told her, his smile dazzling.

Her heart skipped a beat as she basked in it, feeling inordinately proud of her husband. "Och, ye look so braw, I'm so lucky tae have such a fine and handsome husband!" she declared, feeling almost reborn.

"I tried me best tae dae ye justice. Ye're so beautiful, Agnes, 'tis me who's the lucky one." He kissed the end of her nose as they stepped out of the double doors onto the broad terrace, where the wedding breakfast had been laid out, because the weather was so fine.

A small figure carrying a basket hopped out in front of them. "Congratulations!" Roisin shouted, dancing with excitement as she showered them with dried rose petals.

Saoirse was standing to the side, looking splendid in her pale green frock, her auburn hair flowing down her back. She shrugged at them with an apologetic smile. "She had some left that she said she was saving fer somethin' special."

Roisin had been thrilled to be the flower girl at the wedding, walking before Agnes up the aisle scattering rose petals, in her fancy dress with a net skirt and embroidered silk bodice that echoed Agnes' own dress. She had practiced diligently to make sure she did not make any mistakes, making her parents both swell with pride.

She was so excited, she took off running around the terrace among the other milling guests, many of whom were her new-found cousins, who were all pouring out onto the terrace and being served drinks and small savories by an army of servants.

"I dinnae think I've ever seen her happier, Conrad. Look at her, she's glowin'," Agnes said, tears of love and pride pressing at the back of her eyes.

"Aye," he replied, dashing a tear from his eye. "I'm so proud of our wee lass, Agnes. Apart from ye, she's the best thing that ever happened tae me."

"I love ye so much, Conrad!" she whispered, standing on tiptoes to kiss him.

Suddenly, Roisin appeared before them, minus the basket. "Did I dae it right?" she asked, looking up at them both with her little gappy smile, hands behind her back, shifting from one satin slippered foot to the other.

"The best. Ye made it perfect, Bláwthin," Conrad said, calling his daughter by her favorite pet name, the Gaelic for Little Flower. "Come up here and give me a cuddle." Needing no second bidding, she practically jumped into his arms and scrambled into her position sitting on his arm, which had become her customary perch with her adored father.

Agnes' emotions swelled in her breast once more. The memory of a few weeks ago, when Roisin had asked why they were getting married again, and she and Conrad had decided it was time to tell her he was really her father, came back to her now.

Conrad was a huge man, a veteran of many battles, a mighty warrior who killed men brutally, without a thought in the service of his clan. He had killed MacDonnell to protect her and Roisin. To see him with his tiny, fairy-like daughter perched on his knee, their blonde heads touching, reading to her, teaching her little songs or rhymes, showing her how to tie a knot, always moved Agnes beyond words.

"I wantae tell her mesel'," he had told her. "But ye stay in the room, just do ordinary things, so it feels normal."

So, Agnes had busied herself about the chamber, providing a background normality, while he took Roisin on his knee and explained to her in simple terms she could understand.

"A long time ago, before ye were born, Mama and me were very young and in love. Because we loved each other, we made ye together. I'm nae yer stepfaither, Bláwthin, I'm yer real faither. Ye're me daughter. Ye've always had a faither, and that's always been me."

Agnes watched from the corner of her eye, uselessly rearranging things on the table, holding her breath. Roisin seemed confused, as well she might. She had never asked why she didn't have a father. Agnes had planned to say he had died when she did ask, but life in France had been so sheltered, it had not come up.

"So, I had a daddy all along, since I was born?"

"Aye." He nodded.

"But where were ye? Why did ye nae come and see me and Mama?"

"Well, just before ye arrived, I had tae go away tae fight some bad people, and I was away a very long time. I couldnae write tae Mama, and she couldnae write tae me. So Mama couldnae tell me ye'd been born. Well, when I finished fightin', I tried tae come home tae find her, but I got a bit lost on the way."

"So, ye couldnae find us?" Roisin asked, gazing up at him with exquisite trust.

"That's right, and I only found ye that night the bad men attacked the carriage. That was the first time we met, was it nae?"

The child smiled and nodded. "Aye. But why did ye nae tell me straight away that ye're me daddy?"

"Well, Mama hadnae seen me fer a long time, and because she's a very good mama and she loves ye so much, she had tae make sure I'd be a good daddy fer ye and nae a bad one before she told me. So she thought about it fer a little a while first before she decided I would be a good daddy tae ye."

"Oh," Roisin said, understanding in her tone. "I'm very happy she did that, because ye are a very good daddy."

Agnes gripped the edge of the table tightly, biting her lip so as not to cry.

"Thank ye, Bláwthin, that means a lot tae me," Conrad said, his voice husky with emotion. Roisin did something totally unexpected then. She clambered up on his lap and put her arms around him, hugging him. "I'm sorry ye got lost, Daddy. But ye found us in the end, and now we're all together. 'Tis like a story with a happy endin'.

When Conrad's arms enfolded her, their blond hair mingling, she resembled an elf being hugged by a giant. He rocked her gently, like a baby. "Ye're the best lassie in the world, I'm very proud of ye, and I'm proud tae be yer daddy. From now on, I promise, I'll always be here tae look after ye and Mama," he told her in choked voice.

"Agnes? Agnes? Are ye all right?" She came out of her reverie smiling at her mother.

"Maither! I'm fine, I was just thinkin' what a lovely day it is and how happy I am. Did ye enjoy the ceremony?" she asked brightly.

"Och, it was beautiful, pet, ye look so lovely. I went through two hankies, I was cryin' so much." Agnes laughed, they embraced and kissed. Her father loomed over her mother and shook Conrad's hand enthusiastically, flashing one of his rare smiles.

"Ye make sure ye look after them properly, lad, or ye'll have me tae answer tae," he told him.

"Ye ken I will, me laird," Conrad assured him, beaming at Agnes.

Her father surprised her by swooping down and kissing her cheek. "Ye look a right picture lassie. Ye dae us all proud. I ken ye'll be very happy together."

"Thank ye, Faither, that's kind of ye." She was stunned when he winked at her. She had never seen him wink at anyone in her life. He pinched Roisin's cheek and ruffled her hair affectionately, making her giggle. Agnes' heart warmed to him even more for trying to show his love for them even though it was hard for him.

Duncan was next to come pushing between their parents, to plant big kisses on both of her cheeks and hug her, then pump Conrad's hand. "Congratulations, ye two. May this be the last time ye get wed."

Eileen appeared beside him. "Well done ye two, ye've really tied the knot now and there's nae goin' back," she joked.

Agnes shared an emotional hug with Soairse as well. "I could nae have done any of this without ye," Agnes told her, brushing tears from her eyes.

"Wheesht! Like I'm always tellin' ye, ye can dae more than ye think! I'm so happy fer ye, me lady. The future looks bright now, eh? Did I nae tell ye that anythin can happen? Well, I was right, eh?"

The party was well underway now, with music and the smell of roasting meat wafting on the air. Everyone had a drink in their hand and was smiling. Roisin was playing happily with her cousins.

"What a perfect day, Conrad. I dinnae think I'll ever be so happy as I am now," Agnes told him.

"Well, I'll see if I can work on that and come up with somethin' fer later," he replied jestingly, and kissed her soundly on the lips.

Agnes was proved wrong a few minutes later, when Roisin raced over to them, excitedly shouting, "Daddy, Daddy!" to Conrad. It was the first time she had called him that in public. To Agnes' astonishment, everyone cheered and clapped. Seeing the blush of pleasure on her husband's face and Roisin's pure happiness as her father caught her up and swung her high into the air was the pinnacle of her joy.

EXTENDED EPILOGUE

September, Moy Hall, five years later…

"'Tis wonderful tae have the family all together like this. They're quite an impressive bunch," Agnes said, squeezing Conrad's arm in hers as they strolled across the grass.

"Aye, I suppose they are, but they have a tendency tae have very noisy bairns," he pretended to grumble, eliciting laughter from Agnes. She was looking out over the lawn at their family, all gathered together, in the gardens of Moy Hall.

It was a balmy September day, and gentle music from a harpist floated on the air, along with the excited shouts and laughter of children coming from somewhere out of sight. The Mackintosh clan had come in numbers to celebrate Roisin's tenth birthday, two generations of them, Conrad's cousins and their parents, his aunts and uncles.

On a flag-stoned area to the side of the lawn stood a long table loaded with the remains of a lavish birthday tea, all manner of drink, plus the remains of a large, iced birthday cake. Lounging around the table, drinking and chatting were her parents, Duncan, Eileen, Evander and May, and two of Conrad's uncles.

Seated on one side of the table was his cousin Kathleen and her husband Blaine, along with their daughter Anabel. Kathleen, the daughter of Conrad's uncle Bran and his wife Illyssa, was a stunning, auburn-haired beauty, rather wild in nature, and a renowned horsewoman. Her long auburn tresses mingled with Blaine's dark, unruly locks as they leaned together, sipping wine, talking and laughing with Conrad's other cousin the more restrained Diana.

Agnes liked Diana, a maverick, who was interested in the healing arts despite her noble position. She was serious, practical, and kind, and adored by her enigmatic husband Lorne, a man of few words who was obviously smitten with his wife and right now cuddling their baby son Diarmaid.

Not far from them, canoodling shamelessly, was Conrad's striking cousin Kieran. Rather like Conrad, with his blonde hair and stormy-grey, Kieran was imperative to look at and charismatic. Yet he seemed to have found his match in the beautiful, spirited Alina. They watched their twins, Nathaniel and Eloise, running around and teasing each other like only a brother and sister could.

Their parents were present too. Alec, Laird of Clan Mackintosh was leaning a mighty arm on the table, his long blond hair tied back from his face, a slightly older version of Evander. Also there was Bran, Alec and Evander's brother and the clan's advisor. They were large, powerful, good-looking men, as were all the Mackintosh men, it seemed to Agnes. Their respective wives, Kira and Illyssa, had taken off their shoes and were dancing on the grass nearby to the harp music, giggling and looking rather tipsy.

"Ach, they look so pretty, eh, Conrad, like flowers in their beautiful dresses," Agnes observed, smiling and waving at them. They waved back merrily, both looking a little worse for wear. She liked them both enormously. Kira was funny and bold, while Illyssa was terribly mischievous and always dreaming up pranks to play on the men.

"Agnes, Conrad, come and join us," Ilyssa called to them, waving them over.

"Aye, come and have a wee dance," Kira said and hiccoughed. "Och, pardon me, 'tis that new wine from France ye've been plyin' us with, Conrad. 'Tis a little too moorish if ye ken what I mean. I'm a wee bit tipsy, I think." As if to prove it, she spun around and bumped into Illyssa, sending them both into paroxysms of laughter.

"Disgustin' display of drunkenness," Conrad complained. "I'm nae letting me wife consort with the likes of ye two. What sort of an example are ye setting fer the young folk?"

"A bad one, I hope," Ilyssa said laughingly. "They should grow up learnin' how tae have a little fun. What is this wine ye've given us, Conrad? I declare, it's gone straight tae me head. I think I'll have another wee glass of the stuff."

"'Tis a new import from the region of Champagne in France. I'm interested tae hear what ye all think of it, seein' as 'tis our new family venture," Conrad replied before flicking his eyes at the servant manning the drinks and holding up four fingers. The man nodded and hurried to pour.

"Well, I love it," Kira said. "It makes me wantae dance."

The fresh champagne arrived and the four stood chatting for a few minutes. Another of Conrad's cousins, Lavinia, a delicate but feisty blue-eyed beauty, and her husband Ian, Laird

MacBean came to join them with their son Archibald. The MacBean's and the Mackintoshes had long been allies and friends, and growing up, Conrad had spent a lot of time with Ian. Conrad and Agnes continued the stroll, taking their wine with them.

Not far away, Conrad's beautiful Aunt Catreena, known as the ice maiden because of her stunning Nordic looks, was dancing in a clinch with her husband, Illyssa's brother Tad, Laird MacBean. Tad's large frame and fearsome dark looks were the perfect contrast to the slender Catreena's icy, blondeness, which concealed a warm, generous heart. She and Illyssa were best friends, and she often laughingly complained that Illyssa led her astray and got her into trouble.

At that moment, the excited shrieks of what sounded like a horde of children grew suddenly louder, and they burst out onto the lawn from some shrubbery. There were nine children in all, with the birthday girl being the eldest at ten. Going on twenty, Conrad often teased her. They adored each other and of all their three children, she most resembled her father. Their youngest, little Rhiannon, was only two. She was having nap back at the castle under Saoirse's watchful eye.

At the head of the explosion of children was Conrad's Uncle Dunn, sporting a wide grin and carrying on his broad shoulders Agnes' and Conrad's three-year-old son, Sullivan, named after his great-great grandfather.

Dunn was the clan's chief scout and, though quite scary to look at, was full of fun. Whenever the family got together, he was always the one organizing the games that kept the children entertained. They loved him and as far as they were concerned any party without him was a disappointment.

Now, he came trotting over the grass, holding onto Sullivan's fat little legs, while the lad shouted and laughed merrily. "Gee up, horsey," he cried happily, tugging on his uncle's ears.

Dunn saw them and made an agonized face, as if fearing their son would pull his ears right off, which set them both giggling.

The tribe of high-spirited children scattered over the lawn, noisily engrossed in their games, or rushed to the tea table to top up on treats or lemonade. Their parents smiled on them indulgently, perhaps under the benign influence of the champagne they had all being drinking.

Coming at a more leisurely pace behind the others was Elayne, Dunn's lovely young wife. At seven months pregnant with their second child, she was glowing. Like Dunn, she adored children. "I cannae wait tae have a whole tribe of them," she was fond of saying. And Dunn would always make them laugh by saying he was going as fast as he could but would be happy to step up production if it pleased her.

Holding Elayne's hand was Roisin herself, in her new, white, broderie-Anglaise party dress, of which she was mightily proud. Today, she had insisted on Soairse doing her hair in a plaited crown, like Mary Queen of Scots, she said. She was a very happy girl, because that morning, she had been presented her very own pony, a little piebald mare she had immediately christened Patches.

"Och, she looks quite the wee lady, eh, Conrad?" Agnes said proudly, waving at her daughter.

"Aye, she daes, but I'd prefer it if she stayed at ten. Ten is old enough. I dinnae want her tae grow up. I wantae keep me sweet Little Flower sweet fer as long as I can."

"Och, ye great soft thing," Agnes said affectionately, pulling him down to kiss his lips. "But aye, 'tis sad that they grow up so quick," Agnes said wistfully. "I suppose there's only one solution tae that problem."

"Oh, aye? What's that then?" Conrad asked.

"Why, keep on havin' more of them, of course." She gave him a smile that said she had a secret.

His eyes widened. "Nay," he said, halting them on the spot.

"Aye."

He gave a great whoop and seized her around the waist, lifting her off her feet and whirling her about until she begged him to stop because it was making her dizzy. Carefully he placed her on her feet. She grabbed at his arm, her head spinning.

"When's it gonnae arrive?" he asked, putting his arm around her shoulders to steady her, pulling her close as they resumed the walk.

"Around Hogmanay, the healer thinks," she replied, thrilled by his reaction.

They reached a stone bench in an alcove cut into the high box hedge. It was a suntrap, so they decided to sit down. Conrad crossed his legs and put his arm around Agnes. She leaned against him happily, her hand resting on his thigh.

"So, what d'ye think of this wine?" he asked, holding the crystal glass up to the light and admiring the pale golden liquid. He had recently formed a business importing the wine from the Champagne region of France, in exchange for the single malt whisky he produced in the distillery he had constructed in the castle. It was proving most profitable.

"'Tis delicious but it goes tae me head real quick. It makes me feel quite… frisky," Agnes confessed with a twinkle in her eye.

Conrad quirked his brows. "Daes it now? That's very interestin'. I may havetae dae some further research intae that aspect of it."

"I'm sure ye will," she replied. They sat quietly for a few moments, bathed in mutual contentment, sipping their champagne and looking out over the happy children and the entire Mackintosh clan. Agnes was enormously proud of her family. She loved being a part of it. And so did Roisin, for she had so many cousins to play with and was never lonely.

"Aye, the Mackintoshes are quite an impressive lot," she mused.

"Aye, nae a bad bunch, I suppose," Conrad agreed with a nod. "But personally, I find a certain MacDonald more tae me taste."

"Oh? Who d'ye mean?" she asked coquettishly.

In response, he bent down and pressed his lips to her decolletage, sucking on the skin gently and grazing it with his teeth.

"Oooh," Agnes tittered excitedly. "I'm feelin' even more frisky now."

He shook his head. "Woman, curb yersel'. This is nae the place and time. We're at our daughter's birthday party. Much as I'd like tae drag ye behind a bush and ravish ye, it wouldnae be proper."

"Well, we're nae the only ones. Look at Bran and Illyssa."

Conrad looked and burst out laughing. His uncle was in a

clinch with his wife and was slowly dancing her into some flowering bushes, obviously with nefarious intentions.

"And the others are nae much better," Agnes pointed out. And indeed she was right, for all the elder Mackintoshes were dancing now. Alec and Kira were welded together and kissing, Tad was spinning Catreena about under his arm. As they watched, she fell into his arms, and he peppered her neck with small kisses. Even Dunn and Elayne, who were sitting with the children, were mooning at each other.

Conrad held up his glass again and examined the champagne. "It certainly daes see tae have an effect," he said ponderingly. "Drink up, wifey." He swallowed the last of his wine and stood up, putting the glass on the bench and then giving Agnes his hand. She followed suit and placed her glass next to his on the bench.

"Where are we goin'?" she asked as he steered them down a little path through the box hedge, away from the party area.

"Foe a wee walk. Somewhere quiet. Somewhere where I can show ye how much I love ye in private."

"Show me?" she asked, her pulse starting to race.

"Aye. We Mackintosh men are nae always so good with words. But were very good at action."

"Conrad, the way ye're talkin', I'm thinkin' that ye're feelin' frisky as well," she said playfully, looking up at him with an adoring smile. "'Tis that French champagne I tell ye!"

"Nay. 'tis ye, Agnes, me beautiful wife. Mo Ròisín. I love ye so much, and ye've given me a happiness I never dreamed could be mine. I want tae show ye me appreciation."

"Och, I love ye with all me heart too, me darlin' man, forever and ever."

"Grand, I'll never get tired of hearin' ye say that."

She screamed with laughter as he suddenly scooped her up in his arms and carried her off down the pathways, in search of that quiet place where they could show each other the deep enduring love they shared.

A SURPRISE!

Your love and support for my books has meant the world to me. As a way of saying thank you, I wanted you to be one of the first to know about my upcoming book:

The Laird's Dangerous Prize, the first fiery chapter in **The Highland Sisters' Secret Desires** series, is officially available for pre-order—and you're among the very first to know.

If you're drawn to danger, desire, and dark-hearted Highlanders, *The Highland Sisters' Secret Desires* will steal your breath—and it all begins with **Isolde & Ciaran**.

In **The Laird's Dangerous Prize**, a masked lady on the run crashes into the arms of the laird she was never meant to touch. Hunted, haunted, and hiding more than her name, Isolde ignites a fire Ciaran MacCraith can't put out. What begins as a rescue turns into a reckoning of secrets, sacrifice, and seduction. She was meant to bring ruin. He never intended to fall.

All you need is to scan this QR code with your phone...

to be the first to dive in.

I can't wait for you to fall as hard for **Isolde & Ciaran** as I did.

—Lyla

DO YOU WANT TO SEE HOW THINGS STARTED?

If you enjoyed *Scot of Ruin*, turn the page to dive into the first chapters of the first thrilling installment in the series, *Scot of Deception* , which will explore **Kathleen & Blaine 's** story.

Lady Kathleen Mackintosh refuses to be controlled. Forbidden from attending her best friend's wedding, she sneaks away. But when enemy soldiers ambush her, she's ready to meet her end… until a rugged Highlander comes to her rescue. He's fierce, brooding—and entirely too tempting. Yet secrets lie between them, and if she learns the truth, she may never forgive him… or herself.

SCOT OF DECEPTION

CHAPTER ONE

Moy Hall, Inverness
March, 1714

Kathleen's boots sank into muddy patches of earth as she snuck around the castle grounds. It had rained earlier that day, leaving the land moist and soft, which only served to make the silent, stealthy trek to the stables even harder for her.

It didn't help that she had to carry everything she would need in one oversized bag. Both her travels and her stay in Castle Stalker would be short, but she would need several changes of clothes and even more accessories for her looks. A lady of her rank could not be seen in any state other than perfection, especially for an event as important as a wedding.

The early morning air was crisp and cold, the chill stinging her face. Her fingers were already frozen and with her free had, she tightened her wool cloak around her shoulders, holding the fabric tightly. Every step she took was laborious. Not only because of the weight of her bag, but also because she had to be on alert, watching carefully around her for any sign of guards.

If they caught her, they were bound to take her straight to her father, and when he found out that she had left home against his explicit orders to remain where she was, he would not allow her to leave Moy Hall for the rest of her life.

But it was a risk she had to take. Her best friend, Fenella, needed her more than ever, and Kathleen refused to deny her her presence when she knew how much it would help her. The letter she had received from her a week prior spoke of a terrible fate—an unwanted marriage, an unloving husband, a lifetime of torment ahead of her. Ignoring the risks of travel to make sure she was there for a friend was only natural for Kathleen.

She had fought tooth and nail to be heard before deciding to leave secretly. She had tried to reason with her parents, to explain to them that Fenella needed her at her wedding, but they had refused to allow her to go. Even when Kathleen had asked for guards, pointing out that she would be safe with them, her parents had not given in. Clan Campbell was preparing for war, they had told her. there was a good chance they would soon attack, and every Mackintosh had to be in the safety of the keep when that happened.

Naturally, Kathleen hadn't listened, for she was determined to go help her friend.

Nothing but the last light of the moon was there to guide her as she walked towards the stables. Soon, the flicker of dawn would wash over the castle and it would be impossible to hide from prying eyes. She had to leave as soon as possible, before she was discovered.

Just as she rounded the corner in the narrow path that led to the stables, a hand shot out and grabbed her, and Kathleen couldn't help but yelp. She muffled the sound with a hand over her mouth, but it was already too late—not only had she been caught, but the sound rang out across the gardens before she had managed to cover her mouth.

"Where dae ye think ye're goin'?"

The voice was painfully familiar and Kathleen didn't need to turn around to know who her captor was, once the first wave of her panic had subsided. Her heart was still thundering in her chest, her hands shaking from the fear that she had been discovered, and she couldn't help but look around her for a moment to see if anyone else had heard her.

Only once she determined there was no one else around did she manage to breathe again. With a roll of her eyes, she smacked Devon's hand off her and turned to face him, her features twisting with indignation.

"What are ye daein'?" she demanded, giving him another push for good measure. "Ye gave me a fright, ye fool!"

In the dim light of the moon, Devon was little more than a shadow. Only his blond hair shone in the moonlight, but she could tell he was terribly pleased by the sound of his laughter.

"Did I scare ye?" Devon asked, and there was no hint of regret in his voice.

"O' course ye did!" Kathleen hissed. "It isnae funny."

"I disagree," said Devon. With a satisfied smile that was barely visible in the dark, he began to walk backwards towards the stables, nodding in their direction. In an affected voice, he said, "Come. Yer steed is prepared fer ye, me lady."

It had been a struggle to convince Devon and Kieran to help her with this. At first, she had had no intention of asking for their assistance, but it wasn't long before the two of them found out about her plan, when she had been making arrangements with the stable boy regarding her horse. Kathleen had narrowly escaped a terrible fate—Kieran revealing everything to her father out of concern for her well-being. Convincing the ever-serious Kieran that it was something she had to do had been far from an easy task. If anything, she suspected the trip in itself would be easier than convincing them to let her go to Castle Stalker.

With Clan Campbell threatening war against Clan Mackintosh, everyone in Moy Hall was on high alert. No one was supposed to leave the keep, not even for an event such as an allied clan's wedding, and so when Kathleen had received Fenella's invitation—along with the letter she had secretly folded within it, which was meant just for her—she had known her parents would never allow it. So, in the end, she did what had to be done.

If she had to do it alone, then so be.

Kieran and Devon had agreed to help her, preparing her horse for her and sneaking her out of the castle so she could depart undetected.

Once in the stables, Kathleen blinked as her eyes adjusted to the light of the torches that lined the walls. Kieran was already there, finalizing the last preparations and ensuring the saddle was properly placed on the horse.

Kieran and Devon were identical twins. Had it not been for the different way they wore their hair—Devon's longer and messy, always tangled from the wind, while Kieran's was shorter and neatly tied back at all times—Kathleen doubted anyone would be able to tell them apart unless they opened their mouths.

"Are ye both out o' yer minds?" Kieran asked in that smooth baritone voice of his. Frazzled, he stomped over to them and pointed an accusatory finger at them both. "Dae ye ken what will happen if anyone finds out we're daein' this?"

"They'll find out eventually," Devon said with a small shrug, entirely unconcerned.

"It was his fault!" Kathleen pointed out. "Devon's the one who scared me!"

"Ye're actin' like a pair o' bairns," said Kieran. "I dinnae even ken why I agreed tae this."

"Because even when ye complain, ye always wish tae help," Kathleen pointed out.

Kieran didn't try to deny that, though he rolled his eyes as if to protest. He really did simply enjoy complaining. Silently, he held out his hand for Kathleen to hand him her bag and once she did, he strapped it on the saddle.

"Remember... we're only allowin' ye tae dae this under the stipulation that ye send us a letter every other day," Kieran said sternly. For someone who was only two years older than her, he could certainly assume a fatherly air with frightening ease. "If we dinnae receive one, we will come after ye."

"Then maybe ye can come tae the weddin' too!" Kathleen teased, but while as Devon snorted with mirth, Kieran gave her no reaction.

"This isnae a laughin' matter," he said.

Devon cleared his throat, scratching the back of his neck as he tried to hide his grin. After a few moments, though, he appeared a little more serious, a little more restrained.

"Kieran is right," he told Kathleen. "Ye should be careful. But it isnae as though ye're walkin' intae a death trap!"

"Perhaps it isnae a death trap, but it isnae safe either," Kieran said flatly.

"Ach, we've done much worse than this," said Devon. "Remember the time when we snuck out o' the castle an' went tae that tavern—"

"I think that's enough!" Kieran exclaimed, slapping a hand over Devon's mouth, much to Kathleen's chagrin. She would have like to have known what had happened in that tavern, but chances were, they would never tell her.

At least Kieran wouldn't—if she played her cards right, maybe she could yet get the truth out of Devon when she returned.

Both Devon and Kathleen struggled to stifle their giggles as Kieran shook his head in disappointment. After a moment of hesitation, when Kathleen wondered if she was doing the right thing after all, she hugged them both and then took the horse's reins from Kieran, ready to start her little adventure.

Sneaking her out of the castle was no easy task, as there were guards everywhere, but naturally, all the guards knew Kieran and Devon well. And with Devon's easy charm and friendliness, they slipped past even the most suspicious of them. By the time they made it to the rear gate of the castle, Kathleen's heart was beating fast, her eyes searching for any signs of anything or anyone who could prevent her from leaving. The closer she got to her freedom, the more she feared that it would be snatched right out of her hands. In the end, though, no one stopped her.

After saying her goodbyes to her cousins and promising them once again that she would write to them every other day, she stepped out of the castle walls and into the wilderness that stretched behind it. Castle Stalker was approximately four days' worth of riding away, and Kathleen was determined to make the most of it, travelling as fast as she could.

Dawn broke in the distance as she rode away from the castle, the imposing building getting smaller and smaller over her shoulder as she left it behind. A dull blue glow fell over the land—the first light of the day as cold and biting as the wind. Around her, there were nothing but trees and open land. The first birdsong of the morning reached her ears and for the first time in days, she allowed herself to believe that perhaps her plan would work out, after all.

An hour had passed by the time she couldn't bear the silence anymore. The dull dawn had turned into an even duller day, the sky gray and domed with clouds. The emptiness all around her gave her no comfort. She had never travelled alone before—she had never even been this alone in her life.

Kathleen began to hum a song to herself, one that her mother had sang to her when she was a child. It helped a little; she didn't feel so alone, so isolated from the rest of the world.

But then, just as she took a turn on the path, the thunderous sound of hooves echoed all around her. Wide-eyed, Kathleen looked frantically around her to locate the source of the sound, though she couldn't see any signs of danger—not until three men rushed out of the treeline just ahead of her, heading straight towards her.

And in that moment, she understood that being all alone on that path would have been a blessing.

CHAPTER TWO

Kathleen's shriek pierced the morning air like a bell announcing war.

In an instant, the three men had gathered around her, surrounding her from all sides. Two of them jumped off the horses as the last one reached for her, pushing her off her saddle just before she had the chance to escape.

Had she managed to stay on her horse, perhaps she could have fled. Now, though, she had no chance of escape.

All the men were dressed in the blue and green shades of Clan Campbell—colors familiar to her and anyone in those parts, as there was no greater enemy to the Mackintosh Clan.

Her parents had been right. The danger was more real, more palpable than she could have ever imagined. And now that she had fled the castle without anyone knowing, there was no one there to save her.

Even as Kathleen was being dragged by the arm, she didn't stop putting up a fight. When her captor tried to hold her still, she kicked at him and thrashed in his grip, wild and furious. Maybe if there had only been one man, she would have managed to escape him all on her own with how willing she was to fight, her desire to flee stronger than any lack of strength or skill. But with three men against her, there was nothing she could do other than scream and kick uselessly at them, only prolonging the inevitable.

Frustrated as he was from her fighting, one of the men who were trying to control her punched Kathleen straight across the cheek, so hard that her head whipped to the side with frightening speed. Pain exploded all over the side of her face —a blinding pain that made her ears ring and her head spin, her vision turning to black for a few moments.

And that was why the strange voice was a surprise as it echoed behind her, announcing the arrival of another man.

"Ye wish tae fight?" he called just as he jumped off his horse and balled up his fists, stomping over to the three men. "Then leave the lass an' fight me."

The man holding her didn't move, but the other two were quick to go to him, meeting him halfway. With her vision restored, Kathleen watched in horror as a fight erupted among them, the pain that still lingered disorienting her and making it difficult to keep track of the men.

The first blow came from the larger of the two, a young man with pale eyes and a red face, his mouth twisted with effort. The strange man avoided his fist, lunging to the side, and swiftly delivered a blow of his own, one that caught the man in the stomach.

Just as Kathleen thought it was going to be a fist fight, though, the other man pulled out a small blade and immediately, his fellow soldier did the same. Drawing in a deep, steadying breath, the stranger took a few steps back from them to do the same, grabbing his dirk from where it was strapped around his waist, fingers wrapping tightly around the hilt.

The more the pain subsided and clarity returned, the more Kathleen's desire to fight back grew. Soon, she was thrashing in her captor's grip once more, kicking and twisting as she tried to escape his grasp.

She didn't rest for a moment, at least not until she heard a loud thud and saw that the stranger had rendered one of the Campbell men unconscious, a small cloud of dust rising around his body as he hit the ground.

Stunned, Kathleen watched as he did quick work of the second man, rendering him unconscious with a single punch across the face. And then, once he too was laying on the ground next to his friend, he turned his sights to the man holding her.

Slowly, he let go of her, raising up his hands as if in surrender. Now that she was free, Kathleen wasted no time before she ran as far from them as she could—but not far enough to escape entirely.

For a moment, the two of them simply stared at each other. The stranger narrowed his eyes at the Campbell soldier, as if suspicious of his intentions. In the end, his suspicion was justified, as the man rushed towards him, fists balled up and ready for a fight.

With a feint to the left, the stranger let him run right past him before he spun around and kicked him. The force of his kick was strong enough to throw the man off-balance, making him fall to the ground, and the stranger wasted no time before he hit him on the back of the head as well, making sure he wouldn't move before he pushed himself back up to his feet.

Standing above them, the stranger's chest heaved as he tried to catch his breath. With the men unmoving on the ground, he turned his sights on Kathleen.

I should have fled.

What if he, too, wanted something from her? What if he had only saved her from those men to have his way with her or because he wanted to rob her?

He was… handsome. *Very* handsome. She wanted to keep her mind on alert but he was proving to be distracting.

It took her a few moments to realize the wheezing sound filling her ears was coming from her own chest as she tried—and failed—to breathe. She slid down to the ground, curling up on a patch of green grass as she tried to catch her breath, but no matter what she did, she did not seem able to draw in enough air.

When the stranger approached her, her fear bubbled over.

"It's alright," he promised. "I willnae hurt ye. I promise."

"Who are ye?" she demanded.

"Me name's Blaine," he said. "I was headin' down tae the valley an' saw ye get attacked, so I thought I'd help ye."

"Why?"

Blaine frowned, as if he didn't understand the question. "Well… because ye were in danger. I wished tae help."

Kathleen observed him with narrowed eyes, taking in every detail of his face—the deep green eyes that seemed to draw one's attention immediately, the sharp lines of his jaw and his nose, the dark strands of hair that now fell over his forehead, tousled after the fight.

He was the most handsome man Kathleen had ever seen, and warmth spread over her body at the sight of him. Her cheeks heated and she couldn't help but drop her gaze, her embarrassment getting the better of her.

It wasn't often that she was embarrassed, but she wasn't knowledgeable in the ways of men and women.

Blaine had saved her life.

He is not only handsome, but also me savior.

However, she was still a little apprehensive; how could she not be? He was a complete stranger to her. But when he offered his hand to her to help her up, she accepted it, standing to her feet.

"Thank ye," she said, her voice thin but unwavering as the first wave of shock began to subside. Absentmindedly, she began to dust herself, trying to get all the dirt off her thick cloak in vain, just to distract herself from the terror of her recent experience.

"Come," Blaine said gently, nodding towards his horse, which had obediently stayed nearby, munching on a bit of grass. "I have some ointment fer that cut on yer cheek."

"Ach! Is it very bad?"

"The cut?" Blaine asked with a frown. Hesitantly, he reached for her and Kathleen swiftly pulled back at first, frightened. Then, she froze, her eyes staring up at him, her rosy lips parted ever so slightly as he pushed a strand of her hair back to reveal her cheek. "It isnae very bad. It will heal in nay time."

For a moment, she said nothing. She only stared at him in silence, breath catching in her throat.

No one had ever touched her like that before. No man had ever gone so close, and to have a stranger displaying such intimate tenderness towards her now brought her mind to a complete halt.

When Blaine spoke again, it took Kathleen a few seconds to understand what he was saying.

"What's a lass like ye daein' alone in the woods?" Blaine asked.

"I'm... travelin'," she said, a little hesitantly. She didn't know just how much she should tell this man when she knew nothing about him at all. "I'm goin' tae a weddin'."

"A weddin', is it?" Blaine asked. "Alone?"

Kathleen looked around her as if searching for someone else.

"Are me guards nae here?"

It seemed to take Blaine a few moments to realize she was joking, but once he did, he chuckled softly. Before they could say anything else, though, a grunt came from the ground near them and one of the men began to stir. There was no time for talking. They had to get out of there as soon as possible.

"We must go," he said. "Can ye get on yer horse or dae ye need help?"

Kathleen's only answer was an amused smirk as she ran to her horse and jumped on with ease and the kind of grace that came from a lifetime of practice. Behind her, Blaine chuckled again, shaking his head as he headed to his own horse, the two of them rushing down the path.

After a few minutes of riding, she called out over the wind, "Kathleen."

"What?" Blaine called back.

"Me name," she said, "is Kathleen."

Blaine smiled. "Pleased tae make yer acquaintance, Kathleen."

CHAPTER THREE

They had been riding fast for about half an hour when Blaine decided they could stop. It was a plausible amount of time. Now, he only had to work on gaining some of her trust—just enough to make her feel comfortable in his presence and urge her to desire his help. At the sight of a small lake, he turned from the main road down the overgrown path that led there, Kathleen following close behind on her own horse.

"Let us rest here fer a while," he called to her and saw her nod before she dismounted her horse. Blaine did the same, leading both creatures to the water, where they could drink and rest. Then, he rummaged through his bag, producing a small jar of ointment. "This should help with yer cut."

Kathleen still eyed him and the jar warily, but she said nothing as Blaine approached her, where she stood under the shade of a large oak. The dappled light seemed to set her auburn hair on fire, the strands glittering under the sun, her eyes following his every move as though she expected an attack.

Instead of an attack, Blaine dealt a gentle caress to a strand of hair that had fallen over her cheek, where the man's fist had cut her. He pushed it behind her ear and he could have sworn that her cheeks were suddenly painted with the subtlest shade of pink, so soft that he would have missed it had it not been for the light.

Blaine dipped the pad of his finger into the ointment and applied a thin layer over the cut. At the first touch, Kathleen drew in a sharp breath, the pungent ointment undoubtedly stinging her. Blaine knew the sensation well—he had used the ointment many times, and so he knew the sting. But it was well worth it, none of his cuts had ever been infected.

Blaine could have stayed a few steps back. He could have kept some distance between them, but instead he had chosen to stand close to Kathleen; close enough for them to share the same air, for him to look into her eyes and see the gold flecks in the pools of blue.

From the gap in her cloak, Blaine could see her chest rise and fall with every breath. The pale expanse of skin over the neckline of her dress drew his gaze no matter how much he tried to fight it, his eyes straying back to it time and time again. There was something irresistible about her—not only her looks, but her aura, or something Blaine couldn't name.

His heart beat faster in his chest. His skin suddenly felt hot, restrictive, as though it could hardly contain him. When Kathleen's gaze met his, those blue eyes staring right through him, he felt as though he would burst right out of it.

What am I thinkin'?

A man like him could *never* have a woman like her. Not only that, but he most certainly couldn't have this specific woman.

He should never even dare think about falling into the temptation.

Abruptly, he pulled back from her, leaving a small smear of ointment on her skin. He didn't mention it; sooner or later, it would be absorbed, so he didn't have to touch her again. He didn't even need to be so close to her. He turned on his heel, heading back to the horses to place the ointment jar back in his bag, just so he had something to do.

"Should I take ye back tae the castle?" he asked her, without even turning around to glance at her. Instead, he focused on fiddling with the clasp as an excuse to not turn around just yet. The exchange, short as it had been, had excited him far more than it should have.

"How dae ye ken I'm from the castle?" Kathleen asked, a hint of tremor in her voice.

Damn it tae hell.

He had done so well up until then. If Kathleen was going to start asking questions, he had to be careful about what he revealed to her.

One wrong word and she could find out the truth.

"Well, a lass like yerself can only be noble born," Blaine said, without missing a beat. He didn't enjoy speaking much, but when he did, he thankfully tended to say the right thing. "Look at ye… just yer cloak must cost as much as me horse. Moy Hall is the only stronghold around here, so I suppose that's where ye came from."

His heart beating wildly, Blaine turned to look at Kathleen to find her cursing quietly as her gaze slid up to the sky with a frustrated sigh.

"It's nay wonder the Campbell soldiers recognized me, then," she said, as if speaking to herself. "I thought I would be safe, especially so close tae the castle, but…"

Blaine had to swallow a sigh of relief. He had said the right thing, after all.

"Ye shouldnae have come out here without guards," Blaine pointed out, this time giving her the warning he hadn't managed to give her before. It didn't matter, of course; it was far too late for that. "How did yer family let ye travel on yer own?"

Now Kathleen's blush was clearly visible, her cheeks heating wildly. "They dinnae doesnae ken," she said. "But I must go tae this weddin'. It's very important tae me… tae me friend."

"How important can a weddin' be?" Blaine asked. "More important than yer safety?"

"Very important," said Kathleen. "It is almost a matter o' life an' death."

Blaine was quite certain that was far from the truth, but he didn't tell Kathleen so. Whether she went to the wedding or not was of no importance to him. If anything, it would be better if she didn't, but he didn't try to convince her to head back to Moy Hall. He only shook his head and refilled his water canteen in the lake as he heard Kathleen's light footsteps behind him.

"I wouldnae mind travelin' with ye if ye're headin' the same way as me," she said, sounding a little hesitant. "It's better tae travel with company, is that nae so?"

Blaine smiled to himself before finally schooling his expression into a neutral one and turning to face her. "So it is," he agreed. "I'm goin' the same way. I dinnae mind makin' sure ye're safe."

Once again, that seemed to be the right thing to say, as Kathleen gave him a small, shy smile. Blaine returned it, jumping on his horse and waiting for her to do the same, then heading back up the path to the main road with her close behind.

He deeply hoped she didn't notice that he had not asked her the direction she was going, nor had she told him.

Her savior was a strange man.

A strange, handsome man.

Kathleen stared at him openly as the two of them trotted up the path, since he couldn't see her anyway. She could only gaze at the back of his head, his shiny dark hair, his broad shoulders and tapered waist. His arms seemed strong enough to lift her right off her feet as though she were a feather. She felt her heart racing in her chest. His green eyes, the sharp line of his jaw and the strong, slightly crooked nose—even the faint scars on his face and hands whose origin Kathleen couldn't help but question—all worked together to give him a striking look.

And yet, the most striking thing about him was not his appearance, perhaps, but rather his behavior.

The moment they were back on the main path, Kathleen caught up to him, falling into step right next to his horse.

"How dae ye ken where we're goin'?" she asked. "I didnae tell ye where the weddin' is."

For a moment, Kathleen could have sworn that she saw a flash of panic in his gaze, in the clench of his jaw. But then, he turned to her with a smile and a shrug, both so disarming that she forgot all about it.

"I saw ye head down the path afore ye were attacked. I wasnae too far from ye," he said. "An'… I'm guessin' we're goin' tae the same weddin'."

Kathleen frowned at that, tilting her head to the side in confusion as she looked at him. "The same weddin'?"

"Aye," he said. "I can only imagine ye're a Mackintosh, since ye're in these parts an' dressed the way ye are."

Kathleen was uncertain of whether or not she should take offence. Looking down at herself, Kathleen decided that it was a fair assessment—no commoner would be dressed in the luxurious fabrics and rich colors she was wearing.

"I'm goin' tae Fenella Stewart's weddin'. Is that where ye're goin'?"

Kathleen's eyes narrowed at him in suspicion. It all seemed a little too convenient for her, being saved by a man who was going to the exact same place as her—the wedding of a noble woman, no less! Who was this man? Kathleen observed him closely, taking in every detail about him; his clothes, the way he carried himself, his countenance. Had she ever met him before?

"Aye, that's the one. From which clan did ye say ye come?" she asked, hoping his response would shed some light on the mystery.

"I'm a Farquharson," Blaine said without hesitation. "Out o' all the Farquharsons, they decided tae send me tae the weddin', so… here I am."

As he spoke, Blaine turned to smile at her and Kathleen found herself smiling back.

This explains it. Couldnae he have said so sooner?

The Farquharsons were good allies of the Stewart Clan, and it was no wonder they had been invited to the wedding. If Blaine had been sent as their representative, then that could only mean he was from a noble line—perhaps not an heir to the lairdship himself, but surely the son of someone important. Their lands were also close to the Mackintosh lands, and the only road leading from their keep to Clan Stewart passed through Mackintosh territory, so luck had brought them together at just the right time for him to save Kathleen from those savages.

"I've been tae the Farquharson lands," Kathleen said, remembering her brief travels there with her father. It must have been a great occasion—another wedding, perhaps, or some sort of celebration which had required her presence. It had been a while since then and she couldn't quite recall the purpose of her visit, but she could recall having a great time. "It's a very bonnie place."

"Och aye, that it is," Blaine agreed. "When did ye visit? I imagine we would have met each other there."

Kathleen thought so too, but she was certain she would remember a face like his. But Blaine seemed to be a good decade older than her by the looks of it, with the crow's feet that appeared around his eyes when he smiled and the faint lines on his forehead. She doubted he would have given a young girl much attention. Had they met briefly back then? Had she not given her much attention either, too preoccupied with her peers to spare him a second thought?

"It must be over a decade now," she said. "I was a very young lass back then."

"I see," said Blaine, nodding slowly as if to himself. "Then perhaps our paths never crossed."

Perhaps it was better that way. Kathleen would rather Blaine know her as the woman she was now than the girl she had once been. She doubted she had even come of age when she had visited Clan Farquharson, while he had most likely been in his twenties.

"Dae ye ken me faither, then?" Kathleen asked. "Laird Mackintosh?"

"Aye, I ken him," said Blaine. "I've met him afore."

"An' me cousins?"

"Nay, I cannae say that I have."

"An' Fenella?"

Blaine turned to look at her, dragging his gaze off the road slowly, the corners of his lips ticking up in amusement. "Nay," he said. "Dae ye always ask so many questions?"

Heat creeped up Kathleen's neck, all the way up to her face. She snapped her mouth shut and moved her gaze to the road, but Blaine only laughed softly.

"I didnae mean tae offend."

"Nay offense taken," Kathleen assured him.

And yet, as they rode together down the path, their horses side by side in a leisurely pace, she kept the rest of her thoughts to herself.

CHAPTER FOUR

*E*ven for a seasoned rider like Kathleen, the seemingly endless hours of the journey wore her down before they reached the next town. They had passed several villages on their way but decided not to stop, as the day was still young and Kathleen wanted to reach Castle Stalker as soon as possible. Yet, after a long few hours of riding, they both needed a good rest—even if just for a short while.

Just off the path, they found a small clearing that seemed to have been used by other weary travelers, as there was a makeshift pit in the middle of it, just big enough for a fire. Kathleen followed Blaine there, the golden afternoon light falling on the trampled grass and the shrubs that surrounded the clearing, making their leaves glow.

It was an unusually bright day, and yet the chill still seeped through Kathleen's clothes, all the way to her bones. As she sat by the roots of a large tree, Blaine quickly gathered some wood and lit a fire with the kind of speed and ease of someone who had done that very thing countless times before.

Kathleen couldn't recall a single time when she had had to light her own fire. Whenever she was cold, there was always a maid or, if she was traveling, a guard or servant to light it for her.

Now, she watched Blaine through the flames as he sat at the other end of the pit, pulling out his blade. At first, she almost recoiled, wondering why he would need it, but then he began to sharpen it with slow, methodical movements, his rhythm almost hypnotizing. The entire time she watched him, he never once looked up, though Kathleen couldn't tell if that was because he didn't notice her or because he was simply ignoring her.

He was clearly a warrior and if she had learned anything from her cousins, it was that warriors had a sense for those around them. They knew when they were being watched, they knew when something was amiss.

So he's simply ignorin' me.

Kathleen was not particularly used to that. She was a social girl, someone who liked to talk—too much, according to her father. But Blaine, though sitting right next to her, seemed so distant that she didn't even know how to begin to reach him.

With a sigh, she leaned her head back against the trunk of the tree, her gaze roaming around the clearing. Some of the bushes around them bore berries, but she didn't know if they were edible. The fire crackled pleasantly. The birds flitted from branch to branch, twittering happily.

Then she noticed a tear in her cloak.

When her gaze fell on it, she cursed under her breath and thumbed it, frowning to herself. When had that happened? And where would she find thread to fix it?

Upon closer inspection, she noticed that her cloak had not been torn, but rather cut, along with her sleeve and the skin under all those layers. The bleeding had long since stopped, but the blood had dried off all over her clothes and Kathleen couldn't stop herself from cursing again. It was far from ladylike, especially in front of another person, but she couldn't show up to Castle Stalker like that. She was hardly presentable!

Only moments later and as Kathleen was still inspecting the wound, a small, wet cloth landed in her lap. Across from her, Blaine stared at her for a moment, before he resumed his task, sharpening his blade without a single word.

Kathleen said nothing as well, as she grabbed the cloth and pressed it to the small wound, dabbing up the blood. She did give him a grateful smile, though, small and shy.

She didn't know if he noticed.

For a long while, silence stretched between them. Kathleen busied herself with the cloth, trying to get as much of the blood off her clothes as she could before finally giving up. A wet cloth would do nothing to help with the stain and even if she managed to remove the blood, the rip would still be there.

In the end, she simply held out the rag for Blaine to take, but he shook his head.

"Dinnae make me stand," he said. "I'm an old man."

"Hardly old," said Kathleen, laughing, as she found the mere notion ridiculous. Her father was old; Blaine was simply *older*.

"Older than ye," said Blaine.

That much was true, at least. She realized just how different their lives had to be. They were in such different stages, after all—he, a man wrought and tested in battle, with all the responsibilities that came with being, if not the head of his household, then a senior member; and she, a young woman who knew little of the world outside the curtain walls of the castle.

It occurred to her then that, even though she had been thinking of Blaine as someone much like her cousins, that stage of his life was already far behind him.

"Dae ye have a wife?" she asked, her curiosity getting the better of her.

Blaine barked out a surprised laugh, his eyes widening ever so slightly. "Quite forward o' ye, dinnae ye think?"

Heat flooded Kathleen's face, from the base of her neck to the tips of her ears. For a few moments, all she could do was stare at him in horror, her embarrassment too great for anything else.

It had been an innocent question. Kathleen had never even imagined Blaine would take it as anything else and now she didn't know what to think. Was that where his mind strayed? Could it be that he had taken her innocent question as permission to take more liberties with her?

"That's… that isnae what I meant at all!" Kathleen said, her protest coming out as a shriek rather than the dignified tone she was aiming for. "I was only curious! I never meant… I would never… how dare ye assume a lady like meself would ever suggest such a thing? I hope ye're nae deluded about me…me intentions!"

For all her protest, Blaine only laughed, shaking his head. "I dinnae have a wife," he said, still shaking with mirth. "I travel too often fer me duties tae have a wife. Me long absences would only be cruel tae her. An' dinnae fash. Ye shouldnae fear I'll dae anythin' o' the sort tae ye."

Those last words reassured Kathleen a little, though she didn't put her guard down entirely. She still eyed Blaine a little warily and kept her distance from him, fearing what he would do if she got too close.

Fearing what *she* would do if he got too close.

Instead of dwelling on it, she scrambled for something to say to ease the tension, asking the first thing that popped in her mind. "What are yer duties then, that keep ye away from home fer so long?"

Blaine frowned to himself, idly scratching his chin. He seemed to be in deep thought for several moments, which they spent staring at each other in silence, until he finally spoke.

"I'm afraid I cannae share that with ye," he said, much to Kathleen's disappointment. After all that time he had taken to think, she had expected to hear something much more exciting than this. "It is confidential. I'm workin' close tae some very important members o' the clan."

The secrecy itself seemed exciting to Kathleen, at least. It gave Blaine an even more mysterious air, which added to the mystery of his scars and his quiet demeanor. He didn't seem to like sharing things about himself. Everything Kathleen had learned about him so far had been through specific, targeted questions she had asked him, and he never shared more than he absolutely had to.

She couldn't decide whether this was something she liked about him. On the one hand, it gave him an almost irresistible allure. Kathleen itched to learn more about him, to figure out what she could about that strange man. On the other, it frightened her somewhat. She was traveling with a man about whom she knew very little. And the little he had offered, had hardly been enough to allow her to form a rounded opinion about him.

Kathleen wanted to believe that he was good. After all, he had saved her from the Campbell soldiers and she owed him her life. But she was still a woman travelling alone.

He hasnae tried anythin' so far. If anythin', he's been the perfect gentleman.

Surely, he wouldn't risk his or Clan Farquharson's reputation by acting less than honorably towards her.

Once again, silence fell over the clearing as Kathleen didn't know what else to ask him and Blaine didn't seem to be in any hurry to speak. The only sounds were those of the flames in the pit, the birdsong, and the rhythmic scrape of the sharpening stone against Blaine's blade, all of them working together to lull Kathleen into a half-sleep.

She didn't know how much time had passed when she felt a nudge against her shoulder. At first, she couldn't help but jump away from it, startled; but then she saw it was only Blaine, trying to wake her.

"We should continue," he said, frowning as he gazed into the distance. "It's gettin' late. We dinnae wish tae be out here when it's dark."

Kathleen nodded and swiftly pushed herself up to her feet, rubbing the stupor from her eyes. It was still bright and the sun didn't seem to have moved too far, so she could only assume she had only closed her eyes for a short time. Even so, Blaine seemed to be in a terrible hurry, rushing as he got the horses ready for them once more to get back on the road.

Silence was their third companion as they headed down the path once again. Blaine may have been lost in his thoughts, paying Kathleen no mind, but she had no such luck. She kept wondering about him, about his behavior. Who was he, truly? What was his role in the clan, which required so much secrecy?

As they traveled, the sky above them darkened the farther they got. Clouds gathered over the treetops, dark and heavy with rain, and when they finally came across a small inn, Blaine was quick to steer them in that direction.

"Let us spend the night there," he said. "It'll soon be dark."

The sun had not yet set in the horizon, but it was low in the sky. The promise of a warm room and a hot plate of food was more than enough to entice Kathleen to stop for the night, even if they could keep riding for a while. Besides, she didn't know if they would find another such place in time, and the last thing she wanted was to be traveling in the dark, even more so if the moon and the stars would be hidden behind the clouds, or it would start raining.

The inn was a squat building, just big enough to house a few guests. Light poured out of the small windows, orange and warm and inviting, but when Kathleen opened the door, she came to a sudden halt.

Every pair of eyes in the room turned to stare at her—all of them men of varying ages, all of them stunned to see a woman alone there at that time of the day.

Behind her, the sun was setting. Inside, the room was dimly lit, the air heavy with the stench of spilled ale and wine.

When Blaine appeared behind her a few moments later, the men who had been staring so openly at her went back to their bowls of stew and their mugs of ale, suddenly entirely unbothered by her presence.

It's so easy fer him tae command respect. All he needs tae dae is walk intae a room an' look around.

It was not as easy for Kathleen. She was a young woman that men saw as an object; a pretty thing for them to stare at.

With a steadying breath, she stomped over to the innkeeper behind the counter, placing her hand on top of the dark wood—and immediately regretting it. She quickly removed her hand from the sticky surface, clearing her throat as she stared him in the eye, mustering all the commanding energy she could.

I willnae let Blaine dae everythin' fer me.

"We would like two rooms, please," she said with the kind of authority that was neither expected nor desired from her.

The innkeeper gave her a bored look, placing a single key on the counter. "There is only one room available taenight."

Kathleen barely stopped herself from cursing out the man, the inn, and the entire day. After everything she had been through, she craved the comfort and privacy of her own room and she desperately dreamed of her chambers back home. But home was far away and none of her misfortunes had led her to change her mind about attending Fenella's wedding. This was just another obstacle she would have to overcome.

Before she could come up with a solution—suggest that they look for another inn, perhaps, or at least ask Blaine what he thought they should do—he slammed a few coins on the counter and grabbed the key without a word.

"What are ye daein'?" Kathleen asked, head whipping around to look at him, stunned.

"Payin' fer the room," said Blaine, as if it wasn't perfectly obvious.

"I'm a lady!" Kathleen reminded him. This was not the best conversation to have in front of all the patrons, but if Blaine thought she would share a bed with him, then he was sorely mistaken. "I cannae share a room with ye! It's… it's inappropriate is what it is."

Blaine gave Kathleen an unimpressed look, before grabbing her arm to drag her aside, away from prying eyes and ears. Kathleen fought him all the way, trying to plant her feet on the floor, but Blaine was much stronger—and much more stubborn.

"If I wished tae have me way with ye, I could have done it already," he said, as though that was meant to give Kathleen any peace of mind. If anything, it only frightened her more, the open acknowledgement of the power he could exert over her. But when she tried to point that out, Blaine continued before she could speak. "Ye're safe with me. In fact, ye're much safer with me than without me. Have ye seen how those men are looking at ye?"

Aye… as though I'm naethin' more than a piece o' meat.

Kathleen stared bitterly at the men, though none of them dared to look back at her—not with Blaine watching. Then, she dragged her gaze back to him, making sure that her displeasure was clear in the sour twist of her lips.

"I still cannae share a room with a strange man," she insisted. "I dinnae even ken anythin' about ye!"

"But ye ken I have nay desire tae harm ye," he told her. When she said nothing, only gritting her teeth in response, Blaine rolled his eyes with a long-suffering sigh. "Fine. I'll sleep in the stables. Will that make ye feel safer?"

Kathleen wasn't certain whether it made her feel safer or not, but she did know one thing; after everything Blaine had done for her, making him sleep in the stables was far too cruel. He deserved the warmth and comfort of a proper room. Besides, a man of his station surely wasn't used to sleeping in the stables with the horses. Even in his roughest travels, he would at least have some comforts.

"Nay," she said. "Ye cannae sleep out there in the cold."

"I've done it afore."

Kathleen's mind scrambled to find a good enough reason that had nothing to do with her own desire to repay him for his help. "Because... because if ye sleep out there, ye might catch yer death an' then what will I dae?"

There! Now he daesnae ken I care.

Blaine responded with nothing but a soft, surprised chuckle. He stared at Kathleen in silence for a few moments, as if he was considering her words, and then he gave her a small nod. "Alright. I'll sleep in the room, then."

Ach! O' course, what other choice daes he have? It's either the room or the stables!

Kathleen had pushed herself into a corner, but she could do nothing other than reluctantly accept it. "Alright," she echoed. "But ye'll sleep on the floor. I might have nae choice but tae share the room with ye, but I willnae share me bed!"

With that, she turned on her heel and stomped up the stairs, the bright sound of Blaine's laughter following her.

DO YOU WANT TO READ MORE?

To read more, scan this QR code with your phone!

ABOUT THE AUTHOR

Lyla Rosewood is an American writer who crafts captivating tales of Scottish historical romance. Born on June 27, 1969, in the city of Santa Clara, California, Lyla's childhood dream was to become a writer.

Lyla felt stuck in a job as a ticket agent and travel clerk, when the support of her husband, Jason, and of their two children, Mary and David, pushed her to pursue her passion.

Now, still living surrounded by the beauty of Santa Clara, Lyla spins tales of Scottish romance filled with history, intrigue, and turmoil. Like her characters, her journey reflects her courage and determination. Through her stories of love and adventure, she demonstrates the transformative impact of pursuing one's dreams.

Note from Lyla

I'm always happy to communicate with my readers. So if you want to stay up to date with my newest releases and win little treats, please subscribe to my newsletter, and you will always be the first to know about my newest Scottish novel.

To subscribe to my newsletter, scan this QR code with your phone!

Thank you, your friend Lyla ⚔

If you want to keep in touch...

Follow me on Social Media:

Printed in Dunstable, United Kingdom